My Name Is Julia

A Coming of Age Novel

Priscilla J Paquette

Contents

1

The Return

I was returning . . .

I looked out through the small glass window and fresh tears seeped from my eyes. I folded my arms against my stomach to lessen the knot of pain in my belly.

The deep blue Atlantic Ocean with bobbing white surf, wasn't calming my heart like it usually did. Because I was remembering . . .

This was the place of my deep wounds.

And the place of my greatest victories.

This was the place of my childhood.

My childhood wounds go deep like the roots of the trees I used to play under by the riverside. Like the spread-out roots of the Samaan Tree. I had spent many hours playing with its red flowers and its pods with my school friends.

Life had been simple . . . but only when I was looking back at the past through the best filters—filtering out the pain, the wounds, the struggle of growing up on this island I called home.

I looked out through the narrow window of the plane and felt the strings of home tug on my heart.

Her majestic towering mountains. The million shades of green. The white caps on the deep blue ocean crashing onto the rugged northeast coastline.

We were approaching the airport. The same airport I'd flown in and out of during my days at Cave Hill, and later for work-related travel. I'd left over ten years ago and hadn't been back—not once during those ten years.

The landscape looked the same. A few houses peeked through the dense green trees. I knew what to expect on the approach. We were flying over the ocean on an inbound flight from Antigua to land at the same old Charles Douglas airport; the long-promised international airport remained an unrealized dream.

We were almost there but I was keeping my eyes on the heavy bank of clouds hanging over the runway. Would the pilot land from the sea or from the mountain? My vote was from the sea; the lower approach meant better visibility.

The clouds were dark grey and ominous, heavy with rain. Same as the emotions roiling inside me. I was coming back after a long hiatus as a diasporan. Dark heavy sorrow settled like lead in my stomach. My eyes turned blurry with tears.

I distracted myself with the clouds, convinced the pilot would land from the sea today. I'd been on many of the De Havilland Dash 8 planes—too many times to count over the years. And there had been many an approach from the sea in weather conditions such as this.

I gasped when the pilot made for the mountains. I watched the slideshow unfold—green trees, green grass, a few houses peeking through—over miles and miles of banana trees. It was "green gold" once. Now it was only green, thanks to free trade and lack of foresight from the leaders.

We were going to go through the bank of dark grey clouds to land.

Why did the pilot choose this path?

It was my last thought before our descent. On the descent for touchdown, the plane rattled, people screamed with fear, with regret. It was brief and the black wheels touched the black tarmac—we'd landed.

People were shaken.

Voices rose in protest. "Why did they fly us from Antigua to put our lives at risk?"

I smiled inwardly. These were the same voices who'd demanded, "I want to go home no matter the cost. They better get this plane to Dominica!"

One moment of fright erased their earlier protests.

I was home.

These were my people.

I gathered my tan leather bags to disembark, paying no attention to the welcome message from the pilot. My mind was consumed with the long drive ahead.

The long drive to bury my mother.

The long drive to bury our unreconciled differences.

The long drive to bury the past.

The long drive to take full responsibility for my sister Juliette.

This is our story of survival.

2

Before Things Fell Apart
(1984)

My mother told me I had been a breech baby. Because of it she had declared for years I would have good luck and be super smart throughout my life. My sister Juliette, four years older than me, was smart too, and she wasn't a breech baby.

Whenever I asked my mother to explain the contradiction she would laugh, throw her head back and snap, "You ask too many questions Julia—too many."

Before I turned seven, she had stopped making her declarations.

I asked a lot of questions.

Who was my father?

Where was my father?

And the question I asked the most: when was he coming back?

She hated that question. It turned her into a fidgety, speech-bumbling, shifty-eyed woman. A woman I didn't recognise. She would turn her face and squeeze her lips together to make sure no words escaped.

At seven, I didn't know what to think. We had Daddy Julius—the man who'd stepped in to love my mother, to love Juliette and me—but I wanted to know my "real" father. Did my mother have something to hide? I didn't understand her retreat into silence whenever I asked about him. Velma Alexander, my mother, was well known for outtalking our parliamentary representative—he could speak for an entire day at the House of Assembly, using words like "pontificate" and "great development"—but still she wouldn't tell me about my father.

My mother's reluctance acted like a lighted match thrown onto kerosene-coated coals. It ignited my need to know into an inferno. But after the superstorm Hurricane David in 1979, I stopped asking; my father didn't come back, he didn't write, he didn't send a box or a barrel.

At seven, I began my first love/hate relationship. I hated my father because I was convinced he didn't care. I loved him because I *was* him. He had made me. I wanted to know all the parts that had created me. He had left the island, my mother said, to make life better for us.

We didn't get better.

We got Hurricane David. It had destroyed the house we had occupied in the middle of the village of Loubiere. The wind had taken the roof, and then the sea had taken the little house and everything in it. I watched the roof fly away from the house across the road, then our own roof went and then we'd had to make our way to another shelter.

I learned hurricanes not only destroy homes and roads and trees—it destroys hopes and dreams. It destroyed the dream of my father riding in to pluck us out of the hurricane rubble. And it birthed my silent revolution.

I made a simple vow.

I would do better, be better at saving our family.

After months of communal living in the chapel, Daddy Julius, our hero—negotiated for the house in the yard we began living in after Hurricane David.

The yard was a collection of four square houses made of scrap wood, according to Old Man Maurice. Each house was like a box with cut outs for windows and doors. The cut outs provided little ventilation and at the height of the daytime heat, the houses became ovens.

Four families occupied the yard. To the side of us Cheryl and Annya lived in the one-roomer. And at the back of us, Aunty Maureen, the seamstress, and her twins, Samson and Samuel, lived in a two-roomer—a replica of our box house. Then there was Old Man Maurice—the yard's money man—and Ma Titre. Technically, Ma Titre lived across the street from the yard, but I couldn't deny her membership in our little square.

And for my last four years of primary school, we lived in what Old Man Maurice described as "these houses built with ration board." "Thief!" he would say. "They thief these boards. They are *volé*."

And he would laugh uproariously every time he said it. Everyone was a *volé* for Old Man Maurice. He even called my Aunt Vignette "a thief, a *volé*" whenever she visited us. And he always said the English word and then the Creole word.

The sea was our backyard. And the road was our front yard. The front yard was my favourite because it was dominated by a black stone with a flat surface on which five persons could sit. Juliette, Samson, Samuel and I had christened it "the big stone."

The big stone was in turn dominated by a tamarind tree which bore tamarinds so sour our mouths filled with water the moment our tongue touched the brown skin. We had no idea how this large rock had embedded itself in the front yard. But it was where all the yard folks congregated and where Juliette and I spent many hours talking and dreaming.

In July 1984 I said goodbye to my primary school where I'd been nurtured for seven years. Seven years of penmanship, composition, mathematics, phonics, reading and dictation, science, social studies, grammar and spelling culminated into a single exam to determine whether I continued to high school.

Maybe because I was a breech baby, or because I studied so many hours on the big stone, I secured the number twenty-three position on the common entrance pass list for high school. I'd studied to make sure I passed. I didn't want to be a statistic. I wanted to be the child who would take my mother and Daddy Julius out of the yard.

Daddy Julius came from a long line of fishermen. He worked hard, and yet there had been little money beyond the basics for us. At one time my mother had cleaned houses a few days a week, but she stopped after Hurricane David because so many houses had been destroyed and no one wanted a cleaner. Five years later she hadn't resumed cleaning people's homes, and we were forced to live on the money Daddy Julius made from fishing.

And the lack of money forced us to live in a yard. Four houses of dingy clapboards—some splashed with remnants of green paint, but most were the mud-brown colour of the river after heavy rainfall. Narrow dirt paths connected the four houses. I hated slipping and sliding through mud after a rainstorm in my red push-in slippers, so eventually I convinced Juliette, Samuel, and Samson that we should pack the paths with millions of tiny pebbles from the beach—after which it became my job to maintain it.

We occupied the house in the front with two small bedrooms, an even smaller living room, and a narrow kitchen outside in the yard that housed decrepit shelving, countertops, and appliances. There were no pipes with running water, and there was no bathroom. It was not the kind of house that anyone dreamed of living in.

I vowed to get us out.

I was twelve and hadn't entered high school, but it didn't deter my conviction. A few months before the common entrance exams which determined my high school fate, our class had a visit from a man who'd attended our primary school. He'd spoken to us about his job as an accountant.

He recounted how it took long hard years of study to become a professional accountant but if you loved arithmetic, you were a logical thinker, you liked to ask questions, you liked to read—then this was the profession for you. "I guarantee you will find a good paying job in the country and in the region. I was a poor boy like many of you growing up and now I earn enough to take care of my family, buy a house and a car, and still have extra to save."

By the end of the talk, I had purposed in my heart to become an accountant.

I returned home that day and spent hours with Juliette on the big stone in the front yard talking about becoming an accountant, while she spoke about becoming a doctor. I recounted the speech to Juliette—how every skill our guest speaker had pointed out applied to me. I embraced his message like he'd been sent by God to deliver it personally to me. I christened it "my special message."

And for the first time I knew what I wanted to do when I grew up. I was going to become an accountant. I was going to make a lot of money. I was going to get us out of the yard.

But I almost didn't make it to high school.

My mother wanted me to go to Juliette's school, the All Girls High School, but my heart had been set on day one to attend a mixed high school. My primary school had been mixed and I couldn't come up with good reasons why I should attend a high school with only girls.

For months my mother had told everyone she met I would be joining Juliette in September at her school. Whenever I was near, I'd piped up, "Mamie, you know Grammar High School is where I want to go."

"Nonsense, no smart daughter of mine is going to go to that school."

"'That school?' What do you mean, Mamie?"

"You're going to go to the same school that Juliette goes to. One, nobody smart goes to that other school. Two, it's not a church school. Three, it has boys."

"But, Mamie, my church primary school had boys."

"The answer is no. You will attend the same school with Juliette."

MY NAME IS JULIA

She never explained why she didn't want me to go to a high school with boys. And it confirmed for me there were no good reasons.

In the end, on the day of registration, she refused to go register me at the Grammar High School. It had been Daddy Julius who had intervened, unknown to Mamie, and unknown to me. He'd gone to the Ministry, the place of the government headquarters, and asked my Aunt Vignette to get me registered at the Grammar High School.

Aunt Vignette, my father's sister, visited the day after she'd registered me. I watched the interaction between my mother and my aunt from my position against the open kitchen door. I'd propped our rickety, dirt-coloured stool against the door to ensure I wouldn't slip off like I often did. I fell so often that Samson teased me daily about being clumsy.

My mother occupied the doorway like a soldier keeping watch, and Aunty Vignette sat on the back step with her flared floral yellow dress tucked between her legs. Her hair was pinned into a perfect puff in the middle held in place by a million pins. Her makeup and gold jewellery were perfect enough for her to grace the front page of Cosmopolitan Magazine.

My mother's once-favourite red dress with the big white bleach spot in the middle of the skirt was a direct contrast to my aunt's magazine-ready appearance. My mother always remarked on how much time and money my aunt put into her appearance but still couldn't find a man of her own. That day, though, she attacked Aunt Vignette for what she considered an interference.

"Vignette, I don't understand. Make me understand. *Fe mwen kopwann*. These two children. These two girls. Do you know how they're eating? Does your brother know if they are alive?"

"Come on, Velma. The girl didn't want to go to that school—why you want to force her? And *Julius* came to *me*."

"Julius. You mean Julius turned a crook?"

"No, he wants Julia to attend the school of her choice. She's going to be there for five years. *Papa Bondyé*, the child should attend a school where she will be happy."

"Happy? People go to school to be happy? Vignette—you and Julius—you're crazy and he is mad. *Fou épi fal*," she said and placed her hands on her round hips. Julia is a smart child and should go to the best school."

"She will be going to the best school," Aunt Vignette stated in a challenging tone. She backed up her tone with a frown and narrowed eyes.

"Vignette, I don't know why Julius involved you in where Julia goes to school. That's a matter for me, her *mother*. Where is your brother?"

Aunt Vignette tilted her head back and looked up at the sky and didn't speak. It looked like she was counting the white cloud formations.

"You can look at the sky all day. Where is your brother, Vignette?"

"I don't know," she replied, and pursed her lips. "*You* don't know. *I* don't know. Look, you moved on with Julius. What do you care about Julian? I come and look in on you and the girls from time to time. That's why Julius came to me."

"Yes, you bring us your hand-me-downs," my mother snapped.

"What's the noise? I could hear you all the way from the bridge," Julius called out from the road.

"You are a crook, Julius," my mother shouted before he came into view.

"Stop your drama, Velma," he said when he came to where we stood. He placed his repurposed flour bag on the ground. It was riddled with jagged holes which emitted slow streams of water. Inside several fishes were still thrashing around trying in vain to prolong their lives as if they knew we would be eating them for supper later.

Daddy Julius directed his full attention to my mother. He glared at her, and she glared back. Unperturbed, he continued, "I want Julia to attend the school she wants to attend. You say she was born smart. So she's smart enough to choose the right school to attend, not the school you think she should attend. She don't have to go where all them rich people going. She don't have to go to that church school. She go enough church school already. Let it be the last time I hear about this. I, myself, will take Julia to buy her uniform and her shoes," he said, and climbed the two back steps into the house.

I had watched his retreating back with the largest smile of satisfaction and said a silent prayer of thanks for Daddy Julius being in our lives. He was the only father I'd known. And because of him I would attend my high school of choice.

On the first morning of high school, I was restless and woke up early. My imagination was more overactive than usual—imagining my new friends, my new teachers. Imagining me no longer in this yard and in this house. I felt my chest tighten when I tried to rein in my mental wanderings. The future ahead of me seemed both exciting and daunting. I was twelve years old and I had to get ready for school, the first step on my journey to adulthood. Though I wanted to stay lost in my fantasies, I knew that I had no choice but to take this leap into the unknown.

About the time Old Man Maurice's cock started to crow, I couldn't lie in the bed I shared with my sister for another minute. I gave in to the sea of energy riding through my veins.

That Monday morning in early September represented a new beginning—from primary school to high school. My childhood days would have no choice but to recede into the past. I was on my way to being a big girl. I was also getting closer to where I really wanted to be, which was away from the cardboard two-bedroom lean-to shack in a yard. Right on cue the other neighbourhood fowls joined Old Man Maurice's red and black crow. They began their morning serenade and eliminated the peace of the early morning.

The sun was still behind the big mountain in the distance, casting dark shadows into our silent bedroom. I lay in bed, conflicted between my desire to go and explore what the new school year had in store and the fear of venturing out into an unknown environment. I was the only one awake in the house, Juliette was still asleep beside me. Although part of me longed to stay in the safety of our bedroom, I knew that I had to face the day and start my new journey in high school.

With a deep breath, I tiptoed around the house, avoiding any creaky floorboards, careful not to wake anyone up. I was bursting with excitement for this new chapter in my life—high school.

I tiptoed my way barefooted onto the dew-wet grass to the narrow sliver of floor space which passed for a kitchen. Inside I turned on the single bare bulb dangling from the ceiling on a black cord matted with years of dust. Two open shelves, unpainted and unvarnished but covered with dents and stains from long use, contained all our pots, pans, plates and cups.

A slab of scrap wood held up by a drum passed for the counter where food preparation took place. A second counter on the opposite side of the wall held the two-burner stovetop.

In this strip of a kitchen my mother Velma tried her best to deliver poor-man gourmet. Next to the door stood the world's smallest fridge, whose origins were dubious. One day it appeared in its exalted position all worn and dirty and when I asked Mamie where it came from she refused to answer.

It wasn't a simple life.

It was a hard life.

"Julia," Daddy Julius's deep voice startled me. I should not have been surprised because he was always the first to wake.

"Yes, Daddy Julius? You frightened me," I replied.

"Girl, why you like to frighten? You too like to dream, Julia," he said. I tried not to roll my eyes or sigh. But one glance at Daddy Julius told me he wasn't serious because his eyes twinkled with mirth.

He had on the red t-shirt emblazoned with the words "Have a Coke and smile." It had become his uniform since he'd gotten it from the Hurricane David rations. The white letters on it had faded. It was torn around the armpits, but it didn't stop him from wearing it. My mother often threatened to throw it away and he would respond, "Try it if you're a woman."

"You ready for school, Julia?"

"Yes, Daddy Julius. It's why I couldn't sleep."

"I heard you get up. It's a big day for you. You're growing up. You were about a year when your mother and I started loving. You are my daughter, Julia."

I stood there and smiled at Daddy Julius. It wasn't usual for him to get so sentimental. It was like he had just realised I was no longer a baby.

"You are all grown up, Julia," he repeated and pulled up the shaky wooden stool. I didn't understand why Daddy Julius refused to ask his friend John to fix the stool. The stool needed new legs, new paint, new scent. It smelled of sweat and every food ever cooked in the kitchen. He sat down and let out a sigh. He looked at me for a long time, from my toes to the top of my head.

"Why you acting so funny, Daddy Julius?" I asked and the words came out slow and shaky. Daddy Julius had left most of the child-rearing to my mother. He had never beat me or Juliette. He intervened when my mother went overboard with the tamarind whip on our backsides. His scrutiny caused me to lick my lips which had become brittle like dry leaves. I shifted my eyes to look at the linoleum covered floor; the white spots were spreading from the vigorous scrubbing Mamie had us do every Saturday.

"Look at me, Julia," he commanded, his voice like a heavy echo in the small kitchen.

I looked up at him. I swayed a bit and planted my feet firmer against the floorboards. I was dressed in my flowered nighty, a relic from Hurricane David relief supplies. This new Daddy Julius was unexpected.

"Julia, listen to me well. You see I made sure you got into the school you wanted to go to. I only want you to promise you will study your book and you won't allow any boy in that school to touch you."

I laughed, relieved that's all Daddy Julius wanted to say to me. Of course, I had no intention of letting any boy touch me at school. I had only one goal: to make it through high school with success.

I looked around the bare kitchen. On the grease-spattered shelf was a pound of sugar in a brown paper bag, sharp edges intact. It hadn't yet been opened and poured into the small Nido tin. The tin once had powdered milk, but it was repurposed like the butter container and biscuit tins my mother had begged from Ma Titre.

In the newly arrived battered fridge were the repurposed rum bottles filled with water, and butter containers making ice. A month ago, we'd had to buy ice or beg for it. The ice took long to make, and the water was never chilled like the soft drink from the shop.

I loved nothing more than to sip on a chilled fizzy orange soft drink, and when the freeze went straight to my brain, I would close my eyes and say "ahh."

The other shelf had enamel plates and cups with dents and chips. Beside the sugar and Nido tin were rice in a brown paper bag, a tin of sardine and mackerel, Maggi chicken stock cubes, and the yellow-orange cooking butter I loved to put on hot bread and hot green figs.

I'd only had to look around the kitchen for my inspiration to succeed at school. I hadn't needed this talk from Daddy Julius.

But he was determined to have this talk. Even though he looked as uncomfortable as I felt. Maybe my mother had put him up to it. I was relieved he didn't have more to say, and I was touched by his interest in my welfare and Juliette's welfare was real.

"Promise me, Julia," he said, his face super serious. "Don't let any of those little boys touch you."

"I won't, Daddy Julius. I promise," I said, my words strong and confident this time. And in a move he had never done before, he took my hand and squeezed it. The new Daddy Julius had resurfaced.

"Julia, why you got up so early?" My mother's voice rang out as she came through the kitchen door. She stopped in the doorway and glared at me and Daddy Julius. Daddy Julius released my hand. My mother's glare didn't faze me for she wavered between glaring and joking. Her two sides were always at war. After twelve years I couldn't gauge what side to expect.

"Julia, you ironed your uniform."

"Yes, Mamie, since last night. You forget . . ."

"Take the bucket and go and get water for you to bathe, unless you want to go to the river," she shouted at me. I didn't know why she shouted. But that was my mother, she tended to overreact most times.

I left to get the bucket. I wanted to avoid the freezing river on the first day of high school. I skipped on the way to the standpipe. I smiled like I'd come first in the common entrance exam. I swung my black bucket and whistled. I felt free and happy.

A warmth spread over my body. The very idea Daddy Julius and my mother cared about my well-being had broadened my smile. They hadn't had the opportunity to attend high school. Both were born at a time when social and economic factors in the then-colonial state prevented many from accessing a high school education. Many parents simply didn't have the money. And many didn't see the value of an education.

I was fortunate. A lot had changed since 1978, the year we gained independence from Great Britain. More people were invested in attaining their own independence. On the one hand, I felt proud to be living in a newly-independent country, but on the other, I couldn't help but remember the years of hardship and struggle that denied my parents and so many others before them the opportunity for a high school education.

A few hours later, the little black clock on the tiny window ledge in our room struck seven o'clock, and I tied the lace on my second shoe.

My mother shouted from the outside kitchen, "Julia, child, hurry up. You have to catch the bus to get to school. You better hurry."

"Oh, Mamie, I'm dressed. I was coming for you to tie my shoelaces for me, but I tied it myself."

Juliette, who remained buried under her cover, laughed aloud.

"What are you laughing at, Juliette?"

My mother joined in with her laughter. "She must laugh, Julia. Oh, *Lawd*, Julia, you must learn to tie your shoelace. You're a big girl and on your way to high school. How you going to tell your friends your mother tying your shoelace?" she said, and broke into a round of boisterous laughter.

"Why would I have to tell them anything about my shoelace and how it got tied? No one will ask. You will see," I said, unable to keep from laughing with them. It was true, I couldn't tie my lace.

"Hurry, Julia," she snapped when I reached for my brand-new bag. "You know I made arrangement with Angus to carry you and I will pay by the month. You have to be by the road by seven fifteen."

I quickened my pace, and, powdered, combed up, laced up, and bagged up, I left the house. My mother had contracted with Angus, the fastest and safest bus driver in Loubiere. Everyone called him Lightning—so he'd painted a bolt of lightning on the front of the green bus, and the word "Lightning" in big letters on the sides.

I made it to the bus on time and it was packed with others like me wearing khakis, bright white shirts and shirt jacks stiff with starch. The uniforms were crisp, and those made with polyester had an extra gleam. I saw a lot of happy and proud faces on Angus's bus. I was happy for my brand-new shoes, and sure everyone else on the bus felt the same way. Our school items were bought with money scraped and saved over the year, and some came from overseas in a box or a barrel.

Bob Marley music blared from the loudspeakers of Lightning's bus. And He drove at the speed of light to get us to our new schools.

By the time I got to the school grounds, my stomach was tied up in knots and I licked my lips every other minute. My brand-new green haversack, my brand-new pen, and my brand-new exercise book didn't increase my confidence.

I made it to my new schoolyard on legs shaky as jelly. My confidence plummeted when I surveyed the large open green space. The L-shaped school building dominated the space—row upon row of doors, with two floors of classrooms. This was very different from the ten classes grouped around a small courtyard which had been my primary school.

I swore everyone had arrived before me. It was a sea of white shirt jacks and khakis, interrupted by the colours of the parents who had accompanied their children. I was alone. My mother had shifted from her original position enough to secure passage on Lightning to take me to school, but not enough to attend the first day of school with me. She hadn't forgotten or forgiven Daddy Julius for his treachery, nor me for my disobedience.

I made my way towards the crowd on the grassy field located next to the staffroom. I looked around for the one familiar face that should be there—that of my former classmate. I didn't see her in the crowd. I sighed, unsure of what to do next. I turned to walk away and ran into two girls. They were mirror images of each other. They had the same height, their hair was in pigtails with brown ribbons fluttering in the air. They wore mischievous smiles on their lips, like they were amused by what they saw around them.

Before I had the chance to say a word to the twins, a tall, big man with a round stomach came out of the staff room with the school bell—*pling, pling, pling*—and my first year in high school began.

"Good morning, students. I am your principal, Mr Rudolph Langlais. I welcome you to Grammar High School. Let me remind you straight off, you are not here by chance but by design. I and your teachers expect a lot from all one hundred of you."

"Today is a simple day, we tell you in what form you are going to be, who is your form teacher, give you your timetable and then we send you home. When I call your name, you will move to join the form you are assigned to. This year we will have three first forms."

The principal called out the names for form 1–1, then he started on the names for form 1–2.

"Gina Adams."

"Gloria Adams."

"Julia Alexander."

When the principal's booming voice called my name, I jumped and moved on legs as spongy as marshmallows to stand beside the twins. We stood beside each other, looking into the sea of faces to see who else would join our class. My former classmate from primary school, Maria, made it to my class, but I didn't know anyone else.

By the time the principal called our names there were thirty-six of us in line waiting to be form 1–2. Then he introduced us to our form teacher, Ms Bontiff. She would oversee us for the next year. All our problems and worries were to be directed to her. The principal called out the names for forms 1–3 and then we were sent on our way to our classrooms with our form teacher.

I loved our form teacher, Ms Bontiff. We'd gotten the prettiest form teacher. She was very slim, stylish, and wore her hair cut short almost like a boy's hair. But she didn't look boyish. She looked young and vibrant. She'd worn a simple white shirt and brown skirt the first day of school. She made the simple outfit classy.

She led us through the routine of each of us finding our seats in alphabetical order. It placed me in the desk right beside the one with the twins. I didn't see how this was going to work—twin sisters sitting next to each other in class all day. My grade seven teacher, Ms Roger, would not have allowed it.

I glanced at them and smiled my sweetest smile. The twins were as bright if not brighter than me. We could have been triplets—we had the same light tan skin, black curly hair, and same height. We were the tallest girls in the class, and we were sitting at the front of the class. No primary school teacher had placed me to sit at the front of the classroom.

"Julia Alexander," Ms Bontiff announced in a voice which snapped me out of my mental wanderings. "Please introduce yourself, and tell us what school you attended. Where do you live, and what are your likes and dislikes?"

I stood up, uncertain of what I should say. She'd bypassed Gloria and Gina. Why? I swallowed to settle the caterpillars in my stomach. I opened my mouth, and the words came.

"I am Julia Alexander. I attended the St Mark's School, where I was one of forty children. I live in Loubiere, a village not far from Roseau, with my father, mother, and sister.

"There are many things I love to do, like reading all sorts of interesting books. I've already read *The Year in San Fernando*." The entire class groaned.

I should have kept that information to myself. I paused, took a deep breath and continued, "I love going to look for mangoes and guavas and tamarinds with my friends. Most of all I love swimming in the sea and the river."

I took another pause and surveyed the room of unknown faces. Would they laugh at me, if I told them? Maybe. I stood taller, lifted my chin, and made my declaration, "And I already know what I want to be. I am going to be an accountant." And then I sat down to loud applause. It surprised me. I had never gotten such a reaction before. Maybe high school would be greater than I expected.

The rest of the time passed in variations of my little speech. I learned on the first day of high school, if you do something well, others will imitate you.

Ms. Bontiff gave us our timetables and sent us home until

Monday when school would start in earnest. I couldn't wait to carry my new books. I loved the strong clean scent—the scent of the untouched. By the end of the year my books and those of my classmates would be smelling like our breakfast, lunch, perfumes, and hair pomades. Our daily lives would have become ingrained in them. Smudges from food, pencil underlines and shadings would also defile them. And that's why I loved the beginning of a new school year. This one was special for me. New school. New friends.

I made my exit from the classroom, and was accosted by the twins, Gina and Gloria. They both opened their mouths at the same time and asked me, "Do you like our teacher and our class?"

I shrugged my shoulder and said, "It's too early to judge the class, but I like our teacher—she's stylish".

They laughed at my comment and said in unison, "We like her too."

"Do you two always speak at the same time and say the same things?" I asked.

"Not all the time," they both answered together, and then burst into laughter.

"We like you and hope we can be friends," said Gina, the twin with the brown watch. I had pinned their difference down to their watches. Gloria's was black. I had never owned a watch.

By the time I got to the front door of our house my first day of high school I was bursting with excitement. I had so much to tell my sister and my mother. However, no one was home. I took the key from under the stone next to the two steps leading to the front door. Juliette and I had moved the stone from the seashore under the direction of our mother. We had grunted under the weight of the stone to get it into place. Daddy Julius shook his head at our folly and commented, "Some people should make boys".

I let myself into the house and went to the room I shared with Juliette. Our room consisted of a double bed Daddy Julius had made himself from local wood he had cut down by the river. Daddy Julius loved to think he had made the bed by himself but he could never have completed it without the help from John, his carpenter friend.

There was a dresser with three drawers my mother had bought dirt cheap from a family who'd migrated to the United States after hurricane David, from somewhere up in the village. The dresser was divided into two drawers for Juliette and one for me.

In one corner of the room our wardrobe hung from the wooden partition wall on white stretchy wire secured by big silver nails from end to end. It was made from a bright floral print cloth and it housed our uniforms and the three church dresses we each owned, which were all hand-me-downs.

For the first time, my uniform was not a hand-me-down. It had the sharp clean scent I associated with my books. The same for my green haversack, shoes, socks, ribbons. Daddy Julius had ensured my mother bought everything new for me. He had done extra fishing to make it happen. A meal or two had been cut but I started high school with everything brand new.

I had smiled for days and stopped many times to admire and smell all my new things. I hadn't gotten a lot of new things, so the one time I did I made sure to appreciate the scent of them.

My mother blamed our lack on the father I'd never known. I had never even seen a photo of him. I didn't even know if we had photos. There were no photos on the walls of the house or on the table like I'd seen in other people's homes. When I asked my mother for my baby photos and photos of her and my father, she responded, "David took them." She blamed Hurricane David for a lot of things, too.

I took off my uniform and stretched out on my bed to think.

I was always thinking.

Thinking about the future.

Thinking about how I was going to turn our family's life around.

3

A Sudden Change

(1984)

T wo weeks before Christmas of my first year in high school.

The aroma of black local ground roasted coffee and oniony and garlicky sardines caressed my nostrils. The faint strains of Christmas music from the transistor radio in the outside kitchen floated to my ears.

Those things told me Daddy Julius was getting ready for his day at sea. Screech. Squeak. A door opened. Followed by the groan of the floorboards under the weight of Daddy Julius's black boots.

"Velma, *mwen ka kité*. I am leaving," Daddy Julius called out to my mother.

"Where are you going today?" she inquired.

"Gustave, Savant, Ti Gus, and I are taking the boat out to Soufriere and Scotts Head today."

"Why so far?" my mother asked, her voice an octave higher than before.

"It's almost Christmas, we want to bring back a huge load of fish," he replied.

"Be careful, Julius. I don't like when you all go out into the Atlantic Ocean." This time I heard irritation mingled with concern in her voice.

"We are seasoned men of the sea, Velma," he said outside our bedroom door.

"Girls, are you up?" he said, and appeared in the doorway with his uniform red t-shirt. The capital "C" in Coke was gone.

"Yes, I'm awake," I replied and stretched my body under my warm, colourful wool blanket—a remnant from the 1979 Hurricane David rations.

"Juliette," he called out.

No response came from Juliette beside me. Her chest and breath rose gently, her arms were curled around her pillow. I was sure she was awake and didn't want to answer for fear she would be asked to start her chores. I hadn't adopted the trick yet.

"Take care, Daddy Julius, and bring back my favourite fish. Lots of it," I said.

"Those tiny fishes that your mother has to spend hours cleaning?" he called out with a snicker, while making his way back through the door. "I will bring seven."

"Julius, you better not bring any of that *kayi* here today?" my mother threatened.

He didn't reply as he was already out the front door to head up to the village to meet up with Gustave and the others.

We had a ritual in our yard at my favourite time of the day.

It was when the sun began its descent over the deep blue sea before it disappeared below the horizon. Our yard folks would spill out of the small wooden houses to escape the heat trapped in the timber.

On that hot day when Daddy Julius had to bring back my seven little fishes called *kayi*, my mother, my sister Juliette, and I were the only occupants on the big stone. The furnace beneath our skin hadn't yet transferred its heat from our buttocks to the big stone. Grey clouds raced to cover the orange rays of the sun, but we didn't move—we would only move if the rain came. From our vantage point on the big stone we watched other villagers go up and down the narrow green bridge. We weren't there long when the cultural grand dame of the village came into view making her way down the bridge.

"Is that Ma Titre? What's wrong with her?" my mother asked. We watched Ma Titre approach, walking in long halting steps.

"It sure is her," Juliette replied. "You can't miss her white cotton head tie."

"I've never seen her hurry. She's always strolling through the village," I added. "How Daddy Julius describes her walk? 'If I reach, I reach. *Si mwen wivé, mwen wivé.*'"

Juliette's eyes crinkled with laughter. "Yes, he says it like that all the time."

"Mamie, what news you think Ma Titre is bursting to tell?" I asked.

Ma Titre's faster than normal pace became more pronounced with each step, the closer she got to us. Before my mother could remark on it, she'd come to a halt at the edge of the big stone.

She placed her hands on her hips and struggled to get air into her lungs. Her chest heaved up and down with the effort. She sounded like she'd been chased by my favourite village dog Spotty with the black spots, more popularly known as Police Loubiere.

The news she was bursting to tell us escaped through her pores—ten-cent size beads of sweat gleamed below the edge of her staple white cotton head tie. She wore this every day except Sundays. On Sundays, she switched to a colourful madras head tie and long white cotton dress.

"You all heard the news yet from Pointe Michel?" she asked and took a lungful of air to steady her breathing.

"A boat is missing." She expelled the words like a bullet shot from a gun.

"What kind of boat?" my mother asked in a shrill voice I had never heard her use before. I glanced at her and my stomach dropped like a heavy anchor dropping to the floor of the ocean.

Ma Titre replied, "A green boat".

"A green boat?" my mother asked. "You sure is a green boat they said?" She repeated the words in a louder more uncertain tone.

I knew the boat Daddy Julius worked on was a green boat with a name painted on the boat. I couldn't recall the name of the boat while the conversation unfolded between my mother and Ma Titre. My eyes darted from one woman to the next.

When Ma Titre uttered her next words, a chill crept through my body.

"Yes, it is a green boat with the word 'Emelda' painted in black on it."

"*Bondyé*," my mother screamed. "Gustave and Julius boat."

"They said is Gustave's boat," Ma Titre responded in a shrill voice as she came closer to the big stone.

"That's Gustave and Julius boat," my mother repeated.

"I didn't know Julius had share in that boat, and all the time you never said anything?" Ma Titre asked, and rested her large hands against her wide hips, her breath more even.

"Ma Titre, I don't have time for your gossip-searching ways." The skin around her eyes had bunched up and the glare she leveled at Ma Titre had a look I'd never seen in my mother's eyes. The chill in my body increased and my heart started racing.

"Are you sure about the news? Why Pointe Michel?" my mother asked and stood up. "They went to Soufriere and Scotts Head. This morning I told Julius before he left I don't like them going out in the Atlantic Ocean. Look, what happened, now?"

"They've not returned to Pointe Michel, that's what raised the alarm," Ma Titre said.

"I'm here sitting, thinking Julius is in Pointe Michel probably having one or two drinks before he get a ride to come home," my mother said.

"I don't know why Julius had to buy a boat with a man from Pointe Michel. We have enough Loubiere fishermen around here he could have asked to buy a boat with them. After all these years of fishing and coming from a fishing family, he couldn't buy his own boat. And that Gustave like to go to the Atlantic Ocean to fish," Ma Titre spewed as if she were the authority on fisheries' affairs.

"Ma Titre. Not today." My mother stood up. "Let me go put on some decent clothes and shoes and go find out what's happened to Julius them," my mother deadpanned. She hurried into the house with the agility of a street cat. But I didn't miss that her eyes had grown bright with unshed tears.

Juliette and I had sat immobilized through the exchange. I couldn't follow her into the house. The muscles in my legs had become mushy like the mashed *toton* Ma Titre and Old Man Maurice liked to eat. The strength had drained out of my legs. The same thing must have happened to Juliette because she didn't get up to follow Mamie. In record-breaking seconds, my mother emerged from the house dressed for the road.

Juliette and I, however, didn't move.

I couldn't wrap my mind around the news with the fog of panic in my head.

What did the news mean?

Was Daddy Julius dead?

Impossible.

Daddy Julius was the strongest swimmer in the village. The tallest and most muscular fisherman I knew. He knew these waters. From Loubiere to Scotts Head on canoe boats. I remembered the night he told Juliette and me the story of his first fishing trip. He told us when he was seven years old, his father had announced, "It's time to start earning your keep."

He had joined his three older brothers who'd already been indoctrinated. On his first trip his job was to bail out the water from the boat. These waters were his universe. And he was the last—the only one—left from a long line of fishermen. His father and brothers had perished in these waters doing what they loved.

Daddy Julius had disappeared. Impossible. I chose to believe he had gotten lost. The idea he may have been snatched away by the jaws of a water death caused my saliva glands to shut down. It was a mistake. Ma Titre was carrying bad information. She was wrong. They were wrong. Daddy Julius was sitting in a shop in Scotts Head, having a drink or two for the road.

Juliette pulled me out of my thoughts when she grabbed my hand and said, "Let's get up and follow Mamie up the road. We have to find out what happened."

By the time we got to the village centre the news of the missing men and boat had already spread, faster than a bush fire in the dry season. Several people had surrounded my mother each clambering to bring some comfort and to pull whatever information they could from her, to retell.

Rivers of tears streamed down my mother's face. She'd become so pale, like the tears were draining her natural hue, the faint hint of brown, out of her skin.

If Daddy Julius was dead . . .

I couldn't finish the thought.

He could not be dead.

Each passing moment brought no news. By the time it grew dark, there had been no word about the men. We were waiting for the group of fishermen and friends headed by Big Man to return to the village with news.

The wait ended when a blue pickup truck deposited Big Man, whose real name I didn't know, and the others. When I saw Big Man, my heart soared with hope. Big Man was the second-most experienced fisherman in the village, after Daddy Julius.

I stood next to Juliette in the crowd. I wrapped my arms around her waist and my head rested on her shoulder. My throat shrivelled up like sorrel left to dry in the sun. My heart pounded in my small chest, and it felt like my eardrums would burst.

Darkness enveloped the crowd gathered on the road. Onlookers. News purveyors like Ma Titre. Comforters. All leaned towards Big Man to hear his report.

"We got as far as the Martinique passage. No sign of Emelda. No sign of bodies. No sign of nets, dead fishes, or lines."

"Big Man, what you mean?" my mother screamed.

"I'm sorry, Velma, we found nothing. Only darkness."

"So, you all just leave them out there and come back to the village?!" she screamed again.

"Velma, we will go back tomorrow morning—"

She cut him off. "Tomorrow morning! By that time Julius will be dead—eaten by the sharks and fishes."

"Maybe the French fishermen found them," a voice in the back offered.

"Maybe," Big Man replied. "Maybe they entered what the Frenchman likes to think is his territory."

"Where is Frenchman territory?" Ma Titre asked Big Man.

This was too many questions for Big Man. "It's right in Dominican waters. The Macouba Bank. The French fishermen claim it. They go there with their big boats. That's why Gustave bought a bigger boat."

"Gustave and his big boat idea. He got Julius in it. Never trusted Gustave, with his smooth talk and wide smile," Ma Titre said. The crowd grew silent. But Ma Titre wasn't done preaching. "All for money . . ."

"Enough, Ma Titre, enough. We need to find the men. I don't care about Frenchmen. I don't care about fishing boats. I don't care about fishing banks. I need to find Julius alive," my mother cried.

With these words my mother folded like my multi-coloured rag doll Maureen our neighbour and seamstress had made for me. However, Ma Titre, with a strength I didn't know she possessed, saved my mother from falling to the ground. Cheryl and Aunty Maureen, who had arrived during the long wait, rushed to help Ma Titre with propping up my mother.

Juliette, myself, and all the other women of the village gathered around my mother. Some to support. Some to record for retelling later on. The air filled with wails of "*Bondyè*" and "*Papa Bondyé*."

I watched my mother's tears stream down her golden, sun-kissed face. My own heart was breaking. I wanted to cry, but my own tears I locked away. I chose to remain brave and believe Daddy Julius was alive. No matter how much the erratic pounding of my chest seemed to scream otherwise.

When we went to bed that night, my heart was heavy and weighed down with feelings over the future. My hope from earlier faltered and I gave into the tears. I cried until my sobs became dry heaves. Exhaustion lulled me into a restless sleep. And for the first time I fell asleep with my back to Juliette.

Hours later, I awoke and turned to face Juliette lying next to me in the double bed. No radio played. Not a whiff of roasted black coffee floated through the air. Not the squeak or screech of a door. All was quiet. The only sound was the distant lull of the sea on the millions of coin-size stones that lined the seashore. The salty and fishy smell of the sea permeated the air, reminding me of Daddy Julius and that he was still out there on the ocean. I wanted him to come back.

"Juliette," I said, my voice strained like I'd been playing "Who can shout the loudest?" with Juliette and Samson and Samuel on the seashore for days, like we did when we were younger.

"It's so quiet. I don't hear Daddy Julius outside getting ready to head out to sea."

Juliette groaned and turned her face to the windowsill, which held some of our valuables, our combs and brushes.

"I know, Julia," she whispered. "You know he's not coming back."

"How can you say that?"

"Because no one survives the Atlantic Ocean, Julia," she said with great conviction, and I squeezed my eyes shut and whimpered.

I rallied back and said, "That's a lie, Juliette. So many people have survived the passage to Guadeloupe or Martinique on smaller boats. Even Daddy Julius and Gustave and Big Man and so many other fishermen have gone and come back to tell stories."

"Okay, Miss Smarty. Daddy Julius and Gustave and Savant and Ti Gus are not coming back. I just know."

"How can you just know?"

"I have a sixth sense. I can see. I have open eyes. I have a spirit guide."

"Juliette. You're lying again," I said, and got out of bed. I slipped into my red push-in slippers.

"It's no use talking to you. I'm going out to the kitchen to make some cocoa tea."

"You're going to make cocoa tea? Unbelievable." She laughed with a hilarity which didn't suit the interaction and turned back to face the windowsill.

The house was too quiet. It'd never been this quiet in the morning. Daddy Julius's morning routine was the clock by which we woke and got ready for the day. A short jab of pain stabbed my belly. I crept past the door of my mother's room and the quietness there caused me to pause to listen. Silence. She must have fallen asleep in the early hours of the morning.

Last night she'd cried without ceasing, wailing. "Julius, gone dead, Julius gone dead. What will I do? *Sa mwen ka fè?*" The wails had reverberated off the flimsy wooden walls of our little house.

I'd buried my head under my thin pillows. But they'd been useless against my mother's cries of agony. Her tears triggered my tears which seeped into the aged spring mattress. Through the course of the night, I cried. And Juliette fell into a deep sleep.

Through the long night I laid in the dark alone with my grief over the only father I'd known. I hadn't met the man who'd fertilised the egg which formed me in my mother's womb. Daddy Julius had been part of my life from birth. I'd kept vigil all night.

Wishing.

Hoping.

Praying.

I wanted him to come back with a bag of whatever fish was left from the catch. He had promised to bring back my favourite fish. In the dark of the night, I didn't care about my favourite fish anymore. I wanted my favourite father. I wanted my only father. And as the night wore on, I settled against Juliette's warm body. How could she sleep? I had to squeeze my hands to resist the urge to shake her awake to scream at her. For the first time in my life I wanted to scream.

But I didn't.

At about ten o'clock that morning, two heavy knocks sounded on our rickety brown front door. The knock rattled the jalousie louvres, and the front wall. I was reluctant to open the door, but I was the only one in the living room. I got up from the shabby brown table chair and pulled the door open. Two men in plain clothes stood on the front steps.

"Good morning, sirs," I said.

"Is your mother home?" the man with the bald head and bulging eyes asked.

"That's me," my mother answered from behind me.

"We are police officers, we received a call about missing fishermen and we have a few questions for you," said Baldhead-and-bulging eyes.

"Questions? Police? How can I answer questions in my time of sorrow?" my mother asked. The sharp edge to her words made me want to huddle behind her, away from the two men. But it hit me that I was twelve years, and not two when I used to be afraid of everything and everyone. I'd outgrown hiding. I shifted so my mother could stand beside me at the door.

"Ma'am, this is routine." Again from Baldhead-and-bulging-eyes. "I am Officer Andrew, and this is my partner, Officer Luke. We are from the Criminal Investigation Department."

"Routine? Officer Andrew, my husband and three other men are missing, and you are here for routine?" she asked and took a step towards them. She swept her arm through the air and regarded the police officers with a tight expression in her eyes.

"Yes, this is a routine investigation," continued Officer Andrew.

"Investigations? Officer, about what?"

"The boat Emelda," he replied.

"Officer, I cannot take any more pressure. I cannot answer any questions in my state of mind," she said and turned away from them and moved to sit on the chair I'd occupied before the officers knocked.

She waved her braceleted hand, and the noise of the silver bracelets sounded like a lame symphony band.

"Please, officers, have a seat. Tell me why you are here and not on the sea looking for the men and the boat."

The officers sat their bulky frames on the two other puny table chairs that were set up against the green-painted wooden walls. I remained in the doorway. I wanted to stand in their presence. I also wanted to flee from their presence. And I didn't want to sit on Daddy Julius's chair. His black shirt remained in the same spot he'd left it. I was also ashamed in their presence. There was a war within me. My shame came from the state of our furniture—four creaky table chairs.

The officer with the bald head and bulging eyes had a small black notebook with a red spine, and a yellow pencil. His partner, the silent one with big bushy joined eyebrows, sat in silence while Mr Bald Head, Officer Andrew, questioned my mother.

He asked my mother what time Daddy Julius had left the house. What had he been wearing yesterday when he left the house? He asked more questions directed at determining his daily routine. During the entire interview, Officer Silent Bushy Eyebrows Luke didn't ask a single question.

But he looked at my mother without wavering. My mother answered each question in great agony, and in a flood of tears. As I watched my mother's agitation grow, I began to resent the police presence in our home. I felt my mother was being treated as a suspect in Daddy Julius's disappearance by Officer Baldhead and Bulging Eyes Andrew. Who had called the police? Ma Titre? She was always calling the police.

I exhaled the pressure I'd felt building in my chest when Mr Baldhead closed his black notebook, tucked his pencil behind his ear and stood to leave. He promised to be in touch if they received any word from the Martinique authorities.

It meant the questioning was over and we could be left in peace to lament. I stole a glance at Juliette's face; she'd come into the room during the questioning and took the chair across from Officer Silent. I'd seen him glance over at Juliette, his eyes taking her in from her toes to her head.

She'd had no tears seeping from her eyes, but her eyes were red rimmed. It didn't detract from how beautiful she looked; her long black hair cascaded in soft curls around her shoulders. Her blue terry cloth shorts and a white vest sans bra, showed off her smooth light golden skin. And she knew her legs looked perfect in them. It was her favourite stay-at-home outfit. I was twelve but I didn't miss the look Officer Silent had in his eyes when he looked at Juliette. Up. And. Down.

I exhaled after the officers left. My mother went into a fresh wave of crying and bawling that brought Ma Titre from across the road. My mother cried like Daddy Julius was irrevocably lost at sea. Her tears would stop and then start afresh, it was like turning a tap on and then off. Through all of this I remained an observer, watching as scene after scene unfolded before my eyes.

On the second day after the disappearance, I had hoped for a break in the case of the missing Emelda. However, the day ended with no word from Big Man. And there had been no word from the police. My mother ensconced herself on the big stone and talked nonstop about the incompetence of all public authorities.

To me no news was still good news. Daddy Julius was the fittest swimmer I knew. Surely, he was floating or swimming out in the ocean.

I believed in my heart a boat had picked them up and was bringing them back to Dominica. Meanwhile, all my mother did was shed more tears. Her and Juliette's lack of faith had exhausted me. It was only day two and they had already lost hope.

I clung to my hope and fought my loss against the heaviness in my chest and limbs, my lack of energy, the slow movement of time.

I had hope, but I wanted the pain to end.

It was almost Christmas.

And we didn't have any Christmassy things in our household.

But on the day the scent of sorrel, ginger, cinnamon, and bay leaf floated out of Maureen's kitchen into our kitchen, it brought a faint smile to my face. I'd been sitting on the stool, the functional door stopper and the prized seat over which Juliette and I had numerous fights.

There had been no word on the Emelda. I refused to think Daddy Julius was missing. He couldn't be missing. How could four men, strong fishermen, get lost at sea? Aren't there big ships out there to see them and rescue them? Isn't God looking down with his outstretched hand to save them?

While the search for the missing Emelda had gone cold, our kitchen had gone colder. My smile faded when I took in our empty shelf—all our Christmas preparations had halted.

Every year we had to do the purge. Twice. On our bodies before returning to school in September by drinking a bush tea concoction. And on our house before Christmas by cleaning.

I disliked the body purge.

I disliked the house purge even more.

I saw no good reason to put the chairs, the mattresses, the chest of drawers, and the grips out in the yard.

But my mother made sure we carried out every piece of furniture and belonging in our house into the yard for cleaning and to catch the sun's rays. Next, we would attack the walls with scrubbing brushes and blue soap and we scrubbed the dirt of the year away until the floor gleamed.

My mother considered the yearly purge a religion. Everyone in the neighbourhood did it and we were not to be the exception. The end of year also meant buying a brand-new piece of linoleum to put in the sliver of floor space in the kitchen. Not forgetting the four new curtains for the four windows in our house. The print floral cloth had to be chosen and brought to Aunty Maureen for making the curtains which inevitably went up two days before Christmas.

With no news of Daddy Julius and the other men, the yearly purge had been put on hold.

My heart had fluttered with joy. I considered it a heaven-sent pre-Christmas gift. No hard scrubbing brushes. No bending over for a whole day on my knees. No scrubbing at the floorboards. No wiping of the floor with a rag. No aluminium basin next to me. No sweating by the buckets.

I scolded myself for my thoughts. Daddy Julius remained missing, and my mother continued to cry without ceasing. At twelve years, I was more concerned with what happened next in my simple world than with her suffering. At twelve years, many times I'd done what I could to resist my mother's instruction and directions.

But my mother always saw straight through into our amateur tricks. The sharp sting of the tamarind whip against my skin is a memory that will never leave me. The whip was administered for the times I'd tried to go my own way.

In truth, I'd spent many of my days and nights in dreamland conjuring up a different time, place, and parents. I was always dreaming of making money to take us to a bigger house.

It wasn't fair we were stuck in a small house and our father was in the great United States. Sometimes all I felt for the man I didn't know was burning white rage. I would wish for harm or misfortune to happen to him. But I never liked myself after those dark thoughts. It darkened my mood for days and left me with headaches. And then I would return to my desire to get us out—to show him we—no, *I* was capable of success without his help.

In the face of the insurmountable hill I'd have to climb, my resolve would waver. I was like a steamroller going back and forth over the same surface, the same ground, the same issues.

I couldn't quiet my new thoughts and I didn't try. How were we going to deal with Daddy Julius no longer being here? When was my mother going to get out of her crying spell? All she'd done since the news for the last couple days had been to sit on the chair in the living room, bent over with her head buried in her hands, rocking back and forth, crying.

With each passing day it seemed to me she had forgotten she had two daughters who needed her.

Two daughters who needed to be told what to do.

Two daughters who longed to hear her shout and assert her authority again.

My mother, the strong, temperamental woman who demanded and acted. I'd always wondered whether she'd always been a strong willed, temperamental, talkative, bossy and bold and confrontational woman? Or had she been forced to become that way because of the hardships she'd faced in life?

I didn't move from my spot on the stool outside our kitchen. I sat breathing in the savoury aroma coming from Aunty Maureen's kitchen. The air grew heavy with spice today, one today, one week since the disappearance. Aunty Maureen's kitchen produced this savoury aroma turning my taste buds into water releasers. With our kitchen dead, Maureen became our chef, our cook, our caretaker while my colourful mother mourned.

My mother had two sides to her. On one side, she was warm and loving, showering me with her gentle words and sense of humour. But then in a split second, that warmth would disappear; her words like daggers, cutting through the air and inciting the desire in me to flee or fight. Her actions and reactions changed with the shifting tides of time and circumstance. Volatile at times. Manipulative at times. Was it the latter this time? Was her endless stream of tears her way of keeping sympathy going?

During the initial days of the men's disappearance a constant stream of people visited our small house. I noticed several people pressed money into my mother's palms at the end of their visit. Doubtless, people were expressing their concern. And the more my mother cried, the more people came to the house to offer solace.

When was it going to end? Not Until they found the bodies? Not until they found the boat? Not until they returned? If none of these occurred, how were we going to put a closure to this tragedy? These thoughts battered my mind.

These questions and thoughts pressed a bit more of my hope out of my heart. Could we live with a mother who no longer told jokes? Could we live with a mother who no longer screamed at us? Could we live with a mother who spent her days staring into space and bursting into the loud ear-splitting wails.

How long could we endure each new outburst? Each outburst brought Ma Titre out of her gate in a flurry of madras cloth to our doorway.

"Julia, stop dreaming," Aunty Maureen said, as she appeared in the doorway of the kitchen, a silver waiter in her large hands. I smiled. On the waiter were my favourites—*titiwi accras* and bakes. I jerked to awareness and gave a slow guilty smile.

"She's always dreaming, Ma," Samson said, carrying the jug of juice.

"I hope this is the sorrel I smelled earlier," I said in genuine pleasure.

"Of course not, Julia," Aunty Maureen said, laughing. "It hasn't even cool off yet. You have to wait. Christmas soon reach."

"Christmas, Aunty Maureen? I need to drink sorrel today."

"I am with you, Julia," Samson said. "Here is some lime squash in the meantime."

"Lime squash?"

"Yes, Julia, no one has been to the market yet. Today is Saturday, remember. Where is your mother, and Juliette?"

"They're inside," I said, and pointed to the open backdoor. "My mother is on her bed, crying like a hopeless woman, like her heart will never heal. I am tired of seeing her cheeks streaked with tears, a wet ink blue handkerchief clasped in her hands, her hair a tangled mess. And Juliette is gazing at the brown ceiling, a smirk playing at the edge of her pressed-together lips."

"Julia, watch your mouth," Maureen warned. "This is a hard time for your mother.'

"I keep hearing these repeated words like Samuel's jammed taped player he'd recovered from the bay. It's a hard time. Where is the hope? Can't a big ship find them and bring them back? Everyone is acting like they are already dead."

"They most likely are," Samson said in his low bass voice, which I was still getting used to.

"I don't want to believe that," I said, and took the orange plastic jug of lime squash from Samson. *I hate lime squash. Why are they bringing lime squash?*

"I know you don't like lime squash, Julia."

I jerked.

"Can you read my mind, Samson?"

"No, I just know you don't like it," he replied. Laughing. His black afro comb jutted out on the right side of his hair, which was always high.

"You need to cut your hair for Christmas," I teased.

"Not a chance. Before school, I will."

"We will see about that hair," Aunty Maureen said as she made her way up the two steps into the house to see to my mother and Juliette.

While Aunty Maureen tried to revive my mother and Juliette, I helped myself to the accras and bakes. I bit into the crispy fried accras, tasting the saltfish, the burning pepper, the fresh chives, the onions, the starchy smoothness and saltiness of the bakes. I closed my eyes. I was in bakes and *accras* heaven. I said a prayer of thanks for Aunty Maureen.

Aunty Maureen had taken on the job of feeding my mother, Juliette and me, but I didn't know where the money for food was coming from. I guessed it was from all the moneys being pressed into my mother's hands by the many visitors. I didn't ask because I would not have been given a straight answer. I relied instead on my powers of observation and learned as much as I could from the conversations flowing around me.

I recalled the many times Juliette and I were cast out of a room for the adults to talk. "Go out into the yard," my mother would say. There was never any question of us declining to go, what with the tamarind whip hidden on the ledge above the window in the drawing room.

This tamarind whip made many a contact with our backside and other parts of our bodies over the years. It was the eighties in Dominica. People knew how to train their children with the rod of correction. "Spare the rod and spoil the child" was a popular refrain.

My mother had been its biggest proponent, the tamarind whip her rod of correction of choice. She'd tried to whip us figuratively and literally into shape. It was a time when no one questioned whether lashing someone with a tamarind whip was too harsh. Yet, even then I sensed something was wrong about the act. It left my skin with red welts that would take days to heal. It was one thing I desperately wished Daddy Julius would have stopped Mamie from using.

Would she remain in this weakened state? Would the tamarind whip lie forgotten on the window ledge?

I prayed with all my heart she would be changed.

The Saturday before Christmas, my mother recovered enough to remember she had two daughters who needed to be put to hard labour for Christmas.

Dressed in her frilly blue nighty, she opened the door to our bedroom. Juliette's head was still buried under her pillow and my head was buried in my latest Hardy Boys book from the library.

"Juliette," she called out, "you better release that pillow. Time to rise. Time to get to work."

"And as for you, *manmzèl* with the book. Put that book aside. It's time to work."

Juliette stretched, groaned and threw her pillow on the floor and I reluctantly closed my book.

She's back. And she means for us to work. For us to purge.

"Juliette, I want you to go over to fetch some hibiscus leaves from Ma Titre's trees. I want you to help me wash my hair today. And you, *manmzèl* Julia, get ready to clean the house and the kitchen today."

"The whole house, today?" I asked.

"Yes, the whole house."

"But Mamie," I said.

"Don't 'but' me. You girls thought you would escape this year. This house is going to be cleaned like every other house. Do I make myself clear? Come, get up. *Levé.* Get dressed. Start working." She turned on her heel and returned to her room to get dressed.

I looked at Juliette, and we laughed in silence. Open mouths. Teeth shown. But no sound. Under no circumstances would we have laughed aloud. We'd learned that lesson a long time ago.

Juliette left and returned with a stack of dark green hibiscus leaves when the sun peeked from behind the big green mountain miles away. There were no scents floating from Maureen's kitchen. I didn't hear Old Man Maurice's radio, and Cheryl's doors and windows were still battened down.

I watched Juliette from my place on the stool in the kitchen. A stool I'd have to scrub later. I'd already gathered all the supplies we would need for our cleaning job. We'd made several trips to the standpipe to fill the drums of water.

Juliette took a seat on the last step and placed the orange basin between her legs. She folded her orange skirt between her legs and under her backside. She then rubbed the leaves together until the water grew thick and green with the pure nectar and essence of the hibiscus, and its herbal fragrance filled the air.

This was our mother's favourite shampoo. Free. Gentle. Green. Natural. With Juliette's help she washed and styled her black wavy hair. It wasn't much of a style. She had gathered her hair into a single ponytail, leaving the black strands to cascade freely down her back.

Later, she emerged from her room and came onto the backstep in a red dress Aunty Maureen had made for her two Christmases ago. I smiled and clasped my hand to my heart. My mother looked so beautiful. She'd coloured her lips red and had outlined her eyes in black eyeliner. I smiled at her first effort in days to be normal. As if they'd planned it, Aunty Maureen appeared in our section of the yard seconds later, dressed in a red shirt and white pants. From their dressing, I concluded they were heading to town.

Were my mother's tears finally gone? Were there no more visitors to receive? Was everyone else busy getting ready for Christmas? Would I have to listen to one more story about how "they say they might all be in Martinique or St Lucia now?" Did we have our mother back?

I smiled a wide toothy smile when my mother and Maureen hopped onto Angus's bus the Lightning, known to travel at the speed of light. Only God knows why those of us who travelled on the Lightning lived to repeat the experience.

"Time to get to work, Juliette."

"Where do you want to start?"

"You take the house, and I will do the kitchen," she replied.

"Juliette, look at me, the answer is NO! This year we are doing both together. I will not do the larger share of the work."

"Who is in charge here? I am the oldest."

I ignored her and continued, without a trace of humour in my voice, "Juliette let's start with the kitchen. You know we must finish both before Mamie returns from Roseau. You also know we will both get blows if any part is left undone. So, let's get to work."

"Look at the linoleum. It's down to the black parts peeking out. I can't even tell the colour of the carpet. You scrubbed it too hard during the year, Juliette."

"Maybe," she said, shrugging her shoulders, and added, "Let's start by putting everything outside first."

And for the next few hours, while the sun blazed its journey towards the sea overhead, we fortified ourselves with Christmas music from Samuel's salvaged radio and tape player and went to work.

We carried out every speck of furniture to the yard. Armed with the wooden scrubbing brush in one hand and blue soap in the other, we scrubbed every surface in the house while sharing a basin of water. We took turns to fetch water and we scrubbed the floor until we could eat anything off the floor.

When the sun had reached its midway point in the baby blue sky, we started to return the furniture into the drawing room. Just in time. The sudden presence of loud music right outside our door could mean only one thing. Lightning was depositing Mamie and Aunty Maureen from their trip to Roseau.

We opened the front door in time to see Angus pulling out a brown-and-white patterned linoleum for the kitchen. The piece of linoleum Angus handed to my mother looked as narrow as Maureen's seamstress measuring tape.

For the first time since the news of the missing boat and men, my mother smiled.

"Juliette, come and take this from my hand for the kitchen and you, Julia, come and take the shopping bag from Angus."

I don't know why I was called to take and carry the heavier item from Angus. I took the multi-coloured strip shopping bag, balancing the weight in my right arm, its silver handles glinting in the sunlight. Within its depth were brown paper bags of groceries. I had to stretch out my left arm for balance, while I carried the bag down the slight slope into the yard. I stopped in the doorway of our super clean kitchen to catch my breath.

"Julia, why you so weak?" Samson said behind me.

"Samson, go trouble your twin, Samuel, and leave me alone."

"Julia is a weak girl. A weak girl," he sang in his bass voice.

"Samson has a bass voice, a bass voice," I mimicked. "Get away from me with your big voice."

"Samson and Samuel, do I have to carry the groceries you all are going to eat," Maureen called out from the road.

Laughing, I said, "You better get Samuel and go carry the grocery or else you will feel the mortar pestle on your skin."

"No mortar pestle for me. For Samuel, not me," he said, laughing, his knee-length pants flapping in the wind, and, shirtless as usual, he turned to go collect the bags from his mother.

We got groceries and a new linoleum for Christmas. The latter's synthetic scent overpowered the kitchen for days. Where had we gotten this money from with Daddy Julius gone? We had survived in the past on regular earnings from fishing and his odd jobs here and there cleaning people's yards, and my mother washing and ironing here and there, which she hadn't done since Hurricane David. Right now we had only the basics. What would we face as the next fatherless family in the yard?

Aunty Maureen headed her fatherless family in the two-bedroom house behind ours. She was always in trouble with Mr Jones, the landlord, who always came to the yard to quarrel with her for the rent. A number of times my mother intervened and told Mr Jones a couple choice words. Aunty Maureen had a mild personality and accepted her situation with humility and did not use any curse words. Things were difficult for her with the twin boys Samson and Samuel, who were Juliette's age. Their father visited from Guadeloupe from time to time. When he did, he brought with him two boxes of groceries and the yard would feast on jus de raisin, yaourt, raisins and apples. When he left, famine would return until his next visit.

Cheryl, our neighbour to the side, lived in the one-bedroom. Money didn't appear to be a problem for her. She would dress in her finest and leave for town every day. My mother would "hmmm" when she saw Cheryl dressed and heading out.

The wealthiest person in our yard was Old Man Maurice. No one knew where he got his money from. There were rumours his children, who lived in England, sent him money in pounds sterling. He lived alone. He went to the village post office every week and collected the mail for everyone in the yard. He went to town on every Friday. On that evidence the adults concluded Old Man Maurice received his money from overseas. Old Man Maurice didn't work and he sang the same song every day: "Born Free."

What I do know for a fact, Old Man Maurice was the little yard banker. The bank who lent money to my mother, Maureen, Cheryl and maybe a quarter of the village. The banker who kept meticulous notes in his Canpad exercise book. At that point in the yard's history there was never any dispute as to who owed him at any point in time. As far I know up to this day, no one ever argued with Old Man Maurice over what they owed him.

Across the road Ma Titre ruled from behind her hedge like the rich queen of the hill. In my twelve-year-old mind, the little picture of our yard economics spun around my head while I packed the Christmas groceries on our open shelves in the kitchen.

I yearned to live in a bigger house and to have better clothes. How were we going to survive without Daddy Julius? Who would help us? Would Aunty Vignette rescue us? Would the church help us? Would the village continue to show up bearing gifts and money? Would my mother be strong enough in faith? Did she have a plan to help us meet our basic needs?

I hated the sudden change and the unknown future.

4

When Silence Reigns

(1984-1985)

In the two months since Daddy Julius disappeared, we had received only one solitary report—a whisper of a possible sighting of the Emelda in St. Vincent. Since then, an eerie silence had settled over us like a thick fog, choking any hope that remained. Could the boat be in Trinidad? Could it have veered off course towards some other unknown destination? Each day was a new torture as I clung to hope, imagining Daddy Julius clutching onto anything that would keep him alive, but also dreading what might happen if he never returned.

The waiting felt like an endless torment, with each passing day bringing more questions and doubts. What if he didn't want to come back? What if he was lost out there forever? The fear ate away at me like a relentless predator, and I found myself struggling to maintain any semblance of control over my thoughts or emotions.

Also during that time, the visitors dried up. Those who gave money, and those who came to extort information, and those who came to size up our house. All the care and concern left with the last of the visitors; sucked right out of the yard.

I saw my mother hover between dark moods and bright cheerfulness. No one suggested any of us should go to counseling. I buried my pain and assumed Juliette did the same. I went to school each day and came back to a dying house each day.

My mother spent most of those days on the big stone staring into the sky. Her spark came back when Cheryl had her domestic life ripped wide open.

I'd christened Cheryl the "Miss-Sophisticated" one in the yard. She was the fashionista in our yard. She was the most jewelled woman in our yard. She sported the latest fashion and wore matching earrings, necklace, bangles and shoes to her outfits.

In her miniature bedroom, it was a mess, like a hurricane had whisked through it. Clothes spilled out of her zippered black plastic wardrobe, which was hung above the bed and ready to topple onto the bed at the slightest agitation. Underwear, bras, dresses, and socks were scattered on the floor.

Her dresser stood within arm's reach of the bed. It was littered with perfumes, powders and all manner and colour of costume jewellery jutted out of a woven straw basket. Her plastic zippered wardrobe was too small to host all her clothes, so the rest of Cheryl's clothes spilled out of four brown grips stuffed under her twin bed. Cheryl had way too many clothes in the little house. Aunty Maureen who sewed for her living didn't have that many clothes.

Every day Cheryl dressed up and went to Roseau. She was always dressed like she was a contestant in the annual carnival queen show. Her best outfits rivalled that of any queen contestant. Her long hair, always worn loose, flowed like smooth satin down her back. When she didn't accessorise with matching colour jewellery she wore gold—distinct and beautiful pieces around her neck and hands.

Some of my happiest moments were when Cheryl allowed me to try on her jewellery while she laid on her bed wearing nothing but a t-shirt. Annya would be playing with her doll, giggling at pulling off its hair. For the short time I got to play adult dress-up, I smiled, preened, modelled. At twelve I already had an affinity for pretty things. But in our world, money was scarce to buy pretty things. We only had the basics. And I couldn't ask my mother for rings, earrings or bracelets. "Julia, if you want pretty things, go to America and find your father," she barked the few times I'd had the courage to ask for something I wanted. And it always shut me down for months because I didn't need reminders about our father the deserter.

But I never saw Cheryl get up in the mornings to go to work.

I was enamoured of her. Her sophistication. Her sense of style. Her sexiness. I watched her. I looked out for her, whenever I was home from school, because I didn't want to miss what she'd chosen to wear that day for her jaunt to Roseau.

I yearned for the clothes, the jewellery, and shoes to create my own sophisticated image. But I'd had to make do with the few amateur renderings from Aunty Maureen who worked in a school uniform dress shop, and that was only for Christmas and Easter and when our dresses no longer fit or were no longer fit to wear.

We didn't have the luxury of choice in our wardrobe selection. I dreamed of the time when I would have choices. I dreamed of the time I would have money to buy ready-made dresses. I dreamed of the time I would have jewellery on my dresser like Cheryl.

Then there was Annya. Cheryl's six-year-old daughter. Beautiful Annya with the angelic face. She'd been blessed with her mother's beauty. She had her mother's long black curly hair. Her eyes were the colour of liquid gold. Her eyelashes, the longest and curliest. But there were no pretty clothes for Annya. No pretty shoes. No pretty earrings. Her pierced ears remained bare. But her mother had two piercings on each ear, and each held a beautiful earring.

The disparity between mother and daughter raised the ire of my mother on several occasions. After raising the matter too many times and with no repentance from Cheryl, my mother settled the matter. She paid Aunty Maureen to make church dresses for Annya. After that, Juliette and I took Annya to church every Sunday at the chapel. Cheryl never went to church. And my mother's attendance was sporadic.

One hot afternoon after school, we alighted from Lightning, with a blast of calypso music, and laughter on our lips. Samson, Samuel, Juliette and me. On our favourite big stone sat a man as tall as the tallest coconut tree in the village. He was shirtless, his muscles bulging and shiny, his skin as dark as the blackest part of the night.

He glared at us and crossed his massive forearms across his chest. And glared at us again. Silent. It forced us to walk with haste past the big stone and down into the yard. The laughter on our lips died. Samson and Samuel hurried to their house and Juliette and I, without delay, opened our back door to let ourselves into our house.

Once we were safe, I asked, "Juliette, do you know that man?"

"How can I know him when we all saw him at the same time?" she said while she threw her bag onto our bed. *Thud*.

"I thought you may have seen him before. Why did he glare at us?"

"I don't know, Julia. Maybe he likes to glare," she hissed and pulled off her blue tie, followed by her white shirt.

"Did you notice how tall he is? Did you see his muscles? Daddy Julius's muscles never got to that size."

"You are too full of questions, Julia. Always wanting to know."

"Perhaps you don't question enough, Juliette. To question is to learn."

"Perhaps, Julia, you are reading too many books. Look at you. Your bag still on your back. Getting into things which do not concern you."

"What if he is an evil man? Did you see his eyes?"

"You saw his eyes." Juliette flopped onto the bed in her undergarments. I hadn't moved. I hadn't undressed. I remained rooted to the spot with my bag still on my back. Something about that man troubled me.

"After that glare, I wasn't going to look at him for another second. I am sure we will soon find out," Juliette said.

It wasn't long before we heard Cheryl's voice. I'd been surprised she was home given the hour of the day.

I rushed to the window nearest the big stone and peeked through the wooden louvres in time to see Cheryl hand the giant a plate brimming with a variety of provisions and red fish.

"Cheryl can cook?" Juliette whispered.

I said nothing.

Where did Cheryl find this man? He can't be Annya's father. Annya's skin is the colour of porcelain.

The giant smiled at Cheryl, and took the plate of food. It was hot. I saw the steam rising from the large red fish. He took it and immediately forked a piece of purple dasheen into his mouth. *How can some people eat steaming hot food and I can't?* My intolerance for piping hot food was legend in the yard. Samson called me a baby because of it.

"Is he Cheryl's new man?" Juliette whispered again.

"Shhh, too many questions," I whispered back. "Just look."

Juliette glared at me.

"Juliette, you don't like your own words . . ." I didn't finish my sentence. I got distracted by Cheryl's movement.

She'd gone back into her house, and she came out with another plate of food and joined the giant on the big stone.

The domestic scene unfolding before me was so unusual I didn't know what to make of it. In the three years Cheryl had lived in the house I'd never seen a man in the house. She'd arrived with baby Annya and had never divulged Annya's paternity. My mother, Ma Titre, and Aunty Maureen and even Old Man Maurice had tried and they had all failed. Annya's paternity was a high-level secret in our yard. And I knew with certainty the adults hadn't given up on finding out.

But that would have to wait. The more immediate thing to figure out was why had Cheryl brought this giant of a man to her two-room house. The bedroom was the length of a toy car. And the living room was as wide as a shoebox.

Satisfied that they were doing no more than enjoying their meal in silence, Juliette and I moved away from our favourite peek-through spot. I'd seen enough of Cheryl and her giant. I'd seen enough of their little lunch party.

But there were niggling questions vying for attention in my head—one of which was, *Who is this giant of a man who glares at children?*

We'd walked past him without greeting him, a cardinal sin in my mother's book of things-her-daughters-should-not-do.

Several times my mother had had words with me and sometimes more than words whenever an adult complained about my failing to greet them in passing on the village road. Mornings, afternoons, goodnights were high social expectations. Our punishment was words of censure, a beating with the handiest thing available, or both.

"Juliette. Do you think the giant will complain to Mamie that we didn't greet him?"

"I don't think he cares. Look at the way he glared at us."

"He could complain to Cheryl. And you know she would always tell Mamie."

"Julia, I don't think this man is going to say anything about that. And if he does, we'll tell Mamie he opened his eyes and glared at us with bared teeth."

"With bared teeth," I said laughing. "Juliette, I think you are stretching it."

"Of course. We would have to stretch it. I'm not getting words or blows for that man glaring at us. For sure."

"I agree," I said laughing and moved to finally remove my uniform to hang it on the nail on the opposite wall to where our well-made bed stood. Our mother had instituted the "Make your bed every day" rule. Another cardinal rule. Break it and you would meet the tamarind whip. "Poverty doesn't mean untidy or nasty," she would preach in the volume she loved to use for the neighbourhood to hear. And I hated when she thought the world needed to hear her sermons.

"Come on, hurry up. Undress so we can see what Mamie left for us to eat. You know once she gets home, we will get the story about the mystery giant, as you call him."

After Cheryl installed the mysterious man in her little house, she appeared happier. Every day she emerged from her house smiling. Her daily trips to town ended.

With each passing day after the installation of Robert—the name of the mystery man—in Cheryl's house, I'd been forced to listen to my mother, Ma Titre, and Maureen speculate and gossip about his origins. Even Old Man Maurice, the yard's money man, had entered the fray from time to time with words of wisdom.

It baffled me why the three of them had concerned themselves with discovering Robert's origin. They would sit for hours on the big stone discussing his height, his shoe size, and other parts of his anatomy.

One Sunday afternoon, when not a leaf stirred on the trees, the speculation mounted to new heights. I sat between the legs of my mother on the bottom steps for our weekly hair ritual. I was dressed in my thick purple knit t-shirt—a relic from clothes we had received in relief supplies after Hurricane David—and a short black skirt Maureen had made for me.

I closed my eyes when my mother pressed her finger loaded with green grease onto my scalp. With each press of her finger, I got a whiff of the fruity, fragrant, flowery smooth scent of the green grease. I was in hair heaven. Then she would twist a cluster of strands of my hair around her finger and rounded each into a knot she secured with a hairpin.

This process took time because my black hair fell below my shoulders. This was our weekly ritual—washed, knotted, nourished, tamed and softened. Ready for another week of combing for school. I loved the ritual because it allowed me to enjoy the gentle massage of my mother's smooth fingertips on my scalp. It soothed me. It connected me to my mother in an embryonic way.

That Sunday she held my hair in one hand and the comb in the other, and waved the black plastic comb in the air, more than she combed my hair. She declared to her audience of Maureen and Ma Titre, "I'm positive Cheryl is with Robert for his size and his money."

"What do you mean 'his size,' Mamie?"

"Ouch!" I screamed. The hand around the cluster of strands tightened and I felt the comb teeth drag through my scalp and hair. I descended into hair hell.

"'Ouch,' what? Keep your mouth out of big people talk."

"But I—"

"Listen, I was not talking to any children present. You are to hear but not listen."

The comb encountered my forehead in a hard knock. While I rubbed the pain out of my forehead, my mother continued with her story.

"I understand he is into construction, but my sources could not say where he currently works. You all know we won't hear the truth from Cheryl, not with her closed mouth."

"In time we will hear," Old Man Maurice countered.

"I don't know about your source, Velma, but my source told me he is on a construction project in Canefield," Ma Titre said as she adjusted her colourful madras wrap on her head, which she wore every Sunday.

"Hmmm, your source," Old Man Maurice said with a smirk.

Laughing, my mother said, "You know Ma Titre—always the first to find out. Miss Find-out is her name."

"And you! Velma is always happy to receive my find-out news," Ma Titre said looking towards Cheryl's house. "Are they in the house? In the hot sun, doing what you and I cannot do, Velma," she said and laughed, her silver bracelets jingling.

"Close your ears, Julia," my mother said with her mouth next to my ears. Like I could close my ears. Like I didn't want to overhear. Like I ever wanted the conversation to end. Of course I pretended to close my ears, while she moisturised, combed, and knotted my hair.

Like so many times before, I sat silent. Listening to the adult world of gossiping. Aunty Maureen was away from the yard. She'd taken Samson and Samuel to the far place in the east. Her village. Buried in a dead end of Dominica where all the villagers claim to be wise.

"Ma Titre, they're not here. They took Annya and went to the river." My mother's cheerful voice pulled me out of my thoughts. Her voice was always cheerful for gossiping.

"River, again. The poor child," Old Man Maurice lamented. Always short, clipped phrases for him. He unbuttoned two buttons on his grey shirt which he wore every day. Aunty Maureen had removed the logo label from all of the shirts. The shirt had been a gift from his sister living in St. Croix. They were from the oil processing company where his sister's husband worked.

"Ma Titre, have you seen them by the river?"

"Velma, you are asking me if I have seen them? Do you think I'm the neighbourhood news carrier for nothing?" she said and convulsed into roars of laughter. Her twelve silver bangles jostled and jangled like a jing ping band. I had counted them one time.

"Little Miss Julia will have to leave for me to tell you and Maurice. Oh, maybe I should wait for when Maureen comes back."

I couldn't see Ma Titre's face because my head was bent under the ministrations of my mother, but I heard the jesting and mocking in her voice.

"Hmmm, I'm on my last twist," my mother replied. She pinned the last twist on my head and sent me on my way. I walked down into the yard on slow, heavy limbs and didn't hear more of the juicy conversation.

Soon after that conversation, on a Saturday, I was left to watch Annya. Saturdays were reserved for our big river wash day. Cheryl, my mother, Aunty Maureen, and Juliette had all gone to the river to do laundry.

When they left the yard, they each carried a bright coloured basin overflowing with clothes. At the river they would soak, scrub, rub and bleach clothes for hours. And they would talk for hours with the other women who were there to wash. This was my favourite part when I went—listening to the stories about life in the village.

But being the youngest female in the yard I got the easiest job that day. It was almost the law that whenever the yard went to the river, my job was to take care of Annya if she had a cold.

Juliette hadn't been happy I got to escape going to the river to wash. Before they left for the river, she had committed the third cardinal sin—she'd twisted her mouth into the loudest of chupes. The shoe landed on her back from my mother's hand before she knew it was coming.

She should have known better than to cry or protest. I don't know why she thought she could have gotten away with a chupes. No chupes went unpunished—one of the rules my mother had instituted on her list of how to raise two Dominican girls well.

I was glad I got to take care of Annya. It meant free time from chores to read my latest library find, *Green Days by the River*. After reading *The Year in San Fernando* by Michael Anthony I wanted to read all his books. I had to join the Roseau Public Library to borrow the books. I didn't own any books but school textbooks. And we didn't own a bookshelf. I envied Sasha, Juliette's friend; she had books at her home and had access to her uncle's personal library.

That day I was quite happy to watch the gang leave for the river with baskets of clothes and sheets and pillowcases. For once I didn't have my mother threatening me with chores whenever I picked up a book which wasn't a schoolbook. It was like she didn't like to see me reading. She didn't understand the adventures I got to live through the literary books. I was learning far more in those books than my dry school textbooks.

Poor little Annya had been sick the last few days, running a temperature with coughing and sneezing. She'd fallen asleep while the gang had prepared to leave for the riverside. I carried her into Cheryl's house and prayed with all my heart Robert wasn't in the house.

Juliette, Samson, Samuel and I stayed far away from him. He'd never stopped glaring at us. And when he wasn't glaring, he would stare me down. He was a strange man. And I hoped with all my heart he had gone out to work or to town.

I sat on one of two hard straight-back chairs that comprised the furniture in the shoe-box-size living area. I settled Annya on her makeshift bed on the floor of the living room and watched her for a few minutes. She drifted in and out of sleep. Her dark hair spilled flat as a measuring tape against the plain white cotton sheet which covered the sponge mattress.

A few years ago, I'd been this age. Before Hurricane David I'd had no idea four years later I would have witnessed my first category five hurricane. No idea I would spend about four months out of school. And no idea Daddy Julius would disappear at sea. In that moment I envied Annya her innocence.

I stretched my legs out across the bare clean boards and started reading my book, *Green Days by the River*. It was a coming-of-age story. My first coming-of-age story had been *The Adventures of Huckleberry Finn*. I enjoyed reading it and was enjoying this one in the same way. It fed my desire for adventure, for escape, for more from life. At twelve I didn't know how I was going to achieve my dreams. I had been grappling with dealing with Daddy Julius's disappearance, so reading about how young people dealt with their emotions and desires was what I needed.

An hour into my babysitting duties I was revelling in the fact that Robert wasn't in the house, like I'd hoped. My euphoria was short-lived. I felt his presence before I lifted my eyes to his. He had blocked the natural light from the doorway. I looked up from the floor and my eyes connected with Robert's black eyes. He looked at me and he wasn't glaring. It was his strange steady stare.

A chill swept through my blood and my organs. I pressed my body against the floor-boards to make me smaller, to make me disappear. The board pressed into my soft skin. I foresaw that I'd have blue marks on my creamy skin.

I'd never been this close to the giant. A burst of adrenaline sent my heart racing. I gripped my book with a tight fist. And the primal need to flee arose within me. Flee what, I didn't understand. But a still small voice in my head said "Run, Julia. Run." I dismissed the voice. I couldn't run away and leave Annya.

I shifted my gaze down to my book. My hand gripped it so tight I'd need a crowbar to ply my fingers off the book. He was staring me down without speaking. I wanted him to glare at me instead, like he did on the day he moved into Cheryl's house. I pressed my body against the floorboards again but this time my knees trembled, and my palms flooded with sweat.

He was shirtless. Sweat ran down his well-defined pecs. His torn jean shorts left his massive legs exposed. His hairless legs glistened with the sweat running like rivulets down his legs into his white tennis shoes, which were supposed to be white but looked like beach sand. And his feet looked like they belonged to an elephant. My eyes had to travel far to meet his eyes again. The bright glazed look travelled all over my body. Searching. Probing.

"Well, hello, Miss Julia. Good morning to you." His voice was deep and dark and vibrated like a rumble of thunder. Whenever he spoke it sent a shiver down my spine.

I blinked and looked at him with what I hoped was my mean eyes, because I hated when he called me Miss Julia. He knew it and he still did, deriving some sort of perverted pleasure from it. He addressed Juliette the same way and she hated it too. What I didn't understand was why he wanted to call us girls Miss and the adult women he always called by their first name. It baffled me.

His husky voice filled the space. "You are growing out quite nicely, those breasts on you look perky, ready to be touched."

My muscles tightened and my body prepared to run. But I couldn't. Instead, I looked all around me and wrapped my arms around my breast in a self-hug.

I sat in silence for what felt like hours, seconds passing in agonizing slowness.

Why was I shocked? Hadn't I seen his searching eyes looking at me? His eyes bored holes in my body, like he wanted to see if I was made of sugary, syrupy, spicy matter.

My thoughts galvanized me into action.

In smooth fluid motion I got off from my position on the floor. My eyes flew to the door to escape his taunting throaty voice.

I raced out the door and went out into the yard while his booming laugh followed me. My heart rate accelerated faster, and heat flushed through my body.

Why was this man seeking me out? Wasn't Cheryl enough for him? Wasn't Cheryl's worship of him enough? I became perplexed. He'd laughed. I wasn't amused he'd found my reaction laughable. My eyes, ears, hands, and feet were encased in virginhood. He'd made me aware of my female form—I hadn't embraced I was becoming a woman. I hadn't yet grown to appreciate—like—know—all of me.

Juliette had convinced me to disregard the training bras my mother had bought for me. I felt exposed in my colourful blouse with the thin shoulder straps. One of my favourite blouses. I loved it for the thin strings. It kept me cool against the heat that lived and breathed in our small wooden houses. And my cut-off jeans shorts with the threads lying against my legs, bronze from the sun, left me even more exposed.

I was terrified but fascinated by the reaction of my body yet in some perverse way excited I could generate interest from the male species.

Robert materialised in the doorway of the house and yelled to me, "Chile, come here and look after the baby like they ask you too."

"I will not go back into the house until you leave." My voice squeaked. I turned around and watched in horror as Robert's white teeth flashed, followed by a booming laugh. This was the second time he'd laughed at me. Was I his new plaything? To taunt, to tease, to terrify.

"Come here, girl. Get your fresh young tail into this house."

I took a tentative step forward. But in a flash Robert was in front of me. He lifted me with his hard muscular arms, against his chest, glistening with sweat. His sweat was so much it seeped into my blouse on contact and formed a wet patch which became stuck to my breast. My braless breast.

At the realisation, I kicked my legs and flayed my skinny arms against his shoulders. My movements were useless. Robert only tightened his grip on me. He brought me closer to his chest. The action soaked my blouse with his sweat. I recoiled when I felt the drops of his sweat on my collarbone.

Before I could form my next thought, he carried me through the door and dangled me for a few moments before he let my feet hit the floorboards. I closed my eyes—relieved he'd put me down.

In a move which knocked the breath out of me and made the world go dark he forced one large hand between my legs and forced them apart. I hadn't had enough oxygen in my brain to process what he'd done when he cupped my secret part, while another large hand folded over my breast, squeezed, then pinched my nipple.

Before I'd formed the presence of mind to react, he released me and went into the bedroom and emerged with a black cut-off t-shirt on.

"Next time, you will know how to talk to a big man," he growled at me.

I remained rooted to the exact spot he'd dropped me. I couldn't think. I couldn't see. I couldn't feel. My breath busted in and out of my tiny chest at a fevered pitch.

What had happened to me? Had his hands been between my legs? Did he touch my breast? Did he squeeze it? Did he pinch my nipple? In the aftermath a sting crawled beneath the skin in my breast. And I could feel his palm imprinted between my legs.

I exhaled a deep sigh of relief when he walked out of the house. I blinked to clear my eyes and I gulped some fresh air to relieve my lungs which had been screaming for air. I hadn't known I'd stopped breathing. He had left but his rancid sweat didn't leave the room with him. I shuttered my eyes to black out the look in his eyes and to quiet the taunt in his voice. I closed my eyes tighter and willed my mind to produce the words to tell my mother about this incident with Robert.

His words had assaulted my childish ears. His carelessness caused my stomach to recoil. My blood raced like the *milèt* fish in the river. My body grew warm and sweat dampened my armpits. I made my way in slow steps to the straight back chair, with its chipped varnish.

I sat and stared at the innocent and untouched sleeping form of Annya. Her black curly hair spilled out of her hair bobbles. She had curled her legs to her chest and her arms lodged between her legs. Her beauty marred by yellow snot clouding the passage of her nose. I had wanted to crawl into the same position with Annya. I had used the same position so many times to feel safe and comforted.

Instead, I touched the breast Robert had handled. His words replayed on echo in my head. Neither Samson nor Samuel, who were Juliette's age had ever made any remarks on my breasts. The knowledge I'd become an object of enjoyment to Robert's eyes became indexed in my mind.

What had I done? Was it wearing my blouse without a bra? Were my shorts too tight? Was my backside too round? Were my hips too wide? I had begun to fill out. I'd had my first period a month before he had touched me.

After years of envying Juliette her perky breasts, hips, and round buttocks I had been overjoyed I had my own to admire in the broken mirror in our bedroom. And Juliette had given me one of her thin white vests she loved to wear around the house. It had become my new favourite piece of clothing. I wore it sans bra like Juliette. And one unsolicited touch had erased my joy with my feminine form. I couldn't believe I had become attractive to a man already.

This big black man Cheryl had implanted in her house, had cut out a piece of my innocence. He had spoken to me like I was an adult. He had touched me in a way I'd never been touched.

Is this your first touch? Don't you remember the time you played house, with the group down the road? Don't you remember when Isaiah touched you and you never played house with them again?

Don't you remember you never told your mother? Don't you know you are not going to tell your mother about Robert? What do you think she will do? What do you think Cheryl will say?

"Stop," I said aloud. As if that would have stopped the thoughts chasing each other in my head. I buried my face in my hands. My book stood open and forgotten on the floor. Annya remained asleep in her same position. Safe. Secure. Serene.

Are you sure?

To shut down the thought, I bent and picked up my book and tried to go back to reading.

And I never told my mother or anyone.

One week later.

A week during which I'd tried to forget the large hand which had cupped my feminine centre.

Why me?

Why not Juliette? Did he touch Juliette too? Was she afraid to tell too? Was she ashamed to tell? Did she try burying the memories so it would go away?

Every time I came to tell Juliette. My mouth refused to open. My brain circumvented the signal to my lips to part. I lay beside her each night. Remembering. In silence. In pain. In confusion.

Every house in the yard had thin wooden walls. Spaces for air to pass through. There were peepholes created by us children. To see. We heard and saw Cheryl and Robert. We heard Aunty Maureen and the twins' father when he visited from Guadeloupe. We had heard our mother and Daddy Julius. But no one spoke about it. Secret. Taboo. Locked up in memory vaults. And I had my own memory vault.

The yard was empty of people. I had been gifted another Saturday from going to wash by the river. I'd been assigned to clean the house by myself. My mother and Aunty Maureen took Juliette to the river for the Saturday wash experience. Cheryl had taken Annya with her to Roseau on a shopping trip—no doubt a trip to benefit Cheryl.

Since Robert had become a part of her household her daily trips to Roseau had dried up. She cooked. She dressed up to serve Robert his meals. She went shopping on some Saturdays. Samson and Samuel had gone out fishing on their *pwipwi*, a makeshift log raft boat. Old Man Maurice had gone up the village to his favourite domino spot, singing his song "Born Free." Not a soul was around.

So, I thought.

I tuned into the WBS Radio station on Samuel's battered radio he'd retrieved from the bay to listen and groove to all the carnival season calypsos. The opening of Carnival City was next week Saturday. It was time to practice my groove. In time with the rhythm of the song, I started working. I went to retrieve the cleaning bucket at the back of the kitchen; it was always turned over to keep mosquitoes and other insects from taking residence.

I bent to grab the bucket handle. And stopped mid action. I'd felt a wall of hardness pressed against my backside.

"You like to walk around with your tight t-shirts, and your little white vest with no bra."

Robert.

"Is this what you're looking for," he said and he lifted me up like I was one of Annya's dolls and held me against the hard board of the kitchen wall. I could feel the board where my head and shoulder rested. Time stood still.

"Is this what you are looking for," he said again, his eyes boring into mine?

His hand . . .

His hand . . . reached underneath my pink skirt.

His hands . . . travelled up my inner thighs.

I closed my eyes.

Oh . . .

This wasn't happening . . . not to me . . . not again.

His hand clamped over my mouth, I closed my eyes as tight as a tin lid.

And I counted. I counted to keep my sanity.

Then I opened my eyes and, oh God, his eyes bored right into mine. A smirk on his face. I closed my eyes again. Oh God. *Bondyé*. Let him stop. Pain. In my centre. Pain behind my head. Pain on my back and my backside. When I thought I would break . . .

I got the strength to scream, and I bit down on his shoulder.

He yelled and released me.

"You better not tell anyone," he roared in my ears. And I kicked and thrashed to get out from under his giant body which blocked out the sunlight.

The world went light then dark. The sound of my heartbeat thrashed in my ears like the sea crashing onto the shore during a hurricane. I was hyperventilating but I kept thrashing my slim legs. He held on to me like my efforts were useless, like he didn't feel a thing. He was a beast.

"Keep wearing those tight white t-shirts and I will give you more of what you're asking for," he hissed like a boa constrictor in my ears.

He released his hold and left.

I stood motionless against the hard board of our kitchen wall for a long time. My chin and lips trembled like I'd been thrown into the river at dawn.

Why me? Why me? Why me?

For days afterwards all I felt was the invasion. Sore. Violated. I delayed going to pee, because of the burning sensation. But I didn't speak. I locked it away in my memory vault.

On day seven I gathered my white vest and my other tight t-shirts to bury on the bottom of my brown grip. When I clacked open the grip, the sound of the mechanism didn't give me the usual pleasure. The pungent smell of the canfour balls mingled with the thick, sultry air of the late afternoon.

I took out my clothes and the canfour balls from the grip and laid the white vest and my favourite t-shirts on the bottom and then layered them with the white canfour balls. On top of them I piled the rest of my clothes.

I pushed down the lid of the grip. The same way I had pushed down the layers of anger, confusion, doubts, fear, and pain deep inside of me.

Secret.

Vaulted.

Buried.

Afterwards I went to the river and scrubbed my skin seven times and dipped seven times where the water was frothy white and strong.

The incident took place during the festive season of carnival masquerade. A time when calypso after calypso flooded the airwaves. My mother and the other adults usually held heated conversations over which song was the best. The one for the road march. The other who would win the crown.

For me the excitement was in the queen show. Each year it was a religion for me to cut out the pictures of the girls from the newspaper. Each picture went into a special long notebook my aunt had made for me with ruled paper and hard red cover paper from the Ministry.

My aunt Vignette, a civil servant, worked at the Ministry. Everyone on the island calls it the Ministry but the official name is the Government Headquarters. My aunt, by virtue of her working in the Ministry, took certain liberties she sometimes transferred to us in the form of largesse. Old Man Maurice called it stealing from the government. Aunt Vignette called it helping oneself and she insisted everyone did it. Who would miss a few sheets of ruled or plain paper, a few pens or pencils, or even toilet paper or paper towels?

On the occasions when Aunt Vignette came to the yard with the largesse, Old Man Maurice would give her the eye, turn up his mouth, spit on the ground and say, "You is a thief, Vignette. Plain and simple. Stealing from the government. Stealing our taxpayer's money."

Aunt Vignette would try to recover with her usual defence: "If they would pay us the wages we deserve, we would not have to help ourselves to a little something to tide us over."

Carnival season opened on the day of the incident, a day when the rain and sun battled for supremacy. The rain won. But rain had never stopped the festivities. Our yard went out in full force to the opening parade in town. That morning I awoke with anticipation in my bones. Juliette and I had already cut up our t-shirts with Maureen's help for our outfit to attend the opening carnival street parade and the opening of Carnival City in Roseau.

Early in the morning, Cheryl had darkened the door of our kitchen to talk to my mother. She was dressed in a tight stone wash jean and a big white shirt with a large black belt over it. She looked like she was headed to town. I wondered why she was going to town so early in the day, when the festivities did not begin until three o'clock in the afternoon.

"Velma, you going to town today?" Cheryl asked from the doorway, rubbing her hands together with great intensity.

"Yes," my mother answered. "But not until this afternoon. What you want?"

"I want to talk to you, but Missus has to go," she said, referring to me. My mother gave me the look and I took up my cup of cocoa tea and my bread and butter and retreated to the big stone.

I wondered, not for the first time, when they would stop cutting me out of conversations. There were times I could hear, but I could not listen. There were times I had to pretend to be the invisible child. It was a lot of foolishness to me. Because Juliette, Samson, Samuel and I knew far more than the adults thought we knew.

A few hours later, dark clouds continued to rule the sky. Everyone in our corner of the island ignored the threat of more rain—my mother, Maureen and the twins, Old Man Maurice, Juliette, Cheryl and myself. Juliette and I dressed up in our bright orange cut-up big t-shirts over jeans. My mother had chosen a Hawaiian shirt, her favourite staple for the last few years. Cheryl had on her shortest yellow short pants with a tube halter top.

We left Ma Titre to hold the fort across the road, she never went to the opening parade anymore, she said her days for carnival were done. But once we got home she would pester each of us with miles of questions of what we'd seen and done. Robert and Annya were not part of our little entourage.

On the bus ride to town Cheryl made it known Robert had declared earlier he was not going to carnival at all this year. He said he hated all the calypsos, and he was staying away from rum this season, as last year he had lost hundreds of dollars because he'd gotten drunk during the celebration.

She said he'd volunteered to take care of Annya and that's why she'd left Annya with Robert and not Ma Titre. She beamed with joy when she talked about her Robert, how he had changed her life and had promised to take care of her and Annya forever. She'd gone on to talk about how Robert had claimed it was his time of purging and making up for all the wrongs he had done for the year.

I froze on Lightning's bus and tried to block my ears from Cheryl's words. I had imprisoned myself into silence. I still hadn't told my mother what Robert had done to me. I'd camped out in our bedroom since the incident to avoid seeing him. I wondered if touching me and goggling my breasts were considered among those wrongs. Would he be doing one Our Father and ten Hail Marys for each time he did . . .

I couldn't finish the thought . . .

And Cheryl didn't say what kind of wrongs Robert was talking about. I heard my mother say a lot of "hmmmm" during Cheryl's repetition of Robert's almost-confession.

After hours of watching the opening revelry of colour, sound, dancing, and jumping up ourselves, we got on the bus and returned home. We spilled out of Lightning's bus in high spirits and laughter and joked in front of our yard. Cheryl hadn't lingered with us; she went into her house to check on Annya.

While we stood around arguing over which songs played during the parade, a blood-curdling scream filled the night: *"Bondyé! Bondyé!* Look at what Robert . . . My child . . . my child . . . my child . . . "

My mother sprinted over to Cheryl's house, and Juliette, Old Man Maurice, Samson and Samuel, and myself followed her.

Cheryl resumed screaming, *"Bondyé!, Bondyé! Bondyé* . . . Look at what Robert doing! *Bondyé*, my child."

By the time we'd crowded into Cheryl's tiny front room, my mother was coming out of the bedroom. She jumped over a collapsed, screaming Cheryl, while carrying a naked, passed out Annya.

I became immobilised. I saw black spots. My legs grew so weak I wanted to join Cheryl on the floor and scream until my lungs gave out. A naked Annya meant only one thing.

Robert.

That beast of a man . . . What had he done to Annya?

I knew and yet I didn't want to know. I didn't want to believe. Not Annya. Not angelic Annya. Not six-year-old Annya . . .

My heart sank when my mother ran out the yard carrying Annya's small, unclothed body of Annya across the road to Ma Titre's house. She was so small and helpless. Juliette followed her, but I didn't move. I sank onto the bare floorboards and focused on Cheryl—anything to deny the truth of what had happened . . .

I wanted to bounce my head against the floorboards . . . I wanted to rip out Robert's heart. The strength which had possessed me when he'd touched me returned and I wanted to march into the room and beat him down with my bare hands.

I wheezed like a steam engine. I closed my eyes and when I opened them, Cheryl was rolling around on the floor flinging all types of obscene words in the room.

Full body tremors took over me when Cheryl held her head in her hands and began to bang it against the floorboards.

"Bondyé, Bondyé, my child, Robert. My child. Why?" She cried. Her hair was knotted into a tangled mess and tear tracks lined her cheeks.

Samuel had remained in the room with me and he too was immobilised. I stood and we watched Cheryl wrestle with grief Like Annya had died. My tears came hot and heavy against my cheeks.

"Why are you crying too?" Samson asked. He sounded like he spoke to me from a far distance.

And what happened next was surreal.

Shirtless, Robert crawled towards Cheryl on his hands and knees, crying like he had lost his mother. He stopped crawling and he stretched out his long, muscled arm to touch her. Cheryl, startled by the touch, jerked back and fell on her butt screaming, "Don't touch me, Robert! Don't touch me with your filthy hands!" she shrieked, her voice carrying the weight of anguish and repulsion.

"Cheryl, I'm sorry. I don't know what came over me. Please, please, forgive me."

"How could you do that to my child, Robert? You promised to take care of us!" she screamed. "You promised to be a father to Annya!" she wailed and pounded the floor board with both hands. "I left Annya with you and this is what you do?" she bawled at the top of her lungs, her face an ugly mass of tears and raw pain. "Why, Robert? Why?" She collapsed into another round of tears.

When she'd recovered enough, she said, "How could you? She's just a baby. Oh Lord, why must the same thing that happened to me happen to my daughter?"

"Cheryl, I'm so sorry," Robert interrupted, his face contorted with tears.

The smooth and suave Robert had vanished. He began to plead.

"Robert, there's nothing you can say to fix this. Sorry? You know how many times I have heard this word? How many times I've heard 'I won't do it again?'

"You just violated my angel, to the point where she passed out. Robert, I saw you between the legs of my angel and my heart stopped. You've killed my heart. Get out of my house. Get out of my life." Cheryl screamed and collapsed into a fresh round of wailing tears.

I felt the air leave the house. My tears began flowing down my face, but I didn't feel it. Cheryl's pain became my pain. Her revelation struck me.

It had happened to Cheryl too.

She was screaming for herself and for angelic Annya.

I lost reason.

I lost sense.

I jumped onto Robert. The giant, who'd prostrated himself on the floor in fake penitence. He thought tears could absolve what he'd done to Annya and to me.

The strength I'd gotten the day he had touched me possessed me again and I lunged on his prostrated body. I pummelled his body with my hands, whimpering and moaning. My hands felt like I was hitting concrete. I continued to hit him through the pain in my hand. My tears so heavy they blinded me. But I poured out my pain and anger into every blow.

For me.

For Annya.

For every girl.

For every woman he'd violated.

"You are an evil man! An evil man! You are a devil!" I screamed. Julia had fled. Someone else had invaded my body. I bent down and bit his hand and clawed his arm. I bit it hard like I had wanted to bite him when he'd held me against the kitchen wall. I didn't stop biting and clawing him until my mother pulled me off Robert.

I'd had no idea my mother had returned until I felt her hands pulling me off.

"Julia! Julia! Julia!" she screamed. She shook me. I gulped for air. My lungs had constricted. I couldn't breathe. I couldn't see. My mother had taken me outside into the cool night air.

"Julia, what's wrong with you? Calm down. Take a deep breath. Calm down." Her words penetrated my fog.

"Samson, go get a cup of water for Julia."

Samson ran to our kitchen and came back with the water.

I had doubled over and rested my face against my knees. I was covered in sweat and felt clammy. My mother lifted my head and held the cup to my lips. I took a sip and refused more.

"Samson, take Julia over to Ma Titre," she ordered. But I refused to move.

My mother went back into Cheryl's house and her angry voice filled the night.

"Robert, you better get off this floor. You think you can kneel your way out of this. You better get up, Robert. Get up and get out of this house and this yard before we call the police." She paused for a few seconds and continued, "Get up, Robert. Get up and leave," my mother shouted, her voice bouncing off the thin wooden walls of the house.

Like I didn't know what was best for me, I moved to the doorway in time to see Robert get off the floor, his eyes downcast. He made a move to touch Cheryl who was still bent over in pain.

"Leave her, Robert. You just go," my mother bellowed again.

I saw steam and smoke coming out my mother's ears and mouth. Maybe it was the mention of the word police, Robert stopped crying and picked himself up and lumbered out the door.

As if rising from a deep sleep, Cheryl got up and moved like a lion attacking its prey to the makeshift clothes wardrobe she'd had Aunty Maureen make for Robert.

She yanked the stoplight red cloth apart and started flinging Robert's clothes through the open bedroom window into the yard.

In quick time, his shoes and toiletries joined the clothes in the yard. Then, with a strength I didn't know Cheryl had, she lifted his toolbox next to the door and threw it into the yard.

"Get out, Robert, and never come back. Never, ever come back!"

She went back to the bedroom and ripped the white sheets off the bed. She threw them through the bedroom window.

Samuel stood behind me with the cup of water. In the doorway. We were transfixed. My mother threw Robert his bag and it landed with a thud on the hard packed dirt. With drooped shoulders, head bent, he picked up each article of clothing and personal items in slow motion.

"You better hurry, Robert," my mother warned. "For the police soon come"

It was that moment he realised this was the end for him. He had to make his way through Ma Titre and other neighbours. A small crowd had gathered out in the streets. Maybe Cheryl's piercing screams had reached the end of the village leading to town. People had gathered to find out what had happened and why Cheryl had been screaming nonstop.

Because it was the opening of carnival, buses were still running. Samson and Samuel flagged a bus and a mob of angry women—Cheryl, my mother, Aunty Maureen, Ma Titre, Juliette and me—pushed Robert into the bus.

My mother and Cheryl continued to attack him with their hands as he settled into the bus. Samson had to pull them off to shut the door of the bus. And through it all he'd resigned himself to his punishment; he didn't lift a finger to defend himself. He'd become a man defeated by his own demons.

That night I went to bed shaken. Annya had recovered, and clinged to her mother, refusing to let go. She cried each time her mother attempted to put her down. But no one called the police. Had my mother mentioned the police only to put fear into Robert? My pillow became soaked with my tears. I couldn't stop the tears as I remembered the events of the day.

Juliette wrapped her arms around me and said, "Don't cry, Julia, Annya is going to be okay."

"How do you know?"

"Mamie and Ma Titre said Annya will not remember what happened to her."

"You believe them, Juliette? Think."

"She's young, too young to remember."

"Do you believe what you're saying?" I said and I removed her arms from around me.

"You don't have to get upset, Julia. Your spirit is too sensitive."

"Juliette, you never question the behaviour of the adults. Why won't they call the police?"

"Call the police for what? So Cheryl's business can be out in the streets. Think, Julia. People would talk."

"Juliette, when will you grow a mind of your own?"

"I am a realist, not an idealist. You, Julia, need to get your head out of the stratosphere."

"So no one cares what happened to a six-year-old child?"

"Lower your voice before Mamie says stop talking."

"Did he touch you, Juliette?" I asked, and gasped at my own boldness. The night's event had shaken me. The words that had been bottled up in me spilled out.

"Who?" Juliette asked, her voice pitched so low I had to ask her to repeat it.

"Who? What do you mean who? The giant we've been talking about. Did he touch you, Juliette?"

"Go to sleep, Julia."

"Did he touch you too?"

"Go to sleep, Julia. Some things you don't talk about."

"You mean, we are just going to bury this?"

"Yes. There are a lot of buried things around here, Julia. Do you want a microphone to announce it to the village?"

"Why not?" I whispered with a sharp edge to my voice. Then I changed course and said, "Mamie didn't ask me any questions. She just looked at me and went into her room after everyone left."

"What did you expect her to do, Julia?"

"She could ask me why I attacked Robert."

"She will not ask you. She does not want to know what she already knows. She's not going to ask you anything."

"They can't ignore Annya's case."

"The child passed out. They had to do something," Juliette said in her too-calm voice.

My heart was still pumping hard with blood. And Juliette's calm bothered me.

"You were over at Ma Titre's house when Cheryl screamed out, 'Why the same thing happened to me, happened to my daughter?'"

"Maybe the same thing happened to Mamie," she said in the dead flat voice she'd been using throughout this entire conversation.

I didn't respond. I couldn't respond. Deep sobs racked my body. Juliette pulled me back into her arms. I could not be comforted. I cried for myself, for Annya, for Cheryl, for Juliette, for Maureen, for my mother. I even cried for Ma Titre. For all women. I cried the tears of the wounded heart.

"You will learn, Julia," Juliette whispered against my ears as she held me. She held me until she fell asleep.

A chill had seeped into my body and crept through my arteries. I was already learning. What more was there to learn? It couldn't get harder than what I'd suffered, and what Annya had suffered.

Sleep eluded me. I stayed awake late into the night. And in that sacred solitude, my thoughts roamed untamed; going over the memories and aspirations, hopes and fears. I sought solace, understanding, and perhaps a glimmer of our truth.

In the stillness, I wrestled with the weight of the unspoken truths and unanswered questions. I wrestled with the tangled terrain of memory, longing, and uncertainty. With each passing hour in the darkness, I traversed the landscape of my becoming; the vulnerability and the resilience I needed to embrace the uncertainty that lay ahead.

Three months later, Robert came back into Cheryl's house. It floored me. It puzzled me for days. For years.

My mother fumed for days when Robert moved back into the house, and she threatened not to lift a hand if it ever happened again. She vowed she would not be getting into anyone's business anytime soon. She said she could not understand why some people could be so wicked to themselves and to their offspring.

One afternoon she stood on our side of the yard and issued a stream of condemnation and judgment to Cheryl and Robert. Cheryl set her face as a flint after and never spoke to my mother again. A week after that attack, they moved out of the yard and the village, to a village on the west coast. We never saw them again.

And I've never forgotten beautiful little Annya.

I didn't understand Cheryl's decision. I didn't understand how she failed to notice how Annya had become withdrawn and sad since the incident and no longer played with her doll. I didn't understand why she didn't choose to save Annya from future harm.

And I added another goal to my "When I grow up" list—to fight for justice for women.

5

The New Arrival

(1984-1985)

The yard changed after Cheryl took Annya and left with him.

Maybe I changed.

I gravitated daily to the big stone.

I sat alone.

I stared at nothing.

I didn't notice the passing cars. At one time it'd been my favourite fun time activity to sit with my purple-covered exercise book and write down the number of each passing car. Many a rivalry was born out of the competition. The winner was the person with the most car numbers. There were not many cars about, and it was usually a wait, but in the height of the competition I would run out to the road whenever I heard a car. I won often because I always listened and ran out or I would sit on the big stone for hours.

I learned the importance of waiting, of being patient, and the power of accumulation. I'd been proud of my efforts to win the car numbers game.

After Cheryl and Annya left, I struggled.

I wasn't happy.

I wasn't proud.

I was bothered.

I wrestled with the events that had propelled their departure.

Where were they now? Was angelic Annya, okay? Was that beast of a man still laying his hands on her baby's body? How could Cheryl allow this man back into their lives?

The day Robert returned to Cheryl's house, I had jumped on him and I hit his face over and over with my hands, and yelled with each strike, *"Mechansté! Mechansté!"* You're wicked."

Except . . . it didn't happen. Not in reality. But in my mind, I scratched him bloody.

When I saw him, my body had broken out in twitches. My pulse raced as if I was running to escape the claws of the dog Police Loubiere.

Robert. In Cheryl's house. A second time. Thanks to my mother, he was gone. But with their leaving the yard, a part of me, a part of our yard, a part of our lives ended.

I couldn't stop thinking of them. I prayed for them a lot. I prayed Cheryl would get rid of Robert forever. I prayed Annya's real father would show up and claim her. I prayed someone would call the police to arrest Robert.

How long must I pray, God?

I was still praying for Daddy Julius to return to us alive. *God, are you out there? Can you see me? Can you hear my prayers? Do I need more mustard seeds before you can hear me?*

Each day became harder than the last to keep my hope afloat. I could feel my hope leaking out of my heart each day. My prayers were like salt dissolving into water.

What really bothered me . . .

The women.

And their silence.

And my silence.

In our silence we became complicit.

My mother, who loved to talk, who loved to tell stories, buried this story. It made me think that maybe she only told stories she was comfortable in telling. Stories that transported humour and nostalgia. Stories that didn't reveal too much self.

She didn't talk about difficult things.

She didn't entertain questions on difficult things.

Maybe because our lives were difficult enough.

I couldn't let it go how my mother and Aunty Maureen and Ma Titre took no action to rescue Annya forever from that monster. Particularly Ma Titre, a woman known for calling police at the slightest scent of trouble—she went silent.

The silence confounded me further when they didn't call the authorities, when Cheryl moved Robert back into her house.

Then with an audacity which defies logic, Cheryl moved away from the yard with Robert in tow.

Life, however, moved on apace. A new tenant arrived in the yard to take up residence in what I will always think of as Cheryl's house.

It happened on a warm Saturday evening. The heat had forced everyone out of their tiny spaces, seeking whatever breeze might come in from the sea or river. The moon hung high in the sky turning the dark sky into silver. The setting was ideal for a long night of storytelling, to be led, of course, by my mother, Velma. Once my mother took the floor, for hours she embellished story after story, while we sat enthralled.

Before she could begin any of her embellished stories a different story unfolded. The yard had turned out in force—my mother, Aunty Maureen, Juliette, Ma Titre, Samson, Samuel, and Old Man Maurice. Everyone had glued themselves to their favourite spot on the big stone.

But before our bodies had had time to transfer our body heat to the big stone, a beaten blue and black pickup approached on the village main road. It was covered with grey patches of bodywork, and it came to a stop in front of us.

What is the meaning . . . ?

I didn't have to wait long. The first thing I noticed in the back of the pickup was a bed frame and a mattress. There were other household items stacked in a way on the pickup that they overflowed and rattled the rusty sides of the truck bed.

Someone was moving in.

The someone turned out to be a tall, slim, built brown-skin young man. He wore blue jeans and a white t-shirt. But what I remembered that night was his manner and personality. At the exact moment his feet had touched the ground he'd flashed a million-megawatt smile.

No one moved. We waited in silence for the new arrival to our yard to make a move.

"Goodnight, everyone," he said, and flashed his million-megawatt smile. He took a step away from the beat-up pickup and came to stand next to where Ma Titre was seated with all her bangles and her white headwrap. His hands went to his hips, and he lifted one foot and placed it on the edge of the big stone next to Ma Titre's hand. He turned up his smile by another megawatt. Later, I would dub it as his signature ammunition; his weapon of disarmament to get his own way.

"Goodnight," my mother answered for all of us.

"Hi, everyone, I'm Timothy Lafleur and I'm here to move into the house Cheryl occupied."

At the mention of Cheryl's name, I looked at my mother. Her eyes narrowed and her lips parted. I stopped breathing to listen to the question I thought she would ask. *How do you know Cheryl?* But she held her tongue, thank God. She might have scared him out of the yard before he unpacked.

After the short introduction, we all got involved in helping unload the pickup of the few goods Timothy had brought with him to occupy his new house. It not being much of a space, all he needed was his bed, a small table and chairs and the assortment of clothes and household effects necessary for living.

In less than an hour we helped Timothy unpack his clothes and his belongings in the house. My mother took charge. She hung up the curtains. She unpacked the two boxes of kitchen wares in the tiny kitchen attached to the outside of the house. By the time the unpacking was done she and Timothy were friends for life.

I'd seen my mother charm her way into people before. But the speed at which she'd moved with Timothy caused a coil of chill to unfurl like a snake in my belly. I knew my mother. She could talk her way into people's lives. She's the person who goes the extra mile with an extra hand, a shoulder to cry on, and a big mouth to laugh at jokes.

I knew villagers who'd described her as having a slight crack in her head. Crazy. Where's your crazy mother? Some have asked me in the past. Although not one was brave enough to call her crazy to her face.

People were afraid to infuriate her. One minute she was a gracious lady. In the next minute she could go on a vicious attack. If she felt threatened, or if someone tried to hurt one of her girls, or if someone said something or spread some gossip she hated.

Such people had the honour to receive a sound thrashing of her tongue which left them mortified into silence for days. Because Velma, my mother, sometimes said things that would make a fisherman blush like a Sunday school girl. Things I think our priest at the chapel would refuse to hear in the confession. But she had stopped going to confession years ago. And over the years her tongue lashings grew worse.

In the days of the infancy of Timothy's occupation of Cheryl's house, a pattern developed. My mother, who'd become sweet on Timothy from the first night he moved into the yard, continued to play the part without missing a beat.

She sowed her seeds of cooking, cleaning, and washing for him within those first days of his move to our yard. I don't know if Timothy hired her or if she hired herself to the job. But she became the cook and cleaner and washer for Timothy.

Timothy worked at the Ministry. The Ministry where Aunty Vignette worked. I had a clear view of the Ministry from my school—a big square concrete structure with many floors and many windows. That made Timothy a civil servant and it impressed my mother and Aunty Maureen. I lurked in the background the day they discussed Timothy's job status. I made sure to wash the dishes at my slowest pace. My mother had been so engrossed in the conversation with Aunty Maureen she never scolded me for my slowness.

"Velma, you found out what Timothy does for his living?" Aunty Maureen asked in a voice heavy with curiosity.

"Maureen, do you know me to fall asleep on important things? *Mwen pa ka domi*," she said and laughed. "Our Boy Timothy is a chauffeur in the Ministry of Agriculture with the extension people."

"A chauffeur?" Maureen questioned.

"Why you say it like that? How many ministry chauffeurs you know?" she asked Aunty Maureen, her tone heavy with sarcasm.

"None."

"Thought so. Listen, Timothy is a civil servant. He receives a monthly pay cheque. Do you hear that? A monthly pay cheque."

"What's cooking in your head, Velma?"

My mother laughed until tears leaked from her eyes.

They had gone on to talk about other people and other things. But that stilted conversation stayed with me. I couldn't pinpoint why it'd gotten my attention. Maybe it was my mother's laugh. Or her tone. Or Aunty Maureen's question about what was cooking in her head.

It was one of the conversations which sailed over my head, but it hinted something was afoot. I made it my mission to watch and listen to my mother and Aunty Maureen any time Timothy's name was mentioned.

In the early eighties it was considered a good move upwards to snatch a job in the civil service. Although a vast majority of the people on the island worked for the government. It was not easy to get in according to my mother and Maureen who talked often about people who got jobs in the civil service "by a pull string."

My mother's favourite story to tell was how my Aunt Vignette, my father's sister, got her job by pull string. I'd heard her repeat the story to Aunty Maureen about how

Aunty Vignette had gotten her civil servant job through her former politician boyfriend. A married man. A man my mother said people referred to as the "minister *fanm*." The minister of women.

It was a reference to activities outside his official capacity. My mother, Aunty Maureen, and Ma Titre, laughed with gusto any time they said, "minister *fanm*."

My mother, a master at weaseling information out of people, had already learnt from Timothy that his civil servant job was compliments of his politician uncle.

I watched my mother become Timothy's helpmate. I watched Timothy become a daily fixture in our house. I watched Timothy eat the food lovingly prepared by my mother for his lunch every day.

My mother's courtship of Timothy grew, and Juliette and I were reduced to second class citizens in our home. A pattern developed where we had to wait for Mr Timothy to have his lunch before we had our lunch.

Juliette became the food server. She got the opportunity to handle the two breakable plates we had in the kitchen. Our mother was determined to serve Timothy only the best. I didn't want to be a part of whatever was going on, but Juliette had gotten me involved. My job was to carry his lime squash in one of the repurposed peanut butter jars. We had seven of those glasses, half of which my mother had begged off Ma Titre. It was a thing in our yard to repurpose every container from something bought at the supermarket.

I walked behind Juliette and took my cue from her actions. Mamie didn't give us time to change our uniforms. It forced Juliette to serve in her blue skirt and white shirt. She would hand Timothy the plate and smile until a faint pink suffused her cheeks. The whole thing was comedic to me, played out, as it were, in our living room furnished with four table chairs. In return, Timothy rewarded Juliette with his million-megawatt smile. And it turned her into a blushing damsel—face pink like the bubble gum we both loved to chew. And she would relieve me of the glass to hand to Timothy.

I hated the little ritual.

After school I wanted my lunch without waiting. I didn't want to play server girl to our new neighbour Timothy. But I was forced to wait on the wooden stool the same colour of the paper bags on the greasy shelf. Before Timothy arrived, the shelf held one paper bag with brown sugar. Now it had increased to seven paper bags each of white sugar and flour.

We had moved up.

Our improved circumstances didn't stop me from pouting my lips while my mother took her time to share our food. Juliette was my direct opposite in disposition. It seemed she enjoyed serving Timothy. When she returned to the kitchen there'd be a faint glow and a twinkle in her eyes.

Was she too getting sweet on Timothy? The thought tightened my chest.

What's special about Timothy?

I didn't understand why Juliette and Mamie were taken with him. They were both falling over themselves to take care of his needs. Yes, he was good looking, tall and slim. He smiled a lot. He outtalked my mother, something I thought was impossible. And he was generous in dishing out his civil servant money.

My mother had made herself Timothy's helper, but then she went on and co-opted Juliette. It was Juliette she sent over on a Saturday to collect Timothy's clothes for washing at the river. It was Juliette who was sent over to Timothy's shoebox living room to iron his work clothes.

It bothered me because all this took place during Juliette's final year in high school when she should have been studying for her Caribbean Examinations Council (CXC) exams in May. Instead, she was forced to do domestic work for Timothy.

But, Juliette being Juliette, she didn't complain. I loved my older sister, but I had a problem with her nature. Juliette never questioned or raised any argument with our mother. She always agreed to whatever Mamie wanted. She tried so hard not to get Mamie vexed. I think her nature made her a perfect pawn in what happened next in our yard.

If only she could have stood up for herself.

A month to the day after Timothy moved into the yard, I returned from my early morning jaunt to get mangoes at Gillon Estate. There was a guard, but he liked my mother and Juliette and me, and it gave us the freedom to take mangoes. Samson and Samuel weren't so lucky—he always chased them. That morning I filled my bucket with mangoes for the yard.

The ground was still wet with dew and under the mango trees the sweet scent of the mangoes that had dropped during the night permeated the air. Mango season was my favourite time of year. I filled my black bucket to the brim with the freshest mangoes from the ground. I wasn't into climbing trees.

Satisfied I had enough mangoes, I made my way home, hauling my heavy bucket by moving it from one hand to the next. I didn't care about the weight. I was happy and I broke out singing Old Man Maurice's song, "Born Free," and stumbled home accompanied by rustling leaves and swaying branches. In my world we were free to steal mangoes.

I stopped singing when I entered the yard. I placed the black bucket of mangoes on the ground underneath the kitchen window when I heard their voices—my mother and Juliette. And I made the deliberate decision to stay beneath the window to listen to their conversation.

"I see the way Timothy does smile at you. I think he likes you, Juliette," my mother said, in an unhurried, relaxed tone like they were talking about what to eat for breakfast.

"You think so, mother? He smiles at me a lot and tells me I'm a pretty girl all the time," Juliette responded in that quiet, sweet voice of hers.

"You know, Timothy is a good catch," my mother said, her tone shifted to the no-nonsense tone she loved to use.

There was a brief silence. Then Juliette's voice, thin and shaky, answered, "What you mean, Mother?"

"What I mean? Juliette, you're not a child anymore, you are sixteen going on seventeen years of age. You're ready to leave school and you're asking me what I mean. What I mean is Timothy is the kind of man you want to catch before he pass through your hands. If you haven't notice, Julius is no longer around here to support us."

"But mother, I thought my education came first," Juliette whispered.

"Yes, I know I kept singing that in your ears, but things here are different with Julius gone. I had to return to working, and the money I make from cleaning people house and washing people clothes isn't enough to keep us. Plus, I want better for my girls. I don't want you all to suffer like I've had to suffer.

"As I told you all already. Your father left Dominica before Julia was born. He went to St. Thomas to make a better life for all of us. The first six months he wrote me letters and he sent a little US for me to take care of you girls.

"Well, you know the story well. For ten years, neither I nor your Aunt Vignette nor any other family members have heard from him. His parents died and he never came for the funeral. It's like he disappeared from the face of God's earth. You know what your mother had to do to survive. For you and Julia to survive.

"All I am saying, Juliette, is you have to think about your future, and Julia's future too."

For a few minutes they didn't speak.

In the silence the sound of the waves crashing into the stones became amplified. And then Aunty Maureen's voice, loud and clear, called out to Samson and Samuel, "Time to wake up, lazies." I smiled, because every morning Aunty Maureen screamed the same command.

I turned my attention back to the kitchen, to the silence between the two most important people in my life. I wondered what was going through Juliette's mind. Why had she grown silent? It was my mother who broke the silence.

"What I'm saying, Juliette, is to give Timothy a chance. The man is already spending money on you. Do you know it is him who gave me the money for you to register for those extra classes you needed to get ready for your exams?"

In an even smaller voice, Juliette answered, "Really, Mother, was that necessary? I could have done without the extra classes."

"Don't be silly, girl. I explained the situation to the man, and he was more than willing to help. You see, Juliette, me, you, and Julia, we don't have much of a choice. Look around you, do we look like we have money? No, we don't."

"But what about Timothy, he's living in the same yard—in the same small house we live in. Does he have money?"

"Juliette, my child, the man has a job. You know what that means; he has potential."

"He's not going to stay in Cheryl's house, as your sister likes to call it. He's going to move up and you are going to be by his side when he moves right on up. In fact, he has already told me he is only living in the little house to save up money."

I had to strain my ears to catch Juliette's reply.

"Mother, I do like Timothy, but I think my priority ought to be placed on my education right now."

I pumped a fist in the air because this was the first time I'd heard Juliette raise a defence to our mother.

"I know, but it won't hurt you to encourage the man's advances. In fact, he already has my permission to pursue you. Think of your future, Juliette. You don't want to turn out like your mother. You don't want this chance to pass through your fingers."

"But, Mother," Juliette croaked as if the words she wanted to utter had given her an instant flu. "I thought I was supposed to study hard. You wanted me to become a doctor."

"A dream, Juliette. A dream which needs money. And money is in short supply around here. Not even Old Man Maurice have that kind of money to lend us," she said, and chuckled.

"Unless you want to do a search for your father, if he is still alive. Maybe he has the money to send you to school but, as you can see, your mother doesn't have that kind of money. So, we must secure your future a different way. This is about survival, Juliette, not dreams. Dreams are for Julia." And she laughed deep.

I glanced around the yard without noticing the dirt or stones.

I couldn't believe she'd laughed at me for dreaming. My dream was a simple one to take us out from the yard.

After Mamie's long rebuttal, Juliette had lapsed into silence. I marshalled my swirling thoughts into coherent ones. And I decided to make a noisy entrance. I started singing "Born Free" and marched to the kitchen doorway. I found Juliette perched on the tiny bench and Mamie bent over the stove stirring the cocoa tea she had going on for our breakfast.

The rich dark aroma of the combination of cinnamon, nutmeg, bay leaves and coconut milk engulfed the room. I inhaled a deep breath and savoured the whiff of spices. My stomach rumbled in recognition. The sound louder than the spoon swishing through the cocoa in a pot its bottom like black tar.

Embarrassed by my stomach noises—I was always embarrassed—I stopped singing and watched them. Juliette had on the oversized t-shirt she'd started sleeping in. My mother had on a worn-out blue cotton nighty decorated in faded white flowers. Her two good nighties were for her sickness, she said, and they were in the black grip under her bed. Both were so caught up in their own thoughts they both ignored my entrance.

"I'm here," I announced to the room.

"I can see you, Julia," my mother replied. "Do you want some cocoa tea?"

"You're asking me if I want cocoa tea, Mamie, when it's the only thing I drink in the morning. Everything else is unacceptable," I answered in an airy voice.

"You're always extra, Julia," my mother admonished. I didn't respond to her dib. I wanted to move the conversation to what I'd heard in my listening spot below the window. I knew I shouldn't. But I hadn't yet learned how to curb my curiosity. I had to know.

"Why did you stop your conversation when I entered?"

"None of your business, Julia," my mother rebutted.

I turned to Juliette.

She'd bent her head to her knees. Her long loose black curls draped down to the floor and shielded her face. I wanted to see her face, her eyes. I wanted to see the play of emotions on her face. She kept her head bent.

I persisted into no-woman's land with my mother.

"Mamie, why are you setting up Juliette?" I asked with more confidence than I should have had at twelve.

"Julia, Julia, don't try my patience today, with your questions. This is not a conversation for you. Stay out of big people talk."

"Big people talk, Mamie? Do you want Juliette to end up like some of the girls up the road, who have four children before they are twenty years of age?"

"Julia, I told you, don't try my patience."

She cut off the stove under the cocoa tea and turned to face me. I saw a flash of venom in her eyes. She placed her hands on her hips over her blue nighty and I trailed my eyes down to the large brown stain at the bottom to avoid her eyes.

"I'll not have a twelve-year-old, going on thirteen years, under my roof, questioning my judgement, my decisions, my authority. There is only one female boss in this house: I, Velma Abraham. Your mother, who carried you for nine months. I run this household. You and your questions. You always have a question for everything."

"But how am I going to learn, if I don't question things?" I cried out.

"It is not your place to question," my mother replied, her eyes hard and cloudy like the grey sky on a rainy day. "I know what is best."

I turned back to Juliette. She was in the same position. "Juliette, are you going to sit there and let Mamie dictate to you what to do with your life? She's setting you up with Timothy. Do you want to be in a relationship with Timothy?"

Before Juliette could answer, *thud, thud, thud* landed on my back from my mother's heavy hand. "Enough, Julia, you are out of place. You have no respect for me," she said and grabbed onto my arm. She led me out of the kitchen, her hand digging into my arm. I closed my eyes against the onslaught of pain from her grip.

"Go to your room and change into your clothes, so you can start on your chores. And no cocoa tea or bread for you this morning," she shouted. "I will not suffer any rudeness from any child living under my roof. Do I make myself clear, Julia? And that goes for you too, Juliette!" she shrieked, in the middle of the yard between the house and the kitchen. "There is only one boss woman in this yard, in this house, in this kitchen. Everyone else is a child. Everyone else must show respect. Everyone else must obey."

After our Saturday chores were done, I accosted Juliette in our bedroom. She'd been lying on the bed in her panties and bra as she loved to do. I was jealous of her ability to be comfortable in her own skin, but it was the only thing she seemed comfortable doing. Where was the confident girl when she faced our mother? I didn't share in her body confidence and often I kept my body hidden from her eyes.

I made sure not to get dressed in front of her but waited to dress when I was alone in our room. Juliette often teased me. She would say, "We are sisters; why are you afraid of baring your breasts to me. I already know what they look like. Stop hiding, Julia."

There were reasons for my reticence. Silly reasons at first. But since my encounters with Robert, I wanted to hide every part of me. I didn't want anyone watching me. After our last conversation I never discussed my feelings or fears with Juliette. And my mother never asked me about my reaction to Robert. There had been only silence.

I was still getting used to my recent growth spurt of body hair and breasts. I shouldn't have, but I compared myself to Juliette's full-blown beauty.

Juliette's light tan skin had no blemishes, no stretch marks, no birthmarks. Her black hair shone with bronze highlights all the way down her back. Her eyes were the colour of smoke. And she had the most beautiful breasts, just the right size, high, firm and with pointed round light brown areolas and the most perfect round buttocks.

On the other hand, I was a paler version with black hair and gold-brown eyes, with breasts which were mere points on my chest and a less than generous buttocks. But I was taller than Juliette and had legs that went on forever.

For years, there were villagers who referred to my mother as Julius's milk. But that wasn't the worst of it. There was this older guy who would call out to us on the bridge and when we didn't answer he would yell out, "Too beautiful to be poor. Too light-skinned to be poor." Every single time. We couldn't avoid him because he was always on the bridge.

I hated him.

I hated the comments.

I hated that people were so ignorant.

I got angry.

And I didn't understand why it made me so angry. And I didn't understand the constant need of people to comment, to label, to ridicule us for our skin colour.

We were not the only light-skinned girls in the village. But we got all the scorn. Samson and Samuel usually defended us by screaming at Mr-Bridge-guy, "You're just jealous of their hair." And that defence made me feel worse. Maybe I was touchy with my feelings.

I fell next to Juliette on our bed wearing my short black t-shirt. The threadbare sheet chafed against my naked thighs. I ignored the scratchy sensation and asked Juliette the question that'd been burning through my grey matter.

"Juliette, do you like Timothy, and are you going to do as Mamie asked you?" I muttered.

Juliette's face was buried face down on her pillow. And when I asked the question she stopped moving and the frayed strings of her cut-up t-shirt, the colour of the insides of the guavas we went to collect on other people's land, stopped moving. I hated the strings and had threatened to cut them off. Juliette had laughed at my threat.

She didn't answer me for a long time. I thought maybe she hadn't heard my question and I was about to give up when she turned her body toward me and looked at the closed bedroom door. A small smile played around her lips, which were the same colour as the bubble gum she was always popping. The smile softened her eyes, and softened my feelings, and it raised my empathy for her. We didn't know our natural father and the only father we'd known had been taken from us without closure.

"I like him well enough, but I don't know about . . . becoming lovers as Mamie is suggesting."

"Lovers?" I asked in a hush. "What does it mean, Juliette?"

"She wants me to . . ." She stopped, and I could see the gear change in her brain. "You know Mamie has always told us to stay away from boys to make sure we don't get pregnant."

"True. Why is she changing her mind? Where's 'you should stay away from Timothy?'"

"She explained we need Timothy's goodwill."

"But why we need Timothy's goodwill? You mean his money, when Mamie works?"

Yes, she works, but you are forgetting one thing, my dear sister—Daddy Julius is no longer around. He was our financial support."

"It is about money . . . Mamie is willing to . . ."

"Julia!" she shouted and sat up on the bed. "You're such a child, you don't know when to stop, how dare— She wants me to encourage Timothy so we can have a secured future. I mean, Timothy does have a job and we do need the help."

"Juliette, I can't believe you're letting Mamie manipulate you into this."

"Well, Miss High Dreamer, I guess it's me or you and since you're too young it's me alone in this thing with Mamie. It's also to secure your future."

"My future!"

"Our future, Julia. With Daddy Julius dead, we have no one to support us. Look at where we live."

"Look at where we live? Look at where Timothy lives! In Cheryl's house."

"Stop, saying 'Cheryl's house,'" she snapped back, with a sharp intake of breath.

"It's smaller than our house. It's a shoebox house."

"You don't understand. You're a child. What do you know? Timothy is only staying there to save up money. He can afford a better place, but he wants to save up money to buy his own place soon."

"How do you know this, Juliette? From Mamie dearest?"

"Why can't you accept things, Julia?"

"Because I ask questions."

"You are not accepting of who we are. You have big ideas. You have big dreams."

"But, Juliette, don't we have the same dreams? What happened to all the years we talked about you becoming a doctor? About me becoming an accountant."

"Do you know any doctors or accountants, Julia?"

"What do you mean, Juliette? We have a doctor who lives up the road. I don't know, but I am sure there is an accountant up the road, too."

"Yes, up the road, Julia, not in this yard. Look around the yard. Look down the road," she said warming to her subject, she'd turned to face me, and she pointed her long finger at me.

"Juliette, you are only repeating Mamie's views," I replied, my voice breaking under the weight of the words she'd spoken. The reality she'd painted by repeating our mother verbatim made me wince. I couldn't bear to look at her, instead I stared at the rusted galvanize that was our roof.

I grew frustrated with Juliette's reasoning. Frustrated with her repetitions of Mamie's flawed reasoning. Frustrated she was caving in and giving up her dreams.

"Juliette, remember four years ago you were a star—the first scholarship to high school in our family, in the yard, on our side of the village. Remember the joy we all felt on your achievement. How can you give up your dreams?" I asked, my voice shuddering.

"Julia, why do you keep attacking me?" she asked in an exasperated voice.

I didn't let up.

"I want you to see reason. You can't pick Timothy as a lover just because Mamie asked you to."

"I Like Timothy," she said and sat up and got on her knees. Her next move was unexpected. She grabbed my shoulder and pulled me up to her face and shook me hard. My pulse took off like the river when it rains heavily, and it rushes to the sea in swollen glory.

She did it for a few seconds too long because my racing pulse turned into a waterfall down the face of a mountain. She parted her full soft lips and said, "It's either me or you."

The room tilted, I became mute.

What is she saying? What's she's getting at? I took a deep breath and asked, "What about love, Juliette?"

She released my shoulders, hopped off the bed and dropped onto the thin rotting board next to the bed. She wanted to stand over me. This was a new Juliette. Not quite. I wanted to dare her to stand over Mamie in this way. I was not her enemy. I was her friend and sister and I wanted her to want the best for herself.

I didn't know why I thought my mother didn't know what was best for Juliette—for me—for us.

The new temporary Juliette stood above me and aimed a fixed hard stare at me and in a low, firm voice, she said. "Mamie is right, Julia. You have too many questions for a child. These things are above you. It is not your business what lover I take on. I will do as I please. It is my body. It is my life. It is my sacrifice. I'm always the sacrifice. You . . . the baby gets to escape again."

And with those ominous words she walked over to the door, pulled it open with force and let it bang, rocking the wooden partition.

For months afterwards, I was forced to be a spectator in my sister's encouraging Timothy. Over the next few months Timothy spent an increasing amount of time in our house acting as if his match box house had ejected him. Likewise, Juliette spent an increasing amount of time at Timothy's house.

Everyone moved through the stony grounds of the yard from house to house.

Happy.

Every morning I heard Timothy belt out love songs. It became part of his morning ritual in getting ready to leave for work. Every morning on the bed I shared with Juliette she woke up humming tunes, breaking into her favourite Whitney Houston ballad, "Saving All My Love For You." Every morning, my mother whistled while she prepared breakfast for us.

Our yard had become a happy place again.

Along with all this happiness, there was never a lack of food. On a weekly basis, Timothy deposited bags of groceries to my mother. She had become the full-time chef to Mr Timothy. But in truth the groceries, the food, was for our one big happy household in the yard.

No one cared about aspirations.

No one cared about my dreams.

On the Sunday before I discovered the true source of all the happiness, Aunty Maureen and Ma Titre cornered my mother on the big stone. The sun had dipped in crimson glory into the sea. Groups of Sunday strollers called out their greetings when they strolled past us. I sat next to Aunty Maureen, my head buried in my latest library find.

Without preamble, Ma Titre launched the attack. "Velma, do you know what is the word in the village? People are saying you sold out Juliette to Timothy. They are saying you are encouraging vice under your roof. They are saying you couldn't wait for Juliette to finish high school."

I abandoned my book to give my full attention to the attack.

This should be good.

I was certain Mamie dearest was going to blow up.

I looked over at her and sure enough, she lifted her right index finger to Ma Titre's face, her cheeks stained red, and shouted, "You, Ma Titre, better tell your newsagents that it is none of their damn business. *Sa pa zafè, yo.* My daughter is my business. I, Velma, carried her for nine months and no one will dictate to me how I raise her.

"Whoever is telling you any of these things, they better go check *their* children. Juliette's future is secured. Do they have a future? Do they have a high school education? Do they have a man who will inherit land one day? Do they have a man with a government job?"

Aunty Maureen interrupted her. "But, Velma, the girl is still in high school."

"Maureen, Juliette is almost out of high school, her exams are in a few weeks' time. You and Ma Titre have a plan for me today. You all out to upset me, Maureen."

"Velma, you forget. You wanted Juliette to become a doctor."

"Listen, Maureen," my mother said, her eyes narrowed into slits, her finger wagging from Ma Titre to Aunty Maureen. "How am I going to get Juliette to study medicine? Look around you. Four little houses, a tamarind tree, and a big stone, and none of it belongs to us. Answer me; how?"

"Velma, Juliette is a bright girl, she can get a scholarship," Aunty Maureen tried again to bring reason.

"She got a government scholarship to high school," Ma Titre pointed out.

"She got the last scholarship, remember. Julia did better than her. I have no hope for scholarship. The government does not give scholarships for university. And Timothy is a good man, and he will take care of my daughter."

"You sure about the government not giving scholarships? Have you asked Vignette? Remember she has connection to a minister in the government," Aunty Maureen added in a helpful tone.

"Maureen, you're casting doubt on our friendship. Because I can't believe you think Vignette, my dearest sister-in-law, would put my child before her own wants and needs."

"Come on, Velma. Vignette always come around and bring stuff for you."

"Yes, her hand-me-down dresses and shoes, and the things she steals from the Ministry," she said with disdain.

She was going to say more, but Ma Titre cut her off by asking, "Where are they now, Velma. I saw them heading to the river on this blessed Sunday afternoon. You're allowing Juliette to leave your house with a man."

My mouth opened and closed at the news. I thought Juliette had gone up the road to visit with her friend Sasha.

My mother stood up and planted her legs wide apart. Sweat popped out like round fat beads on her forehead and her nostrils flared. And, with a sweep of her hand, she addressed her attackers in a hard voice.

"Now, listen to me. I don't want the two of you to have anything to tell me about my child again. You have not listened to a word I have said this afternoon. My daughter is securing her future. You understand me. The two of you need to drop this."

"How can we drop this? Do you want the girl to get pregnant?" Aunty Maureen asked.

"Maureen, Maureen, you are trying my patience."

"Yes, Velma, you cannot want to see Juliette pregnant," Aunty Maureen repeated.

"It is none of your business," she screeched in response.

"Velma, I hope you have the girl on birth control," Ma Titre declared her own voice hard and loud.

"You see, you two. I'm done with you for today."

Before any of them could respond, my mother marched off to the house and slammed the front door. Ma Titre and Aunty Maureen sat for a few seconds with their mouths agape.

"Julia, why is your mother so vex, so *fache*?" Ma Titre asked me when she'd recovered.

"Ma Titre, I have no idea and I'm not going to ask. I have already received my lengthy talk on minding my business and not asking questions from both Juliette and my mother."

"I hope to God, she has the girl on birth control," Ma Tire repeated in a hot whisper.

Maureen said, "Hmmm."

They'd said their piece to my mother. And my prediction came true—she had gotten mad. It bothered me that neither Aunty Maureen nor Ma Titre had been able to sway my mother from her devious path.

She'd decided Juliette's future and fate.

It was survival over dreams.

Ma Titre and Aunty Maureen continued to talk about my mother and the plan she'd convinced herself was the best one for our survival, our future. And I went back to reading my book to divorce myself from their conversation.

And, maybe from that moment, I decided in the back of my head I was going to be different. I knew I wanted different things. I thought Juliette had wanted those things too.

Was I being unrealistic?

About a week after the confrontation.

Juliette began her leave from school to prepare for her CXC exams, due to begin at the end of the month. For the most part she stayed home to study while I went to school and mother went out to whatever job she'd had lined up for the day.

I came home from school that first week in May expecting to find Juliette buried in her book on our bed lying in nothing more than her bra and panties as usual. I couldn't find her. I went out back to the kitchen and Juliette wasn't there either. Confused, I came out to stand in the middle of the yard wondering where Juliette could be.

It was then I heard her voice, carried on the wind, crying out, "Oh, Tim. Oh, Tim."

My ears perked up, for the sound had the exact cadence of the sounds Cheryl used to make when she and Robert were in the throes of their passion. A heat spread through my body under my khaki skirt and shirt jack. Without delay I rushed to our hiding place under the tamarind tree on the other side of Cheryl's house where we used to peek through the hole Samson or Samuel created.

I was afraid of what I would discover but at the same time a certain excitement crawled along my flesh. I creeped my way to the peep hole and there revealed to my eyes were my sister and Timothy, naked. I watched their passionate exertion, my sister chanting "Oh, Tim. Oh, Tim. Yes, yes."

I stood transfixed, my eyes glued to the peeping hole, watching Timothy and my sister, limbs entwined, tan skin against golden skin, wet with a billion beads of sweat. I stood there peeping until the bodies changed position.

And then my curiosity gave way to anger. The scene disturbed me. What was my sister doing? Why was she enjoying it so much? Why wasn't she studying for her exams? Where was Mamie? Why did my body respond at the sight of the lovers?

Confused, I ran away from the peeping hole, entered our house, and threw myself onto the bed where I trembled from what I had seen. I trembled for Juliette too. I trembled with the fear lodged in my belly.

Why was I afraid? Was this what Juliette really wanted? Did she really want to be a kept woman? Why was Mamie allowing Juliette and Timothy to be lovers while Juliette was still at school? Why had Mamie gone out of her way to encourage the affair?

I didn't know what to do with the many questions that arose from what I'd witnessed through the peephole. Like many things, I keep my voyeurism to myself. I feared the truth that Samson, Samuel, Juliette, and I had been closeted voyeurs when Cheryl lived there. I would take this to my grave. The adults would never learn of the peeping hole.

I never went to the kitchen. I forgot I needed to eat. I didn't bother to get up from the bed. I drifted off to sleep even though the house was hot and stuffy. And my last thought were Ma Titre's words to my mother on Sunday: "I hope you have the girl on birth control."

I couldn't have envisaged then how this one single event I'd witnessed had the power to determine the course of our lives.

6

Homes Are Not Created Equal
(1986)

My third year in high school brought more changes to my home life in the yard. I came home late one Friday afternoon having attended my first meeting of the Debating Society at my school. I'd been declared useless at athletics and so I turned to more esoteric adventures. My friends Gina and Gloria joined me because they were also useless at athletics. In our sports-dominated high school we were outcasts. The decision to join the Debating Society hadn't been hard to make.

On the bus I became lost in thought on Mr James and his militant approach in training us how to debate. I also became lost to yet another world building in my fertile fantasy mind. A world much different from the one I occupied. A world where mothers didn't push their daughters into relationships for financial security. A world where I had my own financial security.

And, of course, I missed when the bus stopped outside our house. Lightning's conductor had to call my name. Startled, I alighted from the bus amidst snickers, and a few heckles from the guys. I was never more grateful for the speed at which Lightning operates. *Peep, peep,* and he was off before the conductor could slide the door shut, taking away the heckles and laughter.

If only time could move at the speed of light, I'd fast forward my way out of high school. With two years of high school left, I felt as if every moment was dragging by. Why did it take five years? Was someone purposely trying to make us suffer by dragging us through more classes than necessary? Did someone enjoy seeing us squirm under the constant pressure of schoolwork and exams? Was it so our society could delay us from reaching adulthood?

I bounced down the pebble track, my bag slung low on my back. It swayed in tune to my steps. I walked past the house to the kitchen. I was hungry and wanted to get to my lunch without delay. Before the kitchen came into sight, I heard the blaring music and boisterous talking.

Among the voices, I heard a new voice. Who was the stranger? Why is there a stranger in our yard? I didn't have happy memories associated with strangers we'd welcomed to our little yard. Terrible things happened. To Annya. To Juliette. To me.

I dispelled my morbid thoughts when Samson called out, "Look who's here, Miss Julia." I had come to a stop in the small clearing we'd packed with fresh pebbles from the sea a few weeks ago. Since then, every footstep generated a *crunch, crunch, crunch*. Old Man Maurice hated it, but everyone in the yard preferred the pebbles over the dirt.

I glared at him. "Don't ever call me that again, Samson. Never again."

His brown eyes widened, and his body froze. He wasn't the only one. Maureen, my mother, and the stranger stopped talking and moving. Four pairs of eyes became trained on me. I didn't cower. I took off my bag and threw it down next to the step where my mother and the stranger sat. I didn't care. Samson shouldn't be allowed to call me Miss Julia. The memory of Robert calling me Miss Julia was too fresh, too painful.

"Julia, what got into you?" my mother asked.

"I don't want Samson to call me Miss Julia. He has been calling me Julia for years. What's with the 'Miss Julia' today?"

"I was just teasing, Julia," Samson offered in a low voice.

"I don't like it," I said, and bent to retrieve my bag and placed it on the step. That's when I noticed the back door to our house stood open and in the middle of the living room stood a big black grip, a shopping bag, and what looked like a toolbox. I squeezed my eyes shut at the construction tools . . .

My breathing became shallow. "Mamie—" My skin felt flushed. In choppy words I tried again, "What are those things?" I pointed to the pile of stuff. "What . . . are they doing in the middle of our living room?"

"Those things belong to Augustus here," she said, and pointed to the man who sat next to her. This was the stranger I had heard from the street.

I stared.

. . . At the Robert look-alike. *What is a Robert look-alike doing sitting next to my mother? Why are his things in the middle of our living room floor? Why is my mother smiling up into this man's face? Why is she looking at me like I am supposed to smile too?*

I didn't smile. I couldn't smile. I wouldn't ever smile. Without a word, I climbed the two concrete steps into the living room and jumped over the things on the floor and closed the flimsy door of my bedroom.

"Julia, Julia. Child, come out this minute. There is only one woman in this house."

I went to lie down on my bed, which I no longer had to share with Julia. I buried my head under the thin pillows. I could still hear her voice. But I pretended not to hear. I didn't respond. I didn't want to even think of her usual words. About there being only one woman in this house. Her usual crutch to establish her authority.

I may have not yet been a woman, but I knew I didn't have to smile, laugh and talk with a Robert look-alike. I couldn't be forced. I was independent. I had my own mind. My stomach churned as if I had eaten stale food. And to top it off, blood rushed to my ears.

Why is this man here? Why should this stranger take Daddy Julius' place? Why did Juliette have to marry Timothy so soon after she graduated, while I was still stuck here at home? What had I done to deserve this? What was God trying to teach me through all these circumstances that were out of my control? Is it wrong to want it to just be Mamie and me? Why did she have to bring this man here? Without warning. Without notice.

I lay on my bed, feeling the hard mattress beneath me, covered with sheets that smelled like camphor balls. My head was heavy with unanswered questions and I felt desperate for answers. I turned and started pounding my thin mattress as a punching bag. Over and over I drove my fist into the mattress to release a piece of the anger in my heart; wishing for my knuckles to bleed it out.

Three weeks later I embraced my first opportunity to leave our house on weekends. My mother had gone and found herself a man. His name: Augustus Xavier. I became convinced my mother refused to live independently.

What reasons existed for her to bring home a new man? As usual, she blamed everything on my father having deserted her, or rather *us*.

Augustus was yet another replacement for the father I never got to know. The father who deserted us. The father who never wrote letters. The father who never sent money.

His lone sister, Aunty Vignette, also hadn't heard from him for the same number of years. Their parents were long dead. Both my father and mother were from the village of Petite Soufriere, a place my mother had refused to take us to visit.

Whenever we raised the subject of going to visit, my mother would become silent, and she would refuse to meet our eyes. She also never answered our questions. We were left to wonder why we never visited the village of our parents' heritage. Although my mother told numerous, embellished stories of growing up in Petite Soufriere, there was always a sense of mystery surrounding it.

When Augustus had installed himself like a fixture in our house, I had to grapple with co-existing in the space with a man that wasn't Daddy Julius. Daddy Julius was the man who knew my favourite fish, and he'd brought it home every time he had gone out to sea—even against my mother's deep protests. She hated to clean the tiny *kayi*fish and complained like a record stuck on the first song.

It'd been almost three years since his disappearance, and I still missed Daddy Julius. I thought of him every day. I didn't know whether he was in Martinique—I knew it couldn't be true because he would have made his way back home already. Was it possible he was in Trinidad, the island at the bottom of the chain of islands in the Eastern Caribbean? I knew I was stretching my imagination, but I wanted Daddy Julius to be alive. I wanted him to make his way back home. I wanted him to come back a hero, full of stories of daring feats. I refused to let Daddy Julius die.

And that left no room for Augustus to manoeuvre into my heart. My memories of Daddy Julius wouldn't let me. I clung to my memories like I clung to my favourite stone whenever I went river bathing, to prevent the current from sweeping me downwards to the sea.

Augustus visited every weekend since his first appearance. During the week he worked on a big project in Marigot—a new housing scheme for the less fortunate like us. There hadn't been any talk of a similar project for our village. I would have gone to work to help my mother pay for one of those houses.

Augustus would arrive on a Friday evening covered in the fine dust of cement—glued to his clothes, his boots, his face, his hair. He not only brought the cement dust—he brought his weekly pay cheque.

Every weekend he spent at our house my mother showered him with attention. They took long river baths in the fading light. She made his favourite meals. She stocked up on his favourite rum.

And I had to concede my mother's joy had increased. She smiled often. She told more embellished stories. She told more jokes. Her laughter drew Ma Titre from across the road, not to soothe her back and wipe her tears like she'd done after Daddy Julius disappeared, but to throw back her head and let off unrestrained laughs. Every day, she turned the volume up on the new black radio Augustus had bought for her. She swayed to the music and worked her way up till she danced until her skin glistened with skinny and fat beads of sweat.

My own happiness should have increased. But I couldn't forget Daddy Julius. I imagined Daddy Julius alive on a strange island, living among strangers. Daddy Julius's bones lying on the ocean floor, his flesh eaten by the vultures of the ocean.

Those thoughts made me unhappy. And my mother's newfound joy, three years after the disappearance of Daddy Julius, increased my struggle.

I wanted her to stop talking. To stop laughing. To stop dancing. Whenever Augustus was in the house, I frowned until the tightness in my jaw caused discomfort. I said chupes a lot and got many a backhand slap in the centre of my back.

The real reason I hated being around Augustus—he reminded me of Robert. He had the same height as the tallest coconut tree in the village. His skin glistened with the deep sheen of midnight blue black like Robert. His differences were his slanted eyes and full pink lips.

His uncanny resemblance to Robert Langlais, the man who'd lived in Cheryl's house, gave me jitters from the bottom of my belly, and made my skin tingle. My body broke out into sweat whenever he got near me.

Why did my mother have to find a man who resembled the man who had illegally touched me. Not once. But twice. Before he did unpardonable things to Annya's little body.

From the day he violated me I'd kept my tight shirts buried under the mountain of camphor balls in my grip under the bed. Because he'd accused me of taunting him with my t-shirt and breasts. I'd retreated to hide my blossoming body. I'd felt seen and exposed. I felt ashamed, but couldn't say why I felt ashamed.

I regretted not speaking up.

Was I better than the grown women who chose not to expose Robert's actions? The anger simmered within me, a steady flame that burned towards my mother, Aunty Maureen, and Ma Titre for their complicit silence. However, I'd become shamed by my own silence. How had I allowed this to happen? I'd said nothing. I, too, had been a participant in the conspiracy of silence, my voice swallowed by fear and uncertainty.

You were a child.

But I couldn't forget. Three years had passed and I couldn't forget how Robert had laid his big black hands on Annya's body. Annya's six-year-old body. Annya, only old enough to play with her dolls, had to suffer under his giant black hands. His giant mouth. His giant black body. He'd violated her fragile frame, and the adults let him live. The worst part—Cheryl took him back. These thoughts haunted me at nights, alone on my narrow bed which, thanks to Augustus's largesse, now had a fat mattress.

I shook my head to get rid of the dark thoughts. I didn't want to break out into shaking, trembling, and shivering until my eyes leaked tears. I found the only remedy was to take deep, steadying breaths to dispel the anxiety. After every anxiety attack, I left for the river to scrub away the shame, the silence, the sadness.

Gina and Gloria were my best friends at school; together we were known as the triplets. By our third year in high school, our friendship had bloomed into one entrenched in sharing, honesty, jokes, and all-around good vibes.

Over the years, I'd shared the stories of our yard with them. Many of the things I described they couldn't understand because they didn't live in a yard like ours. They lived in town and had proximate neighbours, but without the dynamics of four small houses in a small yard.

Their invitation to spend the weekend at their house came when I wanted to get away from my mother and Augustus's honeymoon weekends. I'd readily accepted the invitation, and my mother wholeheartedly agreed, her enthusiasm eclipsing even my own.

When I asked my mother permission to visit Gina and Gloria, I'd expected her to grill me with questions. This was the first time I would spend overnight at someone's house. She had never entrusted Juliette and me to stay with anyone—not even to Aunt Vignette's.

It bothered me.

Was my mother anxious for me to leave the house as much as I wanted to leave? A heaviness invaded my body until my ribs grew tight and restricted my breath with the realisation. Was I in the way of her happiness? Was she choosing this man above me and my needs?

And before I could stop myself my mouth opened to ask, "Don't you care I will be gone for the entire weekend?"

We were in the living room the Thursday night before my visit to Gina and Gloria. I sat on the floor and watched while my mother rolled her hair on big yellow curlers. My job was to hold the plastic bag filled with yellow and pink curlers and hand her a curler when she needed it.

"It is only two days, Julia," she said while she rolled her hair on a big yellow smooth curler. The single light bulb on a black dirty cord hanging from the ceiling in the living room created a soft golden glow.

"Are you going somewhere this weekend," I asked, my voice rising as I handed her a pink ribbed curler this time.

"Not the pink one, give me a yellow one. And why are you asking a grown woman if she is going out this weekend? You won't be here, so you don't need to know."

"But, Mamie!"

"Give me a pink curler."

I pulled a pink curler out of the bag to hand it to her and it fell from my hand.

"Watch what you are doing, Julia!" she snapped at me.

I bent my head and rolled my eyes. My mouth filled with saliva, and I had the sudden urge to leave the room. I wanted to leave the bag of yellow and pink curlers on the floor. I didn't want to share in this mother-daughter routine anymore.

"Hand me a yellow one this time," she barked.

I jammed my hand into the bag and pulled out the pink curler and handed it to her without looking at her and again it fell.

"Julia, what is the matter with you tonight? Do you want me to take my own curlers tonight?"

"No, Mamie," I muttered.

"Then hand me a curler, without letting it fall to the floor."

I didn't know what bothered me the most about that interaction with my mother. Was it her nonchalant response or my response to her nonchalance? I was upset and I couldn't or wouldn't voice it to her. Instead, I jammed my hand into the bag each time I took a curler to hand it to her. But I made sure I didn't drop a curler again.

All I wanted was for things to be as they were when Daddy Julius was alive.

I was stubborn.

Because everything had changed with Daddy Julius's disappearance.

My mother had changed.

Juliette had changed.

Had it changed me too?

Maybe.

I didn't think about it too hard because I'd become too preoccupied with avoiding my mother and her quest for happiness with Augustus.

With Juliette out of the house I should have been at the centre of her reason for living and the centre of her ambitions. Instead, I was set free like driftwood on the surface of the deep blue ocean.

Free to roam.

Free to leave.

Much like the song Old Man Maurice sang everyday, "Born Free."

All I wanted was for Augustus to disappear so life could be how it used to be.

Was I wrong? Should my mother be robbed of her little happiness with Augustus? Should I cease to be the reason for her living or the centre of her ambition? She had married off a pregnant Juliette to Timothy. She only had me. Was it wrong to want Augustus to disappear so life could go back to how it was?

Friday afternoon arrived.

I swayed to the ear-splitting reggae music Lightning blasted on the bus. I ignored the chatter and screaming from my fellow high school mates. I tapped my foot to the beat of "Get Up, Stand Up," a favourite of Lightning. All week he'd been playing Bob Marley.

I liked the song too. Because many times I had wanted to stand up and demand my rights. I swayed and tapped more to the beat and allowed the beat to infuse a heat in my heart and a lightness to my limbs. I got lost in imagining my weekend stay with Gina and Gloria. The rest of the trip on the bus I couldn't bite down on the smile that softened my face. I got off the Lightning high on the buzz of adrenaline flowing through my veins.

I went straight to my room to change from my khaki skirt and white shirt jack, remembering to remove my school crest. I couldn't lose another one down the river. And I didn't want another sermon on the subject from my mother. She'd promised to leave me without a crest the next time I let one go down the river, and not having one would get me a demerit or a detention, which I also didn't want.

I slipped into my cut-off jeans which fitted halfway down my thighs, and a white oversized t-shirt which fell just above my knee.

I set about packing the slim pickings from my wardrobe into my mother's multi-coloured striped shopping bag with metal handles. I dumped my favourite outfit in first; the ready-made orange skirt pant with matching top. Next went in my blush pink church dress, made by Aunty Maureen, with ruffles around the neck and at the hem.

Then in went my pink, blue, and white shiny rayon panties—they crackled when you rubbed them; my blue and white lace bras; and my white cotton nighty covered in a million tiny blue and yellow flowers.

I topped this up with my toiletries which consisted of a jar of Vaseline, my roll-on, a pink brush, and a hard black breakable comb—the one which did more to create friction than it does to loosen tangles. This completed my packing for my first weekend away from home.

My mother waited with me for Lightning, my favourite bus driver. He drove fast, but I was never afraid while riding his bus. My mother sent me on my first weekend out of her house with these words: "Make sure you behave yourself in the people's house. Watch your mouth and eat what they put in front of you," she said to me in her no-nonsense voice. And with that admonition she sent me on my way.

Gina and Gloria lived in the part of town called Pottersville—a mishmash of buildings and winding streets nestled on the outskirts of Roseau beyond the bridge leading out of town. The enclave is bordered by the Roseau River, the Caribbean Sea, and the beginning of Goodwill—that bastion of middle- to upper-class residences.

Men and women of all walks of life dwelled in a variety of wooden and concrete structures, and conducted businesses out of many places fronting the main street. It was a place of constant foot and vehicle traffic, colourful characters, and a variety of shops licensed to sell spirits.

These shops carried the sign on a little black board printed in white, "This shop or tavern is licensed to sell spirits." The results then were men in various degrees of inebriation calling out merrily to passers-by, or who were flat-out passed out on the pavement when the spirits overwhelmed their bodies.

I got off the bus at the Roseau Old Market in the company of a cacophony of noise; horns blaring *peep peep*; music blasting out of buses; pedestrians shouting out greetings in patois and English; bus conductors shouting over each other "Right away, Right away!" And to top it off, the conductors from the cultural capital shouting over everyone else, "South City, Grand Bay, right away."

In this *mélé* I spotted my friends who were standing on the broken steps which were part and parcel of the road, a fixture of the old market square. They were both wearing acid wash jean skirts with red and pink shirts. I couldn't suppress in my smile when I saw them. I crossed the cracked pavement to meet up with them.

When I was within arm's length of them, Gina blurted, "Why do you have a shopping bag?"

"It has my clothes and everything I need. I don't—"

Gloria cut in. "It doesn't matter what bag you have. I'm excited you'll be spending the entire weekend with us."

I exhaled the breath I didn't know I'd suppressed. I hadn't given a thought to using my mother's shopping bag. I couldn't travel with my grip and there were no other bags.

"You know we have a long walk across town, so no skylarking," Gloria continued in a playful voice.

"Of course," I answered.

Gina and Gloria's house was at the very end of the community on the end of the street from the bridge leading out of town right on down to the deep-water harbour. It meant I had to walk across town from the Roseau Old Market, with my striped shopping bag in one hand, to the rhythm of the excited chatter of Gina and Gloria.

At the time very few people had cars. People walked everywhere. Gina, Gloria, and I walked and laughed all the way to their house. It was an upstairs and downstairs structure which housed the shopping centre owned by their parents. By the time we got to the entrance of the shopping centre my hands were turning red from holding onto the metal handles of the shopping bag. The moment we entered the doors of the shop I placed the bag on the glazed concrete floor and began to rub my hands to relieve the tension.

Mrs Adams was at her usual perch at the cash register. Every time I'd visited the shop with Gina and Gloria, she'd been manning the front counter. When we came through the door her eyes widened and she stood up from the tall black wooden stool and scolded Gina and Gloria. "I can't believe you allowed Julia to carry her bag all the way across town by herself."

"But, Ma, we offered to help," they chorused together.

"Girls, I can't hear your excuse. Please pick up Julia's bag and take it upstairs to your room."

Both Gina and Gloria scrambled to take the bag from my hand. Gloria, normally the take-charge twin, pulled the bag from Gina. Gina opened her mouth to complain but one long look from her mother silenced the words before she could utter them.

"You, Gina, take Julia up the stairs and make sure she has something to eat and drink after this long walk in the hot sun. You must be thirsty and tired, Julia," she added in a softer voice than she had spoken to Gina and Gloria.

I watched her switch gears to attend to a customer who'd finished his shopping. She laughed while she cashed for the customer, and at the same time she issued another reprimand. "I raised you girls better, to do better," she growled, the cadence of her voice rising on each word.

I didn't know what to make of her reprimand in a playful tone. My mother's reprimand was always militaristic. Her tone hard and unyielding.

We laughed and Gina and Gloria took me outside the store to take the stairs to the living quarters above the grocery store. We climbed the fifteen green-painted concrete steps to the upper living area.

At the top before she opened the door Gina grumbled, "I told you to let us carry your bag, but you wouldn't hear. Now our mother thinks the worst of us."

"It wasn't a big deal for me to carry my bag by myself."

"See, you so hard-headed, Julia." Gloria piped up to support her sister, and opened the door to their living quarters.

I followed them inside and asked, "Why would your mother think the worse of you?"

"Because she expects us to be kind to our friends."

"Really? But you and Gloria are always kind to me at school. When we go back down to the grocery store you can tell her so, or I will."

"You don't know my mom, Julia. She won't let us off the hook so easily," Gina said, and closed the door behind us.

"But she was smiling and laughing the whole time," I said, and looked around what seemed to be the kitchen.

"Don't let that fool you, Julia. She expects us to fall in line," Gina said.

"You guys have it good; you should meet *my* mother," I said and moved into the kitchen. I stared at everything and hoped Gina and Gloria didn't notice.

"Oh, Julia, you always say that," Gloria responded.

"Your mother tells hilarious stories," Gina added.

"Her stories and her reprimands are worlds apart. They come from two different people," I said in a low, depressed voice.

"You know Julia loves to exaggerate, right, Gloria?"

"I don't," I protested in a louder, stronger voice.

We all laughed because it was true. Maybe I was my mother's daughter. Stubborn.

I walked into the centre of their kitchen and was transported to a different world. The kitchen had white walls. I stared. Who paints the walls of a kitchen in white? Even the cupboards were white. How do you use a smoky kerosene stove and coal pot in a white kitchen?

I turned around to seek out the kerosene stove and coal pot, but my eyes found a stove with an attached oven. A stove with an oven. No smell of kerosene. No black soot on the white walls. Do Gina and Gloria have to purge this kitchen every year?

I couldn't imagine having to clear out this kitchen to purge it each year. There were too many things. Everything looked like it was bolted in place. There were cupboards at the floor and ceiling level. And there was the biggest fridge I had seen in my life. To top it off, there was a sink with a pipe for running water.

This was a dream kitchen to me. I fell in love with the kitchen the more I stared. There were two windows, with matching flowered curtains, through which streamed in endless sunlight, making the kitchen as bright as the sun. Surrounded by the beauty and reality of their kitchen, I grasped the stark difference between Gina and Gloria and myself.

How could I ever invite them to spend a weekend at my home?

The earlier lightness of limbs and the heat in my heart was replaced with heaviness in my stomach. This wasn't my world, this was their world. The realisation hit me like a mud slide down the mountain. We were from different homes, different worlds. I hadn't given much thought to our differences before.

At school we were equals. At their home the gap became blinding.

Our kitchen at my home was nothing more than a shed; their kitchen made me want to linger and study its beauty. But Gina pulled me down a long corridor to the bedroom she shared with Gloria.

The girls should have warned me.

When Gina opened the door to the bedroom she said, "This is where you will be spending a lot of time with us." I realised I'd gained entry to a different world; this time, a heavenly bedroom.

My bedroom would fit five times into this room.

I surveyed the soft baby blue walls. There were two windows, adorned with frilly white curtains, each with a direct view of the sea and the harbour.

Who likes white in this house?

A dresser stood under one window, with its own large mirror in which the girls could see a perfect reflection of themselves. Meanwhile, back at my house my broken handheld mirror reigned. It had broken a year before, and my mother refused to get me a new one. I couldn't help myself, I went to stand before the girls' mirror. My image was live, perfect, and in technicolour.

I glanced at the two double beds and the girls in unison informed me I would be switching beds to sleep with each of them in turns.

I stared.

I remained still.

I smiled.

The room was unbelievable.

I sat down on the bed nearest me because my legs lost their ability to balance the rest of my body. I took up the brown teddy bear with a red heart that rested against the white pillow. I'd never had a teddy bear. And I'd never known I wanted to have a teddy bear. I brought it to my nose, and it smelled like the sweet powder Gina and Gloria splashed on their chest every morning.

I had no words. Tears began to flood my eyes.

"Julia, Julia," Gloria said.

"Why are you so silent?" Gina asked.

"Give me a moment. Let me absorb this," I said, and wrapped my arms around the teddy bear, burying my face in it for comfort.

"You're being melodramatic."

"No, I am in heaven."

"Stop," they said in unison in the sing-song voice they used for their own brand of melodrama.

"Come, let us show you the rest of the house," Gloria announced.

By the end of the tour, it was evident to me that Gina and Gloria's entrepreneur parents were doing quite well with their grocery shop. How else could they afford to have Gina and Gloria live in such luxury?

I considered it a luxury. My only comparison was my house and the other houses in the yard. There were nice wooden and block houses in the village, but I'd not been in any. We played outside by the sea and the river. The only house we had visited often was Sasha's, who was Juliette's friend, to watch TV. They lived in an apartment building which was small, and nothing like the spacious airy house Gloria and Gina lived in with their parents.

At least to my mind at the time this was luxury. Our two-bedroom, wooden house with the flimsy partition, and an outside kitchen, with no bathroom facilities belonged to a different Dominica.

I could never have Gloria and Gina over at my house. No point in lying to myself. They could never be comfortable in a world without running water and plumbing.

I sighed and exhaled a small puff of breath to release the growing heaviness in my chest. I needed to end the comparison of our lives and turn to enjoy the gift of time I'd been handed with them.

At the Adams house everything was different. There were two parents, Gregory and Marie. They'd been married to each other for twenty years in holy matrimony. They'd lived together under one roof, both directly involved in continuously running their business. They owned the building outright which housed the Adams Grocery Centre and their dwelling space upstairs.

Mr Adams did the heavy lifting and Mrs Adams took charge of the cash register and their cheque book, according to the wise sage, Gloria. The shop represented their livelihood but it was not their life, I heard Mr Adams say during my first weekend.

After we'd unpacked my meager wardrobe and hung up my dress in the cavernous wardrobe in the girls' room, we headed back down the stairs to the grocery shop. The Adams Grocery Centre was a convenience store, conveniently located for people on their way in and out of Roseau.

The Adamses kept the store opened right until the ripe old time of seven o'clock. At that time, all the supermarkets in Roseau were long shut down, with the majority closing at four o'clock, the official end of business on the island. Roseau became a virtual ghost town, with hardly a living creature afoot. But at the Adams Grocery Centre the place was abuzz with people going in and out, getting the basic things they needed to survive.

Mrs Adams kept up a lively banter with customers. I walked up and down the four narrow aisles of the shop that first night, taking in the many products on the bare wooden shelves. There were Crix crackers, Shirley biscuits, Nice biscuits, dark chocolates—these were all the things I wanted to eat right away.

The usual basic items—sugar, Quaker oats, Cream of Wheat, Breeze, Cholox, blue soap, yellow soap, cooking oil, Glow spread butter, Mello Kreem, cod liver oil, Ferrol compound . . . and I could go on and on—adorned the shelves.

The store was a virtual bastion of competing scents; the savoury fish scents of saltfish mingled with smoked herring and the salty pig snout. All of the scents combined to create a sharp, fumy, musty, mouldy, dusty scent that permeated all the shops I'd entered in my village. I found the Adams shop wasn't much different. It was just bigger; and it had one, most telling difference—the front wall of the Adams Grocery Centre didn't have the little black tavern sign with the white lettering.

The difference came from their chosen faith. They belonged to the minority denomination of evangelicals. I knew this from the girls telling me at school, but I learned first-hand its true application for the entire household, including visitors to the house.

At six o'clock the next morning in the Adams household, I opened my eyes to the bass voice of Mr Adams. "Girls, girls, it is time to wake up. Time for us to pray, give thanks, and break our fast."

"Oh, Daddy, can we stay in our beds for another five minutes?" Gina said while she rubbed at her eyes with one hand and had her other arm stretched to the ceiling.

"Yes, Daddy. We fell asleep late last night for some reason." Gloria's muffled voice came from under the pink blankets.

"I know you're excited Julia is here. But guess what, girls, some things are constant around here. You know the deal. I want all three of you up and dressed in five minutes in the living room for our morning devotion. Do I make myself clear?" he said in his deep no-nonsense tone.

"Yes, Daddy." Gina and Gloria piped up.

And I said, "Yes, Mr Adams."

I mean there's no way we were going to disobey an order from six-foot, all-muscle Mr Adams with the authoritative bass voice. We got up, dressed, and went to the devotion table.

This was all new to me. My mother's faith didn't extend to family devotions or any devotions for that matter. The only time I remember being awakened was the once or twice she'd decided to make the pilgrimage to La Salette in the years when she'd claimed the whole world was against her.

My mother often declared, "I'm a *bido* Roman Catholic." But her staunchness did not extend to practicing her faith. It'd always puzzled me how one could be a staunch member of a faith and not practice the faith. My mother and her approach to her faith had made strange companions.

In the Adams living room at fourteen years of age, I experienced my first live morning devotion. The five of us sat around the dining room table with Mr Adams at the head. He took charge and directed the morning's devotions. He called on Gloria to say the opening prayer. Then he opened his big black Bible and read from Psalm chapter 23. I remembered this because the Psalm was already well known to me.

After he read the short passage, he expounded on what it means to have a Good Shepherd looking over us each day. Then he asked each of us girls what we thought of the passage. Then Mrs Adams sang the song version and Gina said the closing prayer. The devotions lasted for about thirty minutes. Thirty minutes each day.

I sat there, listened, participated, but wondered what would drive anyone to do this every day. I could not envisage the necessity to have such a family devotion to an unseen God who would make people die at sea, who would make fathers disappear and never contact their daughters again.

I stopped praying after Daddy Julius disappeared. My mother stopped sending us to church on Sundays. Ma Titre or Aunty Maureen had to threaten her with hell's damnation before she'd remember to shout at us to go. I had believed in God. I had prayed so hard for Daddy Julius and the other men to be found alive.

Silence reigned.

It was like God had shut heaven's door on my voice and my cries.

In turn, I shut down my mind, my heart, my soul.

God had forgotten me.

I forgot Him.

More firsts awaited me when I woke to a wet soggy Sunday morning. I awoke to the familiar sound of the waves crashing onto the millions of black and grey pebbles. For a moment I was lured into thinking I was still in Loubiere. But then I opened my eyes, and the grandeur of the bedroom reminded me I was at the Adams house in Pottersville.

Hours later we left together for Sunday school and church service. No one dared raise any objection to attending.

The time spent with Gina and Gloria exposed me to a whole different concept of faith and church. I must admit my discomfort that first Sunday I went to church with them. There was so much singing, shouting, and clapping I got a headache from all the clanging noise.

There were men and women running up and down the front of the church, dancing to the beat of the music. I heard strange babblings from one woman operating under some special force. She spoke in a different language. I became confused—too much was going on during the service.

From the time the service began with the singing, there'd been no sitting for well over two hours. At one point I turned around and noticed a few people had taken their seats and gone quiet, but the majority stood and danced to the music the whole time and shouted, "Hallelujah! Praise God!" over and over again.

Being more accustomed to the very sedate Mass said in the Light of Hope Chapel, the catchy and melodious music filled me with warmth and lightness. I swayed to the music as my mind emptied all my concerns and worries. I was being carried away. Peace. Comfort. And at the same time, I wanted to put my hands over my ears. The noise and the length equaled a sensory overload for me at the Temple House of Worship.

After one hour, Mass would have been done and we would have been free on our own. Free to do whatever we wanted with our Sunday. That first Sunday I visited, Sunday school and the church service ended at three o'clock. I left with ringing ears and the need to retreat into a quiet place and never come out. I was also very hungry.

I promised in my mind I would not visit with Gina and Gloria again. This long, bawling church service was not for me of the sedate faith. Too much music, bawling, and loud preaching in one day.

Gina and Gloria looked unfazed, and I noticed they'd been active participants in the service. They closed their eyes and lifted their arms in worship. The family also sat together in the service.

Were they always like that? Was the phrase "a family who prays together says together" coined in reference to them?

Although I'd been horrified by the length of time I'd had to sit in church my first Sunday, I didn't stay true to my secret threat not to repeat my visit.

The life of luxury and warmth I experienced at the Adams household called to me, offering a solace that I never knew before. It was the first time I realized how different some people's lives could be from my own. Even though I wanted to stay, it filled me with sadness to know that there were such disparities between us. I realised we were from separate worlds.

We were not all made from the same cloth. Some of us had better cloths to work with. The better cloth option was birthed in me in the Adams household. This birthing within my spirit would take me on a journey of new discoveries, life, and pain.

The next time the girls extended the invitation for me to visit, I accepted, though I couldn't brush off the dread of another four-hour service. My dread turned out to have been unfounded because my second service experience there ended up being only three hours long.

Between the time of my first visit and second visit I became receptive to questions about faith and about God. It drove me to seek clarification from Mr Adams during lunch on my second visit. In a trembling voice, I asked Mr Adams, "Why is the service so lengthy, going on for two hours and more?"

"I am glad you ask, Julia," Mr Adams responded with a smile.

"It's like this. In our church, worship is central. We believe in worshipping God in singing, praising, and dancing. Our motto is 'Make a joyful noise unto the Lord.'

"We believe in the baptism of the Holy Spirit, and speaking in tongues. I am sure you have noticed various individuals speaking in unknown tongues during the service. We believe it is the outpouring of the Holy Spirit upon a person. The person is given a message which is relayed in the unknown tongue, and someone is charged under the same Holy Spirit with the interpretation of the tongue."

His answer evoked more questions in me. "So how does one get filled with the Holy Spirit?" I asked, and I attacked the only thing left on my plate, the baked chicken.

"First, you must accept Jesus Christ as your Lord and personal Saviour. You are to confess and believe with your heart he is the Christ and he died on the cross for your sins. You have to believe he is able to forgive you of all your sins. Then you are to live a sanctified life before him following his commandments and statutes as laid out in the Bible."

"How does one know they are saved?" I asked.

Gloria answered, "It is more a matter of faith and believing. And you do feel different; you become more aware of when you have gone wrong."

"So have you made the decision, Gloria?" I asked.

"Yes, we both did," they answered together.

The discussion went on for a few hours and I became intrigued. Julia, the always inquisitive one. Julia, the girl with the questions. Julia, the girl who wants to know everything, showed up.

I couldn't wrestle away the questions. *What does it mean to accept Jesus as Lord and personal saviour?* The conversation fed my hunger to know more. How could I access the peace? How could I acquire the joy? How could I experience the power of the Holy Spirit?

Is any of this true? How can I know the Bible is not just a history book? Would the God Mr Adams talked about allow a father to desert his two daughters? Would the same God bury the only father they knew in the deep blue waters of the Atlantic Ocean?

Back at home, these questions burned through the energy in my mind. I entertained the questions like my many other questions within the four corners of my mind about our life and life in general. I was certain my mother didn't care for my questions of our faith, our hope, our future.

I knew I wanted a better future for me, for my mother.

She'd secured Juliette's future with a marriage—it had led only to children. I was certain I wasn't going to allow her to steer me into such a future when I left high school. I wasn't going to need her written permission because I wouldn't be getting married until way after I turned eighteen.

My mother never questioned me about my experiences at the Adamses' house. The weekends I spent away she could spend uninterrupted time with Augustus wrapping him more around her little finger.

I overheard my mother and Ma Titre one day discussing his history. At least two women had wrapped him around their fingers and extracted all his money from him. One woman had gone to the extreme where he paid for her land and built her house, and then she kicked him out of the house when she found another man.

"You know, Ma Titre, I would never do that. I, Velma Abraham of Petite Soufriere, would never treat the man I love in such a manner. That woman was heartless, totally heartless. An evil witch. A jezebel. But you know me, I am all about loving," she said and threw back her head in a deep raucous laugh.

When she had uttered those words, I stopped listening and vowed to choose a different path from my mother, Ma Titre, and the majority of women in the village. Women bent on living their life to extract something from men, or to wrap men around their little fingers. It never occurred to me then that the men encouraged the women, and they expected to be wrapped.

7

The Stranger Shows Up
(1987)

T he summer at the end of my third year of high school.

I'd been set to enjoy my summer vacation as a recruit in my mother's new enterprise—ice-pop making. Saturdays had been ordained production day.

One Saturday of that summer vacation I sat down outside the kitchen to grate seven coconuts. The day before it had rained the entire day and it'd left the ground soggy. The rain had stopped but the cement-coloured clouds refused to roll away. They hung low and dirty and sucked up the sea breeze.

As a result, the humidity level spiralled and my body responded to the heat in long lines of sweat. They travelled in thin streams down my back under my white t-shirt printed with the words "Hooked on Freedom" in green. It'd been a gift from Aunt Vignette, purchased for me to attend a political motorcade with her a few years ago.

Our strip of a kitchen was always hot. The single window trapped the heat within its narrow confines. Most days our kitchen was like a box oven, like the box oven where Sasha's mother baked bread and cakes and pies. Whenever I'd gone over there with Juliette, there was always a baked treat for feasting.

My task that day was to squeeze every drop of coconut milk from the seven dry coconuts. I grated the coconuts and placed them in water to soak to make it easier to squeeze out the milk from them. After soaking the grated coconut in water, I piled them into the biggest yellow strainer in the world over a big orange basin. The goal for the day was to get the maximum amount of coconut milk. I had to exert great force with a spoon to bleed the milk out of the grated coconut leaving behind dry coconut flakes, which we threw away.

My mother's coconut ice pop enterprise began with the arrival of the brand new two-door fridge which occupied a proud position next to the kitchen door. It made the kitchen even smaller. It replaced the short, one-door fridge. In the world of fridges, we had moved up.

This was one of Augustus's many gifts to my mother, in addition to the new bed and the new wardrobe in her room. I overheard her say to Ma Titre in her throw-her-head-back-and-laugh routine that this was her *"chalè"* money she was extracting. I didn't get what she meant. I wouldn't until years later.

Augustus was also a central figure in the coconut ice pop production. His job was to de-husk the dry coconuts. Augustus was out in the yard with his cutlass in hand surrounded by fourteen dry coconuts to de-husk for the next round of coconut grating. Shirtless, his midnight skin glistened with sweat as he brought his cutlass down to cut away the dry husk from the coconut. Up and down, his biceps and forearm contracting then releasing, delivering the strength to clean every coconut of its hard dry shell.

When he was done, my mother would take each shaved coconut, break it into manageable pieces on a stone positioned, it seemed, as if it was placed there in the yard by God himself for this future use. Next, with her knife, she shelled out the coconut from the shell one piece at a time.

Then the next step in the process was to grate the many pieces of coconut with the aid of a basin held in place by her thighs. And this was the step I didn't get to escape; in a similar fashion, I grated my share of coconut.

I had settled into the rhythm of grating the coconuts, taking care not to grate my fingernails, when I heard the squeal of brakes at the front of our house. It disrupted the quiet of the morning. I thought nothing of it—probably Lightning depositing Ma Titre after her Saturday market shopping. The quiet was further disturbed when someone called out, "Good morning. Is anyone home? I'm looking for Velma." It was a voice I'd never heard before. The accent sounded foreign, and the voice boomed with bass.

I looked up at my mother who sat opposite me. I was surprised at her reaction. Her eyes bulged. Her mouth gaped open. She took a big swallow before she said, *"Bondyé, Bondyé. Julia, go and see who's calling at the front door."*

I obeyed and took the gravelled path to the front of the house.

Why had my mother physically reacted to the stranger's voice?

When I got to the front of the house, I found a tall, fair-skin man. He was not alone. He had a woman and two boys with him. Behind them I saw a blue pickup truck.

I looked at the stranger. He looked familiar. But I was certain I hadn't seen him before. *Why does he look so familiar? Why do his eyes ... look so familiar ... ?*

I froze.

Lightning's bus zoomed past at the speed of light, blasting Bob Marley's "So Much Trouble in the World." A rope of knots formed in the bottom of my gut and twisted my stomach. My thoughts chased each other in my mind.

Who is he? Could it be him? Who's the woman with him? Who are these boys?

I remained glued to the spot.

I took another look at his eyes—eyes I was certain I had seen before. But I had never seen him. So how could I have seen his eyes? He smiled at me. And it was my . . .

I refused to finish the thought. My heart was ready to explode through my chest it was pounding so hard. The noise in my eardrums was like cows in a stampede on the bank of the river.

The stranger was dressed in a white t-shirt, with "I Love NY" emblazoned in red across it, acid-wash jeans, and white sneakers. He looked like he had deplaned from America. The woman with him was a white woman, tall with long black wavy hair, and the two boys could have passed for white with their slick-down wavy black hair. And oh, my goodness, they had the stranger's familiar eyes.

Who are these people? Why are they here?

Before my thoughts mushroomed, my mother called out to me.

"Who is it? What happened, Julia? I can't hear you."

"Ma, it's a man . . ."

"Well, bring him down into the yard," my mother replied. There was a shift in her voice—was it uncertainty?

Before I could do my mother's bidding, the stranger spoke to me.

"Are you Julia? Don't you know me? I'm your father."

I tilted my head to look at the stranger. Did he just ask me if I knew him? This can't be the same man who'd left me in my mother's womb to go to St. Thomas. How could I know him? I wasn't born when he'd left.

I don't know you. You've never existed in my world.

I didn't respond.

My brain had shut down. My pulse pounded like the surf on the shore. My throat tightened, threatening to cut off my breath. I spun around and headed back into the yard on two heavy legs in halting footsteps. I didn't turn back to see if he had followed me. This was a situation for my mother.

I didn't know this man and had nothing to say to him. I couldn't wait to see the expression on my mother's face when she came face to face with the stranger.

I didn't have long to wait and I wasn't disappointed. When the stranger entered the yard and faced my mother, I saw a range of emotions slide one over the other on her face. She placed aside her basin, grater, and coconuts; stood and settled both hands against her waist and addressed the strange man claiming to be my father.

"Well, well, well. *Papa, Bondyé*," she said and raised her arms and face to the clouds. "Look at who is standing before me. The mighty Julian. Julian, I never thought you would show your face to me again. What are you doing here, Julian? What do you want? Who told you we live here? Vignette?"

"I came to see you and the kids."

"The kids? What kids, Julian? *Papa, Bondyé.* You turn American. What kids? They are not children anymore. Juliette is married and has two children of her own. Not kids, but children. Look at Julia over there. She is a big girl, about to leave high school."

"Velma, I can explain if you give me a chance," he said, pleading.

"Explain!" my mother repeated, her tone aggressive. I kept my eyes on her. She moved her hands higher up on her waist and squinched her face into the meanest squall.

"You wait. Your explanation is fifteen years too late," my mother screamed at the stranger.

Augustus had stopped his cutlass work and his head moved back and forth between my mother and the stranger. The white woman who I would later come to know as Ann, turned beet red from embarrassment and fright. The two boys hid behind their mother.

My mother pointed her finger at the stranger and said, "You, Julian, need to get out of my yard. After fifteen years. After you divorced me to marry your white woman. After you never wrote to me except to send the divorce papers. After you never supported Juliette and Julia for all these years you're in America. You show up today and you want to know the kids?

"You know what, if you know what is good for you, you will take your white woman and your kids and get out of my yard. I don't need you. Juliette and Julia don't need you," she screamed like she was in a carnival band. I wanted the ground to open up and swallow me. I wanted to flee to the sea, the riverside, the mountainside. I closed my eyes and wished I could have stuffed my ears. I had the shakes, and I didn't want to see the rest of the scene.

The white woman's eyes grew wider. She took a step back to put more distance between her and my mother's venom. But then she placed herself back in my mother's spotlight when she called out to the stranger in a trembling voice, "Honey, we should leave."

"Honey? You mean you turn Honey now, Julian?" my mother said and threw back her head and laughed louder than she'd been talking. "Lady, before I start with you today, you better take your adulterous body and children out of my yard. You hear me? I don't want you, nor Julian, nor the kids, in my yard. Get out," she shouted.

The white woman turned a darker shade of red and took her two boys out of the yard. But not before saying, "Julian, are you coming with us? You heard her. She's a bitter woman."

"Julian, you better get your woman off my property," my mother said, and took steps towards the stranger.

"But, Velma, please listen to what I have to say," he pleaded again.

"What you have to say? You mean I've not made myself clear. I don't want you in my yard. I don't want you to get to know our daughters, not after they're big. Take your white woman and go on your way," she said, her words sharp and laden with scorn.

"Velma, I want to explain what happened all those years ago," he begged in a shaky voice.

"Go! Leave. *Kité,*" my mother screamed, legs planted wide. She shook her fists at the stranger. She exhaled as if she had run to the river in the face of threatening rain to pick up her clothes left bleaching on the stones.

Augustus stopped his head movements to shout in his slow annoying voice, "Well, Velma, listen to what the man has to say."

She turned around and vented her full fury on Augustus. "Who asked you any question? You have no idea the amount of misery the man left me to see in Dominica with two baby girls. He left to make a new life in St. Thomas through the back door with some Grand Bay people. Not a word. Not a letter. Not a money. The man forgot me and his children.

"Now he's back asking for the kids. What kids? Do you know that five years after he left, he sent divorce papers so he could marry for his citizenship papers? He made promises, and then I never heard from him again.

"For all these years, I, nor Vignette, nor his dead parents knew he had moved to New York. And all that time, not a word. Not a letter. Not a money. Nothing. Now I must listen to him? No. Julian, get out my yard. I have nothing to say to you."

At the end of her tirade, she crossed her arms in front of her chest and stared down the stranger. I had never seen that magnitude of fury in my mother's beautiful golden-hue eyes. The only time she'd been so furious was when she'd handled Robert for Cheryl, and those efforts had been in vain.

In the face of my mother's onslaught, the stranger had no choice but to leave the yard for peace and quiet. My mother's shouting had drawn Ma Titre, Aunty Maureen, and Old Man Maurice. They gathered around her, their faces anxious to learn more.

Ma Titre, dressed in a patterned dress of green, yellow and red flowers against a rainforest green background, and her signature white head tie, was the first to speak. "Are you okay, Velma? I could hear your voice in my kitchen."

While my mother turned her attention to Ma Titre and the others, I tried to follow the stranger out to the road. I should have remembered my mother had eyes at the back of her head. With a strength I didn't know she possessed, she pulled me back into the yard and said, "You stay right here."

I watched the stranger and his family leave the yard and my chest tightened at the thought I wouldn't get to know my father and my brothers. I wanted to leave with them, and I wanted to run away from the scene and go sit on my favourite stone by the sea and watch the waves and whatever boat happened to sail by on the deep blue waters.

They left.

My mother removed her hands from her hips and exhaled heavily. I clenched my sweaty hands to keep from attacking her. I pressed my push-in slippers, with the big safety pins keeping them together, into the ground to stop my legs from trembling.

A war had begun in me.

A part of me wished to know them and another part of me wished they'd never showed up. I'd learned new things about my mother, the stranger, siblings I didn't know I had, a stepmother I'd never known existed.

After they left, my mother held court with Ma Titre, Aunty Maureen, and Old Man Maurice recounting the history of her relationship with my father.

"How old were you when Julian noticed you?" Ma Titre asked.

"Me, I was a slim twenty-year-old in the village of Petite Soufriere, one of the prettiest girls in the village, and Julian the tallest and most handsome man in the village. Well, he had done left the village to work in town and would come up for public holidays. August Monday holiday was the holiday he noticed me by the seaside. He stared at me for an hour before he came across to talk to me."

"An hour?" Old Man Maurice asked. "A man afraid to approach a woman. Hmmm," he said, and scratched his throat.

"Old Man Maurice, he wasn't afraid, because we talked for more than four hours that night."

"Four hours and you fell in love."

"Yes, Old Man Maurice. We fell in love and after that he would come up every weekend to be with me."

"You mean every week he would have money to make the trip to Petite Soufriere. He must have been working for a lot of money," Aunty Maureen said.

"Yes, he had a big job by Phansa Shopping Plaza Centre, the biggest shopping centre in Roseau," my mother replied.

"Big job, Velma. And he left it to go to St. Thomas?" Ma Titre asked.

"You don't understand. Julian use to come up to Petite Soufriere well dressed and with groceries in his hand. Not many people got groceries every week. We used to sit outside on the bench in front of my mother's house to talk, to hold hands."

"Talk and hold hands?" Maureen said.

"Talk, she says. Maureen, you believe that?" Old Man Maurice asked, wiggling his bushy eyebrows.

"Of course I believe. I believe you will live to ninety years," Aunty Maureen said, laughing.

"Yes, Maureen, in those days you had to sit in full view of the parents. My mother would sit a stone's throw away and my father would pass through the yard every time with his pipe in his hand. By October, my father asked Julian, 'What's your intention for my daughter?'"

Julian declared his undying love for me and said to my father he wanted to marry me in December. Without any fanfare we planned the wedding for December. My father killed two goats and we had loads of provision and enough rum for all the men in the village to get drunk."

"You mean so fast you and Julian marry?" Ma Titre said. She nudged the nip in my mother's waist with her silver-bangled hand and burst into laughter.

My mother ignored her laughter and continued with her story.

"What is so fast? Remember Julian lived and worked in town. You know how much money and time he would spend to come and see me. You see Julian had plans to work hard, save his money, and build his own house. His ambition was what attracted me to him, not his handsomeness."

I sat in silence on the back step of the house and listened to their conversation. I rested my head against my knees and tried to calm the churning in my stomach. My rope had broken up into a million knots and they were dashing around in my stomach. In my head, questions swarmed around until I felt dizzy.

My mother's last words forced me to look up to take in the audience of her one-woman show. My mother had a smirk on her face. I couldn't believe it after all the anger she'd displayed when my father—the stranger—had entered the yard. This was a classic swing of her, going from one emotion to the next. She was in her element—storytelling with humour, recounting their start.

She continued, "Julian. Handsome Julian. Ambitious Julian. Declared me the love of his life and promised to take care of me for the rest of my life.

"After we were married, I left Petite Soufriere with the idea in my head I was heading to a better life in town. Well, you should see the house Julian brought me to in River Street. The house had one door, one window, and was big enough to hold a single bed, two chairs, and a tiny table, on which sat the basin with two plates, two forks, two knives, two pots, and two white enamel cups. There was the kerosene stove on which I had to create my culinary delights. A single ledge above the table held all our groceries.

"There were big holes in the wall through which rats or cats could pass through. *Bondyé*, you don't want to hear the worst part. On the east was our neighbour David, with whom we shared a common wall.

"David was a sweet man and had women in and out of his room bawling the whole night at the top of their lungs. The partition used to get kicks and blows, and the bed—couple times it broke down and Julian had to help him fix it the next day and he would be back in action the same night.

"On our right was Hilda. Hilda and her visiting man, it seem, never used to sleep, for the entire night she would be howling like a hyena. So, you can imagine me, a new bride, in that environment. It was January of 1968.

"In short order I became pregnant with Juliette, and in December of 1968, Juliette was born. After Juliette's birth, I had to put down my foot and tell Julian it wasn't the right environment to raise our baby girl. We needed more space and we had to get some peace and quiet so the baby could sleep in the night."

"You mean them people continued carrying on?" Aunty Maureen asked and wiped the tears escaping down her face. She held her waist and a loud, unequivocal laugh escaped her lips. Ma Titre, Old Man Maurice, and myself exchanged knowing looks and keeled over in laughter at the picture my mother had painted.

"What you are laughing at, Julia?"

"Mamie, but you were giving a joke."

"Joke what—I'm talking to big people, not children. What did your father say? Kids. No, I'm not talking to kids. Turn *American*."

I looked at my mother and prayed to God she didn't notice me continuing to laugh.

"The man did take his responsibility and found us a two-room house higher up the road from where we lived. That house was much better.

"The neighbours made noise in the day. The lady on the right of us, Ma John, had six good-for-nothing boys who were all teenagers at the time. I don't know how they slept in their two-room house, because she also had a man visiting her every night with all those boys. I never heard her or the man. But in the day, she would quarrel with the boys over every single thing.

"On our left was an old man and his wife. Their house was a big house with two bedrooms. The man would drink until he got drunk and then he would sing until he fell asleep, which he did every day without fail. And that, my people, marked my early days with Julian."

"So how come he left for St. Thomas?" Ma Titre asked.

"He hooked up with some Grand Bay people at work."

"Why you have to say it like that? '*Grand Bay people*,'" Ma Titre said. "Grand Bay people is good people."

"I did not say they're not good. I just said 'Grand Bay people.'"

"But is the way you said it," Aunty Maureen added and laughed.

"What way, Maureen? Anyway, Julian met these people from Grand Bay at work and became friends with them. They introduced him to the scheme to get to St. Thomas on a boat. I was against the scheme.

"I was how many months pregnant with Julia. I began to worry about what could happen if the boat sank and my husband got lost at sea. But Julian had made up his mind. He convinced me he needed to go so we could have a better life. He said he was tired of living in a one-room house with drunk neighbours for company. He wanted his daughter and child number two on the way to have a much better life than he had.

"So, he persuaded me his going to St. Thomas would be our best bet to make it out of the part of hell we were living in. He would go first and then he would send for me and the children.

"According to Julian they left Dominica in the dead of night to make their way to St. Thomas. I heard from him every month for a while. He left three months before I had Julia, and three months after Julia was born the letters stopped. For those first six months he sent money twice. He told me how hard things were and jobs were not easy to come by."

"What did you do to survive then?" Maureen asked.

"As soon as we'd moved into that first house, I realized Julian wasn't making enough money for us to move out. From the very beginning my thought was to get out of the house, so I found a job as a domestic with a family in Goodwill."

"Velma, you like fancy words, ehhh. 'Domestic,'" Old Man Maurice said and laughed until tears seeped out of his dark eyes.

"I know she means a servant," Ma Titre said. "What's a domestic?" she repeated, and her laugh drowned the sound of the waves for a few seconds.

"You two are just miserable," my mother said, joining in the laughter.

"I became a domestic helper to the Nurse family. The husband had some big post in the police force and the wife was a teacher. They came from St. Kitts but had been on the island for over ten years by the time I worked for them.

"This is how I made my money, and they helped me to take care of the girls when I told them Julian had stopped writing and stopped sending money.

"Then I met Julius, he fell in love with me and moved me to Loubiere, and the rest as they say is history. That is my story, and I am sticking to it," she said and laughed so hard her tear ducts released a stream of tears in reflex.

"That's it, no more juicy morsels?" Aunty Maureen asked my mother.

"No, I am done for the day with Julian. Now, fifteen years later, he shows up with his American wife, his American kids and his American accent, asking me for the *kids*. He wants to get to know the *kids. Chupes, tan*?"

"But fifteen years is a long time ago, Velma. You and the man divorce. You never told us you were divorced, and you're still holding a grudge."

"What do you want me to do, Maureen, welcome him with open hands.

"At least you could be polite and let him speak to Julia," Ma Titre offered, her gaze fixed on my mother's face. Ma Titre hardly ever backed down on being direct with my mother. Aunty Maureen usually held back.

"Ma Titre, your head needs to be examined. I raised my children by myself, no letter, no money . . ."

"Yes, I know, no phone call . . . but he is here, right, and you have to deal with it."

"Give the man a chance," Old Man Maurice chimed in.

"Would you not like to know your father, Julia?" Aunty Maureen asked me. "Answer me, child, don't be afraid of your mother."

"Well, yes, Aunty Maureen," I whispered. I wasn't sure I wanted to know him.

"Say it louder," she said in a firm voice.

"I would like to get to know my father and brothers," I said with a bit more strength. I said yes because there was no way I could have explained my conflicting emotions and thoughts.

"Not over this healthy body of mine," my mother said and she turned on her heel and went into the kitchen to continue her coconut ice pop production.

Over the next couple days my thoughts were heavy with what transpired between my mother and father.

Was my mother still bitter with my father over deserting us? I had learned new information on the day he came to the yard. I'd learned details my mother had never shared with Juliette and me.

Why hadn't she told us our father had served her with divorced papers? Up until Saturday I believed my mother and father were still married.

I had to grapple with the shock of finding out my parents were divorced and my father had remarried an American woman and had two other children. I didn't know how to accept I had two brothers.

Would these strangers and I remain strangers? My mother had been adamant neither I nor Juliette would have anything to do with the man who'd deserted us some fifteen years ago.

I didn't bargain the stranger, my father, was a persistent man.

On the Tuesday after the stranger had visited the yard, Juliette came to visit with her two children, Timmy and Tammy. I recounted the story of the stranger, the white woman, and the two boys.

"Juliette, I prayed for the ground to open and swallow me while Mamie put on her worse behaviour. You know how she overreacts, over embellishes, over demonstrates. She outperformed any Hollywood star."

As I was about to tell Juliette the rest of the spectacle. A *tock, tock* rattled our front wall. Who could be knocking on our door?

I got up to open the door and on the other side stood the tall handsome stranger. Oh my God, he had Juliette's eyes.

"Can I come in, Julia?" he asked in a tentative voice.

"Why should I let you in? My mother says she don't want you around here," I said with my eyes cast to the ground. I didn't really want to say it. But I felt I needed to stand in solidarity with my mother.

"I know what your mother said, Julia," he said but not before flashing me a deep understanding look. "But what do *you* say? Don't you want to know who I am? Don't you want to hear my side of the story?"

I felt two little hands on my thighs. Little Timmy, Juliette's son, was trying to get between my legs to see who was at the door. And then I felt Juliette come to stand behind me."

"Daddy, is that you," she said, her voice cracking. I looked at her and could not believe Juliette's eyes were grey watery pools. She was going to burst into tears. Over this stranger.

Did she even remember him?

She was only three years old when he left. She held one-year-old Tammy in her arms, her legs resting against her stomach swollen with child again.

Juliette, pregnant again. It was her third pregnancy in three years. Juliette, my older superstar sister, always pregnant. I knew it was a mean thought. But I couldn't stop it. I hated what my mother had turned Juliette's life into—a sad movie.

"Why did you leave us, Daddy, and never got in contact with us? I was three years when you left, and Julia wasn't born yet. You left and never came back.

"Do you know how many times I asked Mamie, When is Daddy coming back? At first, she would tell me 'soon,' and then she moved to, 'I don't know.' You never came back. You never wrote. You never sent a photo.

"Why? Daddy . . ." Juliette whimpered and her lips wobbled like the red Jell-O we loved to eat when we were younger.

And for the first time in my life, I witnessed a big man cry. I had never seen Daddy Julius cry. The stranger stood in the doorway of our small house and bawled out his eyes in shame.

What could he say to us? He had abandoned us. Abandoned us for a better life in the United States. Our mother. Us. We never got to share in the better life he went to create.

He forgot his promises once he made it to the other side. I looked outside and there was no white woman or brown skin boys in the vehicle. Good. I didn't want to have to acknowledge them or learn about them today. Dealing with the stranger was enough. It was the same pickup truck from Saturday. And it looked like a pickup truck that carried only bananas, also known as green gold on the island.

"I'm so ashamed of myself," the stranger continued in a low voice, like his voice box had been narrowed to block his sound from escaping.

"I hope you girls can find it in your hearts to forgive me. I didn't forget you, but things were so hard in the beginning. For months I had no job and no money to send to your mother. I became a failure in St Thomas. I was stuck over there with no money to come home, or to take care of myself. For a year I searched for steady work and found only odd jobs. I was desperate with worry. I worried about your mother. I worried about you. I fell into a depression."

He paused. Tears shone like pieces of mirrors in his eyes.

Juliette and I hadn't moved. We stayed in the open doorway. And this was how Aunty Maureen found us. She was returning from up the village and halted when she turned to enter the yard and took in the stranger and the pickup.

"Hey, so what is he doing here? Is your mother here?" she inquired.

"No," I said, "and please don't tell her." I opened the door for the stranger. He came in and folded his over-six-foot frame into our little chair.

I stood up while Juliette sat with Timmy and Tammy on her. I didn't trust myself to sit down to listen. I couldn't stand still. I paced the living room floor while he spoke.

"I was rescued by a white man named Ross, about two years after I arrived in St. Thomas. He was constructing a guesthouse at the time. He gave me my first full time job. I worked with Ross for years and he taught me all I know about construction. Then one year Ross's sister came to visit St. Thomas. We took one look at each other and fell in love."

"But, Daddy, after years of steady work, why didn't you get in touch with us?" asked Juliette.

"I didn't know. I mean, a lot of things had happened. Things I can't tell you. I was sure your mother was so angry with me she wouldn't want to hear from me."

"Do you hear yourself, Mr Abraham?"

I couldn't call him Daddy like Juliette.

"You left a wife with two children in Dominica, and you sit here and say you did not know how to make contact. You were ashamed. Did you ever stop to think of us? Two little girls. You left us for another man to raise.

"Do you know what happened to Daddy Julius? The sea swallowed the man who fathered me. To this day, I hope he's alive somewhere in the Caribbean. But with each passing year, my hope dries up. You forgot us. We needed you. You turned your back on us. What of your vows of undying love to our mother? What about your promise to her father to take care of her forever?"

I remained pacing. The big knots in my stomach I'd experienced on Saturday returned and lodged low in my stomach. My skin tingled as sweat formed a million tiny beads on my sun-kissed skin.

He'd worn an "I love NY" cap and he pulled it down low on his face. He dropped his chin to his chest and continued in a hollow voice. "How could I let this happen? I know you girls will never understand what happened. Even I myself do not have the answers to the question.

"As the years went by, I guess it became more comfortable to think of my family in Dominica in the abstract. It became more comfortable to think you had forgotten me, that you no longer needed me.

"I already knew that your mother had already taken up with Julius. Someone from Loubiere, who had arrived from Dominica and who knew Velma and myself, told me Julius and Velma lived together. I was shocked and devastated to hear Velma had replaced me in her life.

"Even though I had done the same thing. I'd replaced her too. But I was angry at her for not waiting. I had a plan." He mumbled those last words.

He stopped talking. And the only sound in the room came from the small fan in the corner. Was Juliette just going to sit there with her tears?

Timmy and Tammy crawled off her and walked to the stranger. Timmy pulled off my father's cap and waved. "Cap," he said, waved it, and smiled. Tammy stood on his white sneakers and tried to lift his head.

If only I could be curious like them—have childlike curiosity. I was a young woman—I didn't want to be curious about a stranger. But I couldn't let the silence reign, since Juliette was content to cry like a lost little girl.

Why couldn't she stop crying?

"How could you think that, Daddy?" Juliette uttered, her voice wheezy. "Do you know how hard it was for us? It was Daddy Julius who raised us. He bought everything we needed. He placed this roof over our head. He loved our mother and he loved us. Then things got bad again when Daddy Julius died. Don't tell me you never heard our story. Not once did it move your heart to reach out to your little girls.

"Yes, tell us something to wipe away the years of dreaming of you returning to us. Tell us why you never sent for us. Even after you got married, you still didn't reach out so we could get to know you and your new family."

Tired, I stepped to the window to look out through the jalousie. I didn't want to look at his eyes which were so much like Juliette's. He was so handsome. My handsome father had returned. But I chose to look at Ma Titre's croton hedge across the road. His deep voice filled the room again. And I turned back to look at him and Juliette.

"Girls, I'm so sorry. So sorry I failed you," he said with tears running down his cheeks.

"I'm asking each one of you to forgive me. I want to establish a relationship with you. I want you to get to know your brothers too, Justin and Jules, and Ann. I want to get to know my grandchildren," he said, and took a peek at Timmy and Tammy who were back on their mother. Timmy was enthralled with the cap. He turned it over and over.

I was happy my mother was out and we were able to have this airing out with the stranger—our father. I had a hard time accepting his explanation for all those years of silence. I would never understand why he never came to see me. He never asked for a photo of me.

I posed the question to him, and he hung his head in further shame. Should I embrace the bitterness of my mother? Should I forgive this man who never tried to get to know his own flesh and blood? Was there room for me to get to know him when I was about to enter my fourth year of high school? What could I possibly gain from striking up this new alliance?

These were the questions that filled the grey matter in my head.

You could finally get to know the father you have never known. The father you have dreamed would ride in on his white horse to rescue you from Dominica and take you to America. The father you dreamed would wrap you in his arms and tell you that everything will be all right. The father you dreamed of every night calling you his beautiful little princess.

I wasn't that little girl anymore.

I was a teenager.

I had outgrown these childish dreams.

Had I really?

I watched the tears make wide tracks down the stranger's face.

I found out I couldn't deny the stranger who was my father. I found out my little girl dreams hadn't died. They were alive in my heart.

I was torn between my old emotions of wanting to know my father and hating him for his desertion. All of my life I had wrestled with those feelings. I wanted to say yes. I wanted to say no. In the end, the deep desire to know him overrode my ambivalence. He held a key to unlock more of my identity. I couldn't deny myself the opportunity to get to know the stranger.

Juliette and I agreed to give him a chance to get to know us. He rewarded us with a deep smile and promised he would introduce us to Ann and the boys.

I smiled back at him even though I had low expectations that we'd become one big happy family. I worried that my mother would stand in the way with her disapproval.

However, later, under the canopy of a million stars on the big stone, I asked her, and she surprised me when she agreed. After fifteen years I still hadn't learned my mother could be full of surprises, running hot and then cooling down to reason. After the high drama of Saturday, I'd thought Juliette and I would have to fight her to become acquainted with the stranger—my father.

During the hottest days of the summer vacation of '87, I went around Dominica with my father in the Toyota Hilux pickup he'd borrowed from a friend. Just as I thought, the friend was a banana farmer, which meant the vehicle wasn't available to my father every day.

On the days when it was, Justin, Jules, and I would ride at the back sharing jokes on the hairpin winding roads that were characteristic of Dominica. The roads were black and smooth with no potholes from the ongoing road rehabilitation which had started a year ago, but many times in the back of the pickup Justin's and Jules's eyes would bulge with fear, or they would close their eyes whenever we got close to the mountains on one side and precipice on the other side.

I laughed at them but grabbed and gripped the side of the vehicle until the blood drained out of my knuckles. The New Yorkers were accustomed to flat, straight roads and tons of concrete buildings. In Dominica they were afraid. I was in my element; at one with nature. At one with the thousands of shades of green.

Justin and Jules were born one year apart. And at the time of their visit, they were turning nine and ten years in September. Justin, the more animated one, spoke freely of their life in New York, while Jules would back him up here and there with a grunt and a yeah.

Jules I perceived as the smarter of the two; he read more than Justin since he boasted to me that he had brought five Hardy Boys to read and Justin had only brought three. At the time we had this chat he'd read his five and was waiting for Justin to finish his three books so he could read them.

With each passing day spent with my newfound brothers, my reluctance to know them faded. I struggled to suppress the anger that simmered within me. They were as much a victim of our father's choices as I was. I decided I would allow myself to get to know my brothers. Despite this internal struggle, I couldn't help dreaming about spending time with them in the US and finally having a family to depend on.

For the first time since Daddy Julius died I felt the glimmer of hope that things were about to get better for me, for my mother, for Juliette and her family. But what if my father returning only brought more chaos and pain into our lives? Was it worth risking everything for a chance at pursuing my dreams? My mother's cynical outlook on higher education was still ringing in my ears, reminding me that even with my father back, success wasn't guaranteed.

But despite these doubts, something inside me refused to give up. Even though my father's return could bring complications, maybe there was a chance for things to get better. Maybe I could become an accountant like I always wanted. Maybe this was the opportunity I had been waiting for all along.

The thought of pursuing my aspirations sent shivers down my spine, but a warm feeling settled inside me as well. And I chose to believe my father would do whatever he could to help me achieve my dreams.

At the end of the two-week expedition around Dominica—the Glo Cho, the Emerald Pool, the Cabrits, the Coconut Beach lime—all these were embedded in me as memories made with my father and his family and Juliette, Timothy, Timmy and Tammy. My father left us with promises to write and keep in touch with us. He took our addresses, and they gave us theirs. By this time, we were at the hugging and kissing stage—they had Americanized us with their easy display of affection.

Our father's parting words to us were, "Girls, I will never forget this time I got to spend with you. It has warmed my heart to have received your forgiveness and I promise to file for you." I'd been so happy to hear those words—*I will file for you*.

His promise destroyed what my mother had filtered into our thoughts for years. There was a way out for Juliette and her children, and for me. I began to paint pictures in my head—visits to America—me graduating from university. My faith had been renewed in a father I hadn't known. I envisaged a future with a father, a stepmother, and two handsome brothers.

I felt an immense surge of hope, like a wave rushing to shore during a storm, or the water rushing down the face of a mountain. It erased years of fear. Fear my mother would force me into an early marriage. Fear I wouldn't be able to attend university. I was ready to fly like the yellow butterflies I chased as a little girl by the riverside.

And for the first time I could identify with Old Man Maurice's love for the song "Born Free." He had told me he sang the song everyday because he was totally free to do what his heart desired. "Julia, in life you have two freedoms. Freedom to follow your heart. Freedom to follow others. Choose which one will make you free."

Since then, I'd claimed Old Man Maurice's song and sang it often to remind myself to follow my heart.

Three months after they returned to America, I received a letter from New York with "Ann Abraham" at the back of the envelope at the post office. I turned the thin envelope in my hand. Puzzled. Why was Ann writing and not my father? This is what the letter said.

Dear Julia,

I wish I was writing to share some exciting news with you but I write this with my heart still laden in sorrow. You see, two weeks after we returned to New York your father went back to work at his latest construction site. It was there he met his untimely death when he tried to save one of his men who had gotten trapped under a collapsing scaffolding. While trying to rescue his worker, the rest of the scaffolding collapsed and trapped both men underneath. Your father died on the spot. You do not know the joy your father felt on getting to know you and Juliette. When we returned, he talked a lot of you girls and he started putting in place plans to get you to New York. The boys are devastated by the loss, but they send their love to you and Juliette. I know you have not known me long, but I promise to fulfill in any way the dream your father had envisaged for you. I am so sorry this tragedy has occurred when your father had just found you. This will be upsetting news, but these are the hard curves life throws at us.

Accept my love, Ann.

Before I finished reading the letter, the ink ran and saturated the pink paper from my fat droplets of tears. I cried for all my little girl dreams. I cried for the future I would never have with my father. I cried for Juliette, Justin, Jules, and Ann.

God can you see me? Why am I experiencing so much loss as a youngster? Are these lessons? Why do I need lessons on going through loss?

Another piece of my heart died that day.

After Daddy Julius's disappearance, I thought I would never get over the pain and the void. How could the world be such a cruel place to do this to me again? This was the second time, no, make that the third time I was losing a father. The first time, the father who left me in my mother's womb and never came back. Then Daddy Julius, the father who'd raised me, had been swallowed up by the sea. My father came back from the dead, only to return to a real terrible death trying to save the life of another.

Oh God, why am I experiencing so much loss in my young life? Why are you taking away the fathers who have loved me? Why are you leaving me orphaned of fathers? My heart is dying. I can't take any more losses. When will it end? Are you there, God? Do you see the pain? The pain tears me apart. Will you deliver me from this wretched body of pain and grief?

I gave in and cried for hours.

8

Hope Forever Destroyed
(Sep-Dec 1987)

When my mother got home the night I received the letter, the sky had darkened. No moonlight, only a few scattered stars. The black sky was as dark as my soul felt, torn apart as it was by loss.

When she came through the door, she found me with the bad-news letter in my hand and little-girl tears dripping from my eyes. I'd kicked off my new green push-in slippers onto the large light green straw mat my mother had recently bought from Tropical Crafts, and curled my legs underneath me on the brown settee—purchased by Augustus. The worn-down dining room chairs were gone. Our drawing room settee had moved up.

"What's wrong with you, Julia?" She placed her bag on the floor and lowered her body into the matching armchair across from me. She reached down and began rubbing the weariness out of her calves from standing all day at The Fashion Store where she had started working as a store clerk.

"What's with the letter in your hand? You're holding it like it is your death sentence."

"This letter is from Ann," I whispered. Too drained of emotions to raise my voice.

"From whom? Speak up louder; I cannot hear you, Julia."

"Ann, my father's wife," I replied, unable to hold back my sniffing and wiping at my nose.

"Oh, you mean your father's white woman."

I narrowed my eyes, unable to suppress my frown.

"What! Your father left me to marry a white woman."

"Perhaps because you failed to wait for him long enough. He'd found out about you and Daddy Julius before he met Ann."

"Oh, he came here to feed you lies. He wanted an excuse for his behaviour."

"Mamie, will you stop it." I waved the letter in the air and said, "This letter in my hand is from Ann. Do you want to know what it says?" Two lines of tears trailed down my face, until it fell onto the letter in my hand, further smearing the ink.

I opened my mouth to speak, and my voice croaked as if I had no strength. I had to tell her, and so I began, "Mamie, my father died in an accident at a construction site trying to save one of his men. He is dead. Mamie. He died. He is gone. I will never see him again. He will never visit Dominica again."

My lips trembled like a flame tossed by the wind. I swallowed and continued, "We'd just met and he is gone. Mamie, why is this happening? Why am I fatherless again?"

I bowed my head and allowed my tears to wet my face. I allowed the pinpricks of pain to roll through my body. The pain rolled into my heart and grabbed and squeezed it so hard the room blurred and then spun.

I grabbed the armrest and took a steadying breath. My vision cleared a few seconds later and I looked at my mother. She had released her hair and was running her hands through the soft black curls. Her eyes were closed. Her movement, unhurried. She acted like I hadn't told her that her former husband had died. My father had died.

I glared at her and my whole body tensed. I had to say something.

"Did you ever love him, Mamie. Did you?" I lashed out at her.

"What you mean, Julia?"

"You didn't wait for him," I cried out.

"Wait." She repeated and threw back her head and laughed. "You foolish girl. You *sot*."

"Less than a year after he left you took up with Daddy Julius."

"Because I had a baby to feed and a young child to send to school. Your father had stopped sending empty letters. He had stopped sending money."

"A year, Mamie. You didn't wait."

She stood up and placed her hands on her hips. She had removed her ring comb and her hair fell in heavy waves around her shoulders. She curled up her thin lips and her eyes had sharpened to daggers.

I met her gaze head on. I didn't care. The news of my father's death had killed a lot of my hopes.

Hope of knowing him better.

Hope of moving to America.

Hope for a better life.

"Listen to me, Julia. He came and filled up you and Juliette's head with lies."

"Lies? You took up with Daddy Julius and didn't wait for your husband to make it."

"Julia, you think your father waited? You think he didn't find a woman to satisfy him? You think I didn't have needs to satisfy too?"

"What needs you talking about, Mamie?"

"Julia, you think you know things. You know nothing about life. Your father went to St Thomas and left us to look for a better life. He failed, Julia. He didn't tell you about the Dominican woman who took him up and was feeding him and giving him sex. That's how he survived before he met Ann. I had to do my share here for us to survive."

"You're lying," I screamed and dissolved into more tears.

"Lying. You think life easy, Julia? No. It's hard, and we have to make hard choices. Your father was homeless in St Thomas. His friends bailed on him. Every man had to fight for himself. And he did. He didn't tell you that. But he told you about what I had to do to survive. I am not ashamed. Because you would have died from hunger. Never forget Julius is all you saw. Not your father.

"You know how many years he met Ann? How many years he left St Thomas and he in America?"

"But you divorced."

"Yes. We divorced for him to marry Ann to get his papers, and then he was to divorce her, marry me again, and file for us. "

"What!"

A deep chill hijacked my spine.

"You're lying," I shouted with my eyes closed. I didn't want to see her face.

"*Ou tann sa mwen di.* You heard me. I kept my end of the bargain. He didn't. He stayed with Ann. He made children with her. He forgot us. You think he was going to file for you and Juliette. You think you were going to get your papers. Guess what—death has saved you from disappointment."

"I don't believe a word you're saying," I cried out in a weak voice.

"You don't have to believe. Truth is truth. You don't have to believe, Julia. You foolish girl. *Sot.*"

And with that she grabbed her black bag off the chair and marched off to her room. She slammed the bedroom door so hard it rattled the thin partition and threw the picture frame of the Sacred Heart to the floorboard.

Ping.

Crack.

She didn't open her door.

And I didn't move from my chair.

The broken glass lay scattered like the broken pieces of our life.

I forgot it and turned my mind to wrestle with my mother's revelations.

The man who had at one time loved my mother. A slim twenty-year-old girl from Petite Soufriere to whom he had pledged his undying love. A few years later, he had reneged on the pledge.

He was gone forever.

He'd left us much too soon. The opportunity to know him had galloped out of my needy hands. At a time when I needed my father the most, he had transitioned to eternity. One part of my brain registered he'd had no chance to choose in the matter. He'd responded with a spirit of chivalry and it had caused his death. That thought gave me no comfort. I felt cheated. I'd only had seven weeks---not months—not years.

I didn't understand.

I couldn't understand.

My mother's revelation had shaken me more than Ann's letter. Everything I thought I knew about our life—our origins, our future—had been a lie. Their stories were different. I didn't know who had lied the most to us.

Did I know my parents?

Had they ever loved each other?

How had they both messed up so much?

All in the name of self-advancement.

Juliette and I had been left fatherless by a man chasing the goal of a better life for us. I felt like my heart had fallen apart like the broken glass of the Sacred Heart. My body grew heavy as if I had drunk gallons of water and the water had replaced the blood in my veins.

I stopped breathing.

I wanted the same thing too—self advancement.

My father had wanted more for us.

I wanted more for us too.

My father had wanted to give us a future away from this yard, away from this newly independent island nation.

I wanted a future too.

Away from the hardship.

Away from the poverty.

Away from the yard.

I had received the dreaded news a day before our ninth anniversary of independence from Great Britain. As a student, I always looked forward to Independence Day. For the Independence School Rally. For the cultural shows. For the military parade. For Creole day, to dress up in colourful madras and white cotton creations.

That year, I took no notice of the parade of uniformed groups, the march pass, on the morning of the third of November, Independence Day. An event I always looked forward to each year. I had nothing in me to drum up excitement.

It all seemed pointless to me. We were independent but my father had to sacrifice his young family, his unborn child, to migrate—for advancement. And he died, and Juliette and I hadn't had the benefit of his advancement. Juliette should have been at university in America. Instead, she was a pregnant, barefoot housewife. Filled with my father's promises, I had started counting down the months to the end of high school, eager to attend university in America. My hope died with Ann's letter.

I stayed home on the ninth anniversary of independence and stared at the ceiling in my bedroom. I listened to the song of the birds flying overhead—dogs barking, waves crashing on the rocks and pebbles—until I grew tired. It was only then I tuned in to WBS radio to listen to the march pass. It didn't hold my interest. It failed to drown out the words swimming around in my head fighting for a foothold into my consciousness. I fought to keep my thoughts inaccessible. An impossible task for me, a thinker.

A day later, at the end of community day of service, my disposition and outlook on life had not improved. I refused to take part in the community service project in our neighbourhood. I stayed in my room and stared at the ceiling.

My mother paid little attention to me. I roused myself from my bed when she began getting ready to attend the block-o-rama in Roseau. A street jump-up event built around something called a "sound system," with giant black speakers. It'd taken music amplification to the next level and had become a favourite with the party and jump-up crowd. The block-o-rama had been introduced to signal the end of community day of service and the end of the Independence Day celebrations.

My mother and Maureen had never missed one since its introduction a few years ago. She and Maureen got dressed up in their stone-wash jeans with a big shirt and a big belt around their waists. This was the pinnacle of fashion at the time. Maureen had made their shirts. I would have had on a similar outfit if I'd been moved to participate. Before they left for town, my mother went on at length about Wadicole being the best—better than Scientific Rolls—and described how she planned to dance to the Wadicole sound system.

She left me in my self-inflicted misery and went out to town to enjoy herself block-o-rama style with Augustus, her beau.

After they left I moved back to lie on my bed. My new favourite place in the house. It was bare. Nothing like the princess, starry room of Gina and Gloria.

Alone, I wondered whether my mother wasn't too old to be excited over a block-o-rama and to be arguing which sound system was the best. It was like they lived in the moment and for the moment. I was from Mars because I thought about the future. My mother didn't care. She had secured Juliette's future with Timothy. I got angry every time I remembered the conversation in the kitchen and every time I saw Juliette looking tired and harassed. Juliette's grey eyes had become as dull as cold ashes.

I sank my head into my white pillow; thoughts of the father I hadn't known overtook every other thought. My father, buried under construction rubble in a foreign country. The father I lived with and knew, buried somewhere in the deep waters of the Caribbean Sea or the Atlantic Ocean.

Why didn't I get to say goodbye?

Why didn't I get to say goodbye to my fathers?

These questions became lodged at the base of my heart like a big heavy dumpling. With a heavy sigh, I rolled over and curled into my favourite feel-safe position: my knees to my chest, and my arms between my knees. In my feel-safe position I allowed the pain to wrack my body, until I fell into what I hoped would be my first dreamless sleep since I received Ann's letter.

Before I lost consciousness, the "why me" question plagued me. *Why am I losing all my fathers?*

No one in my class had lost a father.

I had lost two.

Weeks dragged by and the weather became cooler. Heavy rainfall. Muggy soil everywhere. Early sunsets. Darker nights punctuated the days after the Independence Day celebrations and the close of the hurricane season.

They were days when everyone breathed easier and took things slower. I joined and moved slower too. My body had been invaded by a heaviness which refused to leave.

A thick mental fog shadowed my mind every day. School, once an enjoyable place, became a place I dreaded. It started in my third year. My English classes had saved the school year for me. The book *Animal Farm*, by George Orwell, became the only thing that lifted my lethargy.

Gina, Gloria, and I had fun with this book. We'd assigned the animal names to our unsuspecting classmates: Napoleon, Squealer, and Snowball. Our favourites in Animal Farm had made better sense of their world than I'd made of my world. They'd been sensible to overthrow their farm owner, take over the farm, and run it as they saw fit. That'd been the simple plan. But the book showed that humans are never simple in what they desire. In the end the leaders who took over from the farmer became worse than the farm owner.

And in my fourth year, things continued on the same way, but the heaviness was winning out.

I became moody. I hated everything. I stopped eating. I hid from my mother to dump my food into the rubbish pail. My clothes drooped from my body.

Gina and Gloria tried to intervene.

One day at school they asked me what was wrong with me. I screamed at them, "Leave me alone. Let me suffer and cry alone. Let me die alone."

The teacher stopped talking. The class became silent. Thirty-six pairs of eyes fell on me. The model pupil. I knew that was what my classmates called me behind my back—*the model pupil*—because for the first three years I'd received both the prize for academic excellence and the prize for leadership at our school's annual graduation.

My subject teacher intervened and took me outside for a short conversation. I refused to speak to her and she threatened to report the outburst to Ms Kentish, my form teacher. She carried out her threat, and Ms Kentish, in turn, asked the guidance counsellor, Mrs Henry, to intervene.

I left school with a note in a sealed envelope from Ms Kentish to my mother. During the ride home on Lightning's bus, the note felt like a stone in my green haversack. Curious,

I took it out to decide whether I should open it before my mother. Did I want my mother to see the contents? It was probably about my outburst in class today.

The unknown contents of the letter preoccupied me. I didn't hear the chatter and laughter. I didn't hear the words of "No Puppy Love" by Tiger. It was one of my favourite dub songs for the year, and although Lightning played it at ear-splitting decibels, I didn't move a muscle to the beat. Things were not ordinary. I was carrying my first note from school to my mother.

I placed the brown sealed envelope on the centre table for my mother. I had to wait for the five o'clock hour—the time she usually got home from work. I tried to predict my mother's reaction but she was always unpredictable.

Would it be a mild response? Would it be anger? Since the arrival and installation of Augustus I'd seen less of her angry responses. And I hoped she wouldn't get angry. I decided to do something to sway her.

I swept the yard until every pebble ended up in a neat pile and the dirt was crisscrossed with the markings made by the hundred sticks of the coconut broom. My mother could not get angry with a clean yard, a clean kitchen, a clean house—the bargaining chips I selected for the note lying on the centre table.

The sun had begun its descent, dipping over the horizon into the sea, when my mother alighted from Lightning's bus at five o'clock. From my perch on the big stone I tried to gauge her mood. I couldn't. So I wasted no time.

"Mamie, there is a letter on the table from my teacher."

"A letter from your teacher? Why?"

"It's on the table. I didn't open it."

"Julia, why do I have a letter from your teacher? This has never happened before."

I didn't answer. She opened the front door. Seconds later, she called to me.

"Julia, come here. Explain this note to me."

"What does it say?"

"What does it say? You had an outburst in class today. Why? Why Julia?"

"I don't know, but Gina and Gloria were asking me too many questions."

"What kind of questions would cause you to shout in the classroom?"

"I lost my patience."

"But these are your good friends. They're concerned. I don't see why you must lose your patience."

"Their questions irritated me," I muttered

"Julia, now you have a spoilt record. Now you have to go see the counsellor. Since you got the news about your father, a man you didn't know, you have not been yourself," she said, her tone hard like the sharp volcanic rocks found on the island.

"Mamie, how can you say this? You have been insensitive to my feelings. You moved on like you were never married to him."

"Julia, you come back with your nonsense. Let it go. Your father left us in Dominica and soon forgot we existed. He showed up last year with his white woman and children and I'm supposed to mourn him for months? Next, you are going to tell me I should wear black for a year like a good Catholic."

"He didn't forget us. You moved on. Both of you messed up. You and my dead father were so concerned with progress, with survival, with advancement. Look at us. Look at Juliette. Where is the advancement? And you, Mamie, you are cold. Don't you have feelings?"

"Feelings? For your father? Your dead father? No, Julia. I'm sorry he died but I'm not going to pine away like you are doing here. Time to stop pining. You, Julia, need to pull yourself together. You need to toughen your skin. You can't let this affect your schoolwork.

"And you insist on dragging up the past. Julia, you will learn about survival. You were a newborn baby. I had Juliette at pre-school. Your father went to St Thomas and he met hard times."

"Why didn't he come back to Dominica?" I screeched. "Why?"

"With what? After he paid his way, he wasn't going to come back in shame, "she screeched at me.

"I don't understand you and I don't understand my dead father. Look at us, we're still dirt poor."

I leaned against the door. My mouth went slack. The tingle in my chest spread fast. "Mamie, you are just impossible."

"No, Julia, I am a realist." She sat down and removed her shoes. "You need to get your head out of your dream world. The real world is for tough people. Toughen yourself up, girl, if you want to make it in this world. Time for you to end the tears." She stood and opened the door to her bedroom and left me in the living room.

She came back.

"I am a survivor. And you are a dreamer. And you will learn the hard way."

She marched back to her room.

And I remained slumped against the front door, my thoughts scrambling to understand.

Was my mother unhinged? How could she be so cold? How could she remain unaffected by my father's death?

Except for the day when I told her about Ann's letter, she'd shown no remorse, no grief. I love my mother, but sometimes conversations with her led me to more questions, more uncertainty.

I picked up the white sheet of paper and read the words until they got blurry. And then I threw it on the centre table as if it'd been lit with a match. I was scheduled to begin counselling sessions with Mrs Henry.

The day of my first counselling session arrived. Me, Julia. In counselling. The hours leading up to my session passed in a blur. My model pupil image lay shredded. But I thanked God. Because my classmates got to see I was like them. Scared. Uncertain. Discouraged.

I hurried along the long corridor to Mrs Henry's office at the end of the ground floor of our school building. The closer I got to Mrs Henry's office, the wetter my socks became in my ripped brown shoes. I didn't know what to expect. I'd never been in her office before.

I didn't want counselling.

The adults were forcing me.

I took a deep breath and knocked on the opened, bright yellow-painted door. Mrs Henry called out, "It's okay, come in, Julia, and close the door behind you. Please take this seat." She said it with a warm understanding smile. I had never seen a smile so welcoming and so full of reassurance. Certainly not from my mother. Mrs Henry's smile drew me into the room.

I sat down on the hard wooden chair which had a thin green padded seat as green as a bay leaf. I took in Mrs Henry with her short boy cut, large gold hoop earrings, and her long nails painted bright red. She wore a matching skirt and short sleeve jacket the colour of dark chocolate. We'd christened her our school's fashion icon. She won best dressed teacher every year.

She leaned toward me and blessed me with another dose of her smile. It was softer. It was kinder. It was as if she was reeling me in to her. I wanted to resist. I wanted to retreat. I did neither. Mrs Henry waited. Like she expected me to talk first. I sat with my sweaty hands folded in my lap. My stomach churned and my heart thudded against my ribcage like a trapped animal seeking to escape. There was no way I would speak before Mrs Henry.

"Welcome to my office, Julia. I want you to feel relaxed. We are going to converse as friends." I nodded at her but my mind raced with doubts. *I can't converse with you as a friend. I don't want to be here.*

"How long have you been at the school, Julia?"

"This is my fourth year at the school," I said in a barely audible voice.

"Good. This is your first time in my office. I see from your record you're an exemplary student. You have never been on detention. You have no demerits. You have more merits than all your other classmates combined. Julia, I do not understand, therefore, the reason you're in my office." She waited for my response, her hands clasped beneath her chin. Her bright eyes never wavered from me.

"Miss Kentish, my class teacher, recommended I come see you."

"Yes, she did. But I want to hear from you. Why are you here?"

"Mrs Henry, I don't know . . ."

"Julia, cooperate with me, will you? I want to be able to help you, but you must be willing to let me in. Miss Kentish indicated to me that you had an uncharacteristic outburst in the class last week. Is it true?"

"I wouldn't call it an outburst," I replied and clenched my hand.

"You wouldn't? Then what do you call shouting 'Leave me alone' for the entire class to hear?"

I couldn't reply, I looked down at my hands and twisted each finger on my left hand with my right. I didn't want Mrs Henry to see the shame in my eyes.

"Julia, I am waiting for your answer."

"Mrs Henry, do I have to do this?" I asked, my lips twitching.

"Yes, we are doing this. It is for your own good Julia. You understand we are very concerned about you."

Who does she mean? All the teachers? The principal, Mr Langlais?

"I want to help you, Julia. What is going on at home?"

Home. *I won't talk about my home. Never. She's prying. Why does she want to know our home business?*

"Never put the business of this house in the street," my mother had warned Juliette and me on repeat.

"Nothing."

"Nothing? Are you and your mother agreeing?"

"We have our little differences, but we are okay."

"Any recent dramatic changes at home?"

I could have said my mother had a new boyfriend. It was stale news at the time of my meeting with Mrs Henry.

My long-lost father came home during the summer to get to know me, then he went back to New York and died on his construction worksite and I was left without a father. Instead, I stared at Mrs Henry's large gold hoop earrings. She looked at me. She waited.

Are we going to play this wait and see game?

I continued to stare back.

She smiled at me, and her face and eyes softened.

"Julia, I know it is difficult to talk of your doubts, fears and confusion. I have a hard time at first expressing what hurts me the most. Once I start talking it gets easier and the burden within my heart begins to lighten. Don't you want the heavy load, stuck at the base of your heart, to be lifted away?"

I felt my nostrils flare. My pulse sped up; my heart pounded and sounded like a pack of horses running through the hills. Mrs Henry had come way too close to my pain. How did she know there was a heavy load at the base of my heart? The pain was digging deeper and deeper tracks into my heart. I continued to rub my hands together.

I refused to speak to her.

She didn't speak again.

I shifted my eyes and fixed them on my fingers. I fought to keep the tears from falling by blinking my lids like blinking headlights.

"Julia, it is okay to feel pain. It is okay to admit you are hurting. It is okay to say 'I am angry.' It is okay to say I need help. I can help you if you let me."

I burst into tears and Mrs Henry allowed me to cry until my sobs subsided. I thought she would continue with her probing but she spoke and relief flooded my body. I lifted my eyes to hers again.

"Julia, we will end today's session here. We made some inroads today. At your next session we will talk more about what you feel."

I left her office feeling a little lighter.

I turned my face up to the sky and allowed the warmth of the sunshine to further lighten my mood. I walked across the basketball court to get to my classroom, like my feet were weighed down by all of the thoughts and feelings that I was trying to process.

The following Friday brought the end of regular class time and my second appointment with Mrs Henry. I entered her small, cramped office. The government-assigned wooden furniture were all from the brown family—cinnamon, coconut husks, cocoa beans. The only bright spot in the room—Mrs Henry. She looked sophisticated in her dark green forest suit with a yellow and blue geometric scale scarf along with her signature large gold hoop earrings.

"How are you feeling today, Julia?"

"I feel fine."

"Do you remember what I said the last time? It is easy to be released from the pain by talking. Have you been able to talk with your mother?"

"My mother. No," I said, shaking my head. "Why would I?"

"Don't you want to open up to your mother?"

"Mrs Henry, at my home we don't get all emotional and get in each other's business."

"Julia, I am trying to get you to trust your mother with your heart and with the things which trouble you. Do you understand?"

"Mrs Henry, you don't know my mother. We don't talk on that level."

"How, then, do you talk?"

"My mother tells me what to do and I'm supposed to obey."

"But, Julia, at this point in your development, the conversation between you and your mother should be genuine and should cover a wide range of concerns."

"Mrs Henry, my mother would have to be like you to make it possible."

"Okay, Julia, tell me what's weighing you down?"

Silence hung in the room while I contemplated my ten fingers before providing an answer to Mrs Henry. I looked up to her smiling face.

"I want to write down my answer."

Mrs Henry's eyes held mine for a beat, then she gathered a writing pad and pen and passed them over to me.

I was taken aback with her suggestion to write it now.

"Now?"

"Yes, now, Julia," she said in her soft soothing voice. She smiled and her genuine concern softened her eyes.

"Can I do it at home? I have a diary."

I wanted to go home to write stretched out on my bed. It was my favourite position to write in my purple diary. I didn't tell Mrs Henry it was buried in my white vest surrounded by white camphor balls in the grip under my bed.

She gave me a warning look to kill any further protest I'd been about to make. I took the pen and this is what I wrote:

"Dear God, can you please let me know why Daddy Julius and my father had to die in the way they died?"

Then I slid the paper over to Mrs Henry. She read what I'd written on the paper and then looked at me.

Is that pity in her eyes? I don't need pity.

"Julia, I am so proud of you for taking this first step. Don't you feel better?"

I nodded my head in agreement. I had begun to feel a little bit lighter but far from feeling like my old self. But I didn't tell Mrs Henry I wrote to end our counselling session. It had been the last day of regular school. I wouldn't have to see her until the next term.

"Julia," Mrs Henry said, her voice soft and soothing. "I want you to continue writing these notes over the Christmas break in your diary. Every day, I want you to chronicle what you are feeling in your heart and in your mind. This should be a no-holds-barred writing. Try and write down seven thoughts, reactions, actions you want to take. It will help you work through your feelings."

"Do I have to?"

"Yes, Julia."

I pressed my lips together to keep from groaning aloud. I didn't want to follow Mrs Henry's instructions.

Mrs Henry leaned forward and smiled. Her smile was so emphatic it thawed my resistance. I found myself answering with a faint smile of my own. My lips softened and I stopped twisting my fingers.

"Julia, we all want you to get through this grieving period. I want you to believe you are going to be okay. Your first term exams are in a few days and I want to wish you the very best in them. Remember we all care about you. You're one of our outstanding students and we want to see you continue to do well. Miss Kentish, your classmates, and everyone loves you. You don't have to go through this painful time alone. Will you remember all I have said to you, Julia?"

"I will try, Mrs Henry," I said.

"Please do, Julia. And when you return to school next term, I will schedule a session. You may leave," she said, and beamed another warm smile full of concern and care.

And, for the second time, I left Mrs Henry's office feeling a bit lighter. A little edge had been taken off the pain and darkness in my soul. My mother had been right; I had started dreaming of the life that awaited me in America. I had believed my father would file for me.

The day after I saw Mrs Henry was a Saturday. I awoke curled up next to Gina on her bed. I listened to the waves roll into each other onto the millions of round pebbles on the seashore in the quiet of the morning, and the patter of the rain pelting the galvanize roof. A cool breeze off the sea brought the smell of salt through the windows of Gina and Gloria's bedroom at Pottersville.

I had succumbed to the girls' invitation to spend another weekend with them on the pretext of studying for our exams. They had asked me twice before and I had refused both times. The second time, Mr and Mrs Adams came up to visit the yard to find out what was going on with me.

Both girls had reported to Mr and Mrs Adams I'd been acting funny for the last couple of months. I had listened to them express their concern and stayed quiet the whole time. Mrs Adams had prayed for me, and I felt some of the stiffness leave my muscles. But I refused to budge from my home.

Until this weekend.

Like clockwork at six o'clock, Mr Adams knocked on the bedroom door to call us to devotions. We read from the book of Matthew. All who are heavy laden can come to Jesus for rest. Mr Adams explained it as having a burden, a heaviness of heart, a pain lodged at the base of your heart.

Mr Adams spoke to my heart and to my need. In between studying and talking with Gina and Gloria, I contemplated his words.

How could Jesus take away the heavy burden and the pain? Would he be able to take away my ache? How would he do it?

The questions lingered in my mind when I went to bed later. I remembered the next morning would be church, and I wasn't looking forward to the long and noisy services, and ending up more tired and hungry than blessed by the end of it.

A few hours later, Sunday morning, we prettied ourselves up for church. I sat between Gina and Gloria and we sang for hours before the pastor began to preach. I don't recall everything he said that morning, but I do remember the text. It was the same text from Matthew in our morning devotions—come to Jesus for rest from all heavy burdens.

Was this message crafted for me? Two different men. The same message. *Is my heavy heart begging to be released? To be set free? Is it time to stop feeling depressed?* I wanted to be the old me, high spirited and sure of myself.

The pastor also spoke on sin and the power of the blood of Jesus Christ to wash us and to cleanse us from our sins. He pressed on his clear message that Jesus can give the peace and joy that surpasses understanding.

His words touched the deepest part of my reasoning. It forced me to respond. It was my moment of enlightenment. A lightness spread through my chest. I found I needed and wanted this everlasting peace and joy. I didn't want this heavy weight around my heart, dragging me down—I wanted to soar.

When the pastor gave the invitation to the altar, I ran out of my seat with tears streaming down my face to accept the peace and joy that Jesus my Saviour offers. I accepted that Jesus died on the cross so I could live an abundant life. Six other persons responded to the altar call. Mrs Adams came to stand with me with tears running down her face. I dared not look back at Gina and Gloria at that moment, but when I went back to my seat, I saw the signs of tears of joy on their faces.

By the end of the prayer, the tears streamed down my face as I poured out my pain, despair, depression, anger and bitterness at the foot of the cross.

I acknowledged the emotions I had been denying for the last few months. When I went back to my seat, I felt like I could go out to conquer the world.

The liberty felt real and wonderful. Before we left, the pastor led the congregation in song. "I've been changed," I sang, believing I truly had been.

9

Juliette's Choice
(April 1988)

Juliette's twins elected Good Friday 1988 to make their grand entrance onto the world stage.

They'd chosen a great year to be born. The year Dominica celebrated the two-figure coming of age as an independent country. Ten years of independence from our former colonial master, Great Britain. It was a big year organised with pomp and ceremony and chock full of activities in each month to celebrate what we had achieved as an independent nation.

Nineteen eighty-eight represented not only reunions, but renewals and reversals. But I couldn't have known it the night the twins were born.

At the time the twins were making their entrance, I kept watch at the house Timothy and Juliette had moved into before their first-born Timmy had arrived. Timothy had declared his son wasn't going to be brought forth in a little one room house, so he'd moved them to a three-bedroom house in the Canefield Housing Scheme before the birth of Timmy. My mother had been beside herself with pride—satisfied she'd married her daughter well. Her daughter had moved into a house with indoor plumbing, with bathroom and toilet.

My mother attended the birth at the Princess Hospital to provide moral support to Timothy. I knew my mother and I imagined her ordering the nurses. When she came to the house from the hospital, she reported the birth order; Teddy came forth at midnight, followed by Tommy five minutes later.

Timothy didn't come home from the hospital with Mamie.

The morning after the birth of the twins, we were surrounded by a mountain of baby and toddler clothes in Juliette's living room. Diapers, vests, socks, booties of various colour and texture littered every chair surface. I cleared a small spot next to me to place the folded items. I placed the last of over two dozen white cotton diapers, and got ready to attack the white cotton vests.

My mother attended to Tammy, Juliette's one-year-old going on two, who was stripped down to take her bath. Timmy, her two-year-old brother going on three, was hitting his hands up and down in his bath water in a big old yellow basin. When Mamie stretched her hands to lift him out, he opened his mouth, closed his eyes and hollered, his wail bouncing off the walls. She left him in the water, though it was uncharacteristic of her to allow children to have their own way.

This was vintage Timmy—he loved to exercise his will. He'd close his eyes, open his mouth wide and let out piercing shrieks, until whoever was in the path of his assault would relent and give in to him. In the middle of this chaos my mother related what took place at the hospital last night.

"You should have seen Timothy; his eyes were red the whole time he held Juliette's hand and the nurses were saying push, push," my mother said, laughing.

"So how did Juliette do this time? Did she scream like the last time?"

"Child, remember it's twins and giving birth is not easy. She screamed double times, treble times."

"Okay, Mamie," I said, chuckling. "I hope this is the last time Juliette gives birth."

"Wait! What's your trouble? Are you the one supporting the children? That's between Juliette and Timothy. They will decide when to stop. What do you know, Julia?"

"The only breadwinner is Timothy and the prices of everything in the store is going up and up."

"You forget Timothy works for the government. His job is secured. His money is well secured." I heard the smirk in her voice and when I looked up from the white diaper in my hand, her full pink lips had parted, but her smirk was so cold, her teeth looked like icicles.

"Yes, but times are changing, Mamie. Shouldn't they consider high school and college for each child?"

"Julia, this is the day after Holy Friday and you're here bothering me about the future. You and Juliette both went to high school on scholarships. Smartness is in their blood. Timmy at three reads well. He will win a scholarship to everything."

"Yes, Mamie, how about this—shouldn't Juliette be at university? Why is she on baby number four?"

A slap landed on the right side of my face, it rattled my teeth and my brain cells.

"Mamie, what did I say?" I cried, holding my hand against my face. I rubbed it to dull the pain, certain the right side of my face would be stained red tomorrow.

"You're not a big woman. Remember you're still a child under my roof." She glared and it turned her beautiful eyes into hard deadwood.

"But, Mamie, I'll be turning sixteen years soon."

"Sixteen years is still very much a child to me."

Without thinking, I blurted out, "Wasn't Juliette sixteen when . . ."

"Stop!" she shouted and this time she bared her teeth like a lion. "Don't go there, Julia. Don't try me today, Julia. Don't you know your place?" Her voice was loud enough for the neighbours to hear and loud enough it frightened Timmy into tears. He'd stopped playing with his bath water and started wailing.

"Look at what you caused, Julia." She bent to pick up the screaming Timmy from the water again. Distracted by my thoughts I didn't have time to react before she lunged into her next attack.

"Leave Juliette and Timothy's business alone. Juliette is coming home in a few days and you're going to spend the week with them to help her with the babies."

Unfazed by her earlier outburst, or maybe I'd become immune to them after almost sixteen years, I launched into my next complaint in the form of a question.

"There are so many babies. Which babies—the newborns, or Timmy and Tammy? Why did they name the twins Teddy and Tommy? Who gives their children these kinds of names?" I said it at the speed of a space shuttle exiting the surface of the earth.

"Julia, you better hush your mouth. Don't be giving them any back chat or advice. Too many of them library books you're reading. Too much Bible reading, with them 'Jesus save' folks. Too many ideas in your brain. You're confused. This is Dominica, not America—the land where your father went to make a better life for us and instead he got married to a white woman and forgot us. And then he died."

I looked at my mother, careful not to narrow my eyes to thin slits. I picked up the folded diapers, went into Juliette's room, to place them into the varnished chest of drawers. It took me five minutes. I delayed because I didn't want to go back out to face my mother.

How could she be so cruel with her words? She should have known how sensitive I was about my father's death. I wiped the tears out of the corner of my eyes. My mother's cold reminder of what happened to my father always chilled my body. Whenever she did, I would come close to disliking her for those callous asides. I was not left long in my misery.

"Julia, you better come out of that room. I'm done bathing the children and they are all dressed and powdered up. I'm leaving for home and later I will run up by the hospital to check on Juliette and the twins. I am leaving you in charge here."

"Yes, Mamie. What time will Timothy be home?"

"I don't know; he should've been here already because he left the hospital before me."

"I haven't seen him for the morning at all, Mamie."

"Hmmm, I wonder what Mr Lafleur is up to, the scoundrel."

"What!" I shouted.

"You just watch the children and stay out of big people business, you hear me? You and your fancy ideas. I'm gone."

A few days later, Juliette came home with the twins.

The first night the twins were home, Timothy kissed Juliette on her cheek and told her he would be back in a few hours. The few hours became six hours overdue. At the six-hour mark I changed into my baby blue nighty. Juliette and I had long since put the children to bed and they lay resting in their white double crib next to their mother's bed.

Before going to bed, I went into Juliette's room to gaze on the sleeping faces of the twins one more time. They were so cute. Innocent. Empty vessels given to Timothy and Juliette.

Are they going to fill them up with our culture, customs and traditions? I wondered whether Timothy and Juliette recognized the privileged task God had granted them as parents?

While the twins rested in peace, Juliette looked weary like she hadn't recovered from giving birth. Under her lifeless eyes were inky shadows. She rubbed her hands across her eyes over and over like she wanted to rub out her weariness. Her beautiful black hair spread out on the pillow like fine silk behind her head. Her gaze was pained and unfocused.

I sat down on the bed beside Juliette. "Are you okay? You look tired."

"Yes, the babies need a lot of attention."

"I noticed. I also noticed you gave little attention to Tammy and Timmy today."

"Julia," she groaned. "As you can see, my arms are too short to hold all my babies," she said, extending both arms in the air. And my husband is nowhere to be found."

"Yes, Juliette, where's Timothy? It's over six hours since he left the house. Is he coming home? Does he do this often?"

"Oh, Julia," she said with another groan. "Too many questions. I'm tired. I need sleep before the twins wake up for their feeding. Please, go to bed. Tomorrow morning, we can talk."

Without another word she turned over on her pillow and closed her eyes. I had no choice but to leave her bedroom. I called it a night and retreated to the small room I shared with Tammy and Timmy.

The next morning, my mind took its time to catch up with my body. I didn't move. I stayed on the bed and stared at the ceiling. The room was bathed in shadows because outside was gloomy as a horror movie. I groaned instead of enjoying the small luxury of peace.

The gloom meant it had rained or would rain soon. I said a silent prayer for it not to rain. There were too many baby clothes which needed washing and drying. But on this island, a lot of days, rain was more a certainty than sunshine. The green rainforest that covered much of the island was a testament to that.

I rubbed my eyes and tried not to groan at the thought it might rain. I looked across the room for Tammy and Timmy. I saw an empty twin bed. I had slept in longer than the babies. Moreover, I'd slept through the night. Some help I was to Juliette.

Creak, Creak. Creak. Was that the front door being opened? I stopped moving and listened. Footsteps followed. It was Timothy. Coldness seeped into my body. I couldn't believe Timothy had just returned home.

"I can't believe no one's awake in this house," he said in a loud grating voice.

"Juliette, Juliette, you're still in bed, woman? Lazy. Get out of the bed," he screamed into the quiet house.

I covered my ears against the onslaught. I gasped for breath. The nerve of Timothy. This man spent last night out of his house, left his wife alone with new-born twins. What's going on here? Why would Timothy stay out all night? I waited to hear Juliette's response. Silence. I decided to remain silent, too, to see how this would play out.

"Juliette, Juliette, wake up," Timothy called as he entered their bedroom. "Woman, what are you doing sleeping? Why are the children in the bed fast asleep? How many times do I have to tell you to send them back to their beds when they come into our room? Can't a man have any privacy in his own room?"

Juliette didn't answer any of his questions. She followed up with a question of her own in a timid, shaky voice, "Where have you been, Tim? Since yesterday you left."

"Juliette, don't start with me. You haven't answered my questions. Why you're in bed at this hour of the morning?"

Juliette's voice became stronger. "Tim, if you haven't noticed there are two more babies in this house. They got up four times last night for feeding. I had to handle the twins by myself. You were not here, and I was exhausted. I'm catching up on my sleep. Where were you, Timothy?"

"Well, Juliette, you're feeling it now. You wanted more children. Remember, you stopped taking your birth control. You failed to tell me about it. This was after I told you specifically we shouldn't have any more babies. But, no, not for Miss Juliette. You got pregnant. Now we have twins. Four children in three years. Juliette you're on your own. Deal with your double trouble."

"Timothy, you're so selfish. These are your children."

"Yes, children I didn't want," he shouted and slammed his hand on the door. It rattled. I balled my hand into a tight fist. I tensed my body to keep my mouth from opening. I wanted to get out of the bed to confront Timothy.

No.

What I really wanted to do was to hit some sense into his head with a broomstick.

"But you were happy, the day they were born at the hospital," Juliette countered, her tone weaker on each word.

I couldn't believe this was the life of my twenty-year-old sister. I hadn't moved. I couldn't trust myself to move or to speak. I dug into my hand with my nails and came close to drawing my own blood.

This was all the fault of . . .

"Happy? Look, Juliette, I cannot forget how you tricked this pregnancy into being. I cannot," he said, his voice rising on each syllable.

A few minutes later, I heard him walk out of their room. He entered the shower in the hallway. The next sound in the house was the water falling from the overhead shower onto Timothy's body. Juliette went silent. I didn't hear the children. Unbelievably they'd slept through the ruckus made by their father.

I remained glued to my bed in disbelief. What kind of life was my sister living? Was this the life my mother had envisaged for Juliette? Juliette who had been so obedient. Juliette the original "model" student. Was this why Timothy had moved them to Canefield? Where Juliette was isolated away from people who would speak up to defend her. I hated to think my mother would not have intervened.

That scary thought galvanised me into action. I couldn't stay on the bed. Timothy finished his shower, and I heard him through the thin concrete walls moving around in their bedroom getting dressed. Juliette begged him to forgive her and to pay attention to the babies, her voice rising in desperation. Timothy didn't respond, but continued dressing, whistling a loud tune like there weren't sleeping babies in their house. And then he had the audacity to start belting out the lyrics to "Mr Lover Man" by Shabba Ranks.

I seethed with anger and waited for Juliette's response, yet none came.

And I lost my cool.

I couldn't remain silent.

My rage boiled over.

I had to say something.

I found the courage and got off the bed and ventured into the living room. At the same moment, Timothy emerged from their bedroom. He'd dressed in dark brown pants and a white shirt. The pant leg had a knife sharp seam. I was certain Juliette had laboured for hours over his clothes. After all, our mother had taught her how to iron a man's pants as part of her instructions to Juliette right before the wedding.

Timothy looked at me and flashed me his signature megawatt smile. His perfect white teeth glistened. His grey eyes twinkled. His long eyelashes danced. Both Timmy and Tammy had inherited his long eyelashes and bottomless grey eyes. Despite my annoyance with him, I responded to his smile and hated myself for the response. Timothy had that effect on people. Perhaps one of the reasons my mother had thought him such a good catch for Juliette three years ago.

"Julia, sorry you had to hear our little argument. Things are bad here for now," he said to me, his smile in place. He said it without a flicker of emotion in his eyes. It dawned on me then that Timothy didn't care.

He threw three twenty-dollar bills on the table and shouted to Juliette, "The money is on the table. Send Julia to town to get the groceries. Make sure she gets my eggs, my stout, and my protein powder from Charlie Pharmacy. I'm off to work."

I couldn't get any words out my mouth. My mind racing, I couldn't keep up with my search for answers.

Timothy slammed the front door. And the door rattled and one of the babies started crying.

Later the same afternoon, I sat down with Juliette on the brown suede settee in the living room. It'd been a long day taking care of four babies. Timmy and Tammy at three and two were considered baby toddlers. We took the time off our feet to catch our breath and to enjoy tall glasses of brown sugar lime squash topped with ice and a dash of vanilla essence. I took a sip and enjoyed the ice-cold liquid gliding down my throat.

"Hmmmm." I closed my eyes for a minute to enjoy the liquid sensation. "Refreshing," I said, and opened my eyes and looked at Juliette. Grey eyes looking into gold eyes. Confusion and pain stared back at me. My sister at twenty. This was her life.

"Juliette, what's going on with you and Timothy?" I asked.

"Don't look at me like that. And what do you mean 'what's going on?' This is my life, Julia."

"How long has this been going on?"

"Look, Julia, I don't feel like being lectured to by my little sister."

"Juliette, you're twenty years of age. You already have four children. From the looks of it, your husband does not show you any respect or love. You're overweight. Why did you want more babies, Juliette? All of this sounds like a sad movie."

The tears leaked out the corners of her eyes. I suspected she was weighing her answer to my tirade.

"Look, Juliette, you need to do something about what's going on between you and Timothy. It's not right. Not for you and not for the kids."

With a bitter smile, she said, "How did my little sister become so wise? You think you know anything about anything? You think you can come here and tell me about my life? I love Timothy and he loves me, we are just going through a rough patch; a little hump in the road."

"Really. So, it's true then. Did you trick Timothy into this last pregnancy? Is that why he's so angry? Why does he stay away from the house for hours?"

One of the babies announced its need for feeding with a long wail. Juliette got up to get the baby. I didn't rise. My hands stayed wrapped around my glass of lime squash. I enjoyed feeling the little beads of cold sweat on the glass. I stared into the glass trying to find the answers to the questions I'd asked my sister.

Is this love and marriage?

I thought about Daddy Julius and my mother. They hadn't married but I'd never heard them in this kind of quarrelling. My mother did on occasion raise a storm with Daddy Julius about something he failed to do. Like the time he'd refused to demand his money from the woman who owed him for twenty pounds of fish. She got mad and called Daddy Julius out. She'd advised him to switch his vocation from fisherman to missionary. She'd accused him of being afraid of his shadow. She'd assured him people would take advantage of his good nature.

My mother had been in full effect. She hated people taking advantage of others. But here was Juliette, her daughter, in a less advantageous position.

A position she'd put her in. I couldn't forget our mother had orchestrated the relationship from start to finish. It wasn't finished yet. Juliette had been catapulted into a private hell.

What would she say if she were here?

At about six o'clock we heard a vehicle come to a stop in front of the house. Juliette and I ran to the window which faced the street to look out. I pulled back the curtain and both of us saw Timothy get out of a brand-new vehicle.

My mouth formed a silent oh. and Juliette blurted out, "I can't believe it. He did it. Impossible!"

"He did what?"

"Look, he took all the money and bought the pickup. Even after I begged him to put the money aside for us to buy a piece of land to build our own house. That was what he had promised me and Mamie."

Before I could respond, the door opened, and Timothy entered, his smile leading the way.

"Come, girls, come and I see my new baby. It's a Toyota Hilux pickup. Brand new and fresh off the port," he said, his voice light and humorous.

I went to the doorway and looked at the midnight blue four-wheel drive. Juliette turned and walked away to go into the kitchen.

"What's wrong with you, Juliette," he asked and followed her, "Don't you want to see the pickup I bought to carry you and our many children?"

"Stop it, Tim," she shouted. "We talked about the money you got from your grandfather's estate, remember? It was to add to the savings to buy a piece of land."

"What're you talking about, Juliette? That's your bright idea, not mine. What did I tell you? Yes, my grandfather left me the money and the farm. Me, not you. I told you I needed to replace the old broken-down pickup to continue to work the farm."

"But the pickup wasn't old and broken down. That's what your grandfather used every week to transport his bananas to town. And you promised from the beginning to get our own house."

"Yes, but I need a vehicle to travel back and forth to Delices every weekend. The old vehicle is for Jason and the guys to carry the bananas to the port. I need a vehicle here and they need a vehicle on the farm."

"So, you took all the money and bought a vehicle. It's all about you. What about our children and their future?"

"Juliette, is that all you can think about? The children, including the additions you schemed to have, will be fine. They will inherit the land in Delices."

"But we could have used this money to buy a piece of land. I told you about the lots being sold at Wall House."

"Oh, you mean your dream of living on the Morne in Loubiere. You fancy yourself living on the hill. It's not going to happen, Juliette. I make the money in this house, and I will decide how it's spent."

"I can't believe you, Tim. That's what you are saying to me? You're the one preventing me from working. And have you forgotten your dream—our dream to have our own house?"

"Yes, Juliette, the plan was for you to stay home with the two children—not the four we have now. You schemed. How are you going to work now? You want to put them in the day care? You want to leave them for your mother? You have sealed your deal, Juliette. Your little plan of deception backfired."

"Tim, when are you going to stop throwing this at me? Have you looked at the boys today? Go to the room and look at them. Look into their innocent faces and tell them the things you've just told me. They are here and they are your flesh and blood and they're the image of you."

Timothy started to clap and said to Juliette, "Nice little performance. But you have not shaken my heart yet, Juliette. I don't know when I will get over your treachery. Right now, I am going to take a bath, get dressed, and get *my* new baby on the road."

Juliette cried, "Tim, why are you doing this to me? Why? Why?"

Timothy ignored the pain in Juliette's voice and came out of the kitchen. I confronted him.

"Timothy, why are you treating my sister like this? What's wrong with you?"

He looked at me and what I saw in his eyes turned my blood into red frosted ice. I'd never seen this Timothy before.

"Julia, you better stay out of this. You're a guest in this house and I don't need you on my tail as well. I don't need this."

He walked to the bedroom, opened and slammed the brown hollow door so hard the door handle fell off. It woke up the children.

I ignored the crying children and went to Juliette. I walked into the kitchen and found her doubled over, her body vibrating with the force of her uncontrollable sobs. She waved me away when I got close to her. I wanted to comfort her, but she pushed me away.

Tammy and Timmy came out of their room crying for their mommy. Amid this chaos Timothy walked to the bathroom with a blue bath towel around him. Determined to get to the bathroom he brushed off Timmy and Tammy who'd tried to cling to him. Then he stopped long enough to place a weak kiss on each forehead. "Go to your mother," he said to them.

I stood transfixed. Heat flushed through my body, and sweat formed on my upper lip. I wanted to punch the walls. I wanted to punch Timothy. I wanted to punch Juliette for this mess.

How could two people who claimed to love each other behave in this manner? What caused this fight? Was this a new thing? How long had these fights been going on? I needed to understand the reasons for what I'd witnessed.

I wanted to understand what my twenty-year-old sister was experiencing in her three-year-old marriage. There was this new passage I learned in the book of Philippians about the strength to do all things. How could I help to strengthen Juliette? She needed strength and I sent up a silent prayer right to God to give Juliette the strength she needed to get through this "hump" as she called it with Timothy.

Fifteen minutes later, Juliette managed to calm down Timmy and Tammy enough to eat the supper I'd prepared while she nursed Tommy. We sat on the settee while the children sat on the floor with their bread and cheese. Timmy took his cheese out of the bread, his bread in one hand and his cheese in the other. He studied each before he decided which one would go into his mouth first. Tammy watched her brother and decided to do the same thing.

Juliette and I looked at each other and laughed. It reminded me of the many times when I followed Juliette in the same fashion. Here, we were with Juliette's children replicating our early interactions with each other.

In this serene lull, Timothy emerged from the room dressed for his night out with his new baby. He took one look at the scene, looked at the newborn babies in our arms, lifted Timmy and Tammy and kissed them and said goodbye to them. He looked at us again, said, "Goodnight girls," and walked out the door, slamming the front door behind him.

The last day of my Easter vacation and my stay with Juliette arrived too soon. About ten a.m. Timmy was out in the backyard playing when he fell and got a gash on the side of his face. With Timothy in Delices, Juliette had to rush to the casualty department on a bus. Timmy's blood had dried where he'd fallen on the dirt outside. All the babies were bathed, powdered and dressed for sleep. And yet there was no sign of Timothy from Delices.

"What time is Timothy getting home?"

"Why are you asking me this question Julia? You have been here for a week. What have you observed?"

"Timothy comes and goes as he pleases. Don't you have a problem with that Juliette?"

"Yes, I have a problem with it, Julia, but tell me what I can do. I have four babies. They consume my energy all day. I can't bother myself too much about Timothy."

"Juliette, I don't understand. Are you telling me you accept Timothy's behaviour towards you?"

"It's not a matter of accepting it; what choice do I have? Don't you see I am trapped?"

"Trapped?"

"Yes, trapped. I am trapped in this marriage."

"Isn't marriage about love and trust?"

"Julia, you wait," she said with a soft chuckle. "You will learn. In this marriage Timothy is the man and I am the woman, and he reminds me every day in one form or another."

"How can you sit there and allow him to do it?"

"Because I am the wife, I must submit. You turn a Bible girl, you should know."

"Does 'submit' mean the man gets to treat you without regard for your feelings? Timothy is mean to you, Juliette. For the week I have been here, all I have seen you guys do is fight. Then Timothy leaves the house for hours. Stays out all night. He does nothing in the house, except to play with Timmy and Tammy. He ignores the twins. He complains when the house is dirty. He wants his supper on the table when he comes home. He complains you are too fat. Where's the love, Juliette?"

"Love?" she questioned in a raised voice. Love is at the beginning. Love is in the romance books. Remember the Mills and Boons romance novels I read by the ton load? That's where love resides."

I never took my gaze away from Juliette's face as she uttered the words. I saw the deep pain flick through her grey eyes. Hope was vanished. Love was running out of her reach. Love can't be fights every day. I see how the Adamses interact with each other. Juliette and Timothy did not have to live this way.

"Juliette, I think you and Timothy need help. Have you told Mamie what's going on with you two?"

"Mamie?" Juliette said with a laugh. She reached out, took both my hands, and looked me straight in the eyes. Grey eyes looking into gold eyes.

"Hear me, little sister. Our mother have me in this mess."

"What!'

"Hear me out. You were there, don't you remember?"

I shook my head. I remembered it all too well. I was shocked Juliette was acknowledging it. I'd listened to their conversation beneath the kitchen window. Later I'd confronted my mother and Juliette. I'd never forgotten her words: "It's either you or me." The most frightening had been her declaration, "I am always the sacrificial one."

She squeezed my hands and continued.

"Timothy moved into Cheryl's house. He was older. He was handsome. I was smitten and fell in love with him. That's my version, I believe. Do you know our mother encouraged me to have sex with Timothy when I was still in high school. Don't you remember Timothy bought our groceries? Do you know why? It was because of the sex our mother had encouraged me to give him. I loved him. I enjoyed the sex with him. But get this; to our mother, Timothy represented our meal ticket. Don't you remember the confrontation you had with her in the kitchen? Don't you remember I got pregnant in school? I graduated pregnant thanks to our mother dearest."

"I remember too well," I said in a voice heavy with emotion. I remembered too many things. Mamie scolded me that day. I was put in my child's place.

"We have to admit our mother is quite the character, Juliette."

We sat in silence. Each of us remembering.

I took another look at Juliette's face. Her mouth was pinched and her eyes had the flat look like the ocean when there's no wind. She either looked past me or stared at her hands. And she squeezed her eyes shut every few seconds. The sorrow and hurt in her eyes felt familiar—I'd seen it before . . .

Secretly I always thought Mamie favoured Juliette, although I had no concrete evidence to believe it was true. Guilt and anger raced through me as the pain and regret in Juliette's eyes reminded me that reality was more complicated than I had thought.

All of it made my heart heavy. This must have been a figment of my own insecurities and longing for my mother's love. To hear Juliette speak of Mamie setting her up to have sex with Timothy for economic benefit was a blow to the confidence and trust I had for our mother.

"Listen to me, Julia," she said, and squeezed my hands between her calloused ones. "Our mother did this because we had nothing after Daddy Julius died. Our natural father was a long way from rediscovering us. She did it for us to eat and survive."

"Juliette, do you realize what you're saying, our mother prostituted you so we could eat and survive. But she worked, Juliette. She had a job," I said as one big fat tear fell down my cheek.

"Yes, a job cleaning people's house at the time. It was not enough for us to survive on. Why do you think she had a relationship with Daddy Julius? You think it was for love. One day I overheard her say to Aunty Maureen she was done with love after our father deserted her to pursue his American dream. She stayed with Daddy Julius because he loved her and agreed to take care of us."

"Do you think she meant these things she stated?"

"Why, little sister, it's time you open your eyes and learn what the adult world is about. Your turn is coming."

"My turn for what?"

"Oh, sorry, you will be spared, because Mamie has Augustus taking care of her. Don't pretend you don't know this. You told me about the fridge he bought and the bed and all the other stuff. It's about economic survival."

"What about love, then?"

"Love is for our imagination, Julia. Look at the people we know—what love do you see them exhibiting?"

"I see love between Gloria and Gina's parents."

"Yes, because they are different. They are from a different world."

"How are they different, Juliette?" I cried, the tears streaming down my face.

"They are rich, Julia."

"What does that have to do with anything?"

"You will learn in time." She looked toward the front door and shook her head a little. She turned back to me and her eyes involuntarily closed and she swayed from side to side. She looked like she wanted to cave in. And in a subdued voice she said, "Do you know why Timothy stays out all night? Because he has another woman."

"What! How can you say this so calm?"

"I have four babies."

"So what? All the more reason . . ."

Juliette cut me off by squeezing my hands tighter.

"Do you want to know what our mother said to me? 'He is a man; this is what men do. Suck it up.'"

I leaned back in the chair as if lightning had struck me in the chest.

"Mamie knows."

"What, Julia, you think she doesn't know what Timothy does with his spare time?"

I shook my head to dispel the dizziness threatening to turn me into quaking jello.

"Mamie said that to you? 'Suck it up?' Juliette, what year are we living in? Are you just going to suck it up? Aren't you going to demand love and respect from Timothy?"

"Oh, little sister, have you not heard anything I have said? Look at me; do I have a choice? Look at me. You think about what I have said in that pretty head of yours. Think about it long and hard. You have the chance for a different life, little sister, and I hope you will choose it. For me, my path was determined when I obeyed our mother's command to give myself to Timothy. I am done here for tonight."

She released my hand and left me with tears streaming down my face. I closed my eyes and allowed my hot fat tears to fall.

She came back and said, "My path was determined even before Timothy. She'd sacrificed me before Timothy."

"Juliette! What are you saying?" I jumped off the chair and followed her to her bedroom.

"Talk to me, Juliette," I said, my voice frantic. "Who? When? Why?"

I thought my eardrums would explode, the roar was so loud. I wanted to fall off the ledge Juliette and I were perched on to end the roaring noise.

"Go to bed, Julia. You're the spared one. Your life will be better than mine. Under no circumstances let Mamie or anyone force you into a relationship. I don't think I even need to tell you this. You're not like me. You're a fighter. You've known what you wanted to be from primary school. Fight for it, Julia. I want you to achieve your dreams. I want you to become an accountant. One of us deserves more than this pain brought on by my choice."

She stopped talking and threw herself down on her matrimonial bed and collapsed into loud sobs.

I threw myself on top of her and held her and wept with her.

"Juliette, Juliette, Juliette," I chanted.

She'd said so much. *Sexually sacrificed.* My chest tightened at what those words could mean. It brought back memories of Annya and what Robert had done to her little body. It brought back memories of his vile hands on me. I asked her and she'd hushed me up. What did she mean, she was sexually sacrificed? And to whom? I wanted to know and at the same time I didn't want to know.

I couldn't take anymore revelations. I stretched out beside her and held her through her tears and my tears. We cried buckets for all the pain and loss we'd endured in our young life.

I retreated into the resilient corner of my mind and vowed again to be the catalyst to lead the Alexander girls out into a bigger and better and more stable life. I decided Juliette would have to leave Timothy.

My trust and confidence in our mother to guide and protect lay shattered. My belief that love could conquer all was shaken to the core by Juliette's revelations. It gave a new picture of our family.

My blood raced through all parts of my body. I didn't know who to target. Our very alive mother or our very dead father. They were both responsible for our current station in life. The decision my father made to desert us because of his own shame and his feelings of inadequacy was ricocheting off our lives.

According to Juliette's revelation we belonged to the class of people who battered their daughters for economic advantage to survive. Maybe I needed to get out of my little bubble. I'd seen all the things Augustus had bought.

I'd heard my mother's comments to Ma Titre and Aunty Maureen. I don't know why hearing it from Juliette created this well of sadness in me. Juliette said she was trapped in the marriage. I prayed God would help me to take a different path. Because I knew with certainty I didn't want to be trapped in Juliette's hell.

I wrapped my arms tighter around my crying sister and prayed for my mother, for Juliette and Timothy, and for myself. I prayed to God he would take me along a different path, a path leading me far away from the revelations made by Juliette's choice.

10

When Strangers Become Family
(1988)

A few weeks after I'd stayed with Juliette, on a scorching hot day in 1988, I got my first and last detention. It happened during the fifth period of the day; English with Miss Daniel. At eleven a.m. sharp Miss Daniel's colourful bangles announced her arrival before she arrived at the doorway. She was preceded, of course, by her usual pile of books weighing down both her arms.

Every time we had class with her I looked forward to two things; her choice of bangles for the day and the number of books she carried. Some of my classmates found the bangles distracting. To me they portrayed that the exacting English teacher had a flair for colour and drama in her jewelry. A form of self-expression denied to every student. Our only form of self-expression for five years amounted to white, khaki, crest, browns, blacks.

"Good morning, Miss," the class replied in unison. Twenty-five pairs of eyes watched her skinny arms unload all her books onto the rickety desk allotted to the teacher. I watched the desk tremble under the weight of the books.

I waited, along with my twenty-five classmates, for the next part of the customary routine. Once the desk stopped trembling and the books stilled, Miss Daniel would place her skinny arms across her waist—the world's smallest waist—while she surveyed the twenty-five faces in the room. Every class with Miss Daniel began with the customary salute.

She picked her dictionary from the pile on the desk and held it up for the salute.

"Class, do you see my dictionary? I want you to lift your dictionary with your right hand."

All twenty-five of us raised our hands with our Oxford or Cambridge dictionaries. No Websters were allowed. Miss Daniel declared Webster's illegal from the first day of fourth form English. Anyone who came to school without their dictionary could be seen scrambling to get one from friends in the other fourth forms. I happily lifted my arms with my dictionary high in the air and looked around to see whether anyone had come up short, because if anyone did, the verdict, without trial, resulted in a guaranteed detention. No one fell short that day.

"I will collect the short stories. Once I have collected them, I will give each of you a story of your peer to grade during this class," Miss Daniel said; her demanding tone left no room for dissent.

And my heart pummelled my ribcage like a hammer against a nail, my pulse galloped at breakneck pace.

Homework? What homework?

My palms began to ooze water.

I had forgotten my homework the night before the class. I tried to think of an excuse to give Miss Daniel, but at the same second realised I had none, except I had simply forgotten.

The night before the class I'd been consumed with excitement over Bible study. The discussions on love, marriage, and divorce over the last couple weeks had ignited my thirst to know more. I wasn't the only young person there intrigued with the studies; other young people flocked in numbers to Wednesday night Bible study.

While Miss Daniel made her way down my aisle, I pretended to look in my bag for my book which was already on my desk. I grabbed a book without looking. Think of a lie. No, I couldn't lie. How could I tell this lie as a believer? Would I have a Christian witness after? Sweat began to trickle down my back. My palms grew wet and I couldn't stop my hand from shaking. I accepted my fate—a detention.

Miss Daniel got to the edge of my desk. I exerted great energy to lift my head to look at her.

"Can I have your homework, Julia? This is not like you. You never forget your home-work, unlike some persons who always forget," she said, her voice higher after each word like someone was turning on the volume on the PA system of her invisible microphone.

A few brave souls attempted to laugh and stopped mid laugh when Miss Daniel turned around. She narrowed her eyes until they were fierce and warlike and in a voice full of authority she said, "Who dares to laugh?" The room went silent. I used the lull to mumble an answer. "Miss Daniel, I got . . ."

She interrupted right away. "You forgot your homework. You do know the rule in this class, Julia."

"But it's my first time," I said in a voice that sounded weak and childish to me.

Hot tears gathered and pooled in my eyes, and I fought hard to keep them from falling. I widened my eyes as wide as saucers so the pool could spread and not fall.

"Julia, the rule is a strict rule. Once you fail to produce your homework in class, it's an automatic detention. Therefore, you leave me with no choice but to book you for a detention. I am sorry, Julia. I know you are consistent with your homework, but simply forgetting will not get you off the strict rule," she said in a matter-of-fact tone.

Again a few of my unwise classmates attempted to laugh, and one or two "huh hmmm" coughed behind me. The attempts were brief and I'm sure were quelled by Miss Daniel's look. I kept my head bowed in shame and I continued to stretch my eyes wider to prevent my tears from falling onto my book. I stared at my book while I contemplated that my classmates were rejoicing in their minds how the great Julia had fallen.

Miss Daniel moved on from my desk and reminded the class of the rule. "No homework equals a mandatory detention" was applicable to all who defaulted.

I realized not only would I be going to detention for my first time, but I had to go home and tell my mother I'd gotten a detention. And the realisation stilled my breath. My mouth went dry as the Sahara Desert and my vision blurred because I'd stretched the walls of my eyelids to prevent my tears from falling. I lost the battle—my eyelids collapsed and fat tears seeped out and created wet spots on my Canpad exercise book.

Six o'clock rolled around the night I'd received my first and last detention, and my mother hadn't arrived home from work. Her delayed arrival forced me into a restless pattern, moving from the chair to stand by the window to look out. My temperature kept rising like the round disc of flour dough for bakes when it meets the hot oil in a frying pan.

I jumped at every sound I heard outside our doors because I interpreted every sound to mean my mother was home. And then I would be relieved my hour of reckoning hadn't arrived.

Like Miss Daniel, my mother also had a strict rule.

Juliette had gone through high school never having broken the detention rule.

I sat there in the dark in our tiny living room which was stuffed with a new three-piece dark brown settee; it left a sliver of floor space to move around and the front door unable to open fully. All our furniture was new, bought with Augustus's money. Time went by and sleep overtook me. I regained consciousness when my mother stood over me shouting.

"Julia, Julia, wake up. What you doing sitting in the dark? Child, it's not like our electricity isn't paid. We are not like some people I know who steals electricity," she said, her voice rising an octave higher on the last words.

I rubbed my eyes, then stretched my arms above my head towards the ceiling to remove the vestiges of the short nap from my body and to give myself time to react to my mother's greetings.

"Mamie, what's all the talk about people stealing electricity. How can they steal electricity?"

"Julia, my dear, some people are wicked, bare face and boldface, and think they are very clever, so they do these things. All around us you will find these things."

I tried to ask another question about this electricity business, but my mother cut in quickly and asked, "How was your day at school?" She flipped the switch for the light bulb shaped like a test tube. It buzzed and I squinted against the sudden flicker of glowing yellow light in the room. She folded her weary limbs into the single chair stuck arm-to-arm with my chair.

"You haven't answered me, Julia."

"I was waiting for you to sit down, Mamie."

"Speak. I'm waiting."

Before I lost the courage I'd been building up for the moment, I turned to look straight ahead at the front door.

"Mamie." I swallowed to moisturize my dry throat. "Today I received a detention for failing to do my homework."

"A what!" my mother said, and turned her body in the chair to look at me. I kept my face trained on the front door.

"Look at me, child. You got a what! Don't you know detentions are not allowed in this house? Juliette went to school for five years and never, never, never brought home a detention report."

"Yes, but she brought home a report of pregnancy," I retorted in a rush of words.

Without hesitation, *blaw, blaw,* my mother delivered two slaps to my face with so much force my face turned to the side on each slap.

"Julia, you're getting too big for your panties. This is about you, not Juliette," she said loud enough for Ma Titre to hear her across the road.

"But you're the one unfairly comparing me to Juliette," I said, my voice sounding shrill to my ears.

"Do you want me to give you another slap?" she said, her tone serious and authoritative.

"Listen to me. You know what's the worst thing—you got a detention for not doing your homework. Tell me, Julia, what prevented you from doing your homework?" Her voice lifted an octave higher and her gold eyes narrowed on the word's "detention," "homework," "prevented." I sensed serious trouble ahead for me. I felt the tear gates opening at the back of my eyeballs.

"I forgot, Mamie," I said and the tear gate broke releasing two lines of warm tears over my rounded cheeks.

The two lines of tears did nothing to weaken my mother's tirade. She continued in her dry authoritative tone.

"The only business you have to remember right now is to go to school and do your homework. Last night you went to Bible study, at your little church. After you had spent the whole afternoon reading your little Bible. You think the people in that little Bible study going to sit your exams for you. Look at what has happened. You got a detention for not doing your homework. Is this what you want, Julia?" she asked, her volume increasing higher than before.

She stood up to tower over me in the chair. She waved her right forefinger across my face and my eyes moved with her finger.

"Listen, I don't want you to go to that Bible study anymore. Weeknights are for you to do your homework. This is the new law in this house."

"Mamie, I need to go to Bible study. How else will I grow as a Christian?" I said, my tone sounding childish to my ears.

"I don't care. For no reason you joined a Christian church, talking strange things, singing strange songs, reading strange books. You're saved. You're reborn. What can these people do for you? All they're doing is filling up your head with all kinds of strange rules and strange teachings. I guess soon you will be speaking in tongues, too."

The words poured out of her like water gushing from a faucet. After the last word she pivoted and stormed into her bedroom, then came back out right away.

"Look at me, Julia, please remember the new law. No more Bible study for you. As a matter of fact, I'm expanding the law. No more of your little Christian church for you.

"From now on you will go to the church of your real baptism, your first communion, your confirmation. And if you disobey me, even your dead father will hear of it."

The finality in her voice slammed something hard and cold into my stomach. It forced me to wrap my arms around my stomach to cushion the pain I felt. It wasn't enough. I hunched over and rocked back and forth. I wanted to escape the glare of my mother's eyes and the effect of her new law.

There would be no escape for me.

This was my new sentence.

I gave in and sobbed.

She left me slumped and sobbing and went into her bedroom. Augustus was nowhere in sight. Not that it mattered. I'd already formed the opinion that Augustus was afraid of my mother. Afraid of her tongue-lashings. I'd been the subject who had suffered under it many times. With Juliette gone I was never spared the brunt of her words. This was a classic performance.

And it worked. On trembling legs, I made my way to my room. To my thinking place. To my reading place. To my sanctuary.

I stayed awake for hours in the dark. I cried my heart out to God.

Should I give up my newfound faith and joy to obey my mother's laws? Was she still the most important authority figure in my life? I had committed my heart to follow scriptural injunctions. Obey your parents . . . I didn't finish the verse in my thoughts. Whom should I obey or disobey? The choice came down to temporary sanctions versus eternal sanctions.

And in that moment, I understood choices are sometimes very hard to make. I understood my mother and father a little better, and the choices they had had to make. I was being pulled apart by two powerful desires. I wanted to be good. I wanted to make the right choice. I wanted to do the right thing. I wanted to belong to something greater than my goals.

That night, I cried until sleep claimed me and left me without the answers to my questions.

The next day I went to school without taking a bite of my breakfast. My stomach was too twisted up in emotions and my throat had constricted in joint rebellion.

I couldn't swallow my favourite hot fresh bread from the bakery with cheese and thick cocoa tea, rich with milk, cinnamon, nutmeg and bay leaf. I brought the cup to my lips, smelled the spices and couldn't drink it.

Throughout the day for all my classes, I suffered from a lack of concentration. My mother's new law stayed on repeat. I schemed and planned the escape route from the house during every lesson. At the end of the school day, I'd learned nothing from mathematics, social studies, integrated science, principles of accounts and principles of business. However, I'd confirmed in my mind to attend the next Youth Meeting at church.

I was scheduled to make my solo debut later that night. I'd planned on inviting Mamie and Augustus—wishful thinking on my part, because even before last night's new law my mother had declared she would never put her foot in my little Christian church. I knew I would be making my singing debut without any visible support from my family. But it didn't stop me from yearning for the support. I wanted my family to experience the new birth with me.

As the clock ticked closer to Youth Meeting time, my nervousness translated into restless movements, even though I knew the song I was going to sing. I chose to spend the time lying on my bed clad in a shabby white t-shirt I'd worn for physical education in school last year. I held my Canpad exercise book with the words to all my favourite songs. I dared not sing out, satisfied to rehearse the song in my mind. The nervous energy went out of my body through the silent tapping of my bare feet against my mattress. The emotion of the song welled in me, increasing the tapping of my feet.

About 6:30, my mother and Augustus came in from the kitchen. My mother said to Augustus, "It's time for us to get dressed to attend the party in Newtown tonight."

I listened and I felt the smile of good luck split my mouth wide open. My body went still and I tuned my ears to listen to the movements of them getting dressed. Moments before they left the house their individual choices of scent permeated the air. Soft flowery scent for my mother's perfume, and strong, musky scent for Augustus's spray deodorant. I realised they would soon be out of the house. I jumped up and down on my new double bed which had taken up almost all the floor space in the room.

A few minutes later, at seven o'clock my mother appeared in my doorway. "Julia, Augustus and I are going out to a party. Remember what I told you last night," she said with a hard-edge tone.

I didn't answer.

Wrong move.

"Am I speaking to the room? Julia, you will answer me when I speak to you."

"I remember your decree, Mamie."

"Decree? I said law, child. Break my law and we will see who's the woman in this house. We will see who's in charge in this house. I expect to find you sound asleep when we return home." And with those parting words she and Augustus left the house.

I marvelled at how God chose to shine upon me that night. I had plenty of time to get ready and to attend Youth Meeting on time without having to execute the escape route I had schemed and planned all day.

I was disobeying, yes.

I made my choice.

I chose the temporary consequences of disobeying my mother. What would Jesus think? These thoughts assaulted my conscience before I left the house. I paid no attention. I left the house.

Hours later, I sang my heart out at Youth Meeting and was hailed as the new songbird of Full Gospel Fellowship by my peers. I got occupied with enjoying the lavish praises from church leaders and friends.

I failed to notice the Youth Meeting had run beyond the scheduled time. At the back of my mind, I hoped my mother and Augustus would be at their party until midnight. And I had figured I'd be safe and sound in my bed, before they got home.

After the service ended, I arrived at the front door singing the lyrics of the song, "The Grass is Greener on the Other Side." But before my hands could reach for the doorknob, the door opened. And I stared into the angry face of my mother, her eyes lit like golden flames. I had no time to react before she hissed, "You're sleeping outside tonight."

And she slammed and locked the front door in my face. I stared but I could not see. I stood rooted to the spot. I gripped my Bible until my fingers ached from the pressure. My heart galloped like a car out on the racetrack and caused pains to fill my chest. My mind rallied to process what my eyes had witnessed, and my ears had heard. It failed.

A minute passed and my heart rate slowed to allow me to form a coherent thought. The strength returned to my legs, and I moved to knock on the door.

This is all a misunderstanding. My mother cannot intend to lock me out for the night.

I knocked for a long time. My knocks became louder. It didn't work. The door remained shut. I shifted to pleading in a high-pitched voice

"Mamie, open the door for me.

"Mamie, open the door for me.

"Mamie, open the door for me!"

I screeched out those words—in vain. No one stirred inside the house.

I switched to Augustus and it didn't stir him.

Is he going to lie next to my mother and allow her to lock me outside?

Daddy Julius. My mind grasped for Daddy Julius. Daddy Julius would not have pretended he didn't hear me. Daddy Julius would have never lain there silent. He would have opened the door for me even though he'd have suffered my mother's wrath for the act. And in that moment, with me pounding and pleading, my respect for Augustus took a steep nosedive.

My saviour came in the person of Aunty Maureen. She came out of her house in her baby blue worn-out nighty and asked me, "Julia, why you making this crazy noise knocking on the door at this hour?"

"My mother—she's locked me out, Aunty Maureen," I replied, my voice weak from my earlier shrills.

"Velma, open the door for this child," Aunty Maureen screamed. She did it again and again and no one stirred inside the house.

While Aunty Maureen tried to get my mother to open the door, I collapsed into a crumpled heap on the ground, heaving hard and heavy sobs.

"Come, child, get up. You will sleep with me tonight. Your mother is a wicked woman. I knew that from long time, but tonight she has gone too far," Aunty Maureen screeched. It was impossible my mother didn't hear her. I knew Old Man Maurice slept like the dead, like Samson and Samuel. I thought Ma Titre would come running from behind her croton hedge.

No one else came.

At dawn the next day, Aunty Maureen confronted my mother in our kitchen. I heard their raised voices. I'd slept in one of Aunty Maureen's big, long t-shirts she'd made herself.

"Velma, why did you lock your daughter outside last night?'

"I've no daughter who disobeys me."

"Do you know she cried all night even in her sleep?"

"My heart is not troubled. You see, Julia thinks she's a big woman. And you know what, two big women cannot stay in one small house."

"Velma, you are being unreasonable. What's wrong with the church? Would you rather see her on the streets all night like many of the girls in the village? Is that what you want for her?" Aunty Maureen asked, her tone demanding an answer from my mother.

"No daughter of mine can be on the streets, Maureen. You ever saw Juliette on the streets? The problem with Julia—she wants to have things her own way. Which is fine, but she's not going to do it in this house."

"What are you saying?" Aunty Maureen asked her.

"If Julia wants to continue going to her little Christian church then she can find her own place to stay."

"Velma, the child is in fourth form, what foolishness are you talking?"

"You heard me right—she can find her own place to stay. I warned her. I set my law and I'm standing by it. *Alé*. Go, if you cannot abide under my law."

"I don't believe you! What law you're talking about?" Aunty Maureen said, her voice escalating on each word.

"I told her, Maureen, the night before. 'No more of that little wayside church for you.' I warned her to be in bed when I got home. But no. *Woman*. She *woman now*. Julia, go and find your own place to stay," she shouted.

I rolled onto my side and clutched my belly, my mother's words like fresh lacerations on an open wound. I pressed a fist to my mouth to stop the scream in my throat but could do nothing about the tears which welled up in my eyes rendering me blind with pain. A heavy feeling crawled from the bottom of my stomach and lodged into my core. For the second time in hours, I'd crumpled under the pain of my mother's words into the camphor-ball-smelling milk-white sheet of Aunty Maureen's bed.

"You're a crazy woman. *Ou fal*, Velma. You cannot do that to the child."

"I cannot? I'm a very serious woman, Maureen."

Moments passed in silence and then I heard Aunty Maureen, sweeping her yard with the broom made from the branches of the coconut tree. And I thought back to the time I'd helped her make the broom.

We'd sat on the big stone and peeled the dry leaves off each stick. We'd raced each other to see who could have the most *kokoyé*—the spine of coconut leaf—at the end of the day. I was proud of Aunty Maureen's thick *kokoyé* broom made from hundreds of coconut sticks. It represented hours and hours of working, talking, and laughing. It was an odd thought to have while I contemplated the words uttered by my mother.

I remained on Aunty Maureen's bed, too heavy with fear to move. I didn't understand why my mother was taking such a hard-line approach to my newfound faith. I also could not understand why she would want me to leave her house because I refused to follow her unreasonable decree.

My spirit sank lower when I heard her enter Aunty Maureen's side of the yard to ask for me. Their voices were much lower than they had been earlier, so I didn't catch all what was said. I didn't have long to wait because Aunty Maureen entered the room a few minutes later and said, "Wake up, Julia, your mother was asking for you. She left for the market and then work. She wants you to break ten coconuts and to grate them by the time she gets home from work this afternoon at one o'clock. I think I got her to change her mind about you leaving the house."

"*Bondyé*, how I'm going to grate all these coconuts before one o'clock?" I said.

"I will help you. Girl, please go over to your place."

I left Aunty Maureen's house fortified with faith that she would help me to get all the coconuts done. But fate intervened. Or God's hand intervened. Or my hard-headedness, my own mind, my own will, my own way intervened. All of these accusations my mother had thrown at me over the years converged that Saturday and changed the course of my life.

At eight o'clock, Sister Alice came by and reminded me it was our turn to clean the church. I'd put my name on the roster of cleaners and was paired up with Sister Alice, who had six children; five boys and one girl. I couldn't in all fairness allow Sister Alice to go and clean the church by herself. I had to honour my commitment to volunteer. I left the house without telling Aunty Maureen.

The two of us took two hours cleaning the church because Sister Alice insisted that we wiped down each wooden bench twice. We mopped the floor twice and polished the pulpit until our holiness reflected in the harshly beautiful shine.

By the time I got home the clock had approached eleven o'clock and I had not started the coconut grating enterprise. I went into panic because Aunty Maureen was nowhere to be found and she had promised to help me. I could smell more trouble coming. It would be near impossible for me to finish grating ten coconuts in two hours. But I had no choice but to start work. I broke each nut. I took out the jelly with my knife and sat down on the bench in the yard with the big orange basin and aluminum grater.

Three hours later, my mother got home and found me in action with half of the coconut done. She passed right by me with her bag of groceries and market shopping and went into the kitchen without saying a word.

My eyes stayed glued to my fingers on the coconut against the grater. My hand trembled. My throat turned dry.

I heard the fridge door open, and she started to put things away. Then she walked past me again and went into the house. She came back out again and this time she stopped by the coconuts and me.

"Julia, I want to know why you're still grating coconuts," she said in a soft tone I'd never heard her use before. My mother never spoke in a soft voice. I started to feel dizzy. Time slowed to a halt.

I stopped grating the coconut and lifted my eyes to face her. And I resolved to tell the truth no matter the outcome.

"Mamie, I had to clean the church with Sister Alice and I came back later than I expected," I said, squeezing the words out of my narrowed voice box.

"You did what? After last night you still went back to that church?" she said in the same soft voice of earlier.

I blinked to ease the tightness around my eyes, and I averted my eyes from hers. I couldn't look at her. A heavy line of sweat trailed down my back. An empty feeling in the pit of my stomach blossomed and I wished for time to speed up in this encounter with my mother. It was unusual behaviour for her when she got angry, she tended to shout, not whisper.

"This is the last time you'll disobey me under my roof." And she turned and went back into the house.

Within seconds she appeared in the doorway with my school bag and threw it at me. Then she went back and came out with my books and threw them at me too. Next it was all my clothes, then my toiletries and, it seemed, everything I had in the room except for the bed and curtains and wardrobe.

She threw it all at my feet.

The yard became littered with my things. Strewn as if flung there by hurricane winds. Indeed, my mother had turned into Hurricane Velma because the speed and force with which she threw these things took her only a few minutes.

Through the entire process I sat there numb. My body froze like I'd been turned into a pillar of salt like Lot's wife. Unable to move. The coconuts lay forgotten. I stared in dazed disbelief at every article I owned. I rubbed down on my breastbone to ease the pain trapped in my chest. It threatened to send me to an early grave.

But my mother still had a final blow to deliver. She had to finish my annihilation. She reappeared in the doorway, this time with nothing in her hand.

"From this day forth I have no daughter name Julia. You are a big woman, and two big women cannot stay in the same little house, so go and find a place to stay."

Words.

Sight.

Feelings.

Deserted me.

I closed my eyes and allowed my tears to spill out. I didn't know how long I'd sat there with my eyes closed. My things thrown like trash in the yard. The coconuts halfway grated. It was Aunty Maureen's voice which brought me back from the edge of the abyss.

Aunty Maureen entered the yard then and screamed, "*Bondyé! Papa Bondyé!* What's going on here? Velma, you are a crazy woman. How can you do that to your own child?"

"Mind your business," she said, and slammed the two-sided door and went into the house.

Aunty Maureen went for Ma Titre, who tried talking to my mother, but she never answered or came out of the house. They helped me pick up every item and brought it across the street to Ma Titre's house.

I called Juliette to tell her what our mother had done to me. Her response further devastated me. Juliette, my sister, urged me to obey our mother and to beg for her forgiveness. She didn't even want to hear what happened. She told me with haste I couldn't come live with her and that I had better think of a way for our mother to take me back in.

Distraught, I called my friends Gina and Gloria. Their mother answered the phone. I was at my weakest point and I exploded into a flood of tears at the kind voice of Mrs Adams. I told her my story with many stops, starts, and stutters, and I'd never stuttered before.

At my lowest hour a stranger came through for me. The Adams family came for me that afternoon in their new car they'd recently bought, and I left for Roseau with them.

Mr Adams tried to talk to my mother, but she never answered or came out of the house.

My mother, never one to be short on words or emotions, had become deaf and dumb.

But what rocked me to the core was Juliette's plain refusal to offer me even temporary sanctuary. I understood she was overwhelmed with her growing family, but I didn't understand how, in the short time of starting her family, I'd come to mean so little to her.

We were sisters, me and Juliette. We were bound by our bloodline and the crucibles we'd survived together. Our father's abandonment. Daddy Julius's disappearance. Our fight against our poverty. Our struggle to understand the adults. Had we really been one united force?

On the car ride to Pottersville, the place of my future home, I realised Juliette and I had always been on opposite sides with any coin that had our mother's face on one side and the face of reason on the other. Juliette inevitably chose my mother's side.

I should not have been shocked that she'd taken the path where there'd be no falling out with our mother. She wasn't concerned about right or wrong. She wasn't concerned about fair and unfair. She wasn't concerned about family solidarity.

I'd been expelled from the family.

The first two people I'd ever loved.

Why would a mother abandon her daughter in deference to a religion she rarely practiced. For a rule she created on the spur of her anger.

For the first time I faced the possibility that my mother's mental health was fragile. It was easier for me to hold on to this premise—easier to forgive her once I'd accepted this premise, whether it was right or not.

I didn't want to face that I'd be going through my last years of school an abandoned daughter. When the car came to a stop outside the Adams house, I wiped the tears off my face and purposed in my heart to fight; to show my mother I wasn't made of sugar and spice, but spirit and steel.

I would complete my high school and A levels.

I would make it to university.

I would become an accountant.

I would not become Juliette.

11

Win, Lose Or Draw-The Great Debate

(1988)

Three weeks after the forced departure from my home, I got selected to be on the final team to represent my school at the National Schools Debate Finals. It'd been the hard, gruelling regimen I needed. I threw myself into all our practice sessions and the elimination rounds.

But it didn't help the pain of my mother's abandonment; the pain crystallised to an inflamed sore. I tried writing even more in my new purple diary as a way of coping. This one wasn't buried in my grip, it was on the nightstand next to the bed in the room I shared with Gina and Gloria. In my diary, I worked through my emotions by writing seven things: thoughts, actions, or reactions—a practice Mrs Henry, my guidance counsellor, had encouraged a few months before. But no matter how hard I tried, there was nothing that would erase the searing hurt in my heart.

But I had to try.

And so I embraced the opportunity of preparing for the debates to work on my perseverance muscles. I had big goals to achieve; I considered the debates my training ground.

The training for the competition allowed me, sometimes, to forget the sore; nonetheless it remained, and its pulverizing pain penetrated my soul. But I couldn't let down my team members or my school. I committed and prepared for every round of the debates.

In the lead-up to the finals we practiced every afternoon for three hours with Mr James. At that time, the fashion was these extra baggy pants that narrowed to the ankles so tightly we called them "gun mouth pants." Mr James was our bright-shirt, gun-mouth pants-wearing drama and literature teacher. He'd gotten us into the debating competition from the drama and literary club. Gloria, Gina, and myself had joined the drama club because we didn't have athletic bones or muscles. And the debating team comprised Gloria, Rommel, and me. Rommel—the charmer, singer, football player, book lover, all weaved together—was the male dynamo of our class.

We made up the team charged with bringing home the trophy to the Grammar High School this year. My teammates were intense. Perhaps not as intense and determined as I was to bring the trophy home. Rommel approached debating with fire and intensity. My friend Gloria, who I had grown to consider as my sister, the crowned Miss Competitive of our class, possessed the same qualities. She rejected the competitive label for herself but had no trouble projecting it onto me.

In practice, Mr James charged each team member to coin three points in favour, three points to oppose and at least three points on rebuttal. In the first hour Mr James made us research the question of the day in the school's library, a dusty dark room with shelves of books and only four tables. I saw no other students during the weeks we used the library.

The questions for our mock debates ranged from "Exams should be abolished in high school" to "Is Dominica's culture dying?" Once the research was done, we sat together to speed-write our speaking notes in half an hour.

For an hour and a half Mr James allowed each of us to debate the topic for, and against. He acted the part of the opponent and within the gruelling hours we learned to think fast by responding to the sharp darts Mr James hurled at us.

At the end of each session, I went home tired but exhilarated. Nothing a half hour nap couldn't cure. After my nap I'd attack my homework with zeal. The pep talks on winning and confidence building from Mr James energised Gloria and me to commit even harder to our studies. At the very beginning of the competition Mr James had threatened to pull us off the team if we didn't maintain our grades. It was our high grades which had cemented our places on the team.

At nights Gloria and I continued our practice sessions in our bedroom before our audience of one: Gina. We practiced our delivery, to ensure we had the proper diction, tone, and emotions.

I wanted us to win so badly I even practiced debating in my dreams. Every night I dreamt of the finals. I envisioned Gloria and me putting forth our points with more passion and force than our opponents. We listened carefully and jotted down our points for rebuttal and then we would deliver one strong punch after another to the delight and loud cheers from the audience.

Every morning leading up to the finals I awoke to loud cheers of victory ringing in my ears. The cheers would stop as soon as my eyes adjusted to the dim light in the room revealing the sleeping forms of Gina and Gloria under their pink blankets.

Every morning I awoke in my new home in Pottersville, I listened to the sounds of the neighbourhood. The steady rhythm of waves crashing against the stony beach. The cock crowing from its favourite fisherman's boat. The loud barking of dogs across the road. The neighbour's radio tuned into the nation's station, the WBS radio, pitched for everyone in the neighbourhood to hear whether they wanted to or not.

And every morning, I thought of my mother and her angry words and wondered if she ever thought of me and hoped she'd stop hating me.

After many practices and hours of research and more practice, the morning of the debate arrived. I awoke about four o'clock to darkness outside the bedroom window. I was in the bed that used to be Gloria's. We'd cried and laughed and hugged on the day they decided I should have my own bed.

All was quiet. Even the sea breeze hadn't awakened because the pink curtains hung flat against the open louvres. The sea lapped rather than crashed against the shore. I closed my eyes and reviewed the images of our victories over our rival schools in the quarter finals, then the semi-finals.

Our team had come up against the best, but each time, our training pulled us through to triumph. I gave up falling back asleep. I was ready like a hunter seeking its prey—in my case I wanted to bring home to our school the gold trophy for the National School's Debate Finals. When the clock struck 4:30 I decided to wake Gina and Gloria.

"What time is it? It's still dark," Gloria said, rubbing her hand across her eyes like she wanted to rub out her eyeballs.

"It's 4:30. I couldn't sleep."

"What?" they both said.

"I'm going right back to sleep," Gina said, pulling her blanket over her head. In a muffled voice from under the blanket, she continued, "You and Gloria can sit and talk about the debate until the sun comes over the mountain."

"Come on, Gina."

"Okay," she said, and flung her blanket to the floor. "Come over here on our bed."

Gloria remained under her blanket, still rubbing her eyes. "Why you're up so early?" she said.

"I can't sleep. You think Kane and Abel are still asleep? They're probably poring over their notes. Going over each word of their arguments so it's etched forever in their grey matter."

Laughing, Gloria replied, "Julia we were up till midnight poring over our notes as you say. Four hours later you are worrying about what the competition may be doing at this hour."

"That's right. It's a competition. Remember what Mr James chanted every day—'It's a war.'"

"Julia, Julia, don't tell me you bought into Mr James's intensity. It's a good thing there is only one of him at our school," Gloria countered.

"Not so fast; you forget Miss Daniel. Talk about intense," Gina added and laughed until she fell against her pillow.

"Girls, girls, how can I ever forget my detention under her strict rule? 'No homework equals one detention,'" I said in an overemphasized sarcastic tone and I laughed until I held my belly. I'm still upset Gina that you won't be with us in Portsmouth today. Why must your music exam be today?"

"Call London and ask them," Gina replied.

"You guys, I'm going back to sleep. Stop the chattering," Gina said, and pulled her blanket to cover her entire body.

"You can't go back to sleep, Gloria. Come let's go over our notes again."

"Julia, you're on your own. I need more sleep to function."

And Gloria flipped her pillow back into place and covered herself with her blanket from head to toe.

"Gina, I'm going to make some Milo; would you like some?"

"Sure," she said from under her cover. At the same time, she pulled her blanket tighter against her body. I shook my head and a smile crept across my face in appreciation of their antics. My chest glowed with warmth at all the memories I'd been creating with my new sisters.

I left the bed and groped my way to the kitchen. A few minutes later when I returned to the room, Gina and Gloria were lost to the land of sleep. I placed Gina's cup of Milo on the nightstand, dropped on my bed and curled my legs underneath my bottom to enjoy my big steaming cup of Milo.

Hours later, outside the school's office, I waited alone for the bus hired to take us to the finals in Portsmouth, when Mr James emerged from the office.

"Julia, are you ready for this afternoon?" Mr James asked.

"Yes, sir, I am," I said, giving a smart salute.

Mr James laughed aloud and guffawed, "Really, Julia, have I been drilling you hard?"

"Yes, sir, at times it felt like we were training in the army."

"Julia, this is war. Today you are about to face your strongest opponents in the competition. Do you know who you come up against today?"

"Kane and Abel," I answered.

"Yes, the brothers Kane and Abel who are a force to reckon with. They are aggressive; they know each other's mind; they each feed off the energy of the other; and they are determined to win. So far in the competition Kane and Abel have been able to dominate every aspect of the scoring. Today you have to be excellent in every round, and in the rebuttal, to beat Kane and Abel." He pulled in a deep breath and released it, then looked around. "I don't see the rest of my team," he said, spinning around. "They need to be here, for the bus will be here soon."

As if on cue a white minibus with the word "Blessings" splayed in large black capital letters on the front entered the yard and drove right up to the spot where Mr James and I stood.

"Julia, please, you better go find Gloria and Rommel and the cheerleaders who are coming with us, and your form teacher Ms Kentish."

I ran to our classroom to find Rommel and Gloria and the five students who had volunteered to come cheer us.

Mr James gathered us beside the bus for a last-minute talk in his drill sergeant voice.

"What day is today?" he asked.

"The finals, sir," we answered.

"What do you plan to do today, troop?"

"We have every intention of winning, sir."

"Why do you want to win?"

"Because we want to bring the trophy back to our school, sir."

"Okay, remember we are on a mission. Let us get this winning train to Portsmouth."

The drive to the second town took us along the coast and was punctuated with hair-pin turns, blind corners, villages tucked under hills, villages glued to the sea. On my left, cliffs with jutting branches, twigs, grey rocks, dry tarish, or wet brown dirt towered over the bus. And on my right the blue waters of the Caribbean Sea foamed and crashed against rocks speckled with dirt, or glistened against billions of tiny shiny grains of black volcanic sand.

About halfway through our journey someone decided to raise a song to pass the time. I sang and kept my eyes trained to the passing scenery. We had just cleared the west coast village of Salisbury. Everything seemed to be going past my window at super high speed. I sent up a silent prayer and asked God to keep us safe on the smooth road.

None of the adults seemed to care about the speed. A few years ago, the national road rehabilitation project had produced smooth road with no potholes, all the way to Portsmouth. It'd been an island-wide project. We'd had to walk home from school for weeks.

I could see we were about to go sailing past a bend in the road. As the bus approached the bend, a white car appeared leaning more towards our side of the road than his side.

Our bus driver had to swerve the bus away from the oncoming car to avoid hitting it. I felt when the bus started to slide towards the embankment of shrubs and trees on our side of the road. And my heart fell into my stomach at the speed of rushing water. We all screamed as the bus continued to ride through the brush of trees, sliding down the embankment, until it came to a stop. It was over in a flash. The sliding bus stopped and the screaming stopped at the same time. Perched and held up by the trees, the bus didn't move. In the silence I heard Mr James, in a faint voice, ask, "Everyone okay?"

It seemed such an odd question to ask at the time since none of us could have been okay after the scare we'd received. Gloria and I had gotten thrown together so we were like twins in the same amniotic sac; our limbs entwined, our heads resting on the side of the bus.

The bus had come to rest on the side with the doors facing up. I didn't see how but Mr James and the bus driver, Bolo, managed to get out through the front of the bus. Mr James then wrestled the damaged door open. When he did, I saw a gash on his face, oozing blood.

I found my voice and screamed, "Mr James, you are bleeding." Mr James ignored my screams and pulled me out of the bus, unpacking me from Gloria. Then he pulled Gloria out in a similar fashion.

Between Mr James and the bus driver, they pulled everyone out of the canting bus. Once we got out of the bus it was just a short way up the embankment. Thanks to the trees, the bus had not fallen far. When we got out on the road, I looked for the white car which in my mind had caused the accident. It stood a few feet from the bend—plunked in the middle of the road without a single scratch.

The driver of the car spoke to Bolo, our bus driver, about settling without calling the police. He knew he was wrong but didn't want the police involved.

I didn't have a scratch on me and neither did Gloria. But Rommel had an ugly gash on his righthand trickling blood. Miss Kentish looked dazed. She sank to the grass and stayed with her head down. Three of our cheerleaders were crying hysterically, and the other two looked dazed like Ms Kentish. M. James took command of the scene and begged all of us to calm down.

"Everyone, please stay calm. We are all alive. No one is seriously hurt. We're going to be okay. Look! Here comes a vehicle."

I turned and saw a yellow bus with passengers. It stopped where our group had gathered. The door of the bus flew open and five people scrambled out to check on us.

"What happen?" the bus driver asked.

"A little accident. I swayed to avoid hitting the white car and ended up where you see the bus," Bolo, our driver, responded.

"I see people bleeding and you say it is a little accident," the bus driver said.

"It's okay. Just bruises and cuts, and some of the children are in a bit of a shock, but they will be okay," Mr James intervened.

"Are you all headed to the finals of the school debate?" one of the female passengers asked. "Because that's our destination. Driver, we can take them if they are up to continuing." Maybe our uniforms gave us away or maybe she knew Mr James, why she guessed correctly where we were headed.

Bolo turned to Mr James. "You heard the lady, sir. What say you?"

"Let me ask the students what they want to do," Mr James said, his tone sympathetic, very different to his earlier demanding and authoritative tone.

Mr James herded us together and asked, "Can you all go on and compete after this?"

"Yes," I whispered.

"I can't hear you. I want each of you to watch me eyeball to eyeball and tell me, 'Yes I want to win the competition today.' If each of you can do it, then we will be on our way."

Rommel, Gloria, and I repeated the words to Mr James, eyeball to eyeball. After he announced our readiness, he wiped the blood from his face, which had miraculously stopped bleeding.

Two girls from our school and Bolo the bus driver left with the white car to head back to Roseau. The rest of us piled into the bus bound for the debate finals. I had been shaken by the accident, but I remembered the hours we had put into our preparations; the schools we had defeated to get finals; the energy and trust Mr James had invested in training us.

I decided I couldn't let down Mr James, my school, or myself. Thoughts of my mother surged through my mind, and I felt the hole in my heart opened up and a fresh wave of pain flooded my heart. And then I remembered my resolve to show my mother I could achieve all my goals without her help.

When we got to Portsmouth the clock had gone past the 2:30 start time for the finals. It turned out our rescue bus contained all the officials for the debate competition. A discussion occurred over the time the debate should start and the officials decided 3:30 p.m. would be the new start time.

When I got to the hall my eyes searched for my prey. They were easy to pick out for they were the only ones on the podium. The twin brothers Kane and Abel were also basketball players for their school. They were both over six feet tall. They paced up and down the podium, their hands buried in their pant pockets. They stopped every few inches to look at the audience.

When we entered the room, everyone in the hall erupted into applause. Apparently, the audience had been under the impression we had abandoned the debate. I picked up on the energy of the crowd and the adrenaline started winding its way through my body.

Gloria, Rommel, and I moved to the podium and took the desk and chair the brothers had allotted for our use. We deposited our research materials onto the small desk—six textbooks, three writing pads each, pens, pencils and sharpener. Out of the corner of my eye I noticed the brothers' raised eyebrows at the sight of the books, and I smiled. On their desk was a tattered white notepad covered with blue ink writing lying askew in the middle of their desk.

We'd brought our books to paint a picture of force. Our desk looked like it could crumple under like a sugar dome flooded by water. Mr James had assured us the book tactic would create psychological fear in our opponents. I lost confidence in the tactic every time I glanced at the tattered notepad. It screamed it had been well utilised, and our unused books looked like they were begging to be opened.

The chairperson, Mrs Paul, one of the women from the bus, took the stage to announce the start of the competition. She invited all persons to have a seat in the auditorium and to be attentive. I used the time in which she gave general directions to the audience to reflect on the question, the opponents, and on my desire to win.

I thanked God I hadn't received a scratch in the accident, and for courage and strength to do the debate. I listened as the chairperson enumerated the rules of the competition, and I rearranged the books on the table. To my right, Gloria fixated on the official as she read out the rules. I glanced at Rommel who was in the first row of seats. He was looking at the bruise he'd sustained from the bus accident. I could see little beads of perspiration forming along his upper lip.

On my body I could feel a trickle of water sliding down the middle of my back. Across the stage our opponents stared straight at the audience. I didn't miss the small smile around their eyes and lips. I got the impression they were unaffected by the rules, the audience, and the pressure of winning the trophy.

"Ladies and gentlemen, boys and girls, I am pleased to declare the finals of the School National Debates open. The topic for this afternoon; 'Do beauty pageants serve any useful purpose in our culture?'"

A ripple of snickers spread through the room.

The chairperson continued the toss of the coin. "The St John's Academy will present the arguments in support of, and the Grammar High School will oppose.

"There are two speakers to a side. For the proposition side we have Kane Lawrence who will speak first and Abel Lawrence who will speak second. For the opposition we have Julia Alexander who will speak first, and Gloria Adams will be the second speaker. The replies for the team will be given by Kane Lawrence and Julia Alexander, respectively, for each team. I invite you to give your attention to each speaker during the debates."

Kane swaggered to the podium. I studied his chiselled nose, thin lips and grey eyes to see if they would reveal anything useful about him. What I saw was a face in deep concentration when he glanced down at his notes on his ragged pad. I missed his opening remarks since I'd been intent on studying his face and notepad. However, his deep, strong, vibrant voice cut through the fog in my brain. It called me to listen to him.

"We have seven points we will raise in support of our proposition; beauty pageants do serve a useful purpose in our culture. I will present four of these points and Abel will present on the other three."

Then he launched into the definition of culture they were adopting for the debate. I took note they were using a comprehensive definition of culture to include art, music, theatre, festivals. I scratched furiously across my notepad jutting down Kane's points.

While on his feet Kane argued that beauty pageants are a viable form of entertainment.

I made a note. We didn't need beauty pageants to keep our oral storytelling tradition alive. There were daily radio programmes which showcased this aspect of our culture, and our Independence cultural festival had kept the oral tradition going. The annual calypso competition is more than sufficient to keep the oral aspect of our entertainment culture going.

I jutted down those points and returned my attention to Kane's arguments. that beauty pageants are an integral part of our two major cultural festival traditions: carnival and Independence. He went on to argue in his deep melodic voice that it adds diversity to our cultural fare. And that culture must be diverse for it to keep growing. And his final point was that beauty pageants provide an avenue for the personal development of the girls who participate.

At the end of his deliberations Kane threw his notes onto the desk and took his seat. As if to signal that this was already the end of the debate. Unperturbed, I stood up to present our opening case.

"Ladies and gentlemen, you have heard from our opponents and their case is that beauty pageants serve a useful purpose in our culture. We, the opposition, have under-taken to show you today that beauty pageants serve no useful purpose in our culture. And more, that beauty pageants are harmful to Dominican society in several ways."

I went on to make my points with supporting data and survey. I paid attention to my diction and made sure my voice reached the back of the room. At every point I grabbed the upper portion of the podium with a stronger grip for support with my left hand and with my right hand I turned over my notes. I also kept my eyes on the three judges, all of whom were scribbling on their notepads.

By the time I took my seat I vacillated between being drained and being elated that we still stood a chance of winning the debate. I took my seat and couldn't deny the sweat I felt running down my legs. I beat my fingers against the desk and wrote a note to Gloria. "How are we holding up? Do you think we are still in?"

She wrote back, "You did well, but I have this feeling that their points are coming across stronger than ours." I answered, "You prepare yourself, for the next round is coming up in four minutes."

The debate progressed with Abel and Gloria who both ably presented their propositions. During their presentations, I spent the time rubbing my hands up and down my uniform skirt and wishing for the time to speed up. I wanted that empty feeling in the pit of my stomach to go away and when the last word was spoken by Gloria, I exhaled my pent-up feelings.

After Gloria's speech, the chairperson, Mrs Paul invited first Kane and then me to give our replies in four minutes. After Kane spoke, I was afraid to stand lest my knees buckled under me. He was fast, strong, and hit their main points on the target. I got up and emulated his style, leaving out all surplusage and hitting home our main points.

We waited about fifteen minutes for the judges to come back with their decision. During the wait, I wrung my hands together under the desk.

Gloria and I avoided speaking to each other. Mr James approached our table once and said, "You girls were great. Let us hope the judges have the same view."

Rommel also came over. He seemed unable to keep from touching the ugly gash on his arm and said, "Hey, I think we are taking the trophy back to school tonight." I gave him a weak smile in response.

Deep down in my stomach I felt that Kane and Abel's arguments were stronger than the ones we had presented. Where Kane had been aggressive in tone and body language, Abel had been smooth and calm and deadly on point.

"Hmmm," I said.

The PA system crackled with life and the chairperson's voice spilled through the black speakers. "We have the results of the finals of the National Schools Debate 1988. I will call one of the judges to do the adjudication."

The judge went to the podium. It was one of the gentlemen from our bus ride to the venue.

"Ladies and gentlemen, boys and girls, it is my pleasure to share with you the judges' findings on today's proceedings. I will start with the team for the proposition, Kane and Abel.

"We find Kane and Abel had a good strategy between the speakers. They started with their most powerful points and the points were evenly distributed between speakers, that is they were both able to make very good points in their arguments. The different speaking styles were used effectively. We found both speakers to be fluent, articulate, and very confident. Their arguments were strong and supported by good use of statistics. Overall we found they proved their case as a general proposition.

"On the other hand, we found the team against the proposition did not disprove the proposition's case. The arguments were too weak to disprove what the proposition had contended. The arguments appeared to be indistinguishable and were flavours of each other, and they tended to prove the same point. We found the speakers to be articulate and confident.

"Overall, both teams showed strong evidence of research, the strong use of language, they were grammatically correct, they spoke with good posture from their notes and the pronunciation and enunciation was excellent by both sides. I think this is one of the better finals we have seen in years in this competition.

"Let me say we found all of you to be very good debaters and that you should keep practicing the skill. I turn over to the chairperson who will announce the scores."

Having just heard the judge's adjudication I anticipated what the results were going to be.

"We have the Grammar High School who was adjudged very good with seventy-two points overall and the St John's High School who was adjudged excellent with seventy-seven points. The best speaker award goes to Kane. The winner of this year's national School's Debate is none other than Kane and Abel for the St John's Academy for the second year in a row."

The hall erupted into cheers of jubilation and high fives. Kane jumped to his feet and threw both hands in the air and Abel stood to face the crowd with a broad smile on his face and lifted one hand in salute. The chairperson continued, "Unfortunately, these guys still have another year in high school, so you know what this means. Congratulations to all of you, you are all winners today."

I closed my ears to the last statement, swallowed my disappointment, took Gloria by the hand and walked over to our opponents to shake their hands and offer them our sincere congratulations. We fought hard, but the judges determined the winners that day.

We had one more year of high school and I resolved to beat Kane and Abel using their own strategies next year. I was here for every fight.

12

Juliette's Travesty
(1988)

On a wet and soggy Saturday afternoon after school closed for the summer vacation on my fourth year of high school, I went to visit Juliette at her home in Canefield.

I flagged down and hopped onto a music-blaring minibus. Loud bass-driven sounds rattled the thin walls. I couldn't hear myself breathe. The bus driver overtook more than five vehicles in less time than it took me to tie my shoelaces. He was far worse than Lightning. I missed riding Lightning these past few months. I missed my mother. I missed the yard people—Aunty Maureen, Old Man Maurice, Ma Titre across the road.

I smiled when my stop came into view. I'd never been happier to disembark a minibus, leaving behind the noise and the ten unaffected individuals on the bus. My smile died once I stepped off the bus because the skies opened and poured out rain. I'd refused the umbrella Mrs Adams had handed to me. I made a long dash for Juliette's house from the bus stop. By the time I got to her house the gutters were overflowing with brown swirls of water.

Despite my valiant run, by the time I got to Juliette's house my hair and my clothes stuck to my wet skin like they'd been drenched in school glue.

Once inside Juliette's house, she ushered me to her bedroom to change into warm clothes. The only option turned out to be Juliette's dresses from before the babies. While Juliette searched the Mount Diablotin of clothes piled in one corner of her bedroom, Timmy and Tammy pounded on the door with what sounded like shoes. "We want to see Aunty Julia," they cried in unison.

Juliette ignored them and I followed her lead. I looked around the room; articles of children's and adult clothing dominated every square inch of surface in the room. Baby clothes, unfolded clothes, dirty clothes. *How does Juliette find anything in this mess?*

I observed Juliette before I changed into the black dress she had pulled out from a pile and handed to me. The dress looked like fungus had sucked out all the black dye from the cloth. Afterwards, I walked and stood within an inch of her. I looked into her eyes. And all I saw were gray eyes that reminded me of the rows upon rows of gravestones in the church cemetery in town. My chest tightened and I rubbed at it to relieve the tightness.

Since she'd gotten married, I'd seen my sister go from being fashionable slim to plump after the first two babies, to flat-tire belly and rolls a year after the twins, Teddy and Tommy.

From my point of view, this marriage had turned out to be for Juliette's worse and not her better. Maybe that's why marriage comes with the vow "for better or for worse." It's for when things get really worse; you remember it, you stay put, you fight for it. After all this was what she'd signed up for on her wedding day.

At the Adams house, it was different. I saw peace, order, companionship, friendship, and love. I noticed it flowed freely between Mr and Mrs Adams through looks and touches and acts of kindness.

In Juliette's house the stench of bitterness hung like heavy smoke in the house. It got worse whenever Timothy was present. The tension between Juliette and Timothy sucked out all the good vibes, leaving behind an atmosphere of acute tension so thick that only the sharpest butcher knife could cut through it.

This became my sister's life and I hated it for her. Every time I visited with her, I wanted to ask pointed questions to better understand what was going on with her life. But she usually retreated and resisted my nosy attempts. I always left filled with tension from her lack of response. I was concerned about her welfare and it strained our relationship. I continued to visit her because she was my family. Even though she'd point blank turned me away when Mamie threw me out.

A year after throwing me out of her house, my mother had little to say to me. I'd turned to Juliette and created the "me and Juliette against the world" sisterhood. It was only real in my head; Juliette's world had been reduced to Timothy's bitterness and anger and the needs and wants of her four children. My world was still evolving with all the uncertainties of the future. I had another year in high school to sit the CXC external exams.

The house looked like a category five hurricane had attacked. Clothes, shoes, toys were strewn like litter. The children ran, tackled each other, and threw toys and clothes, and alternated between crying, laughing and shouting. That day I had another pointed conversation with Juliette. I prayed it wouldn't be the dance of retreat and resist we had had in the recent past.

"Juliette, let's go to the living room, so we can sit and watch the children play," I said in a neutral tone. "How long have the twins been asleep?"

"Not long. I just gave them their morning bath in some Glory cider, which is why they are asleep," she said and the tiniest smile played at the corners of her mouth. My stomach tightened like a coil rope because it hit me that Juliette seldom smiled. I couldn't remember the last time Juliette wore lipstick.

"Glory cider, Juliette," I said, laughing. "That's what Mamie bathed us with when we were younger. She always said it was good for rash and heats."

"Julia, it's the exact reason I'm bathing the twins in it. We do what we learned," Juliette said. "I've found myself doing a lot of things because I observed Mamie when you were a baby," she said in a nostalgic tone.

I saw it reflected in her eyes too. A longing for when life was simpler. When we were innocent. When Daddy Julius was alive. So many things changed for us after Daddy Julius died. Juliette's predicament, orchestrated by our mother, was a direct outflow from Daddy Julius's death. An act of survival is what she had called it.

I couldn't help pointing out to Juliette her age at the time. "But you were young, Juliette. You can't possibly remember," I said, my tone playful.

"Of course I remember, Julia. I'm four years older than you. Trust me, at four years you remember things, and I was an inquisitive four-year-old," she said with a small laugh that softened her face. I saw some of her burdens, her heaviness, her concerns slip out on that laugh.

I should make her laugh more. When last did she really laugh? When was the last time she had time to catch up with herself? When was the last time she went out with Timothy and had some fun? I dismissed the questions and returned to our conversation. I felt I was making headway with Juliette.

"Yes, you kept reminding me of our age difference, every nanosecond," I said, really enjoying this playful banter with Juliette. We were seated on the stained sofa—it looked worse for wear since my last visit. It was too quiet though. Where were the kids?

Laughing in response, she said, "You were the prettiest baby I'd ever seen. I wanted to hold you all day like you were my own favourite doll. But Mamie didn't allow me to hold you. You had the longest eyelashes and perfect eyebrows. Look at you. Your eyelashes are longer, your eyebrows are so perfect they don't need to be tweezed and your signature gold eyes are bigger and brighter than mine. Tell me, sister, any man in your life?"

"Man?" I responded at high volume.

"Yes, like a boyfriend?" Juliette repeated, laughing at me. Her hands trailed through her long dull hair, and her eyes sparkled with life. And it made me hopeful. The sister who had teased me. The sister who had looked out for me. The sister who had defended me. Could she reclaim her joy?

"No, Juliette, there's no boyfriend. I'm still at school. And besides, very few of the girls in my class have boyfriends," I replied.

"I would not put too much trust in that, if I were you," she said with a smirk.

Was she trying to convey to me there were other girls like her? Other girls who'd been cast in the role of prey for economic advancement by calculating mothers.

"That's the problem; you're not me. Look at you. Where's my sister?"

"Julia, do not start with me. Tell me about your exams and the debate finals."

She stood up and walked over to the kitchen to fetch Timmy and Tammy who had been very quiet.

I jumped when Juliette shouted, "What are you all doing playing in the soap powder?" I had never heard her shout at that volume before. It forced me to my feet.

I ran to the kitchen and stopped short in the doorway. Timmy and Tammy had created a disaster zone. They both sat on the floor with the whole contents of the big bag of soap powder spread across the floor. Both of their hands were dirty white with soap powder. I picked up one on the right and the other on the left and carried them to the bathroom sink to wash the soap powder off their hands. I encountered another Mount Diablotin pile of clothes in the bathroom. I had to walk on clothes to get to the sink.

Bondyé, when is Juliette going to be able to bring this under control? What does Timothy do to help? Why doesn't she ask me to come help her more often? So many questions fuelled my desire to help, my desire to fix. But first Timmy and Tammy needed attention.

Juliette remained in the kitchen armed with a brush and dustpan she salvaged what she could of the soap powder. I washed the soap off the hands of Timmy and Tammy. They giggled and wiggled and tried to get out of my grasp the whole time. Both were oblivious to the fact they had decimated the soap powder their mother had bought for the month. And she mightn't be able to wash their clothes for part of the month. Then it hit me Juliette had not yet delivered a slap or two to their skin.

Back when I was about six years and Juliette was ten years. We tried a similar thing with our mother's white scented powder. The powder existed in the prettiest pink bowl with the prettiest pink powder puff I had wanted to claim as my own. I wanted to see it on our window ledge which had served as an extension of our dressing table. Our room had had little furniture, but it had been clutter free. Velma didn't tolerate sloths.

On the day in question, we'd contented our little hearts by taking equal turns with the pink powder puff. We lathered each other's body with powder until our skin shone white and the sweet scent of the powder hung heavy in the room. Yes, we'd taken off our clothes for the experience.

Our mother had returned home from the river, where she'd gone to wash clothes, and found us in a state of bliss revelling in the powdered perfume. And for our moment of sweet bliss, she rewarded us with strokes from the tamarind whip she'd asked Daddy Julius to prepare earlier in the week for when she needed it.

She used the tamarind whip to make dang dang on our skin and our bottom tail caught on fire. It turned out to be an afternoon we never forgot. We both cried ourselves to sleep. After that day we refused to even glance at the yellow powder dish which replaced the pretty pink one.

I brought the children to the living room and told them to sit quietly on the rug while I rounded up a few toys for them to play with. Then I sat down on the battered brown sofa. There were two holes in the faux leather cover and white stuffing flowed out of it. Juliette saw my gaze fixed on the hole and said, "Timmy was the one who did it with a nail he found while Tim was trying to fix a shelf in the kitchen."

"How, Juliette?"

"He took the nail and jabbed it into the chair multiple times, he stopped when he saw the stuffing started to come out. It seems he wanted to know what was in the chair."

"Did you beat him?" I inquired.

"No, Julia. Tim and I decided early on we wouldn't beat our children."

"But Mamie beat us all the time," I said in a matter-of-fact tone.

Why wouldn't they discipline the children?

"We talk to them and explain to them what they've done wrong."

"You really think this is going to work, Juliette? Even the Bible says spare the rod and spoil the child."

"Julia, Julia. I'm not going to raise my children with tamarind whips, broomsticks, leather straps, guava whips, electric wire, and mortar pestle. We cannot keep ourselves enslaved to the mentality of the past." Her voice rose on each word like an orator.

My sister, the orator.

"Are those your views, or Timothy's? By the way, is he helping you raise the children?" I asked with genuine concern in my voice.

"My husband and I speak with one voice. We are one parent. Not two. We will not divide and rule in our house."

"You haven't answered my question, Juliette. Is Timothy helping you? Do you know where Timothy is right now?"

"Yes, he told me this morning. He said he would be taking his woman to the village of Scotts Head to visit her family."

My jaw dropped, my eyes bulged, my throat tightened, my muscles went numb. I squeezed my eyes shut to give me time to deny the spoken words. But the words from Juliette's mouth dangled in the air between us. They refused to drop. I opened my eyes slowly to seek her eyes. What I saw caused an arctic freeze to crawl through my body. Her eyes looked away into nothing, without focus. Her cheeks were heavy and shiny. Her grey eyes had lost every spark of energy they once reflected.

I leaned against the battered chair for support and tried to quiet the rapid blinking of my eyes as I tried to process what I'd heard.

The news Timothy had a mistress was unbearable, but that he would tell Juliette where he was taking her was reprehensible. And the worst part for me was hearing Juliette repeat it with such calm. For a few moments neither one of us spoke. I looked at Juliette and Juliette looked at nothing.

"That's not all," she whispered. "The woman, she calls the house often. She tells me about Tim. She tells me what he likes. She tells me where they've been. She tells me what they've done. She taunts me. 'He no longer loves you,' she says."

"What!"

I struggled to find the right words to say to Juliette.

"Why are you allowing Timothy to treat you as if you do not matter?"

"What do you think I can do, Julia? Keep him tied to the bed. Report him to the marriage police? Report him to the priest?"

"There you have it. Report him to the priest. Let the priest hammer his obligations into his swell head until it deflates like when we pulls the plug of the innertube after we go swimming."

"Haha. He would never go to the priest. Even if he did, he would paint me as the evil wife and he the saintly husband. You know he can out-talk and out-lie even the best politicians and preachers."

"Oh, Juliette, for the sake of the children and your own sanity, you must do something. Demand that he stops. Threaten to leave if he does not stop."

"Ummmmm, not so easy, girl. Not easy at all. Tim is convinced it's his right to choose to take a mistress. He claims every married man in Dominica has a mistress."

"And you've done nothing to persuade him otherwise?" What does he mean by 'every married man?' You can't just sit there and accept this hurt from Timothy," I said, my voice rising with indignation.

How dared Timothy treat my sister like she was inconsequential? I tried to recall whether Mamie knew about this and what she had to say about all this. She started this. She had placed Juliette on this path. She made Juliette reliant on this man. And he was treating her like she was dispensable, of no value. The mother of his children. His wife.

"Listen, Julia, Tim is an adult. He is given a free will which he chooses to exercise every day. He's chosen to deliberately destroy our marriage. And there is nothing I can do to stop him from exercising his free will every day. This is my life," she says, and she went back to staring at nothing.

I struggled to comprehend the things Juliette said. I stood up. I had the sudden urge to move. My blood was boiling like the Boiling Lake in the Roseau Valley. I wanted to find out whether my movements would dislodge the heavy weight nesting at the bottom of my belly like a cast aluminium ball. But it didn't. The heavy ball moved with me. And my thoughts moved with me. I walked past Juliette with her troubled thoughts and went to stand on the porch outside.

Directly across the road I observed a house under construction. The men were shirtless, sweat running down like streams on their muscled arms. They'd formed a bucket line to pass along the concrete mixture in gray rubber buckets to pour into the prepared decking.

I watched the men work until the light started to fade and the orange-red glow; the colours of sunset, began to creep down into the edges of the Caribbean Sea. I stayed outside to delay my return to the horror of Juliette's life. I wanted to delay putting my thoughts and questions into words. I wanted to delay hearing Juliette's words in response to my questions.

The day had already wrung out of me so many emotions on behalf of my sister. How was she going to survive Timothy's betrayal, pain, humiliation, and shame?

I watched the men, and I watched the sunset, but it was the vacant stare of my sister I saw. I couldn't unsee it.

The afternoon gave way to sunset, and sunset to dusk. All the orange got erased from the sky and still Timothy didn't come home. I decided to go back in to check on Juliette. I turned the doorknob and entered the house. I didn't get beyond the doorway because Juliette had the black phone in her hand. Her lips moved but I heard no sounds. I watched her face crumple, her body turned into a chain reaction of tremors; her hand with the phone trembled like a shaking puppy.

The swell of all the emotions erupted from Juliette in a primal, piercing scream. The phone crashed to the floor with a loud clatter; the sound galvanized my feet into action. I leaped to where Juliette stood and caught her in my arms. She screamed, she howled, she blubbered. I didn't know why she was crying. The children didn't understand why she was crying. And the children and I began to cry with Juliette.

I cried from fear as I held her. I cried because the children were screaming. I struggled into a position sitting with Juliette on the floor.

Speech deserted Juliette. Incoherent sounds escaped her mouth. My pulse raced and the deep sound of my heartbeat thrashed in my ears. How was I going to save Juliette from her howls of pain?

The howling brought two of her neighbours through the door.

"What happened?" her next-door neighbour Sarah demanded. She'd come in with a lady who had the same midnight-coloured skin, thin lips and nose, and wavy black hair down her back. Most likely her daughter.

Sarah knelt beside me and said, "Juliette, what's the matter with you?" Juliette didn't respond; she only screamed louder.

I couldn't stop the shrieks of pain. I couldn't stop my own tears streaming down my face unabated. I tried to reach out again and cried, "Calm down, Juliette, calm down. Tell me what happened. She paused from her wailing long enough to murmur, "Tim is dead."

Then she threw me off her and lay prostrate on the floor and hollered, "Tim! Tim! Tim! Tim!" until her voice became hoarse with grief and tears. She lay on the floor inconsolable, moaning, and whimpering.

I became useless to Juliette and the children at that point. I was hyperventilating. Pain took over my chest, lungs, and throat.

How could Timothy be dead?

What had happened?

My thoughts raced endlessly as I struggled to make sense of the tragedy. I tried to reach out and comfort Juliette, who lay motion lesson the floor, but my arms felt heavy and my words were too weak to express what was in my heart.

Tears slid down my cheeks as I realized that there was no escaping this pain. And even as my heart broke for her, a part of me remained numb, unable to fully grasp the reality of the situation.

Thank God for Sarah. She took Tammy and Timmy to her house next door with her teenaged daughter, who had entered the house with her, to look after them. With all the wailing going on I feared the twins would wake any moment, but they stayed fast asleep.

By seven o'clock, darkness had fallen, and with the darkness, my mother arrived at the house with Aunty Maureen from Loubiere. By then the house had filled with all kinds of curious onlookers. It brought back fresh memories of the night Daddy Julius and the other fisherfolks hadn't returned from their fishing trip. I think every villager from Loubiere, and Pointe Michel had gathered around my mother, the other women and children affected by the disappearance of the men.

A wave of sadness squeezed the valves on my heart shut. There we were experiencing another outpouring of concern and of curiosity. People wanted to hear first-hand for themselves what had happened to Timothy.

Juliette lay on the floor still inconsolable, moaning and whimpering. Her head rested on the lap of Sarah who was doing a good job of rubbing Juliette's back.

When my mother came through the door, she gave the slightest turn of a glance in my direction and went to Juliette.

"Look at my daughter," she said, and her tears were already spilling out of her eyes. "Poor Juliette," she said and she enveloped Juliette in a hug and began to moan and whimper with her.

A slow anger began to burn in me while I watched mother and daughter cry for a dead man. A dead man from Juliette's own account in the last few months had done nothing but deliver sharp wounds into Juliette's heart and soul.

My mother rocked Juliette back and forth. I wondered if she would ever rock me like that again. Her one glance confirmed she was still angry with me. How would we mend this broken mother-daughter relationship-bridge? My heart suffered fresh stabs of pain as I watched my mother and sister at one in their grief over Timothy.

About twenty minutes later, my mother had sufficiently recovered to go over what had happened. She reported Timothy had gotten trapped under a landslide which came down suddenly under the cliff between the villages of Soufriere and Pointe Michel.

A voice unfamiliar to me asked, "The woman was on board?"

"What woman?" my mother asked, like she didn't know.

"You didn't know Timothy had an outside woman?" Sarah asked, her eyes widened in disbelief, and her tone was thick with accusation.

"Juliette, is this true?" our mother asked in a weak tone of voice. It was unbelievable. Of course Juliette didn't or couldn't answer. Not since Daddy Julius's death had I heard such weakness in my mother's voice. Too many shocks. Timothy's death. Timothy's marital offence. It was too much for me. It had to be too much for my mother. And the children. Dear Jesus, the children were now fatherless.

Juliette's response to my mother was to start a fresh round of primal screaming. And I wanted to join her. But I also wanted to stay alert for when the twins woke up. It was unbelievable they were still sleeping with all the commotion.

I watched the range of emotions march across my mother's face. Rage. Indignation. Shame. She looked at Aunty Maureen and Aunty Maureen looked at her. The women in the room were into full storytelling, reporting the more sordid details of Timothy's indiscretion. When my mother had had her fill of the stories, she declared, "God has seen the tears of my daughter and has delivered her from the noisome pestilence."

I looked at my mother, willing her to look at me. In Juliette's small living room with ten other women my mother refused to meet my eyes. She refused to acknowledge my presence. She continued to act like there was no second daughter in the room.

I wanted to ask her if she felt comfortable knowing the part she played in setting Juliette on this path to pain. The question lodged itself in my mind, but my mouth refused to cooperate to let the question escape. My mother who'd thrown me out of her house for my new faith had uttered words from the Bible as a vindication for Juliette's delivery.

Juliette's predicament was the result of our mother's orchestration of the relationship with Timothy. How could she ignore the vast changes Juliette underwent in four years?

How could she ignore the pain Juliette's eyes reflected?

I knew Juliette was not okay. That was so apparent when I stayed with them after the twins were born. Timothy's behaviour had been so reprehensible, and then to find out it was because he'd been cheating the whole time . . .

How was it possible my mother, Aunty Maureen, and Ma Titre had no knowledge of Timothy's cheating? It was impossible. Someone knew. Someone knew and never intervened. They kept silent. The same silence they'd kept with Annya's story. They'd sat back in silence and allowed Cheryl to bring Robert to live with her again.

A fresh wave of disappointment, discouragement, and anger at the adult women in the room raced through me. Maybe my young idealistic mind didn't grasp yet why certain decisions were made.

Why the women had unseeing eyes. Why the women never uttered some stories. Why the women buried stories deep in the ground. Why the women forgot certain stories. Maybe I wasn't like these women. I'd never forgotten Annya. I'd never forgotten that beast of a man. What he did to Annya. What he did to me. The skin on my face heated up as the memories crowded out the day's events.

And then a deep sense of shame lacerated my heart. I wasn't different. Yes, I remembered. But I'd stayed silent too. We were all united in the sisterhood of silence. Silence the pain. Silence the shame. Silence other people knowing. Except the gold standard of silence could not exorcise the pain. And so, we lived life like we had no pain.

A moment later I brought myself back to contemplate my mother's response. With one quotation of a Bible verse she attempted to absolve herself of any moral responsibility. It was all God's doing. I gathered some strength from deep within and prayed from my heart for God to begin mending Juliette's brokenness.

Much later that night, I had lost count of the many people that came through the house to stare at Juliette and to offer their condolences. People came from all over the island. People Timothy worked with. People Timothy had gone to school with. Even people from Delices made it to the house that night.

Through all of it Juliette never stopped bawling. I was amazed at her capacity for grief. I wondered at the source of her tears, recalling the conversation we'd had earlier in the day. I couldn't understand why her tears would not cease.

As if on cue, every half hour our mother joined the chorus of grief. The loud sounds of wailing rose like a mournful symphony. It was as if every half hour the chorus knew it needed to let loose with one more decibel of sorrow before falling silent. And my mother was the most skillful instrument, her voice rising higher than any others in the chorus. The sound shook me to my core, and I was torn between wanting to join in their grief and running away.

At about nine o'clock someone suggested they should take Juliette to the hospital so they could give her something to put her to sleep. The person was neither a doctor nor a nurse, but my mother and Maureen happily pounced on the suggestion. Sarah's husband, who had been keeping guard by the door and who was reported to have been one of Timothy's party buddies, volunteered to drive them to the hospital.

Four hours later they were not back from the hospital. The crowd had thinned to the next-door neighbours. My eyes were pregnant with sleep, and I felt like an alien on its first visit to earth. Although we had been down this territory of loss as a family, this one felt unfamiliar in its intensity.

In addition, I was just scared for Juliette. Juliette, left behind with four children. Juliette who had never worked since she left high school. Juliette who'd lost all desire for higher education. Juliette without dreams.

I felt the gulf widen between the axes of my life and Juliette's with each passing year of her marriage to Timothy. With each birth of a child.

What was she going to do? Did she have any desire, drive, dreams? She would need these three to create a new life for her and her four fatherless children.

I couldn't help myself. I was already an overthinker at seventeen. Everyone said I was too wise for my age. I don't know why, but I contemplated things. I read too much, my friends and classmates accused.

But there was so much to learn wrapped up in books. I cracked every book open to learn something new. And that's how I came to have so many questions about the many unknowns Juliette would face.

All the children were asleep, and I longed to crawl into the bed with them and never come out again. Life was cruel. Life was so uncertain. Life had thrown this tragedy at Juliette, and for what? I wondered. Juliette—widowed at twenty-two, with four children under the age of five, and jobless. I closed my eyes, and I asked God, "Why Juliette? Why now? Why like this?" There was no answer, and so I prayed on.

"Father, I ask you tonight to dry up the tears from Juliette's eyes. I pray you will heal her of every shred of guilt and shame. Mend her broken heart and restore her soul. I pray for a double portion of strength for her to get her through this difficult time. Father, I ask that you use this time of loss to reconcile me with my mother. Melt the hardness in my mother's heart. Turn her heart of stone into a heart of flesh. I pray your hands will continue to rest on and protect Timmy, Tammy, Teddy and Tommy. In Jesus's name I pray. Amen."

I opened my eyes the moment the front door swung open and the entourage from the hospital came through. Juliette was no longer crying but her eyes looked like they would shut down at the slightest movement. Aunty Maureen led her to her bedroom Like an obedient child, Juliette followed all the instructions my mother and Aunty Maureen doled out to her. She got on the bed, closed her eyes, and fell asleep. And didn't ask about the children.

Four days later. The grieving widow, the mother-in-law, relatives of the deceased, friends and onlookers gathered in numbers in black and white at the church in Delices.

For some unknown reason Juliette convinced everyone that Timothy would have wanted to be buried on the land his grandfather had given him. His grandfather had been his only family for most of his teenage years after his grandmother died. Timothy's father had died in an accident and his grief-stricken mother had run away to Guadeloupe to drown her sorrows and never once returned to Dominica. It was rumoured that she was in France, married with a family of four children, but had never seen fit to write, visit, or send for Timothy in Dominica. He was dead and no one reported a word from her.

Timothy, being unknown to the priest, got a quick and dry service. But Juliette unloaded a fresh stream of tears and wails during the eulogy.

Earlier there had been a brief battle between our mother and Juliette over whether the children should attend the funeral service; Juliette won that battle. Each child was dressed in black and white, miniatures of their parents, one of whom lay dead in the coffin at the front of the church.

During the service I thought about Timothy and whether he'd had the chance to repent before he drew his last breath. No one could say with certainty whether he had or not. No one could say with certainty whether he was in heaven or hell.

An hour later Timothy's body had been lowered into the ground on Timothy's inherited estate at Delices. His young life had been cut short, suddenly and without remedy.

I held the twins while the grave diggers lowered the purple coffin into the ground and the loud wails of their mother turned on my tears and the tears of every mourner gathered around Timothy's final resting place.

Two weeks later Juliette experienced a total breakdown and had to be hospitalized for weeks. This forced our mother to move into the house to take care of the children. I waited for my mother's call to help, but it never came. And I descended into my own despair, desperation, and depression.

13

A Rite of Passage

(June-July 1989)

G raduation was memorable beyond words. However, for me it comprised the joy of achievement and the despair of loss. Lost were my mother, Daddy Julius, my father. The invitation I'd sent to my mother via Juliette remained unopened on the table, Juliette had reported. I thought of Daddy Julius who would have attended my graduation if he had been alive. I thought of my father and my heart stopped. I couldn't handle the pain of his loss. The chance to know him had been snatched away in the cruellest way.

The first week in July 1989 I marched down the red-carpeted aisle with my graduating class into the People's Action Centre. We marched past the rows of black cushioned seats. My chest grew tight during the march. Even though I'd heard from Juliette that my invitation remained unopened, I'd hoped my mother would come.

I scanned the rows of well-dressed people talking quietly to their neighbours behind their white programs with purple tassels. She hadn't come. And my heart dropped to my belly. After that I averted my eyes and kept them trained on the stage draped in heavy red curtains until we stood in neat rows to take our seats near the stage.

I arranged my brown robe with the gold lapel and settled into the soft cushion. One hundred of my schoolmates surrounded me. But I felt alone, abandoned. Maybe she read my thoughts, for Gina grabbed my sweaty palm and squeezed it. I felt reassured and I turned and gave her a weak smile and stretched my eyes to keep my tears in their ducts.

I didn't want to cry.

I brought my attention back to the graduation ceremony.

Each step my schoolmates and I had taken over the last five years had brought us to this final act. We would receive our certificates stating we had met the graduation requirements of the school. We had been engaged in this fight to the finish. I should qualify that some of us had been more engaged than others. Many of my classmates and schoolmates had been content to coast along taking the easy way out for everything.

I had been to the last four graduations because graduation day was also the day that students who had earned a place on the prize list received their prizes. Over the past years I'd received a purple mesh diary, a Parker pen, a dictionary, a Thomas Hardy book. These were part of my fond memories of having been in high school.

The graduation was a time for speechifying, so we suffered through the speeches of the principal, the education minister, and the guest speaker, who spoke on our theme "Aim High to Achieve."

Mr Byron John, a past student and a practising attorney, had a few words of wisdom to share with us. "You must not be afraid of aiming high. I know 'the sky is the limit' is a cliché, but it is true. The sky is indeed your limit, and you must aim to reach the sky. Have a five-year plan and a ten-year plan and list all the things that you want to accomplish.

"Of course, you can adjust those plans as the years go by as things will change and your perspectives will change with time. But start with a plan and stick to it as much as possible." Then at the end of his speech he said, "I have two words for you that will always allow you to achieve: determination and discipline. Write it on your hearts. Write it in your notebooks. Write it on your walls. That's how important these words are as you aim high to achieve."

At the end of his speech Mr John received a standing ovation. The only standing ovation. His speech had colour, relevance, and wisdom. I remember nothing of the other speeches. I understood that graduation was less about the students and more a time for the school to parade its successes. To show off what it had achieved over the school year. To show off its connection to high-profile past students. To show off its academic superstars who would receive token prizes.

The most important part of the ceremony was when each graduate got to participate in the ceremony by receiving the graduation certificate. One by one we went to the podium for our certificates. I was the third person on the alphabetical list from my class to receive my certificate. With a heart heavy like a crocus bag filled with sand, I walked the stage to receive my certificate from the minister of education, my eyes bright with the tears which threatened to fall. I fought back the tears, shook the minister's hands, took the certificate, and posed for my photograph. My high school journey was wrapped up for me.

I should have been filled with the thrill of anticipation and the joy of completing. But I couldn't shake off that my mother hadn't shown. Each step I took back to my seat, the dagger sank deeper into my heart. The pain stole my breath and brought tears to my eyes during the ceremony.

Then I remembered what I'd purposed in my heart on the day my mother had kicked me out of her house. This was another rung on the emotional ladder to climb. I bargained with myself. *If I get through this then I can get through the next set of challenges coming my way.* I'd proved I had the resolve.

Time would tell if my strategy was foolproof.

It consoled me that Juliette had come for me, and the Adams family. Back in my seat, I watched the rest of my class and the other graduates receive their certificates.

I'd received my last set of graduation prizes; the prize for English, Principles of Accounts, Social Studies, Office Procedures and the Academic Excellence prize for my class. I also received a prize for Debate and a prize for leadership ability. It was seven prizes in total. Gina walked away with the prizes for all the science subjects and Gloria received the prizes in History and Geography.

Between the three of us we left our graduation from high school loaded with prizes. From the feel and shape of my wrapped prizes, I guessed they were books and pens.

Once the ceremony was over, we smiled and posed for over a hundred photos, creating memories to last our lifetime. Mr Adams came armed with his Canon camera and we ended up with two albums of graduation photos. My graduation day turned out to be the most photographed day of my life.

I was glad this aspect of my journey was over and that I could move on to putting down on paper my five-year plan as Mr John, our guest speaker, had admonished us to do. I had a future to plan and I wanted to get on with it with haste.

A week after our graduation ceremony.

A moonlit night provided the perfect backdrop for our graduation ball. The girls and I had spent the entire day primping for the biggest social event of our lives. A night that would only be eclipsed by our wedding days. Our dress designs came straight off the pages of Teen Magazine, brought to life by the finest seamstress on the island, Miss Myrna.

When we got up on the morning of the graduation ball, none of us had a finished dress. Miss Myrna had not finished our dresses after promising Mrs Adams many times she would get our dresses the day before the graduation ball.

Over and over Mrs Adams had said to us, "Girls, you will get your dresses for the graduation ball, but it will most likely be on the day of the ball." I hadn't believed her. I wanted my dress the day before so I could try it on. I had wanted to walk back and forth in front of the mirror.

Panic flooded our faint hearts the day of the graduation ball. There were no dresses in sight. At seven o'clock in the morning, Mrs Adams gave in to three panicky teenagers and left alone for Miss Myrna's overstuffed shop on King George V Street. We refused to go.

I refused to spend the morning watching Miss Myrna's heavy leg press down on the black foot pedal without mercy. Nor had I wanted to watch her two ancient nervous assistants iron or sew on buttons or decorations on the dresses.

It would have been too frustrating to watch while the dress came together one cut at a time. Instead, we spent the morning primping our hair and painting our toes and our fingernails. It was 2:30 when Mrs Adams returned home with our dresses. "What took you so long?" Gloria and Gina squealed together. "Yes, why so long? It's almost time for the ball," I added.

"Girls, girls, girls, patience. Have you learnt nothing about patience? Remember, Miss Myrna is seamstress to the stars."

"What stars, Mama," Gloria asked. "There are none in Dominica."

"Come, Gina. Miss Myrna is in high demand. Every wedding and queen show, she designs and makes the dresses. Many of her dresses have won 'best evening wear' over the years. She also makes school uniforms by the tons. There is a long waiting list. When I arrived at her shop at eight o'clock this morning, she'd already finished two of your dresses, so I sat out and waited for the third one."

"Thank you, Mamie," we all said together, and laughed.

"I have never seen you girls so excited; not even after your win over Kane and Abel were you so high-spirited."

Eager to try on the dresses, we grabbed them and ran to our bedroom to change. I didn't care if Miss Myrna was a seamstress to the stars, I only cared if my dress actually fit me.

Black, gold and white were the base colours for our ode to sophistication. Gina tried on her black dress with a V-neck plunge with thin shoulder straps and a gathered band of gold around the waist. Her dress had a short-sleeve gold waistcoat to go over it. She tried it on, and it fitted perfectly.

Gloria and I were in a hurry and with haste we donned our gowns. Gloria's was a gold top with short puff sleeves and the same V-neck of Gloria's dress with a two-tiered layered black skirt. My dress was white with flyaway sleeves and the signature V-neck with a gathered black band around the waist and a black and white rose on the left hip of the dress.

We were young, bright, and carefree. We twirled around the room admiring our dresses and our youthful figures in the full-length mirror which took up a wall in the living room.

"Do you think our dresses are good enough for tonight?" Gloria asked. The three of us stood in front of the mirror to examine whether our outfits met the sophisticated criteria. I'd piled my hair high on the centre of my head with tendrils of curls dropping to my shoulder. Gina had chosen a pin-up wrap with curls falling on her right and left ears. Gloria looked very different with her million wavy curls.

"Hello. Is this us?" I said.

"No, these are the girls that have invaded our bodies for today," Gloria supplied with a giggle. Gina and I joined in and we doubled over in laughter.

At six o'clock we were ready. But the graduation ball was more than an hour from starting time. We were advised to be in place by quarter to seven so we could be organized on the receiving line to be accepted and greeted by the President of Dominica.

Gina, Gloria and I were all dressed up and dateless for the graduation ball. We'd chosen to go without dates, partly because there were hardly any boys in our class, and probably only two had planned to attend the ball. It wasn't just the boys; more than half of the girls in our class also hadn't planned on attending.

Gina often said that our class had too many special people who had no interest in what was going on around them. I believed that most of the people in our class and school were constrained by lack of money and lived too far away to make it to the ball in town.

When we got there, a line of cars and dozens of giggling teenage boys and girls had converged on the Waterfront Hotel for the joint graduation ball. Unsurprisingly, we were not the only unattached attendees at the ball.

The student organizers soon had all the unmatched boys and girls matched up for the receiving line. I ended up with a boy named Hugh from the Saints High School. A basketball player with long arms and longer legs. When he smiled his teeth shone like white pearls.

We got in line in front of Gina who'd been matched with a boy named Mark, also a basketball player from the same school as Hugh. At the back of us was Gloria with Felix, another basketball player. It turned out to be our night to hang out with the stars of high school basketball.

Soon it became our turn to greet the President. He smiled at us warmly and shook our hands and told us to enjoy our time at the ball. After, we walked to the reception area. Silver and white balloons hung from the ceiling. The focal wall behind the head table for dinner was covered with more sliver and white balloons in a recurring pattern.

Every table had white and silver anthuriums in a clear crystal vase. White tablecloths adorned each table, and the place settings were all perfectly arrayed silver. The setting was a historic moment for me, and I savoured the beauty of the room and of the moment. That night was the last chance to celebrate and leave behind high school desires and dreams.

We went through the three-course meal oohing and ahhing over everything. We had been warned to stay away from wine, so we only had a touch of champagne.

It seems that Gina could not tolerate even a touch of champagne for she was all giggly from the moment the champagne touched her lips. Every word that Mark leaned over and whispered in her ears was punctuated with peals of laughter.

Gloria and I looked at each other with raised eyebrows each time. The guys appeared to be oblivious. They were certainly not watching their liquor content, probably because they did not have parents like Mr and Mrs Adams to impose the "no drinking" rule on them.

Of course, we would never tell that we had broken the rule. By the time we had our touch of champagne, Mark was already on to his third glass.

By the time we got to dessert, I had stopped enjoying the evening. Turned out to be coconut ice cream served with bread pudding and black fruit cake. My three favourite desserts. It was so delicious we went back for two servings. There was some rum in both the fruit cake and the bread pudding; add that to the earlier touch of Gina's champagne and we ended up with Gina falling over with unbridled laughter. She started whispering into Mark's ear, and he responded falling over with laughter.

From that point in the evening, I had a hard time concentrating on anything that Hugh was trying to say to me because I was too busy watching Gina and Mark.

Once dinner was over, we three excused ourselves from the guys and went to the bathroom to freshen up. Every girl at the ball must have had the idea at the same time because there was a long snaking line to the bathroom. We waited in line about fifteen minutes to get in. The bathroom was adorned with white and silver balloons and there was a vase on either end of the counter with silver and white anthuriums. When I emerged from the bathroom, I met Gloria at the mirror reapplying her lipstick. We looked at each other through the mirror and laughed.

"You're having a good time so far?" I asked Gloria.

"Sure," she replied. "I noticed you were enjoying your date."

"What's not to enjoy?" I cackled. "Did you see those teeth? They are so white and perfect they belong in a toothpaste commercial."

"Where is Gina? Did she go out already?" Gloria searched the crowd of girls around us at the mirror, but she was nowhere. "Do you think the champagne has gotten to Gina's head or is it Mark who has gotten to her?"

"I think it's the champagne," I replied without hesitation. "We need to watch out for her."

"You think that's necessary, Julia? Gina can handle things. Besides, Mark looks harmless."

"I saw Mark drink several glasses of champagne."

"These boys are not like us, Julia. They are not sheltered little boys. They are the stars of the basketball team. Handsome. Charming. Full of vigour and strength."

"Please stop, Gloria. This is not the time to be writing the opening lines for a Mills and Boons romance novel."

"Mills and Boons? What are those? Never heard of them," she said, unable to contain the small smirk she'd intended. It grew into a wide smile that softened and brightened her eyes.

"Remember the time principal, Mr Langlais, caught you with one inside of your Integrated Science text? What did he say to you?"

"'Put that trashy book away, Miss Adams. You're supposed to be reading your textbook quietly. You're not going to learn anything from that trashy book.'"

The memory was so hilarious—or maybe it was our touch of champagne—Gloria and I gushed into peals of laughter and left the bathroom in search of our dates and Gina.

We found our dates moments after leaving the bathroom. When I asked for Gina and Mark, they said that they had not seen them, and they must be around somewhere. I was a little concerned at the answer, but we soon fell into crowd-gazing and talking and laughing to each other. The floor had been cleared for dancing, but no one was dancing.

Everyone stood around the square floor waiting for one brave couple to grace the dance floor first. I was nervous at this point because it was three years since I'd last danced with anyone. I stopped going to fetes, block-o's and jams after I became a believer. I looked around the room comparing dresses and hairstyles and shoes.

Some girls were wearing too much makeup and looked much older than their seventeen years. Others were wearing shoes that were way too tall, so they hobbled around all night looking nothing like the graceful ladies they wanted to be. Yet others were in dresses that were too tight and revealed too much flesh so they looked like ordinary street girls out in a carnival band.

I couldn't say much about the boys; they all looked handsome in their black jackets and pants. Most of them had worn ties, and a few had on bow ties. But I could count on both hands the guys who were from our school—Grammar High School.

The Saints High School dominated the ball scene with the girls from the All Girls' High School. The Valley High School and the Hillsborough Girls' High School also had poor showings.

After I'd had my fill of looking around, there was still no Gina and Mark in sight. I got worried and decided to go in search of them. I stole away from the crowd and went towards the back of the hotel.

It was there I discovered not everyone at the ball was interested in people-gazing. Much more was going on at the back of the hotel. I saw several couples engaged in various intimate poses—arms around necks and waist, lips glued to lips.

I walked faster and scanned the area with radar eyes looking for Gina and Mark. And at the same time I was praying that I would not find them draped around each other like these careless couples in the dark.

It wasn't until I reached the darkest corner of the hotel that I found them. Gina and Mark—locked in an intimate embrace. His hands were caressing her backside and her head lolled on his shoulder as if in a dream, oblivious to the hands fondling her behind.

I screamed, "Gina!" and pulled her away from Mark. Gina stumbled into my arms like a drunken woman.

"Gina, Gina," I said and grabbed her shoulders and shook her.

"What's the matter, Julia," she said. Her eyes showed just a slit of white. Her lipstick had smudged.

"Hey, Julia, nothing happened here. We were just chilling," Mark offered in defence.

I bared my teeth and said, "Chilling? Then your hands should have been chilling too. Looks to me like they were raising up a storm."

He lifted both hands, and smiled at me. "See, they're chilling." My nostrils flared and I shook my head and pulled Gina away. I was not going to be able to deal with the cute basketball player who was accustomed to getting his way with the girls.

I found Gloria and gave her a shortened version of how I'd found Gina. I left out the part about his roving hands. I told Gloria that we needed to call her parents to come get us.

"But they will find it strange that we are calling to come home before our midnight curfew," protested Gloria.

"Look at Gina. She looks like she is ready to fall asleep. We need to take her home."

"What are we going to tell them?"

"We will tell them we took a touch of the champagne but it looks like Gina could not handle the amount."

"Are we sure she didn't have more?"

"Look, we don't know, so we only tell what we know. Remember, all three of us had a touch."

We made the call home. Mr Adams answered and sure enough he wanted to know why we wanted to come home an hour early. I told him it was dancing time and that we were not into it and really wanted to just come home."

It was enough to get him out of the house to come fetch us.

Our big night out. Our first night to stay out till midnight. But we were begging to come home. I held up Gina as best as I could while we waited for Mr Adams to show up. Hugh and Felix had followed us out and apologized for the behaviour of their friend.

They were embarrassed at what had happened and they waited with us in the dark chilly night. When Mr Adams got there, I hurriedly pushed Gina into the back seat and Gloria jumped in the front talking with excitement over what we had done and seen at the ball. While Gloria chatted, Gina fell asleep on my shoulder. Mr Adams must have observed us in the rear-view mirror. His question boomed in the car.

"Why is Gina asleep and you, Julia, are like silent night at the back there."

"Oh, Mr Adams, I'm tired," I mumbled. "As for Gina, she's totally out." I hated lying to Mr Adams, but I also wanted to protect Gina from any repercussions. And I knew Mr Adams would be disappointed in not just Gina, but also Gloria and me. So, I lied to protect all of us.

"Are you sure? You guys didn't dance? You all drank anything?"

From there, silence reigned in the car until we got home.

Mr Adams waited until we were safely ensconced in the living room to speak again. He asked each of us to take a seat and went to get Mrs Adams. Gloria looked at me and I looked at her. Eyeball to eyeball we reminded each other of the story we'd agreed to tell. Only the facts known to us. There was no place for conjecture or speculation. Gina had dozed off in the chair, oblivious to the fact she was home.

"Gloria and Julia, please tell us why we have a sleeping beauty on our hands tonight. What happened at the ball?" Mr Adams asked, and settled himself into the armchair, stretching out his long legs. Mrs Adams was rubbing the sleep out of her eyes when she sat down in the chair next to him.

"The truth is, we had a touch of the champagne that was served to everyone," I mumbled.

"Can you speak up, Julia. I barely heard a word you just said."

"We had a touch of champagne."

"A touch of champagne. What does that mean?"

"We only touched the champagne to our lips," Gloria responded.

Mr Adams leaned forward and said, "You only touched it to your lips? You all expect us to believe that? We were once young. Seriously, we are very disappointed in all of you. Look at Gina. She has no idea what is going on. Am I to believe that Gina only had a touch of champagne?"

"Yes, she did. We were all sitting at the same table. We took the touch together," I said.

"I heard you the first time, Julia. But you have broken our trust. We trusted you to obey our no alcohol rule. No alcohol meant exactly that. Not a touch, not a taste, and not a tittle. What of your testimony? Did any of you think about this tonight? Look at Gina," he said again.

Gloria and I hung our heads in shame. We had disappointed our parents. Mr Adams's reaction confirmed my earlier resolve; I dared not tell them how I'd found Gina. It wasn't my proudest moment—lying by omission. But I couldn't convince myself that it wasn't the right thing to do. I doubted if Gina would herself remember when she woke up tomorrow.

Mr Adams had to carry Gina to her bed, his disappointment heavy in the air between us. But the way he expressed his disappointment was mild to how my mother would have responded. He'd sentenced us to a week of working all day in the shop by ourselves. Neither Gloria nor I raised any protest.

We accepted our punishment, which wasn't really a punishment, except we'd have to learn to make decisions on the spot. It would be an opportunity to prove that we were becoming responsible young adults. Both Gloria and I tossed and turned because we couldn't fall asleep; the excitement of the night was still buzzing in our blood. We repeated the promise to keep our lips sealed on what had happened at the ball.

There you go again, Julia, promoting the sisterhood of silence. It was my last thought before I fell into a restless sleep.

The month of August brought our CXC results.

I became restless the moment I heard on WBS radio that our results were on Island. I didn't sleep the night I heard the news. I watched the tiny hands on the poppy-red clock on the dresser until daybreak.

When we made our way to school to collect our results slips, the secretary's small office was filled with students and parents waiting to get their results. A lot of the faces of my schoolmates looked morose. My pulse accelerated and my stomach churned. I wanted to turn and run away.

I looked in the staff room and there were no teachers about. Only nervous students strolled the compound.

Gina, the confident one, was the first to enter the office and collect her slip. When she removed the staple and read the slip, she lifted both arms in the air and said, "Yes, yes. I did it. Thank you, God."

Then Gloria went. She came out of the office with the slip, opened it, then jumped off the walkway onto the grass and did a little dance. By that time, they'd attracted a crowd who wanted to know their results.

Then it was my turn. I should have been confident that my results would be good. My future rested on those results. I had studied harder than Gina and Gloria for those exams.

I walked to the office on wonky legs to Mrs Paris, who'd been our school secretary for our five years at the Grammar High School. She always had a kind word for me and a smile to go with it. Today she had the broadest smile I'd ever seen on her face in the five years I'd known her.

"Congratulations, Julia," she said. You have done our school proud. Here are your results."

When I opened the slip, I stood for a long moment and stared at the results. Out of the seven subjects I had sat, I had gotten five ones and two twos at the general level. I remained immobilized and read the results again.

I became so overwhelmed with joy I collapsed into the old orange plastic office chair. I burst into tears of joy. I'd come this far only by the grace of God and because the Adams family had opened their home to me.

Mrs Paris came around her desk and hugged me. That only made me cry more. I cried because my mother was not here with me to rejoice with me. When Juliette's results had come, my mother had gone to collect them. Juliette had been swollen with child at the time and had refused to go. My mother had willingly gone, and had returned home rejoicing.

There would be no such rejoicing for me. There would be no smiles. She would look at the results and hand them back to me without a smile. I was certain that would be the fate I'd face if I had the opportunity to show her my results at Juliette's house. It was the only place I saw her. And she usually walked out of the room when I attempted to communicate with her. The thought depressed me so much I cried harder.

Mrs Paris left and came back with Gina and Gloria.

They sat on either side of me, and rubbed my back until they too started to cry. We made quite the spectacle that day before our school mates.

It was our principal, Mr Langlais, who broke up the crying; he took me into his office. I emerged ten minutes later all smiles on, ready to face the new world awaiting me.

I was done.

This was the culmination of the five years we'd spent at the Grammar High School. The many lessons, books, detentions and merits were all training to get us to our CXCs, which would determine the rest of our lives. This premise was drummed into our heads by our teachers.

Would this premise hold?

I would find out in the next two years.

14

A Brush With Love

(1989-1990)

Thursday afternoons meant worship practice at church, which meant I got to spend time with some of my favourite church people at the Temple House of Worship . . . and my favourite worship director.

One Thursday night, our worship director, Joshua Joseph—the soul and energy of the group—invited the group out to the Bamboo Tree Restaurant to celebrate his acceptance into Bible School. We were a group of ten and had climbed into the back of Ron's pickup—he was the group's drummer—for the short trip to town.

On Great George Street, the major artery leading out of Roseau, was the Bamboo Tree Restaurant. It had a glass façade and arched bamboo decor framing the door. The restaurant had celebrated its opening three months before the night we visited. It became popular among the younger generation for its chicken and chips and its burgers, which was the exact reason for Joshua's choice.

Joshua had chosen the perfect night to visit, as well. We were the only guests when we arrived. At the door, a waitress, dressed in a pencil-thin black skirt and white shirt printed with pale khaki and green bamboo stripes, greeted us with a dazzling hundred-watt smile. She led our party of ten over to two tables which she pulled together herself, refusing the help of the guys.

By the time we'd settled into our seats, I was breathing in the faint aroma of bay leaf wafting through the air. I liked its understated sweetness. It was the first time I had experienced it in a restaurant. A popular jazz tune floated out of hidden speakers throughout the dimly lit room.

Once we were seated, Joshua said to the waitress, "Looks like we're your first guests for the night."

She turned to him and beamed a smile. "You could say that. We're quite happy to serve you tonight. My name is Miska and I will be your server. Let me get the menu. I'll give you a few minutes and I'll return to take your orders," she said in a soft, clipped accent which sounded foreign to me. I tried but couldn't place her accent to a village in Dominica.

When Miska returned with the promised menus, each person studied it as if for an exam.

"I think I already know what I want," Joshua announced. "I come here for the smoking hot and spicy creole chicken wings. They are perfectly seasoned with an array of local seasonings and the right amount of hot *piman*."

"I bet you do," said Ron, in his usual playful and teasing tone. "You do love your pepper all the time."

"Well, the pepper definitely spices things up and I love that," Joshua replied. "I like my food hot and spicy." And everyone laughed.

"I must say, practice tonight went beyond the normal. Ron, the drums were rocking; you are letting go and letting God lead in the practice. Kurt and Moses, you guys continue to do wonders on the keyboard. I really appreciate you. Jason, you're the man. You control that bass guitar with dexterity. I really do appreciate you guys.

"Your commitment to God and to music is having a positive influence on the worship experience. As for you ladies, your beautiful voices lifted in praise has moved worship to a different level. Two years ago, when we started the worship team, there were many grumbles. People had been accustomed to having one song leader. A few persons threatened Pastor Stewart they would leave the church if he persisted with changing things. And some did leave."

"What was the root of the resistance?" I asked Joshua.

"It's people being resistant to change, Julia. People do not like change when they are comfortable. Several persons felt there was no reason to get rid of the single song leader format. 'Why change the established practice?'"

"But there is so much depth and diversity added to the service as a result of the current approach to worship," Ron said.

"Yes, it's true. And I think people recognize and appreciate the change. There are always people who resist just for resisting's sake. Pastor Stewart believed and held fast to this new direction that God had revealed to him.

"Some older members, like Mother Jno Baptiste and Mother Stedman, the prayer warriors, have been very supportive. As a result of our worship experience, the church is growing. People are becoming more liberated in their praise and worship. But for the church to get to that truly liberated level, the worship team must get there first. The question I want each of you to ask yourself is, what is the quality of my personal worship?"

Stacia, the most recent addition to the worship team, asked the question on everyone's mind that night. "What will happen to the team when you leave for Bible School? You are the pillar of the team."

"I may be a pillar, but I'm not the foundation of the team. Remember, who sets the foundation, also sets the leader. One of you will be raised to be the leader."

He looked first at Stacia, then Meredith, Elsie, and Nina, and finally his eyes rested on me for a few seconds more than was comfortable for me.

He had been doing that a lot lately. He would look at me like a man deciding whether to plummet down a deep well. Within those few seconds I sensed he was trying to transmit to me an unknown message. He shifted his eyes, and I puffed out a tiny trail of air in relief.

I'd trailed off—my mind wondering what was behind Joshua's furtive looks. How had I known he was always looking at me if I wasn't doing the same? Something unknown wrapped and coiled itself in my belly, and it scared me enough to return to the group conversation. I came back to the group in time to hear Joshua pronounce, "Plus, before I go away there is still time for the group to learn how to regroup once I leave, which is months away."

At the end of his statement, Miska appeared and took our orders. Everyone ordered what Joshua assured us were the best chicken wings in Dominica, along with some fries and coleslaw. While we waited for the food to arrive, we talked about the group, the direction we wanted to go, the new initiatives Pastor Stewart had set to accomplish, and then to matters of the heart. We were all young and filled with a lot of youthful desires and energy.

"Joshua, do you plan to find your wife before or after you come from Bible School," asked Meredith, a long-standing worship leader in the church.

"Why are we starting with me?" Joshua asked. "But I have to be honest here; I think I've found my wife already."

"What!" erupted around the table. Everyone looked at each other with enquiring glances and then turned to Joshua for the answer. Joshua shook his head, waved his right hand and refused to say any more on the matter.

My curiosity had been piqued. I mentally canvassed the young ladies in the church. I started with those at the table. Meredith, I decided, was too old, she was almost thirty. Elsie and Nina were younger than me. Stacia was too flighty to be a pastor's wife.

And me; my immediate plans were to go off to university A levels. My mentor, Adrian Hill, a chartered accountant, had mapped out a plan for me to achieve my goal. It included me applying for scholarships and financial assistance. He was helping me by tutoring me and paying for my scholarship applications and exams. I was so relieved I didn't have to look to Mr and Mrs Adams. They had gone beyond kindness to take me into their home. They had provided a safe place to thrive. I liked Joshua, but I considered myself out of the running for the post of wife. And the post of pastor's wife I'd seen was saddled with many jobs, challenges, fights . . . and, of course, joy.

Are you going to ignore the little butterflies unfurling in your stomach?

If that's what that unknown thing was, then yes I'm going to ignore it.

To stop my thoughts, I jumped into the conversation.

"Joshua, we are all curious," I said. "Don't keep us trapped in our own curious thoughts."

"I don't have to give details, Julia. As the days, weeks, and months fall into each other, the answer will reveal itself."

What does he mean?

Miska came back then with our food and the conversation turned again to food. While the others busied themselves with their hot plates of chicken wings and fries, Joshua's brown eyes met my gold eyes and lingered for a minute too long. I looked away first and re-joined the conversation.

Two weeks later, I had lunch with Joshua at *Le Bon Manje*, a tiny, homey restaurant located on Cork Street, to discuss our upcoming youth concert at church.

The interior walls of the restaurant were painted in soft pink and the exterior front wall in pale green. Joshua insisted it reminded him of a halfway ripe guava, pink on the inside but light green on the outside.

However, I wasn't impressed. The place hosted five small square tables, each with four chairs. The floor space was so limited that if I leaned towards the table beside ours, I would be able to touch it without effort. I tried to imagine the place filled with patrons.

Every customer would have to slant sideways, and press their arms against their body to get to their table. Since we were the first customers, we chose the table next to the lone window—no one would have to brush past us sideways to get to their table.

"What do they serve in this tiny pink room, Joshua?"

"The best pelau in the whole of Roseau."

"How do you know?"

"Because I have tasted every pelau in this city."

"Every one?"

"I've come very close," he said, and laughed. His laugh was always so carefree and joyous. It made me forget my sadness over my mother and the situation with Juliette and the children. It'd been a slow road to recovery for Juliette after Timothy died.

Joshua's melodious soothing voice brought me out of reverie, "Let me place our order with Joy-Ann."

He didn't wait for my response. He got up and went to the crude wooden counter and called out to Joy-Ann. Joy-Ann turned out to be tall and wide, with the whitest teeth in the darkest face. He placed our order of two pelaus and came back with an expansive grin on his face.

"What happened?" I inquired.

Laughing he said, "Joy-Ann wanted to know whether my girlfriend wanted a large or a small pelau. I told her you could only handle a small pelau."

"You did what?"

"I answered her question."

"By leaving out the important clarification."

"Perhaps I refused for a reason," he said, and looked at me with eyes that twinkled with mirth.

What did he find so amusing?

I let it go, because we were there to discuss the concert. By the time Joy-Ann brought our food we'd whittled down our to-do list in half. Joy-Ann placed two large green plastic plates with steaming heaps of pelau on the table. I looked at the green plastic plates, which were like the ones my mother owned. Imagine poor man gourmet plates in a restaurant.

Joshua's pelau looked like Morne Diablotin and mine looked like Morne Anglais. Joshua was right—the small plate was enough. I breathed in the savoury scent from the rice. The mixture of sweet peppers, spicy pepper, the chive and parsley, combined with

212 PRISCILLA J PAQUETTE

that sweet savoury scent of the burnt sugar used to colour the rice, wafted to my nostrils. I closed my eyes for a moment when the hot pelau landed on my tongue.

"Hmmm. Delicious. This has the right combination of rice, lentils and fresh seasoning, I admit, Joshua, you were right. This is the best."

"I told you," he replied with a cheeky grin.

"You—"

He cut me off. "No. It's my turn to talk. Two years into the future, Julia, where do you want to be?"

The sudden shift in the conversation stalled me a bit. But I recovered to answer without reservations, "At university."

"How will you pay for it?"

"I have a plan."

"Will you work before? Because I spent the last two years working and saving to go to Bible School."

"Really? I assumed the church would sponsor you."

"The church is not sending me, Julia. And besides, the collection is not as big as you think. Many people don't pay tithes. Sometimes it's a struggle for the church to pay utilities and the parson."

I looked up at him with widened eyes.

"Yes," he replied. "But let's get back to you. What is your plan?"

"Why don't you go first? Why are you going to Bible School?"

"It's not fair; you cannot answer a question with a question. But I will answer. I'm going to Bible school because of the call of God upon my life. I can't explain it to another, but after spending time praying and fasting about my future, this is what God confirmed in my spirit. I became a Christian five years ago at a crusade in Goodwill. I came out of A levels and went to teach as a high school teacher. One night I went to the crusade and the preacher's words spoke to me. His words convinced me I was a sinner in need of a saviour. It was a quiet conviction for me."

"Sounds very familiar to me, a mirror of my own story," I said. "The other night you mentioned you've found . . ."

"My wife. Yes," he said with a slow smile. After a moment's pause, he turned his eyes upward to the ceiling drawn by some interesting artifact that wasn't there.

Was he suddenly shy? I'd never seen a shy Joshua.

"I have found her. I can tell you're dying to know. Are you overtaken by curiosity?"

"Joshua, you're the only person I know who would use the words 'overtaken by curiosity.'"

"Why talk in clichés when the full array of the beautiful English language is available for use?"

"Only you, Joshua," I said, laughing.

"Miss Abraham, I have heard your fancy use of language on occasion," he replied.

"I'm a debater; what do you expect? However, let's get back to your question. Of course I'm curious. I'm not the only one—the others on the worship team want to know too."

"Time will reveal the person," Joshua replied.

"I don't understand the need for all this mystery."

"It's no mystery at all, Julia. No mystery at all."

Later that night at Pottersville, in our room.

Gloria snuggled under her checkered pink and brown blanket, engrossed in a book on critical thinking. It was one of our school text books we used for general paper. She had read through it once and was reading it through for a second time, for a reason that escaped me.

Gina was sprawled out on the mat doing her toenails. She was painting them in fire engine red. The scent of acetone nail polish remover floated in the room's airspace. The sea breeze blowing through the louvers had done little to diffuse the scent. In our acetone-scented room, I leaned on Gina.

"Gina, why are you painting your toenails fire engine red?"

"Because it's an expression of how I feel. Energetic. Happy to be alive. Full of energy."

Gloria chuckled from behind her book, and I lifted my head from the essay I was writing to watch Gina paint stroke by stroke with the glistening red polish. One by one each of Gina's toes emerged fire engine red.

My personal preference was for pastel colours and the near colourless nail polish. I guess I was not as expressive or energetic as Gina.

I decided to switch focus to me.

Turned out to be a classical wrong move.

"Guess who I had lunch with today," I said to the room. The energy in the room paused. Gloria threw her critical reader aside and sat up on the bed. Gina paused midair over her little toe; and a drop of fire engine red fell onto the mat.

"Oh, no," Gina groaned. "Mama is going to pop a blood vessel when she sees this."

"No, she won't," said Gloria. "That's not important. What's important here is the announcement."

"Don't keep us in suspense, Julia. Tell us. I had no idea you had a lunch date," said Gloria.

"It wasn't a lunch date. We met to discuss and plan the upcoming youth concert."

"Let me guess. His name starts with a J. J as in Joshua," Gina said with a loud snigger. She straightened her legs and lifted them off the ground to admire her handiwork—fire engine red toenails. She looked funny with her toes decorated with pieces of white toilet paper pressed between them.

"Joshua, hmmm," Gloria said. "I've noticed his eyes follow you everywhere."

"How? When? Why I'm only now hearing this?" I asked. I threw down my pen onto my book, my essay writing forgotten.

"How could you keep this from me?"

"You sound anxious. Nervous," Gloria said.

"Look at you, your cheeks are turning pink," Gina interjected.

"They always turn pink when you are nervous, excited or anxious."

I studied the animated faces of my friends. Gloria's eyes reflected hidden knowledge and Gina revelled in the sight of my pink cheeks.

"So, are you guys going to tell me what I don't know?"

"You need to tell us what's going on with you and Joshua," asked Gloria.

"Not a thing is going on," I said and picked up my pen to get back to my writing.

"You like him, don't you?" said Gina.

I stopped with my pen midway to the paper and watched as it fell from my shaking fingers. With my left I grabbed my shaking right fingers to quiet the shakes. I turned around to view the faces of my sisters. They were serious and waiting for an answer. I felt my cheeks swell like a tea bag dropped in hot water. I imagined they were no longer pink but as red as Gina's toenails.

With bravery I didn't feel, I declared, "Of course I like him. Is there anyone who dislikes Joshua?"

Gina and Gloria smirked and shook their heads.

"You get off the hook tonight, but I'll be watching you and Joshua," Gloria dead-panned.

Thankfully the stilted conversation ended then. My sisters didn't push me for more. The truth was my heart had raced with the knowledge that they'd noticed his lingering looks.

Who else knew?

Who else was watching?

I'd gotten off easy. I had noticed some of Joshua's lingering lazy looks.

All the time.

Did he really look at me all the time?

I smiled against my will, unable to still the tiny thrill of electricity running through my veins.

Thanks to my sisters, I had decided to become my own spy to discover if those looks really existed.

Was he really looking at me, stealing searching looks?

Was that my heart racing ahead of my thoughts?

Wasn't I watching him too?

I hated to admit it to myself, but it had been growing harder to stop watching Joshua. Be still my heart.

Over the course of the next two months, after each church activity, whether Sunday morning service, Sunday night service, Tuesday prayer meeting, Wednesday Bible study, Thursday worship practice, Friday youth meeting, Joshua and I lingered in conversation. We were always shadowed by Gina and Gloria who were merciless in their commentary.

The night Joshua held my hand in his slender hands outside the church doors, the girls were beside themselves. They declared us in love and on the way to the altar. I had to slow them down. But I could not slow down the *thump thump* beat of my heart every time I saw Joshua. Nor could I quell the nervous tension which invaded my body whenever he stood near me. I would step away from him. This response was triggered by my desire to protect my body. After what Robert had done to me, I hadn't let down my self awareness.

And so the night he held my hand I felt tiny tremors travel from my hand to my body, wrapping itself into new awareness. I was afraid and excited. The fear arose from the newness and the intensity of the feelings. The fear arose from the knowledge I would have to lower the walls I'd build to protect my feelings and my thoughts.

None of these concerns stopped me from doodling his name on all my notebooks during my A-level classes at the community college. I drew stick pictures of us. I daydreamed when I should have been reading and studying. If this was love then I was becoming drunk on it.

Before the talk and rumours could escalate, Joshua visited with Mr. Adams to express his interest in seeing me. He'd wanted to go to my mother, but I assured him my mother had given up her right to give permission. She still refused to see me or talk to me, not allowing me to visit her in the home I'd grown up in. The hurt in my heart remained a gaping hole. I'd gotten to a point in the journey where I'd begun to doubt whether reconciliation with my mother could close the gulf of pain.

Instead, it'd been Mr. Adams, my guardian ,my father for the last three years, who'd laid down the law. Joshua could only see me on Saturday night at our house. He came over and we played card games, dominoes, Monopoly, Snakes and Ladders, or we would watch TV.

Sometimes Gina and Gloria left us to watch TV alone in the living room and we would start out sitting on the long brown couch with space for one person between us. The space would grow smaller until our legs touched. And every time, tiny specks of heat would unfurl deep within me.

And when Joshua turned to face me, his brown eyes soft and full of deep mystery, my heart would stop for a second and then it would gallop faster than a racehorse. Those gazes didn't last long. I was fearful. I didn't want to see too much. We would go back to watching TV and chatting and would spend the rest of the night in a battle to keep our legs away from each other. Well, I would move my leg away from him. But I couldn't erase the wide grin on my face or the lightness that infused my chest.

In December 1989 I completed my first term of our A-level studies at the community college. I had chosen to do exams in Accounting, Economics, and Sociology. Gina, Gloria, and I studied like crazy for these exams, we were no longer in high school and the work was more difficult than it had been for our CXC exams. We stayed up most nights way past the midnight hour taking all the information into our heads.

On the last day of the term, we gathered with the ninety-something other students for our final ceremony of the term. At the end of the ceremony our grade slips were handed to us. Gloria as usual was the first to open her grade slip. I looked at her when she did and saw the smile spread slowly along her face.

"Wow, I passed all," she said, pumping one arm in the air.

"Let me see," Gina and I said together.

"Why don't you two open your own slips? Open yours then I will tell you mine."

I removed the staple from the paper in deliberate motion so as not to tear it. Gloria looked at me and rolled her eyes at my foolishness. My own eyes opened wide when I saw my results. I got eighty percent in Accounting, seventy percent in Economics, and sixty percent in sociology. Like Gloria I did the one arm pump in the air and added a whoop to it. Gina tore open her slip in the same fashion as her sister. I watched for the reaction in her face and was not disappointed when a big grin spread across her face.

"What did you get, Gloria?"

"I got a seventy in accounting, sixty-five in economics and sixty in sociology. What about you, Gina," she asked.

"I got seventy in accounting, seventy-five in economics and sixty-five in sociology," Gina replied.

"Good for you," I said.

"Better for you, Julia. What do we have to do to beat you?"

"Study harder."

"Yeah, right. You're naturally smarter than us."

"Is there such a thing as naturally smarter?"

"Well, you are. We study together. We put in the same hours, and you always come out ahead."

"Maybe my memory is better."

"Yes, that must be it. But now we have cause to celebrate. Let's go to Bamboo Tree Restaurant."

A brisk walk and a few minutes later we'd made our way onto one of the busiest streets in Roseau. King George V Street. I had to avoid bumping into people. Students in school uniforms dominated the sidewalks and the streets.

Vendors adorned every sidewalk, peddling apples, grapes, Starlights, Bandits, bright coloured water guns, toy revolvers, bright red cars, Christmas decorations, clothes, and all manner of household items.

Christmas was one week away. Christmas carols blared from giant black loudspeakers on the sidewalks. It was the storeowners' way of shouting out to passers-by to come shop.

I spotted Joshua, in his white shirt and brown polyester pants, walking with long strides, staring straight ahead like he was avoiding the vendors and their goodies for sale.

"Look, there's Joshua. Let's cross the road," I called out.

"Oh no," they said in concert. I didn't wait to see if they followed. I stepped into the road and almost got knocked down by a car taking the corner. "Joshua," I called. He stopped, turned around and, when he saw it was me, his face broke into a grin as wide as the Indian River. Gina and Gloria were hot on my heels, and they whispered loud enough for me to hear, "The lovebirds."

"What's up?" he said as he approached us.

"We are on our way to Bamboo Tree Restaurant. Are you on your lunch break? Come with us," I said all in one breath.

"Slow down," he said. "I still have some time on my lunch hour. I will walk with you guys to the restaurant."

By the time we got to Great George Street it was almost impossible to find a spot to put my feet. We had to take longer strides to keep up with Joshua's six-foot strides. In our way were more seasonal vendors and people getting their early Christmas shopping done, their arms overflowing with bags.

Above the noise, I asked Joshua, "What do you want for Christmas this year?"

"I have already received my Christmas. You."

Words and breath deserted me.

A line of sweat formed above my upper lip. I licked it away with my tongue. Sweat pooled in my palms, which forced me to rub them on my black skirt.

His simple and profound answer had discombobulated me.

Did he really say I was all the Christmas he wanted? I'd heard him with my ears, but my mind couldn't wrap around what it all meant.

"There must be something that you want, that you have been eyeing all year."

"Do you have money to spend," he asked me.

"I've saved up my scholarship allowance. I have a good bit of money."

"Keep your money, Julia. I have something in mind that we can do to show our growing affection for each other. It is simple. Profound. Free. Let us exchange letters on Christmas day and our current favourite book."

Amid the Christmas shoppers, this boy, almost man, I had fallen in love with wanted to exchange letters and books. How could I not agree to the simplicity of the request?

The deal was sealed by the time we got to the doors of Bamboo Tree Restaurant. As promised, Joshua left us at the door to make our way into the circus that was going on in Bamboo Tree Restaurant.

I followed Gina and Gloria through the crowd. I didn't see the Christmas decorations, the harried parents with crying children. I didn't hear the music in the background. I'd zoned out because my mind reeled with how I was going to write my first love letter.

Christmas day arrived with chilly winds. I'd woken up with a swarm of butterflies at home in my stomach. Even after I prayed, they showed no signs of leaving their temporary home.

I tried but I couldn't trick my mind to forget that I would be having lunch with Joshua and his family. I didn't know if I was ready for this step but when he'd asked me, I couldn't think of a good excuse.

Besides, he had been in and out of the Adams household, so it made sense that I should get to know his family. Under the warmth of my covers in the early hours of the morning, I'd thought about what I was going to wear, what I was going to say, and how I was going to act.

At noon, Joshua came by the house in his father's car. It was a short drive from our house in Pottersville to his house on Rose Street in Goodwill. We pulled up to a house with the most perfectly manicured croton hedge I'd seen. Ma Titre's croton hedge was a shabby cousin at best. And on either side of the walkway leading to large concrete steps were the two biggest snow-white Christmas trees I'd ever seen. Joshua led me right through the brightly decorated house to a large backyard where we found the entire family gathered for the occasion.

Joshua didn't stop walking until we reached a lady wearing a red blouse with white pants and matching red sandals. And I knew he was going to say this was his mother.

"This is my mother, Magdalene. Ma, this is Julia, who I have been telling you about."

"Child, come here," Joshua's mother said. She opened her arms wide and smiled with warmth and sincerity. I walked into her arms, and she enveloped me in the warmest hug. I wanted to stay in her warmth. The beautiful blend of florals that was her perfume added to the intimacy with which she had embraced me. She squeezed me and whispered in my ear, "No one calls me Magdalene. I'm Mags to everyone and that includes you."

And I felt right at home. Her warmth permeated right to my heart and the gaping hole in my heart got a bit smaller. And for the first time I thought maybe I would begin to get over the pain of my mother's abandonment.

"Look at you. Joshua has not done any justice describing your beauty. Your hair is so beautiful. How did you get these millions of curls? And your eyelashes—they go on forever," she said in one breathless rush.

I laughed and told her, "My hairdressers are my twin sisters. They're responsible for the millions of curls you see."

"Your twin sisters? Joshua mentioned you had one sister."

"Yes, I do have one sister. The twins are my adopted sisters. I've been living with them for the last couple years. We're the same age and at school together."

"Well, my child. I'm happy you're here. Welcome to our home. Make yourself happy. Eat and drink all you see. Come let me hug you, my future daughter-in-law."

She embraced me again and my heart soared with happiness. I felt light and energised and accepted. I loved Mags from that moment and hoped everyone in Joshua's family was just as warm and loving.

After Mags, Joshua took me on a whirlwind tour of the family. His father was a tall silent man with knowing eyes. Joshua had an older brother who had gone to university in the States and was living there. He had returned home with an American wife and the two of them held court on how great it was to be living in the United States.

His sister looked more like Joshua and was direct, firm and charming all at the same time. There were many aunts, uncles, and cousins, and two grandparents at the get-to-gether.

I'd never seen so much food in my life.

Mrs Adams normally did a large spread for Christmas with the usual ham, turkey, and chicken, macaroni pie, provisions, garden salad, and black cake.

But at Joshua's home it was more than a spread, it was a veritable feast.

One table was dedicated to every conceivable meat from chicken to mutton. Another had yam pie, breadfruit pie, banana pie, scalloped potatoes, diced sweet potatoes, provisions, rice and beans, rice and vegetables, fried plantain and some other dishes I could not name.

There was a table with red beans, pigeon peas, and four different types of salad. The dessert table was covered with black cake, sweet potato pudding, bread pudding, chocolate cake, upside-down pineapple cake, tiramisu, custard cups, banana cake, coconut cake, and even gooseberry on sticks.

And the drinks. Two of Joshua's cousins managed the bar. There was everything from sorrel to cognac. Lunch went into the night. Family came and left. Friends dropped by and left. The conversations were many and flowed throughout the day. I met so many people the names and faces became a blur to me.

At one point Joshua whisked me away to the dining room. He had carved it out as our time to share our Christmas presents. I took out my favourite book at the time—*Animal Farm*—and he placed his on the table—*The Pilgrim's Progress*.

Two very different books for two different people. They were also similar—both were allegories with dispersed themes. Mine centered on politics, choice, and equality. Joshua's cantered on faith and reaching higher heights in Christ.

"I think we should read our letters to each other," Joshua suggested.

"Now? What if someone walks in on us?"

"Do you hear them outside? No one is going to bother to come into the house. You go first."

"I pulled my pink envelope out of my bag, on which I'd sprayed a few puffs of my favourite scent." I placed the envelope underneath Joshua's nostril so he could inhale and remember the scent.

"Hmmm, nice," he said, closing his eyes.

"You open the letter, and I will read it." I had not sealed the envelope, so it was easy for him to remove the two small white pages I had written. He handed it to me, and I read the following:

Dear Joshua,

Over the last months of this year, I have come to enjoy getting to know you on a deeper, more intimate level. You are no longer Joshua, the worship leader, to me. You are no longer just my duet partner. You have become my friend and my confidant. I enjoy every moment we have spent together. The games, watching TV, sharing our dreams and aspirations, singing together, reading the Word and praying together.

I love the following things about you; your confidence, assertiveness, kindness, concern for others, your zeal to follow God's leading, your charm; your musical and singing abilities; your humility and humbleness; your tendency to put others first; your leadership capacity; your selflessness; your determination to do good and to succeed. All these characteristics make you Joshua. I pray you will never depart from these ideals, and they will be your guiding light as you move to Bible School and later on in your ministry.

You are the first thing on my mind when I wake up and the last thought when I lay my head to rest. I doodle your name all day in class on my notebooks. I see your smiling brown eyes looking at me everywhere. Joshua, you have become embedded in my heart and in my mind. When you are near, I sense it. When you look at me, I don't want to look away. When you take my hands, I don't want you to ever let it go. I could look into your eyes forever for what I see there.

When I'm in your presence, I get excited. There's a tension, a nervousness, and a feeling of belonging. It is also comfortable and peaceful. I am enjoying this journey with you. We are both young and have aspirations we want to fulfil. No matter what happens, this time with you will always have an extra special place in my heart.

Joshua, it is my pleasure to wish you a very merry Christmas this December 1989. I pray God will grant you the desires of your heart in 1990.

Your beloved,

Julia."

When I looked up from reading the letter, Joshua had a lone teardrop from the corner of his left eye. I reached and brushed it off with my finger. He held my hand and placed a kiss in the centre of it. It was a touch of his lips to my hand, but it stirred the silent embers within me.

"That was so beautiful, Julia."

I swallowed to wet my patched throat before I said, "Read yours. I can't wait." I tried not to fidget too much. My muscles were all twitchy and quivering. I willed myself to sit still while Joshua pulled a white envelope from his pants pocket. And out of the envelope he pulled a white legal size note sheet, written on front and back.

My eyes bulged wondering what he'd written in so many words. My two short sheets lay on the table as evidence I had not said enough.

Joshua caught my gaze and laughed. "I had an advantage over you; for months I have written and rewritten this letter," he said.

"I'm ready."

"Okay, here goes."

Dear Julia,

You are the most beautiful girl in the world to me. You captured my heart the moment I saw you that first Sunday at church. The desire to know you sprouted in my heart and grew and spread like grass. You became embedded in my mind.

I have watched you grow in Christ over the last few years, and you've become more beautiful each year. Your zeal is contagious. Your courage in the face of the adversity you have had to face for your faith is exemplary beyond words. Your dedication to the Lord moves my heart and the hearts of others who meet you. You are a gem. You are my rose and you are my lily. You are my fairest among women. Like Solomon I want to say "Behold you are fair, my love, behold you are fair, you have dove's eyes" (SOS 1:15).

I have enjoyed every moment I've spent with you. I live for the times we spend together in companionship. I enjoy your laughter. I enjoy your voice. I enjoy your intellect. I enjoy you. I want always to be in your presence. These past few months getting to know you on a deeper level have been very special to my heart. I look forward to every Saturday I get to spend time at your home. To see your eyes get lighter with laughter. To hear the peals of laughter from your mouth. To beat you at Monopoly and Scrabble. Thank you for the opportunity to be part of this moment in time with you. It is a time I will forever cherish in my heart.

Julia, I don't have the words to convey how special you are to me. You occupy my waking thoughts. You invade my dreams at night. You wake me up in the mornings. You invade my devotion time. I could not get you out my thoughts even if I tried.

Julia, I want you as my forever friend. I want you beside me always. I want to grow old with you. When I close my eyes, it is you I see sitting by my side, our hair grey with age and wisdom. It is what I pray and fast for fervently every week. I say this not to scare you but to let you know how deeply I feel.

I believe God is writing our life story and our love story. I don't know the end, but the beginning has been sweet. I look forward to the months ahead of us. I look forward to spending more time with you. I look forward to hearing your beautiful voice on the phone. I look forward to hearing the beautiful sounds of worship you make. I look forward to a deeper friendship with you, where we can share all our dreams, aspirations, and hopes for the future without fear.

I promise to give more of myself to you. I promise to let you in on the thoughts I rarely share with others. I promise to be kind to you always. I promise to listen to you and to respond to what it is you need. I promise to look out for you. I promise to pray for you always. I promise to be there for you in season and out of season.

Julia, my beloved. My fairest among women. I declare my heart belongs to you on this
Christmas day 1989.
   Your beloved,
   Joshua.

When Joshua was through reading his letter to me. I couldn't speak. I sat immobilised and allowed the tears to roll down my face. We both sat there for what seemed like a long time, holding hands and staring through bleary tears into each other's eyes.

A few days later, several hundred of us, including many visitors, gathered at Mount Hope Fellowship for the end of year service.

In Dominica, everyone makes it to Old Year's Night service, the New Years Eve church-goers. For many it is the second time in the old year and the first time for the new year they will be in church.

At Mount Hope we catered to these many visitors every year by having an evangelistic slant to our service. We do the normal vision and promises for the new year, but Pastor Stewart takes the opportunity to present the salvation gospel to the lost.

We were in fine form Old Year's Night. Joshua was on fire leading the worshippers in song after song. People were all over the auditorium singing with upraised arms. Shouting. Clapping. Making a joyful noise to the Lord. I could feel the sweet presence of the Lord. From songs of praise to songs of worship. In our last worship song, Joshua sang "Open Up Your Heart to Him," one of the songs he had written in the year.

Joshua sang, and many fell prostrate before God with tears, on bended knees. Many stayed face down, while others stood in the presence of the Lord. In this atmosphere the twelve o'clock hour struck. Silence reigned as people opened their hearts before God. For up to five minutes after twelve, Pastor Stewart allowed the congregation to be silent before God.

At the end of the silence. Mother Jno Baptiste, one of the spiritual pillars of the church, spoke. She was a founding member, a prayer warrior, a tongue speaker, and a woman with a word. I waited. Her deep musical voice filled the sanctuary.

"Church, the Lord has remembered us tonight. Truly, the Lord is about to do great things in our midst in 1990. This is what the Lord is saying tonight. Joshua, he says, I have heard your prayer, I have seen your tears, I am going to raise you as a minister in this land and other lands. But I will sieve you before you take up the ministry. You will marry Julia before you enter the ministry. Your lives will be blessed together, and your ministry will be fruitful. This is the word of the Lord."

And she returned to her seat.

At once several people erupted, into, "Praise God, praise God." I sat transfixed. I didn't know what to make of the word. I refused to lift my head or my eyes to anyone. The blood in my veins turned into red ice.

Then Joshua's voice filled the sanctuary, "Thank you, Lord. Thank you, Lord." A hush fell over the church.

But not for long. Mother Stedman, another prayer warrior, took the mike and said, "The Lord has indeed spoken. Joshua and Julia, despite all the obstacles which will come your way, rest assured your lives will be joined together forever."

There was more wailing this time from Mrs Adams, and yet I remained on the floor paralyzed. I wanted to scream. I wanted to cry. My blood raced through my veins. My head swelled into a dull ache. I pressed my head into the concrete floor willing the pain in my head to go away. Willing the spoken word to dissolve into nothingness.

Then another woman of God spoke. Sister Joy, the ultimate spiritual warrior in the church. Sister Joy was fearless and zealous beyond normal. And she simply said, "The Lord confirms what has been said here and it shall be done according to his will and for his holy purpose."

I was the last person to get off the ground. Mrs Adams had to come get me off the ground. I discovered later that Joshua never left the pulpit; he'd remained kneeling in the presence of the Lord.

I sensed there was a joy and happiness with the word that was spoken in the church that night. But I left church confused and with a heavy heart. I smiled in the right places.

I said happy New Year to all the people, except Joshua who had remained kneeling by the pulpit. I was relieved to have learnt this was the case for I could not have faced him that night with that heavy word hanging over our heads.

I had a problem with the word, because I was convinced my plan to study accounting was the one God had ordained for me for that time and that season.

Three months before Joshua was due to leave for Bible School, he took me to dinner, with my parents' permission, to Hibiscus Restaurant in Canefield. We were the only patrons in the walled garden of a hundred types of flowers—hundreds of angel's trumpet, dozens of red anthuriums, and endless red and yellow heliconia, surrounded by a hundred shades of green only to be found in Dominica. It was breath taking, the beauty of the place.

But I had a mixture of emotions—the anticipation of dinner, but also dread. My heart sank with the reminder that Joshua would soon leave and we would no longer have these beautiful moments together. I adjusted the ruffles along my ruby red V-neck blouse and ran my hand down my skirts to curb the fluttery feeling in my stomach.

We ate by candlelight a wonderful meal of dolphinfish served in a creole sauce, with vegetables, on a bed of seasoned rice. We each ate until the white of our plates shimmered in the light. For dessert we settled on the creamiest coconut ice cream. Each spoonful caressed my tongue with the smoothness and sweetness of the right amount of coconut, sugar, custard, and milk.

I was enjoying the evening until I saw Joshua go down on bended knees with a box in his hand. My heart started to race. Sweat popped on my face and down my back. Panic stopped the breath in my lungs. I was afraid of what he was going to ask, because I knew the answer wasn't going to be the one he wanted to hear.

"Julia, I have spoken to your parents and the Lord has also spoken to us. I would like to spend forever with you for all the reasons I told you in my letter. Will you marry me? Will you accept this ring as a promise to marry me?"

I sat for what seemed like a long time, like a pillar of wood.

Bloodless.

Lifeless.

How could I make this decision to get married when God had not spoken to me? I'd received no personal revelation I was to marry Joshua.

I had continued to pray concerning my future and each time the word I received was the one leading me to do my accounting degree. Each time thoughts of Juliette and the children and their circumstances dominated. I couldn't ignore the choices my sister had made and the effect it had had on her life. I'd vowed not to take the same path as Juliette. I didn't want to get married so young.

I couldn't ignore that my sister and her children needed me to take a different path to be in a position to help them. My mother and Augustus were bearing the economic burden of Juliette and her children until Juliette got better. But I feared the sister I knew before Timothy and the babies was forever gone. Her struggle with depression had no ending.

And I wanted different things. I wanted a different path. I wanted to be a change agent. Maybe I would get to do all of those things with Joshua at my side. But not yet. I couldn't say yes to Joshua's proposal without letting him know the fears within me.

"Joshua, I cannot agree to marry you tonight."

"What do you mean?" he said, his face crestfallen.

"There are a lot of things we have not talked about."

"What is there to talk about, Julia, if God has spoken?"

"But God has not spoken to me."

"I don't understand, Julia. What are you saying? What do you mean, God has not spoken? You were in church on Old Year's Night, when three women of faith confirmed the word of the Lord."

"Yes, I was in church. Yes, I heard. But God has not yet given me direction or peace in my heart."

"What on earth are you talking about, Julia?" he said. He stood and sat again in his seat. He tossed the box with the ring into the centre of the table which stood between us like the Berlin Wall before it was torn down stone by stone. How were we going to scale this wall? Would I have to take a hammer and knock off each stone standing in the way of reason?

The waiter who had come to take the picture with the disposable camera, which Joshua had bought for the occasion, moved back into the shadows.

"What about the stuff you wrote in your letter?"

"I meant all of it, Joshua. But the direction I'm getting from God is to pursue my accounting degree at university first. I plan to sit the University of the West Indies scholarship exams next year. My mentor, Adrian Hill, an accountant, encouraged me to take the exams, given my circumstances."

"Wait, Julia. You are blubbering. What does this have to do with my proposal?"

"You want me to become your wife before you enter the ministry. Joshua, I cannot get married while I'm still at school. You will be in Bible School for two years. I will be at university for three years. I want to finish school before I get married."

"Julia, I don't know what to say. You are rejecting my proposal for very selfish reasons. I was not expecting us to marry right away."

"But you are expecting us to marry before you enter the ministry."

"Yes," he whispered.

"Then I can't do it. I have to finish school."

"There is nothing more to say, Julia. I'm very disappointed. All my hopes and dreams were built on this confirmation from God. And you're here telling me you have to finish school before you can get married."

"Why is it so difficult to accept, Joshua? I could say the same thing about you—you are being selfish. Why is it I can't want to go off and complete school? I've shared this dream with you. I told you about my sister and wanting my life to be different. We have forever to be together. What is three years compared to forever? Tell me."

Joshua refused to answer. He kept his eyes on the closed box on the table. I looked at it. A small purple box with gold edges. Was it a single solitaire? How much had he spent on it? Was I being selfish? I closed my eyes. Our first major fight as a couple was over whether we should marry. What an illustrious start. Each unmoving. The waiter returned to the kitchen. Our first fight would not be captured on film.

We sat in silence for minutes. Then Joshua said in a tight voice, "Let me take you home." He grabbed the offending purple box and shoved it into his pocket. He expelled a deep trail of breath and he stood up like a man who'd aged ten years in ten minutes.

My lungs constricted like someone had wrapped their hands around my windpipe. But I couldn't change my mind. I had to be sure too that this was the correct path for me.

Later, in the darkest hours of the night, I couldn't sleep. I wrestled with the issues in my head.

By daybreak, I'd resolved to make an appointment to see Pastor Stewart. I was confused. I was in pain, and I needed some wise counsel. I was in luck, for as soon as I called the church office, Sister Joy set my appointment to see Pastor Stewart at four o'clock in the afternoon.

When I got there, I was surprised to find Joshua waiting in the outer office. His face was twisted with sadness. Misery languished in his eyes. The black t-shirt and jeans he wore added to the tragic air around him. I had worn a yellow sundress, hoping it would uplift my spirit. It didn't work. I felt the same misery rise within me. How had we made a mess of things the night before?

"Joshua, are you here to see Pastor Stewart too?" I mumbled.

"Yes, and you?"

"I'm seeing him at four."

"I'm seeing him at the same time."

We both looked at each other and smiled through our misery. Pastor Stewart had set us up to meet at the same time. He must have sensed we were both coming to see him about the same thing. Just then the door to his office opened.

"My two favourite young people. Why are your faces so long and sad? Come right into my office and let me hear this." He said all of this with a twinkle in his eyes. Like a man who'd seen it all before.

Once we were seated across from his tiny desk which had four neat piles of paper on it, he asked Joshua if he wanted to go first.

"Last night, I proposed to Julia, and she turned me down flat, in disobedience to the word."

"Julia, is it true?"

"I did not turn him down flat, Pastor Stewart. I told him I couldn't marry him until I was through with university. He refused to listen to my reasons."

"Joshua, was last night the first time you heard about Julia's plans to go study?"

"No, we have been talking about our plans for over a year."

"You were well acquainted with those plans and yet still you proposed to her last night?"

"Yes, I leave next week for Bible School, and I wanted to have her promise to wait for me."

"To your mind, Julia will only wait for you because you have placed a ring on her finger. Where is your faith in all this, Joshua? You spoke of the word earlier. I remember Mother Jno Baptiste said before you and Julia become husband and wife God will sieve you.

"Son, he has already begun to do so. You cannot always have your way. Yes, you and Julia may get married before you enter the ministry, but you haven't asked God how he plans to bring it about. You assumed God was going to do it your way. Remember, son, his ways are not your ways, and his thoughts are not your thoughts. Additionally, he has the long-range vision we don't have."

"Thank you, Parson, for your correction. You are right. I wanted things my own way. I was so upset last night with Julia. I called her selfish. I told her she was rejecting the word of God."

"Son, it's okay. Trust me, if you want to spend forever with Julia it is not the last time, you're going to call her selfish. I am sure she also called you selfish last night."

We both chuckled in response.

"Young people, make up and get back on track. You both have great potential and God is going to use the two of you in powerful ways in the church and in the wider community. You are both going to school overseas. Take the opportunity to meet other young people, socialize and argue to your heart's content on campus. Write each other long letters in the interim. Call when you have money. Remember, forever is a long time."

We took our leave of Parson with lighter hearts and a determination to stick to our faith and our belief in God's plan for our lives.

Three months later, in July, Joshua boarded the plane destined for Jamaica and Bible School. I gave him a huge study Bible with the following inscription: "To Joshua, from Julia. May God continue to order your steps . . . Love is as strong as death." SOS 8:6

15

A Season Ends
(1991)

The last official day of my school life in Dominica.

I sat with my other A level classmates in the sweltering heat of the Goodwill Parish Hall dressed in blue gowns and yellow lapels. I gripped the graduation programme and used it like a fan to cool down my face. The minister of education was droning on and on about how he had elevated the state of education in Dominica. Perhaps a future generation would be the beneficiary of that elevation.

I looked around at my school mates—the class of 1991. And not one of them appeared to be listening. Everyone was using their programme as a fan to generate some breeze in the stifling room. But the minister continued, unaware that the July heat had invaded the walls, the floor, the chairs and the very air in the room.

I switched off the minister and his speech. The last two years had gone by like a race car through the months. The memories of the last two years rolled through my mind; my election as president of the student body; the endless debates under the big tree; the Love for All concert I had organized; beach trips; social evenings; and exams after exams.

We had experienced it together and today marked the culmination of our journey. Sadness welled up in me at the thought of never seeing some of my friends after today.

I moved on to happier thoughts. Joshua was back home after a year at Bible School. During the past year we had engaged in a duel of intense letter writing. I don't know how he did it, but I had gotten a letter almost every week from Jamaica. Mr Adams remarked once, "I hope that boy is studying the Bible as much as he writes to you."

Gina and Gloria teased me each time I received a letter. They got me a big white shoe box on which they had drawn two big red hearts. Every letter I received from Joshua went into my special box. The box was stuffed to the top with mushy letters.

Earlier in the year I had taken the University of the West Indies Scholarship Examination. A week ago I received the news from the university. I had passed the examinations and had been awarded a scholarship. The day I opened the envelope with the news, I jumped up and down for a minute and screamed, "Yes, yes, yes! Thank you, Lord!"

Mrs Abraham, Gina, and Gloria came running when they heard my rejoicing. The four of us proceeded to have a party of hugs, tears, and screams. The joy in my heart that day was full and sweet as an overripe mango. I closed my eyes and savoured the sweetness of my victory. I had defied the odds. I wasn't going to become a statistic. And that day I became a firm believer. My dreams were no longer dreams but were taking shape in the reality God had ordained for me.

The same day, I visited Juliette to share my good news. It was one of her better days. Her eyes were lucid, bright with understanding. When I told her the news, tears streamed from her eyes. Panic sprang in my heart when I saw her tears. Juliette was to be shielded from anything with the power to upset her. I thought my news was good news, but it had distressed her. I realized too late that my success would remind Juliette that her chance at a university education had evaporated.

Timothy's cheating and his verbal abuse, then his sudden death, had thrown Juliette into an emotional blizzard. For months after his death, she had withdrawn behind a wall of pain. It took months of careful coaxing by the doctors for that wall of pain to crumble block by block.

At least we thought the wall had crumbled. But then there were days when Juliette preferred the silence. She would retreat to a place where no one could reach her.

Alarmed that day, I moved to the chair where she sat and wrapped my arms around her. Juliette's pain and anguish invaded my heart and my tears spilled. We were two sisters crying for a world of loss. There had been too many losses in our lives. I didn't know any young women our age who had lost all the important men in their lives. Daddy Julius. Our father. Juliette's husband.

And this was how our mother had found us in the waning afternoon light. With red rim eyes I said, "Mother, I passed the university scholarship examination. Do you know what that means? I can attend the UWI, all expenses paid."

She looked at me and then she looked at Juliette.

"Good for you, Julia. Your learning is for yourself. It is not for me. It is not for Juliette. You must be happy. Now you can pursue all those high dreams you have. You and your high morality. Hah, you go on, Julia." Then she fled the house before Juliette or I could form a coherent thought.

I wondered not for the first time if my mother was deranged. Did she, over the years, mask her pain and disappointments behind a constructed wall of bravado? The gaping hole she had created in my heart three years ago expanded another inch.

My mind returned to the graduation ceremony when the minister for education stopped talking. I had tuned out from the ceremony to revisit another wound inflicted by my mother. Maybe this was my attempt to sabotage the joy of my accomplishment. I shifted my mind to more immediate matters. I knew Juliette was somewhere in the auditorium. I'd seen her earlier. Joshua was sitting with Mr and Mrs Adams and Pastor Stewart.

My mother hadn't arrived. In the face of her known hostility, I'd made the trip to Loubiere to deliver her invitation to the graduation. She hadn't been home but I had gotten the opportunity to spend time with Ma Titre and Aunty Maureen. Sadly, Old Man Maurice had passed away a month before the graduation. Samson and Samuel had moved to Guadeloupe to work with their father. This knowledge hung like a heavy cloud over me, threatening to destroy the euphoria of responding on behalf of my class as the Student of the Year.

I struggled to pay attention during the ceremony because I was chanting in my mind, "Please come, Mamie. Please come to my graduation." I half listened to the speeches. I went up to collect my certificate with one thought on my mind. Where was my mother to witness my graduation?

All too soon, Mr Grant, our principal, called out my name. "Miss Julia Alexander, our student of the year, the winner of the prize for academic excellence, the winner of the prize for leadership, and the winner of an academic scholarship to the University of the West Indies. We welcome Miss Alexander to the podium."

When I stood to make my way to the podium my legs swayed like the long branches on a coconut tree on a windy day. I gripped the seat in front of me to stop the sway. I felt Gloria's hand touch the small of my back. At her touch my courage returned, and I turned to make my way to the podium.

With each step there was less shakiness as I pressed forward, my prepared speech in a folder in my hands. I could have said it from memory for the many hours I had spent going over the speech. When I got to the podium, I scanned the crowd again for my mother's face, but I couldn't find her.

I stood before the mic with a bit of hesitation. Then I began, "It gives me great pleasure and I am greatly humbled to be given this opportunity to speak for this year's graduating class. I intend to highlight the many achievements of my classmates over the last two years. I will also speak about the challenges we overcame together to make it to this day. Indeed, this is the day that the Lord has made, and I give him thanks for having brought us a mighty long way."

I stopped for the applause and lifted my eyes to the audience. I saw her then, moving way at the back in a red dress. And my emotional dam broke. I stood before my classmates, parents, and other well-wishers, and the tears cascaded down my face.

Three times I tried to go on with my speech, but the tears choked the sound of the words in my throat. Someone approached me and handed me some tissue to wipe my face. I was told later that Joshua had to be held back from running to me.

After the third time, I regained my composure enough to continue. I apologized to the audience without saying what had made me break down. I gave the speech in its entirety and was treated to a standing ovation by my classmates and the audience. The rest of the ceremony passed in a fog of excitement and a flurry of activity. Two years of hard work, many sleepless nights, study groups, classes, exams, were celebrated in a three-hour ceremony.

At six o'clock we marched off with our certificates into life beyond the school doors. My seven-year journey had culminated in this moment.

For many of my classmates their journey in formal education would end that night. The rest of the camp was divided into the few who would go off to university right away and the many more who would have to fight and scrape at doors to open well into the future.

It was the year one thousand, nine hundred and ninety-one. The internet had not reached our shores; computers were almost non-existent; family finances for further education were unheard of; information on schools and scholarships were in outdated books at the library. I marched out of the parish hall as one of five leaving for university right away. I, Julia, was among the privileged few.

In the face of all the losses and my mother's abandonment, I'd found the courage and zeal to stay in the fight. Because of my friends Gina and Gloria and the generosity of their parents, I'd stood a chance. And my heart swelled with gratitude for their love towards me.

Outside the hall, Gina, Gloria, and I emerged to pandemonium. Photographers took pictures from all angles. Parents, children, and siblings fell into each other's arms. Mr and Mrs Adams and Joshua found us and our group fell into excited chatter.

However, my eyes kept scanning the crowd, looking for my mother. Joshua observed this and asked me, "Who are you looking for."

"My mother," I whispered to him. He looked at me with a raised eyebrow.

"She was here? You saw her?"

"She came in during the introduction to my speech. That's when I broke down."

"I should have known. Come here, let me give you a hug."

He hugged me and I gave a silent thanks to God for this sensitive man he'd placed in my life. His encouragement and prayers were a continual blessing in my life. His love gave me hope for the future.

"We should go look for her, then."

No sooner were the words out of Joshua's mouth than Juliette showed up. She rushed to me and wrapped her heavy arms around my waist so tight she almost choked the life out of me. A chaotic mix of emotions surged through me—joy, pain, sadness—all at the same time.

"I am so proud of you, little sister," she said with tears in her eyes. "Go out there and do your thing, for you and for me." I hugged my sister, who now weighed over two hundred pounds. There was no brightness in her eyes. They were dull with pain and medicine.

"Have you seen our mother?"

"She was here!" Juliette said with a loud voice.

"Who was here?" Mrs Adams asked.

"Our mother was here. Can you believe it? She came to the ceremony," I responded to Mrs Adams.

"Oh, Julia, that must mean she's ready to let go of the past," Mr, Adams offered with a reassuring smile.

"I sure hope so, because we have been praying for her heart to soften all these years. If this is her coming around, then I'm thankful," Mrs Adams said. "But where is she?" she asked, her voice full of concern.

And we began the search for my mother. It ended in disappointment. She had come to the ceremony but fled afterward.

For four years my mother had withdrawn her love, her care and her presence from my life because I had chosen a new path of faith. Because I had disobeyed a rule. Juliette had done far worse. But she had orchestrated and sanctioned Juliette's behaviour.

I hadn't understood why she threw my clothes and everything I owned out in the yard that Saturday. Four years later, I wasn't any closer to understanding the thought process that had led her to that decision. My mother was not a staunch church goer. She went without a sense of obligation.

In fact, for most of the years she had lived with Daddy Julius she hardly graced the doors of the church with her presence. She said the people in church would whisper, "Look *adilté-la*. Look the adulterer."

"They called me the adulterous one," she told me. "I heard one woman under her breath one Sunday in the chapel. I stopped going regularly after that. A bunch of hypocrites. Some of them have two sets of children, some have three. Some have wrong fathers. Some haven't got fathers. But they wanted to call me names. I said to hell with them and their church."

After that she only went on Ash Wednesday, Easter, Pentecost, Christmas and Old Year's Night. She stopped going to La Salette. That one made me happy. During the five o'clock morning trek to Pointe Michel, Juliette and I would be half asleep on our feet. It was not a happy memory for me. I had wanted to stay in my bed and sleep. I wasn't allowed to fall back asleep once we got to the church. Juliette didn't escape, either; she had to pray and roll the beads.

My mother had denounced with bitterness her panel of judges as lacking understanding of her situation.

As far as my mother was concerned, she'd done what was necessary to take care of her two small daughters. Daddy Julius loved her and took care of her when the man she had loved and married had deserted her when he left Dominica to make a better life for us. We experienced the opposite. We went from bad to rock bottom bad like a car going from zero to one-eighty.

I rode back to the house with Joshua. I sat as close as I could to him in the car. He held my hand with one hand and drove with the other. On the drive, we didn't speak. We were content to sit in companionable silence.

When we got to the house, we met the graduation party in full swing. When I entered the living room, everyone began singing "For she's a jolly good girl."

My cheeks stretched into a silly grin, and I was sure my eyes sparkled with unshed tears of joy. I walked into Mrs Adams's outstretched arms. When her arms closed around me, I bawled an ugly cry.

"We love you, Julia," she'd whispered into my ears.

She released me and I turned to face the room of smiling faces. I felt the waters building up in my tear ducts, and at the same time I grinned.

The reception had been planned for me and the twins. That's why Joshua had taken the long way home. I thought he had wanted to hold my hand for a little while longer. But it was to give the guests time to arrive so they could sing the song on my entry.

I looked around the room. Everyone who had touched my life in some way was at the party. Pastor and Mrs Stewart; my mentor, Adrian Hill; all the worship team members and band players; friends from school; Mother Jno Baptiste and Mother Stedman; Joshua's parents; and other friends and family of Gina and Gloria; and Juliette.

Everyone but Velma, my mother.

I knew I shouldn't, but I began to pray for her to show up at the party. She had surprised me at the ceremony. I wasn't asking for too much, I convinced myself. I couldn't think of a valid excuse for her to continue our estrangement.

When I should have been enjoying the party with Gina and Gloria, I spent the first thirty minutes of the party looking toward the door. It never opened. My mother never showed. And my hope for a reconciliation before I left for university shattered. And in that moment, I buried my longing for my mother's presence and approval and set about enjoying the party.

On the wall behind the dining table, ten green balloons surrounded a white banner with the words "Congratulations, Girls" in bold yellow letters. I surveyed the table covered with every conceivable form of finger food. Four types of sandwiches, enough to feed the graduating class, saltfish balls, *titiwi accras* and bakes, cocktail sticks, chicken wings, stuffed eggs, quiche, meat pies, tiny rotis, sausage rolls, tarts, cakes and fruit salad.

By the time I got to the last food item I knew Joshua's mother was responsible for more than half the food on the table. Food was her love and her livelihood. Joshua had told me that she catered parties, weddings, and meetings all over town. I knew we were being treated to mouth-watering delicious food. By the end of the long evening not a morsel of food remained on the table. What had not gone into mouths at the party was making its way home in various colours and sizes of bags.

The part of the evening that caused me to laugh, to cry, to smile until my cheeks ached were the toasts.

Mr Adams's booming voice had brought the room to silence. "I'll go first, because I'm the tallest in the room."

Everyone laughed.

"Hear ye, hear ye, to my three beautiful daughters. We are so proud of the three of you. For your commitment to excellence through your seven years of high school education.

"But most of all we are proud of the moral stance that each of you have adopted. In the next few months Gloria and Julia will travel to Barbados to attend UWI Cave Hill and Gina is going to UWI Mona in Jamaica. I know that you will continue in the spirit of excellence. Your mother and I will be praying hard for you girls. We'll be praying extra hard since we won't be there to monitor you."

More laughs around the room.

He beamed at me and Gina and Gloria and continued, "But I know that you will be fine because you have received a strong foundation based on God's word. I wish the three of you to be in the palm of Jesus's hand. Cheers."

"Cheers!" everyone said, and laughed.

The next person who spoke was my mentor, Mr Hill. I thanked God every day for the mentorship program which connected me to Mr Hill. He'd been a real mentor and had taken me under his wing, under his firm, under his resources. He'd explained difficult accounting concepts, paid for my scholarship exams, and helped me to prepare for the exams by doing past papers with me, which he'd sourced from his contacts.

He came over and stood beside me and took my small hands into his larger hands. The smile of pride on his face brought a fresh batch of tears of gratitude. I couldn't help it. This man, my mentor, had believed in me. I knew I wanted to become an accountant from that day of the career talk in primary school. There were times when I had doubted not that I could do it but whether I should pursue it. Was I like my father, wanting more no matter the cost? I wanted more than survival. Mr Hill made Julia, the dreamer possible.

His cultured voice brought me out of my contemplation. "To Julia. I have been your mentor over the past two years and was charged with providing inspiration and guidance to you.

"But let me be the first tonight to say that you have been an inspiration to *me*. I have never met a more determined, disciplined and passionate person. I hope that you will continue to apply these three characteristics to everything that you do in the future. I expect to hear great things from you at UWI. You have the ability and drive to bring home a first-class degree, and I expect nothing less.

"To Gina and Gloria, the two of you are just as determined, disciplined and capable as Julia and I expect the same from the both of you. I know one of you is eventually going to Jamaica to do medicine; it is going to be hard, but you can do it. Continue to believe in yourselves, and the sky is the limit."

Another round of applause went up. It was followed up with toast after toast and finally we each got a turn to say thank you. I went first.

"First of all, I want to thank God for all the wonderful people he has placed in my life. Without your love, guidance, attention, and correction along the way I would not have made it so far. I want to thank God also for the many gifts he has placed within me that have allowed me to excel in so many areas."

I almost went deaf from the cheers and cat calls.

"Let me continue," I said laughing through my tears. "I want to say a very special thank you to Mr and Mrs Adams for taking me into their home when my mother threw me out. You've treated me as a daughter through the years. And without your intervention in my life, I would not be standing here before you. These two people are responsible for my success tonight, along with each one of you who prayed for me, encouraged me, or helped me in any way over the years. I love each one of you and I thank you all."

And I broke down. Joshua saved me from collapsing to the ground. The tears were of gratitude, joy, triumph. Every face in the room was wet with tears by the time I said the last word.

Next, Gloria and Gina spoke together. They said the same words at the same time. I don't know if they had rehearsed or planned it. What I do know is over the years there had been many occasions where they said the same thing at the same time, or they finished each other's sentences. Their thank you speech expanded the good feelings in my heart. I was sure my face and eyes were the colour of raspberries. I didn't care. We were bringing down the curtain on our childhood in style and surrounded by love.

The gun had gone off on the fast track to adulthood.

Long after everyone had fallen asleep, I stayed awake, too excited to sleep. I kept going over the kaleidoscope of colours that'd been my life. The first nineteen years had been so eventful, with more tragedies than anyone I knew.

What would the next nineteen years hold for me?

There was only one way to find out. I would have to get up each day and live each day moment by moment as it would unfold, with the assurance, with the hope, with the faith that the grace of God was more than sufficient to keep me.

I breathed in deep and allowed the calm and contentment to spread warmth through my body. I'd never felt so comforted, confident, courageous.

16

Leaving Home, Leaving My Island
(1991)

T he day before I left for UWI at Cave Hill in Barbados, I went to reconcile with my
  mother.

She had attended my graduation from A levels. And when I had seen her in the
audience, my heart swelled with hope. But by the end of the graduation ceremony my
hope had withered—she'd disappeared as soon as the ceremony had ended.

Across the seat from Juliette, I shook my head to clear the painful memory. I had
spoken to Juliette the day before and told her I would visit them. However, when I arrived
at the house it wasn't Juliette I met.

The house was in disarray. Even with Juliette living with my mother, the clutter from
having four children running around the house was evident. The appearance of the house
should not have bothered me. But I couldn't stop comparing it to when Juliette and I
were children in this same house. My mother had a strict rule: "We may be poor, but this
house shall always be spotless," she'd preached every day.

My mother had taken over and was managing all of Juliette's affairs—the children and
the finances. After Timothy's death, she'd moved into the house at Canefield and had
even managed to negotiate a lower rent with the landlord who lived overseas. But a few
months after Timothy's death, when Juliette was hospitalised, she moved the children to
Loubiere. And when Juliette was released, she moved back without questions or protest.

In his quest to spite Juliette for her perceived evil action of having his children, Timothy had gone on a spending spree. He left debts to be paid off at the credit union in
Roseau and Delices and the pickup at the bank for farmers. His salary and gratuity from
the government had come to Juliette, but his debts had to be paid. My mother had put
one of Timothy's granduncles to run the farm. He ran it and kept most of the proceeds.
I'd heard from Juliette that Mamie had to visit Delices every month to get money from

him; and she had threatened to sell the farm. Juliette had relayed the news in the dead voice she almost always talked in of late.

After all my mother's scheming and strategising for Juliette's future, Juliette and her children were stuck in the yard.

I picked up a heap of children's clothes off the sofa to clear a spot for me to sit. Only to discover a long gash in the brown sofa—the white stuffing looked like white cotton that had fallen into wet dirt. Augustus had paid for the set. The day it arrived my mother's smile had surpassed the sun in its brilliance. She had danced like she was in a carnival band. And she had regaled Ma Titre and Maureen with the details of how she had persuaded Augustus to buy the living room set and how she had thanked him. The three of them had laughed until they held their bellies and Ma Titre had cried out, "*Moi ka'y pisa an mwen!* I will pee myself!"

I smiled at the memory and sat down on the gash and hoped no wires would poke through the hard material to snag my new blue jeans; I was breaking them in so they would fit perfectly for my first trip outside the Island. Gina and Gloria had called me silly and had laughed at me for a long time. It had irritated me, but now I remembered the moment with fondness. They were right. But I was giddy about the opportunity I had been granted. Going away to university was a big deal for me. The culmination of my primary school declaration to become an accountant was being fulfilled.

My smile dimmed when I took in Juliette's appearance. She was dressed in that ugly loose fitting yellow house dress she'd insisted on wearing these last few months. Her movements were slower than the last time. Her eyes were grey lifeless pools. She'd lost interest in her children; in life; in herself. I closed my eyes for a second and recalled the many happy images of Juliette and me growing up.

"Juliette, remember the good times we had?"

"What good times, Julia. We were dirt poor."

"Dirt poor? Daddy Julius always made sure we had food to eat. We always had fish . . ." My voice trailed off when Juliette started to laugh in a way that frightened me.

"We were poor, Julia. We lived in a two-room house with no bathroom, no running water. And I am back in it with my children."

"Remember we had a fridge Daddy Julius bought."

"Oh yes, your precious Daddy Julius. Your daddy . . .". And she laughed aloud again but her eyes remained dead, unseeing, out of focus.

"Did you take your medication today, Juliette?"

"Mommy dearest always gives me my medication. You came to see her."

"Yes, that's why I'm here. I'm leaving for Barbados tomorrow, Juliette. I can't leave without saying goodbye to Mamie and repairing things between us."

"You!" she shouted, and pointed a finger at me. "You're smart, but so naïve. Naïve. That's you. Naïve Julia. Naïve Julia. Naïve Julia," she chanted.

What is going on with Juliette today?

Lord, please help me, I screamed in my head.

Fear reached into my chest like a large fist and squeezed my heart. I grimaced at the pain it caused.

Where are my mother and the children?

I looked around the room.

"You are looking for her. She's not here, Julia. And she took the children with her. It's just me and you. And I'm going to tell you a little story about your precious Daddy Julius."

The way she said the words, each sounded ominous. And it caused a prickly sensation down my spine.

What is Juliette going to say?

"Your Daddy Julius . . ." she said and pointed her forefinger at me again. This time I noticed there was a long red scar on it. Like she'd cut herself earlier.

"Your superhero . . ."

"Juliette, why are you working up yourself today?"

"Sit back and listen to your big sister," she snapped. "You will listen today," she barked and shook her forefinger like she was waving a gun. I sat back, my heart tripping and skipping beats, like a bad record on a record player.

"Your Daddy Julius, not mine. He started touching me, Julia, when I started high school. When he'd come back early from the sea or when he didn't go out, he would touch me. You would be at school in Pointe Michel, Mamie would be either at the river or cleaning somebody's house. I would be in the house alone."

Daddy Julius did what?

My whole body froze. My breath left my body. The room turned black. I closed my eyes.

"One afternoon Mamie came back early and walked in on us. I saw her. I was facing the door. Her skin became colourless and her eyes darkened, and she left the room without a word.

"Your Daddy Julius went out right behind her. I stayed on the bed just how he'd put me and left me, with my black bra and no panties. I heard her voice through the thin partition. 'If you ever lay a finger on her again. I will kill you with this knife.' That was the week before he disappeared.

"I was glad when Daddy Julius died," she said, her voice low and full of venom.

I opened my eyes to look at Juliette and I couldn't see her. The room was still black. My face felt like flames were in the room lapping at it. And my body began to twitch and twitch and twitch. I couldn't control my body. And my mind couldn't keep up with what Juliette was spewing.

She's lost her mind. What is she saying?

"He could no longer touch me."

I came out of the dark trance and screamed, "Juliette! Stop!"

"He used to touch me," she said in her familiar dead voice.

"No!" I screamed louder. "You're lying, Juliette!"

"He liked using his tongue on me."

"Stop! Stop! Stop!"

She laughed like she'd lost complete control of her brain neurons.

"Yes, Daddy Julius dearest, did the same . . ."

"Stop!" I placed my hands against my ears.

She continued as if I wasn't even in the room. Like she wasn't speaking to me but to some unknown thing in the room with us.

"Yes, the same Daddy Julius you wanted to come back. I prayed he would stay dead and buried at the bottom of the ocean. My prayers were stronger than yours."

My face felt wet. I didn't know when I'd started crying. The childhood I'd been pining for these last few days, while I'd been packing for my move to Barbados to begin university, was being destroyed by Juliette and her revelations.

I would never trust nostalgia and memories again. Two unreliable sources of reality. What I'd known or thought I'd known hadn't existed. Our household had been an unsafe place, a danger zone, a den of calamity and iniquity.

Why?

My brain cells lost oxygen and shut down. Tears rolled down my face like rain sliding down a car's windshield.

"You escaped. I was older. I was the sacrificial daughter. I thought I'd escaped for all time after Julius died. But then Timothy arrived, and our scheming mother cranked up her gears."

The fog of despair in my brain lifted, replaced by fury.

"You agreed, Juliette. You let her do this to you."

She laughed that high maniacal laugh I wished I'd never hear from her again. It held too much bitterness.

"Oh, sweet, untouched Julia. You can sit over there with your virgin purity. You escaped, Julia. I paid the price for your survival."

"You agreed with everything she did and said. You never sided with me when I challenged her. Never. You always sided with Mamie against me. It was me against you both. You were a coward, Juliette."

She laughed that ugly laugh again and I almost lost my freaking mind.

"Stop it, Juliette. Stop!" I breathed in ragged breaths, watching her from my hot, wet eyes. "Why now...why are you telling me..."

"Look at me. Mamie was wrong. Her way failed, Julia. I believed her that Timothy would take care of me. That it was the best I could do. That it was the only way for us to survive after Daddy Julius died.

"I'm messed up, Julia. Look at me. Four children. A dead husband. Look at me."

I looked at my sister, her long silky black hair had been replaced by short black curly hair. Her hair had fallen out after Timothy's death. In the past year, she'd added another twenty pounds to her pregnancy weight. Her stomach protruded; her once-perky breasts were closer to her stomach than her throat. My sister, just over three years older than me, no longer existed. She'd been replaced by a woman I didn't recognize.

Her wounds went far deeper than those inflicted by Timothy. My mother. Daddy Julius. Our father. They'd all failed us. And for what they'd done to Juliette, they all deserve hell's fire. I had let that thought simmer in my mind. I didn't care it was unchristian of me.

I wanted to hurt someone like I was hurting. And like Juliette was hurting. I closed my eyes and wrapped my arms around my stomach and rocked back and forth.

Oh God, make this pain stop.

"You came here to reconcile with Mamie," she said in a halting tone. "You're wasting your time, Julia," she added with a laugh. "She does not want to reconcile or talk to you,

Julia. You defied her and then shamed her when you went to live with those 'Jesus saves' folks. Those Surbrooks people," she lamented.

A rush of adrenaline incinerated my blood. It stopped my tears.

"Juliette, you turned me away."

"How could I have taken you in?"

"You're my sister."

"Timothy refused—it was his decision."

"Nonsense."

"I had no say. No power."

"Velma is your mother and you learned nothing from her," I said, unable to keep the bitter tone from my voice.

"I'm not like her. I'm not like you."

"*I'm* not like her," I shot back.

Juliette laughed loud and long.

I wanted to block my ears with a small stone like we did when we were children.

"I told you some time ago to take your escape and run. Leave Julia. Go back to Pottersville. Board the plane tomorrow and throw three stones behind your back. Do not come back."

"But I can't . . ."

"Let it go, Julia."

"I can't leave you and children in this little house with Mamie. Remember our dreams, Juliette."

"You. Not me. I stopped dreaming when Julius started touching me. Every dream died."

"Why? You could have fought back. You could have told Mamie. You could have gone to the police. You could have told Aunty Maureen and Ma Titre."

She laughed uproariously.

Had she gone crazy?

"Oh Julia. Miss Naïve. You were there and saw what happened with Annya. They all knew Julius was touching me. All. Of. Them. They all knew Robert had touched us too."

"Juliette . . ."

"Mamie knew from day one, Julia. The day she pulled the knife on Julius wasn't the first time she'd walked in on us." And she descended into another round of high, bitter laughter.

"Juliette..."

I choked on the words. They wouldn't come out. The room started spinning. Juliette was zooming in and out from my sight. The things she had said could not be true. They could not be true. My chest felt like it would explode with fire and acid. I clawed at the faux leather chair with my clammy hands. But Juliette wasn't done with me.

"Run, run, run, Julia."

My eyesight cleared and I came face to face with my sister's manic eyes.

All of it was too much. Too much revelation. Too much anger. Too much pain. I stumbled out of the house. I'd been gutted by Juliette's revelation. I stumbled over to the big stone and sat there and allowed my tears to fall. I'd never been more grateful when I heard faithful Lightning's bus. I brushed my hands against my eyes to wipe out some of the tears, then got up and flagged the bus.

The bus ride to Roseau felt like a blur: I saw none of the houses or the people always milling about in Newtown or the cars that zoomed past us. And Angus blasting Brother Bob's "So Much Trouble in the World" only increased the chill that had taken over my body. The pressure in my chest became more intense. The haunting lyrics seemed almost too appropriate for how I was feeling.

Would the struggle to survive ever end? Would the troubles ever relent, allowing a glimmer of hope to pierce through the darkness that surrounded me? These questions echoed within, their answers elusive, leaving me yearning for solace in a world rife with uncertainty.

Juliette had destroyed the childhood I had immortalised. I became like one of the black rubber tubes I'd loved so much for sea bathing—stolen by a big wave and pulled out to the deep blue sea to disappear beyond the horizon.

Juliette's revelations flipped a switch in me. The realisation of our truth.

It turned me, the night before I left Dominica for Barbados, into an inconsolable mess. My adopted family, and Joshua, who would be leaving with us on the same flight to Barbados, tried to comfort me.

It failed.

My head felt like it had grown into a big pumpkin. Thick with the heavy words Juliette had spoken. They were rolling like heavy boulders down the mountainside in my head. And I felt my head would explode from the tension.

But I stayed mute.

I sat next to Joshua on the settee. He had tried to pull me against him again and I resisted.

How could my mother have done this to Juliette? What kind of mother lets her daughter go through so much pain and shame?

She said nothing.

She did nothing.

She sacrificed Juliette.

My eyes filled with fresh tears.

But I couldn't tell them what Juliette had told me.

I couldn't.

I couldn't stop the erratic beating of my heart. My heart, my heart, my heart . . . can't take any more pain.

I slumped forward and buried my aching head in my hands. Joshua tried to rub my back, but I brushed him off.

"Julia, you're making me afraid," he said, his voice tight.

Gina and Gloria were on the floor and Mrs Adams sat on the chair opposite the sofa. I heard her quiet voice. "Julia I'm very worried about you. What happened at Loubiere? What did your mother say?"

I broke my self-enforced silence to say, "My mother wasn't there."

"What? But you called and told Juliette why you were coming," Gloria said.

"I told you it wouldn't work, Julia. Your mother deliberately hardens her heart towards you. Four years, and she won't forgive you," Gina said and ended with a big sigh.

She was right; my mother refused to face me. She didn't want my forgiveness because she didn't want to forgive me. I had gone there to forgive her and to beg for her forgiveness. I had wanted to reconcile with her before I left for UWI at Cave HIll in Barbados. I wanted to hear her say she was proud of me. I wanted to assure her that I intended to keep my promise to get her and Juliette and the children out of the yard.

And Juliette, with her revelations, had erased my resolve to forgive. All I wanted to do was confront my mother.

How could you do this to Juliette? How could you?

Aunty Maureen and Ma Titre—they knew, and they stayed silent. They destroyed Juliette. They let Daddy Julius, Robert, and Timothy exercise power over Juliette.

And when I remembered what they had allowed that man to continue to do to Annya with their silence, I started to scream.

I must have scared Joshua and Gina and Gloria and Mrs Adams. I was past caring. There was a ball of pain in my belly, and I had to scream to get it out.

I screamed and lost all sense of time. I can't recall how long I screamed. At some point Mr Adams came into the room and started to pray. And then the others joined in; that much I was conscious of.

Having lost all sense of time I don't remember when the heaviness which had invaded my body began to lift. The numbness dissipated. And the lump in my throat began to decrease.

I could hear again. The roaring waterfall in my ears had ceased.

Mr Adams interrupted the pity fest I had begun, his baritone full of authority. "Joshua, I think you should take Julia out for a drive and dinner as you had planned. Let her get some fresh air and some time to calm down."

"Daddy look at her, she's a mess," Gloria delivered in a voice high with concern.

"Gloria . . ."

"Mr Adams, I think that's a great idea," Joshua said, his voice not as tight as it was earlier.

I was following what they were saying but I didn't want to join in. I didn't want to make any decisions. I didn't want to feel anything.

I wanted to go completely numb.

Maybe Mr Adams was right.

So I allowed Gloria and Gina to lead me to our room, where they undressed me and put me into the white dress with a flouncing skirt, a narrow waist, and a fitted bodice with cap sleeves I'd chosen. They fussed with my hair and declared me ready. And so I allowed Joshua to guide me down the steps and into his waiting blue car. It was really his parents' car since he'd sold his before he left for Bible School last year.

In the car, Joshua announced we were heading *to La Bel Place*. It was our favourite place for the best fried chicken on the island. I managed a weak smile and turned to gaze out the window. I hadn't wanted to read the frown lines on Joshua's face of him struggling to contain his concerns.

"*La Bel Place* is your favourite place Julia and you're not shouting," he said.

I didn't respond. I continued to look out at the darkening sky. The car was rolling past the blue swells slamming into the rocks along the road. I was looking but didn't see it. Joshua's voice intruded on my dance with my pain.

"You have to talk about it, Julia. You can't keep it bottled up."

"Easy for you to say, Joshua. You've had an easy life."

"Julia . . ."

"Yes, Joshua. You had an easy life." I turned to him, sure my eyes were blazing bright gold like a brilliant sunset.

"You grew up on that hill, that bastion of middle-class privilege and comfort. You don't know what it's like to ration food, to borrow money from Old Man Maurice to buy bread in the shop, to watch your mother manipulate your sister into a romance before she finished high school and then an early marriage."

"Julia . . ."

"No, let me finish." My blood was boiling. I knew I should not have been raising my voice in anger at Joshua. It wasn't his fault. He'd been nothing but kind and loving to me. He'd been patient in the beginning when I hadn't wanted to sit near him or have him hold my hand. Although the memory and effect of Robert's hands on my body had faded, it had left a deep psychological scar. And my default had been to protect myself from being exposed to being hurt again.

The car stopped. We were at the place. But I still turned on Joshua.

"You don't know what it was like, living with my mother. She was broken. My father broke her heart. My father broke her dreams. Do you know she laughed at my dreams? Do you know that?" I shouted."

"Julia, you're crying again and it's breaking my heart," he said and reached for my hand. But I brushed it away. I didn't want to be comforted.

Did I even deserve this man?

I was broken too.

"Julia, what did Juliette say to you today?"

I shuttered my eyes and clenched my hands. I allowed fresh tears to squeeze out the corners of my eyes.

Do I dare tell Joshua the truth? Would he still like me? If I told him about Juliette, about me.

I squeezed my eyes tighter and dug my fingers into the soft flesh of my palms, they were certain to turn crimson red.

And there in the car with Joshua, a pale moon high in the sky, casting the barest glint on the face of the sea. My high school guidance counselor's voice intruded. "It is easy to be released from the pain by talking."

Maybe this was the true test of my rite of passage. I thought it'd been my graduation from high school and A levels. But it was grappling with the silence, the shame, the sin.

Joshua reached for both my hands and I allowed him to take them. If we had a future together, then he should know all about me, all about my family's sins of commission and omission.

It was hard to get the words out. I sputtered. I choked on the words. I cried. I dug deep into my strength reservoir to relay to Joshua what Juliette had told me. I started with Juliette's story because I wanted to delay telling my own.

"And Joshua, remember how I cringed when you touched me sometimes or how I blew up when you would sneak up on me?" I said, between hiccups and tears.

"It was because the giant Robert, who lived next door in Cheryl's house, assaulted me with his hands. And he made it my fault. He said I was walking around the yard without bra and he had to teach me a lesson."

"What Julia!" he said. He released my hands and slammed his against the steering wheel several times.

"What did your mother do?"

"I never told her. I spoke to Juliette and she told me, "Some things you don't talk about." And when I asked her why Mamie hadn't asked me any questions after I attacked Robert on the night he assaulted Annya, who was Cheryl's six-year-old daughter. She calmly told me, "She will not ask you. She does not want to know what she already knows."

"Julia, I am so angry. How could your mother choose silence over justice for her daughters? And they didn't call the police for the six-year-old?"

"No, they didn't. Not even Ma Titre. I have never forgotten, Joshua. Little Annya, passed out."

"What!"

"Yes, my mother and all the women in the yard remained silent and went on living. Maybe what Juliette told me that night is true. Maybe the same thing happened to my mother and the other women."

"Even more reason to protect and defend your daughters. I am so angry right now, Julia."

He continued to hit the steering wheel. His nostrils flared and the vein on the side of his forehead pulsed.

Troubled at his reaction I asked, "Are you angry at me?"

"Not at you Julia. At the adults who were charged with taking care of you and Juliette. They failed you," he growled.

"Do you still want me to be your wife?"

He turned and his eyes were bulging. "What kind of question is that, Julia? You think your story would make me change my mind about waiting for you. No, Julia. It only strengthens my resolve to be there for you whenever you need me."

"I was so afraid to tell you. I was ashamed to tell you. I told myself over and over you didn't have to know. I could just continue the silence.

"But tonight I realised that my real rite of passage to womanhood is to break the silence, break the shame, break the chains. And my guidance counselor was right, talking releases the pain."

"I am glad you did, Julia. But I want to hit someone for the first time in my life," he said and pulled me into a hug against his chest.

I chuckled against his shirt and in a muffled voice I asked, "Do you even know how to fight, Joshua?"

And in a lighter tone he said, "I grew up in a lane filled with boys."

And I laughed for the first time since Juliette destroyed the nostalgia of my childhood.

"Let's get some fried chicken in you before you head off to eat only flying fish."

I complied, secured in my feeling for the first time that my life could only get better.

The time out with Joshua calmed my pulse and heartbeat a bit by the time we made it back to the house. But what I had learned from Juliette I couldn't shake off.

And on the last night before I left for university, after we had finished our packing, I went to bed heavy with sadness. All the joy I had felt on winning the UWI full scholarship;

coming in the third spot of A levels results; it was gone. That dream, that purpose I had planted in my heart at eleven, dressed in my green skirt and green and white checked shirt in that little classroom in the village of Pointe Michel had come true. Me—the poster child for poverty, tragedies, and abandonment—I had been granted the opportunity to pursue my dream of becoming an accountant.

Knowing that it came at the cost of Juliette's life made me question everything afresh. And on that last night in Dominica, I dragged my weak limbs to bed to contemplate whether I could pursue my dreams when my sister couldn't even dream.

Hours later, I couldn't sleep. My body was heavy with tiredness, but my mind refused to shut down. Pictures from my childhood skittered through my mind. Juliette and me going for mangoes up the river. Juliette and me playing skip in the road with other girls in the village. Juliette and me swimming in the sea all day and then the river. Juliette and me competing to make flat stones skip on the water's surface. Juliette and me dressed up for church. Juliette and me fighting over hot bakes. Me wearing all Juliette's hand-me-down clothes.

From the outside it had looked like a normal childhood. I tried to recall when Juliette had changed. I couldn't. I was about three years younger, and my days had been spent playing or buried in a library book or doing homework.

And then I remembered when our dream talks on the big stone ceased.

I groaned and tried to stop thinking. I hadn't yet conquered my tendency to overthink. *Would I ever?*

I placed my hands over my ears and closed my eyes. The room was dark, but the moon was shining its glory on the surface of the sea. A light breeze stirred the white curtains at the windows. Gloria and Gina were buried under their blankets. I was alone with my memories, my thoughts, my pain.

I still couldn't articulate in words what I felt as I lay there enveloped in the darkest hours of the night, and so I resorted to the language God understands—my tears.

I cried for Juliette and what she'd endured under my mother's misguided direction. I cried for my mother and the disappointments she'd suffered, the pain she'd carried, the demons that'd ruled her mind and her choices. I cried for my father who'd failed in his duty to love and protect her and to love and protect us, his daughters. I cried for myself and all my little girl dreams, lost and shattered in a reality I hadn't known existed.

I cried for Daddy Julius who hadn't really existed; he'd been vile and had violated Juliette. I cried harder when I realized that I might have been added to the list if he hadn't died. I cried because Juliette's revelations had inducted me into the sisterhood of silence.

Inside of me had shattered. I had no strength to speak. Shame for me, for Juliette, for my mother rose dark and heavy within me and I cried some more.

Exhaustion claimed me in the early hours of the morning. It didn't feel like I had been asleep long when I jerked up from my troubled sleep. The faces of Timmy, Tammy, Teddy and Tommy had been crystal clear in the dream I'd had. "They are the future, Julia, and you have to fight for them." I'd heard the words so clearly in the dream.

And that's when the heaviness began to lift. I had to follow my dreams so they could have theirs, and my future children too. I remembered Mr Hill, my mentor, and his admonition and faith in my abilities. I remembered my adopted family and all the love and care they'd poured into me the last few years. I remembered Joshua's love and our future promised to us by God.

And right on my bed I lifted Juliette's four children, my mother, Juliette, and myself in seven individual prayers. By the seventh prayer, my tears had dried up and the peace and contentment I'd felt the night of our graduation party returned. The tension left my body and was replaced by a steady, calm pulse and heartbeat.

And I vowed to wipe the tears off my face. I vowed to release the last seven years of my childhood and its disappointments, tragedies, lack, and pain. It was time to take all I'd learned, all I had become, and walk into my future. I vowed to leave Julia the child behind when I boarded that plane to leave for Barbados.

Hours later at the Melville Hall Airport, our six very heavy suitcases were placed on the conveyor belt to whisk them out of Dominica. Each bag was overweight. In each suitcase, we'd placed all the creature comforts that we thought we needed for this next stage of our lives.

We'd packed bags of farine each, a tin of powdered milk, cocoa sticks, nutmeg, cinnamon sticks, authentic Dominican pepper sauce, green seasoning by the bottles, meat pies, gooseberry jam, all flavours of tart, and, of course, bread enough to last us for a month. We also had bay rum and shilling oil, and a bottle of aspirin just in case. To carry all these things we thought we couldn't live without, Mr Adams had had to pay hundreds of dollars in overweight.

With our boarding passes in hand we moved to the restaurant area to wait for our flight to be called.

Gina was on her way to UWI Mona in Jamaica and had been crying all morning. The realization she would be apart from Gloria for the next five years was too hard for her, so she'd broken down and cried, threatening not to go to Jamaica. She wanted to know if she could switch to study law.

By the time we were ready to leave the house, she'd seemed to have calmed down and accepted her reality. She clung to Gloria like her lifeline was about to be cut off. It was little comfort to her that Joshua would be accompanying her to Jamaica; that she wasn't going alone.

"All those who are holding boarding passes for flight 364 destined for Barbados, please proceed to the departure lounge and await your boarding instructions," said the announcer over the telecom.

There was a mad scramble of hugs and kisses and more tears as we said our final goodbyes. Just before I went through the door of the departure lounge, I handed Mrs Adams an envelope and told her it was a letter for my mother I wanted her to deliver.

At 4:50 we boarded the flight destined for our new lives awaiting us in Barbados and Jamaica. Gina and Joshua were going to spend one night with us in Barbados because their flight to Jamaica was not until the next day.

And as the plane climbed the sky, my mind drifted to the letter in which I'd written three simple words.

I forgive you.

I looked out through the windows at the receding green mountains, and the song I'd adopted from Old Man Maurice reverberated in my head.

"Born Free."

About The Author

P riscilla J Paquette is a native of the Commonwealth of Dominica, an attorney, and a lifelong avid reader. With her debut novel, "My Name is Julia," she fulfills her dream of writing a book of literary fiction. Inspired by her experiences living in multiple Caribbean islands, Priscilla is dedicated to showcasing the resilience of her island and its people, as well as the wider region. For more information visit www.priscillajpaquette.com.

Acknowledgments

I would like to express my heartfelt gratitude to the numerous friends and family members who have contributed to the completion of this book, both knowingly and unknowingly.

I want to thank my friend Brenda who read my poor attempt at stories in high school. She read the first version of this book and was gracious as any friend would be to say I should finish it.

I am deeply grateful to Bernard who pushed me to stop making excuses and just get on with editing the book.

Special appreciation goes to Pastor Bailey, who through inspiring conversations encouraged me to pursue my writing goals.

I owe a great debt of gratitude to my editor, Lia, whose dedication in reading multiple drafts of this tome has been invaluable. I am equally indebted to Wendy, whose insightful feedback and comments on select chapters proved immensely helpful. I would also like to extend my thanks to Marah, a new friend whose feedback and enthusiasm to read the remaining chapters provided me with renewed motivation.

I want to thank my family and friends who answered questions about the 1980's in Dominica; my cousin Steve who answered my many mundane questions; my friend Rhoda who asked questions and got answers from third parties on my behalf; my friends Frederick and Neville who also answered questions.

Lastly, I want to acknowledge Eunica, whose unwavering support and encouragement kept me going during the challenging moments of this writing journey. And to my colleagues who inquired about the progress of the book, your interest and support were invaluable.

To each and every person mentioned here, as well as those whose contributions may have gone unmentioned but are no less appreciated, thank you for being a part of this literary endeavour. Your belief in me and your willingness to offer guidance and encouragement have made this book a reality.

Let's Stay In Touch

There are a gazillion titles on Amazon, and I'm glad you've discovered this one. So if you'd like to know when I release a new book, instead of leaving it to chance, sign up for my newsletter. I'll send you an email on publication.

Yes please!

No thanks—I'll take my chances.

Follow Priscilla on

Instagram.com/priscillaj.paquette

Made in the USA
Las Vegas, NV
16 September 2023

77699870R00144